Heaven Bound

Mother's Secret
Book Two of the Heaven Sent Series

D0057850

Heaven Bound

Mother's Secret
Book Two of the Heaven Sent Series

Montre Bible

URBAN CHRISTIAN

www.urbanchristianonline.net

URBAN CHRISTIAN is published by:

Urban Books
1199 Straight Path
West Babylon, NY 11704

Copyright © 2007 Montre Bible

All rights reserved. No part of this book may be reproduced in any form or by any means without prior consent of the Publisher, excepting brief quotes used in reviews.

ISBN-13: 978-1-60162-946-3
ISBN-10: 1-60162-946-X

First Printing October 2007
Printed in the United States of America

10 9 8 7 6 5 4 3 2 1

This is a work of fiction. Any references or similarities to actual events, real people, living, or dead, or to real locales are intended to give the novel a sense of reality. Any similarity in other names, characters, places, and incidents is entirely coincidental.

Submit Wholesale Orders to:
Kensington Publishing Corp.
C/O Penguin Group (USA) Inc.
Attention: Order Processing
405 Murray Hill Parkway
East Rutherford, NJ 07073-2316
Phone: 1-800-526-0275
Fax: 1-800-227-9604

Dedication

I would like to dedicate this story to my two younger brothers, Anthony and Dion. Allow your imagination to soar by reading more. When your imagination has no limits, neither will your life.

Matthew 16:19

. . . And I will give you the keys of the kingdom of heaven, and whatever you bind on earth will be bound in heaven, and whatever you loose on earth will be loosed in heaven."

Heaven Bound

Mother's Secret
Book Two of the Heaven Sent Series

INTRODUCTION . . . a letter to the reader
by Andrew Turner

Readers, the book you are about to read is a candid look into my mother, Andrea's, life. Unlike the book *"Heaven Sent"*, you won't be reading much about my experience in walking with this "gift," but you will see why she decided to keep all these things hidden; you will learn our family secret. She wrote this to me before she died. It took some time for me to decide whether I was going to release this or not, but I feel that to understand what I'm about and what I have to do, you have to know where I came from. I think by reading this myself I have a better insight into my own personal destiny and what my mother wants from me. I hope that this story blesses you and encourages you to fight the good fight of faith and always know that the heavenly angels are always around you guiding you.

Sincerely,
Andrew Turner, son of Andrea Turner

CHAPTER ONE

Dear Andy,

If you have found this letter, then I've probably already passed on . . .

It wasn't my entire intention to leave you in the dark for so long. It wasn't my intention to leave in you in the dark at all. I guess I thought that the gift would pass over a generation and you wouldn't have to deal with all I went through, but what has been prophesied in your life is coming to pass. So I want to apologize to you, your brother, and your father. I do love you so much. I see myself getting sicker and I think you deserve to know the truth. I am of the nephilim. The nephilim is someone who is born half-human and half-angel. You may not quite understand, but what that means to you is that your real grandfather, my father is an angel. His name is Donyel and he's not the type of angel you want to run into; he's a fallen angel. I have certain powers being a nephilim that allow me to do certain things and know things. I have been able to tell you've inherited some of that. As you get older you will see this develop. I'm sorry I won't be there to help you deal with it along the way. I get sicker every day and I think just being nephilim adds to it. Although people like me have power, we're vulnerable to all types of sicknesses and demons. There are no laws against demons for oppressing anyone of my kind. As a son of man, a child of God, you have the defense that you will be considered human so the universal laws of mankind apply to you. But you have angel powers, so, Andy, know this—you are special.

One of my powers is that sometimes I get visions of the past, and sometimes, I can see the future. That's how I knew you would find this letter. That's how I knew a lot of things about you growing up. Remember that time when you snuck out the house to go hang out with that knuckle-head, Mackenzie, to see that movie, "Constantine", that I told you not to see? Nothing could keep you from being interested in all that supernatural stuff, and for good reason. And even though I never actually caught you, I knew exactly what you had done and you couldn't figure out how. Well, now you know why. Sometimes I would simply just know everything about a complete stranger's life. You have this same gift and I pray you use it wisely. So I want to take this time to tell you the story of your family. I want to let you know how it all came to be so you will know what to do when the time comes for you to use your powers. Remember, having power doesn't make you powerful but using your power for the glory of the heavenly Father is far more powerful than any force out there. This is my story and this is your story. It all started twenty years ago when I was seventeen years old and it was a hot summer in Heaven, Texas . . .

The dusty country wind blew the wooden sign that read "The Wallace Family" back and forth as it hung off the mailbox. The old black woman, known to the town as Me-Ma, held her dress down to keep it from blowing up as she scurried as fast as she could to the mailbox to see what the messenger had dropped off.

"Andrea baby, when did you apply to this school?" Me-Ma asked waving an acceptance letter with the details of a full scholarship to Texas State College in Dallas.

I walked outside on the porch squinting through the sun to see what Me-Ma was so excited over. Back then I was a short, petite type girl who was so pretty and mulatto-looking that everyone practically knew that Me-Ma had secrets of her own about my upbringing, but that was just idle gossip around town and I paid it no mind—I loved my mama.

"Let me see that, Mama." I grabbed the letter and skimmed over it real quick. It appeared that I had been chosen out of several students for academic achievement with a full scholarship to their school with one requirement. "I have to take a set of core classes by the dean of the department who requested my possible enrollment."

"Ah, congratulations, Baby!" Me-Ma exasperated and hugged me, grooming my long wavy hair out my face, as if I were going to see the dean right that second. I paid the woman no mind, as to me the letter was like gold. It was my ticket out of a town that just didn't seemed to fit my style. I loved my mama, but I couldn't imagine living the life that she lived and now I had been given the opportunity to spread my wings and go to the big city and get an education—something not too many citizens of Heaven, Texas were able to do outside of high school. So with little thought to the situation, the upcoming fall I would go off to college.

The day was approaching and I wasn't sure what to think. It was the last day of August and all my memories of Heaven were both cheering me on to progress and holding me there at the same time. Heaven, Texas was a small town resistant to change and many of the buildings looked no different from the time they were originally built. The summer was fading away like my childhood and now I was becoming an official young adult. All my life I'd been in the small town of Heaven and thought I'd just die here until I got that letter for a full scholarship to Texas State College in Dallas for academic achievement.

Dallas was gigantic in comparison and I was slightly nervous about the move, but I'd be darned if I told Me-Ma that. I was determined to prove to her that I was a grown woman.

"Andrea, are you sure you don't want me to drive you to the campus, baby? I just don't want any thing bad to happen to you," Me-Ma said as I prepared to leave.

I rolled my eyes before turning to face her because the last thing I wanted was my old country mama in her old fashioned Mayberry looking dress and apron making a scene as I stepped on the college campus for the first time.

"No, Ma, I can make the drive by myself, and if you drive with me, then you'll have to drive back by yourself and you know how you get sleepy on the road."

"You right, Baby, but you make sure you call me as soon as you get there ya' hear?"

"Yes, Mama."

"Did ya pack all yer linens and thangs?"

"Yes, Mama." She still had that worried look in her eyes. Would nothing make her feel okay with me leaving?

"Mmkay..do you got some quartas so you can call me on the pay phone?"

"I have my car phone, mama. Don't worry about me." I kissed her forehead and zipped out the door before she could say another word. I looked back at Me-Ma as I got in the pickup truck full of clothes and boxes. Me-Ma just stood on the porch holding her apron looking like an old country mother. I sighed and thought that I couldn't just drive off like that. I was determined to leave but still . . . that was mama. I pretended to fix something in the glove compartment of the truck and then walked back to the porch steps. She looked up to the sky and examined the clouds.

"I hope it doesn't rain, I have all these clothes in the pick-up," I said looking up to the sky to examine the same clouds she was. She smiled at me and her worried look melted away. Her eyes were so warm and I didn't want to get emotional, but those old eyes were pulling on my heart. She stepped down off the porch and gave me a big hug. I embraced her hug and laid my head on her shoulder. With me gone, she would be alone. Papa had died four years ago from a heart attack and now I was leaving her. Deep down I wanted to be there for her but there was something I knew I had to do for myself. Starting college was a part of my beginnings. Mama looked at me still holding my shoulders and adjusting my sweater.

"Even if a storm comes, baby, you can get through it. I don't believe the Lawd has brought you this far to leave you." She kissed my forehead and I closed my eyes. I remembered a time of the past.

I could see Mama a few years younger with Papa and they were happy together here in the small town of Heaven. She was beautiful, her hair freshly pressed and curled and she was wearing her yellow petticoat. On her head she wore a white frilly bonnet with matching gloves. It must've been Sunday. Holding her hand, I could see Papa as strong and big as could be. He was built like a bear, but had the most beautiful smile in the world; a gentle giant with a hardy laugh. They would stroll Sunday afternoons to Lake Papa Pete and just laugh and talk about what they would do in their life. But I don't see myself in this memory. Where was I? Where am I in this memory?

"Andrea, you aw'right baby?" Me-Ma tilted her head and grabbed my attention. I blinked and looked at her.

"Um, yeah. Daydreaming I guess." I was confused at the thought I had just had; a memory that I had never personally experienced. I missed Papa though. I missed the time I would just lay on his belly while he was sleeping. Of course, back then I was much smaller and laying on his belly felt like I was at the top of giant hill. I giggled within and smiled.

"Well, you get on now befo' these clouds get too thick now."

And so I left and took to the road leaving Heaven behind without looking back. I daydreamed the entire time, hypnotized by the roaring engine of my truck not realizing how much time had progressed. I made it to the campus with nothing but the belongings in my truck and my wits.

I pulled all my hair in one pony tail and rolled the window down to look around. Other students were unpacking their moving vans and moving into the dorms. There was a lot of activity all around me. I wished I had brought some help now seeing that it would be some work moving into the dorm. I pulled an envelope from my sweater and opened it. Which hall was I in? Hughes Hall; that's the name of it.

"Excuse me, sir." I stopped a young man who was crossing the street in front of my truck. He was happy looking, and the first black I had seen on the campus. Plus, he was cute. He was peanut-butter-brown-colored, sported a low faded haircut and he had these dimples in his cheeks when he smiled. He wore these nice brown loafers; I always admired a man who wore nice shoes. He skipped over to my window to see what I wanted.

"Hey, what's up?" he asked brightly. I smiled, trying not to be obvious that I was checking him out.

"Um, I'm looking for Hughes Hall. Do you know where that is?" He smiled at me, which I simply found irresistible to ignore and my high yellow cheeks flushed. He pointed down the street.

"Well, you're on the right path. Hughes Hall is at the next stop sign and then make a left. It's the first building on your right. If you go too far on that road you'll be at Bristol Hall, which is the men's dorm."

"Is that where you live?" Okay I was obviously flirting, but I couldn't help it.

"Yeah, you new here?"

"Yeah, I'm a freshman."

"Well, welcome to Texas State College." He extended his hand. "Maybe I'll see ya around." I took his hand and shook it. *"Mmm, girl you look good."*

"Excuse me?" I asked.

"I said, I hope to see you around some time; what's your name?" I looked at him weird. I know I heard something else, but I hadn't seen his lips move, so it was almost as if I had read his mind. I wrote the feeling off to being tired from the long drive.

"Andrea. . . . Yeah, maybe we'll run into each other again. Well, thanks for the help." He stepped back onto the curb and I drove off in the direction he told me. I didn't even ask for his name, I felt like an idiot. Had I kept driving I would've seen the big sign on the street that read "Hughes Hall next left".

But hey, I had made my first friend. I should've kept him around to help me move my stuff. I parked my truck in front of Hughes Hall and took out my envelope to re-read my room assignment.

Looking at the crowd, something told me I should've taken advantage of the early move in. I had never in my life been around so many other girls. In Heaven, I just didn't relate to the other girls. The average girl was only concerned with her looks and which boy to impress. Those same girls ended up getting engaged after graduation to those same tired country boys. But I didn't want to live and die in that small town. I didn't want to find some country boy that I had known since kindergarten and marry him after graduation, and raise a small litter of chil-

dren on a farm that he inherited from his grandfather—
not really my ideal fantasy. No, Andrea Wallace wanted
more for herself. Andrea Wallace had a scholarship. With
that I would get myself through school and be a psychologist. I loved the human mind and I was the type of person
that people just simply enjoyed talking to. So hey, why not
get paid doing that same thing?

I entered the girl's dormitory to secure my room. I finally made it through the long line to the front desk. I was
surprised to see another young black brotha working behind the desk, and when he saw me, he stopped everything
he was doing and smiled. I looked down at his badge and
on it was written the name Philip. He had curly hair and a
bright complexion. His eyes were blue and if it weren't for
his thick afro-centric kissable lips, one might think he was
white. He smiled at me. *Snap out of it Andrea.*

"Do you have your room assignment and some form of
I.D.?" he asked. I was still speechless as I rummaged in my
backpack for my wallet. I hated carrying a purse and a backpack was the logical solution to that problem. I flipped
open my wallet and showed my I.D.

"Hello, Andrea Wallace, yes, I've seen your file. Philip
pulled my key and a card from the file draw almost immediately. Your roommate is already here. Her name is Karen
Hendricks."

Karen Hendricks? Oh God, please don't let my room
mate be some stupid blonde who is on the cheerleading
squad. Philip took his room check card and my key and
led me through the hall to my room.

"So do you work here?" I asked curiously.

"Yeah, I'm Philip Franklin, your Assistant Hall Director."

"But you're a guy." He laughed at my comment.

"Yeah, I'm very aware of that. If it's any consolation, the
Hall Director is a woman."

I embarrassed myself at being so shallow. I mean this was the 20th century. If women could do men's jobs surely the roles could be reversed. But it gave me a feeling of safety to know that I could call on Philip—beautiful muscular Philip—if there was anything that I needed. We got in the elevator to go up to my floor.

"So, you're from Heaven, Texas."

"How did you know that?"

"We have a file on all our residents. I try to get to know something special about each resident and your file seemed to stand out with the name of that town." I had a feeling that if people kept finding out that my town had a weird name I would be marked as the country girl on campus.

"Heaven on Earth, as they say in my town, but to me it felt like hell."

"Why you say that?" he asked with a hint of laughter.

"My town is really *really* small. The closest thing to a club looks something like a saloon. Could you please not spread it around that I'm from that town? I'd just rather forget about it." He nodded. The elevator doors opened and we stepped out into the hall.

"Agreed. Let me be the first to welcome you to your new life. Fifth floor, Stephanie is your floor assistant and your room is number 510." We walked down maybe a few feet from the elevator to the left and I could hear some music through the door. On the door were name tags. One had the name Karen and the other had the name Andrea. That was pretty cool that my name was already on the door. It made me feel like I was welcome. Philip knocked and then unlocked the door before giving me the key and then we both entered inside. There was a small room, a small multi-purpose sink with a mirror above it, a walk in closet area, and two beds on either side of the room with a dresser in between. To my surprise, a lanky black girl with big permed hair was dancing around the room hanging up posters of Michael Jackson on one side. I walked further into the room and she stopped and looked at me.

"Andrea I presume?" She smiled at me and extended her hand. I could see she had a small gap in between her front two teeth. Her smile was so big like that cat on Alice in Wonderland.

I don't know why I was reluctant, but I shook her hand. "Yeah." I was hoping that living with another female wasn't going to be too much drama.

"Yeah, girl how are you doing? I was wondering when you were gonna get here." Philip chuckled to himself and left the room closing the door behind him.

"Mmm mmm. That Philip boy is some kinda fine, ain't he?"

I laughed. Karen said the things I was afraid to say out loud. I nodded.

"So where's all your stuff? I know you brought more than that old brown backpack?" I put my backpack down on the available bed and sat down. I was tired from the drive and really didn't want to go downstairs *just yet.*

"Yeah, my stuff is down in my truck, but I'm so tired I just need to rest for a second."

"So where you from?" Karen asked. I didn't want to talk about my itty bitty town, so I was already thinking of ways to change the subject.

"East Texas. Where are you from?" Very brilliant the way I flipped the question back to her and off of me. Ten points for Andrea's team. Karen took yet another Michael Jackson poster and began pinning it up on her side of the room.

"I'm from here, born and raised. If you didn't come pretty soon, I was gonna start decorating your side of the room." I looked up behind me at my naked walls. Her side of the room was decorated with so many posters that I thought I may be uncomfortable undressing with M.J. staring at me. I didn't think about bringing any decorations or posters. All I had was my quilt and some books, but nothing to make my side of room interesting. I could just imagine people coming into our room and asking Karen, "Who's the boring plain-Jane roommate you live with?" A sinking feeling jabbed at my gut and I knew I had to head to the nearest store as soon as possible.

"I didn't bring that much stuff. Do you know where I can buy some things for my side of the room?"

"Girl, yeah, they got more Michael Jackson posters up at the Bazaar . . ." She kept talking but I tuned Karen out when she said Michael Jackson. This girl was obviously obsessed. Don't get me wrong, he was a good singer and I loved his songs but his video "Thriller" scared the mess out of me. It reminded me of some dreams I used to have as a kid. Besides, I wasn't about to become one of the many women screaming and crying over some singer. That just wasn't my style—I was too dignified for that. She was still talking about Michael and I began to feel like *maybe* I should be listening. . . . . nah, never mind. Why waste the brain cells? I needed to save my memory on things like these college classes. When I tuned people out it was like watching TV on mute. I saw their lips moving, but my mind was in a total different place; and there Karen was, lips just a moving a mile a second.

". . . and then I saw him wave that white glove on TV, girl, and I just went crazy . . ." Karen continued to talk despite my inability to stay in tune with her. I nodded ever so often to make her think I was listening, but I wasn't. It amazed me how someone could talk so long by themself. I waited for the right moment to interject—you know, when she was taking a breath.

"Looks like you're all in love with Michael." I interrupted at just the right moment.

"Only a little, I already have a sweetheart. You should meet him, he goes to school here, too."

"That's cool. I don't have any friends here."

"Girl, yes you do. You have me!" Karen said, posing like a spotlight had hit her. I laughed at her and she stuck her tongue out at me. Well, Karen wasn't like every girl, so I guess I could deal with having a crazy friend like her to keep me grounded.

CHAPTER TWO

Tired from the drive, I crashed the moment Karen stopped talking. I woke up suddenly realizing that most of my stuff was still down in my truck.

"Whoa, girl what's wrong with you? You waking up all crazy." Karen was by the sink looking in the mirror.

"How long have I been 'sleep?" I searched around for a clock in the cramped little dorm room.

"Don't worry, Andrea, you've only been 'sleep for about twenty minutes." It felt like I had slept for hours. That was some good sleep. "I called my man over here to help you get your things up to the room since it looks like you don't have anybody to help you." Karen was a lifesaver, 'cause God knows I didn't want to take on all those boxes by myself. She continued to primp.

"This guy must be pretty special," I said, watching her primp some more. I was amazed to see how high she could tease her hair.

She glanced at me and smiled. "He's my baby. I love that boy!" She grabbed a large blue can of hair spray and released a foggy smoke screen of ultimate hair control. I coughed and waved the fog from my face. A knock was at the door. When she opened it I was in total awe. The boy that showed me directions, Dewayne, was at the door.

"Andrea, meet my boyfriend Dewayne—Dewayne meet Andrea." Dewayne entered the room and smiled that charming smile and I felt embarrassed that once again I was noticing how cute he was. Wouldn't it just be my dumb luck that all the cute guys always have girlfriends?

"Hey, you!" he said excitedly. "I met her already on her way in." Karen looked and smiled at me.

"Yeah, Dewayne showed me how to get here." This campus was getting as small as Heaven. That's what I was trying to get away from—that small town mentality. There were too many people in too small of a town. Everybody knew each other and knew all of your business.

"Well, isn't this a small world? Well, Wayne, baby can you be a sweetie and help Andrea move her stuff in?" She hugged his neck and gave him a quick kiss on the cheek.

"Do you think you can just kiss me and butter me up and I'm gonna do what you say?" Karen looked speechless at his tone. ". . . Then you're exactly right." Dewayne said and grabbed her around her waist triple kissing her cheek. She laughed and hit his chest.

"Boy, stop playing and help this girl get her stuff!"

They were the cutest couple. Their relationship would either a) make you feel like your own relationship sucked b) make you wish they wrote a book on how to help your relationship, or c) make you hate them 'cause they were so happy. I smiled, remembering I had no one like that. The thought gave me an empty feeling deep in my gut. But I would officially mark Dewayne off the list as a potential. He was cute, but all he could ever be was a friend and I had to accept that. I told Dewayne where my truck was and told him I'd be there in a minute as he exited the dorm.

"How long have ya'll been together? Ya'll are too cute," I said.

"We've been together through high school. I'm surprised we're still together. Most of our friends broke up at graduation."

"Well, it looks like you two are really happy."

Karen smiled her gap-toothed smile and fixed her hair one more time in the mirror and stopped. "Yep. I really love that man." I saw how sincere her eyes were through her reflection in the mirror. I wondered what it must feel like to be in love like that. Every girl wants to find that special guy that adores her and loves her more than anything. Every girl wants to just let go and give her all to that one special guy that will make her feel alive. I sighed to myself and felt like I was doing something wrong.

"Let's get downstairs before Dewayne hurts himself," I said to distract myself. "My boxes are loaded with stuff." We hurried down and just as I said, Dewayne was attempting to lug a box meant to be carried by two. He struggled and groaned and eventually sat the box on the curb, moving it a total of two inches. I walked up to him.

"Dewayne, you can't carry this big box by yourself. Here, let me help you." He grabbed one end and I grabbed the other end.

"Okay," he said, "On one, two . . . three!" He groaned and grunted and lifted the box a couple of feet from the ground. But for some reason I didn't feel the effort that he was putting forth into the box. I picked up my end with the greatest ease. I looked around the box and gave Dewayne a questionable look.

"I don't know why you're looking at me crazy, girl, 'cause this box weighs a ton! You must be an Amazon or something."

"Less talk, more work!" Karen said from inside the truck as she grabbed some boxes of shirts.

"Karen, you have this dominatrix attitude today that I find arousing." Dewayne flirted, puckering his lips as he spoke.

She shooed her hand, "Boy, you are so crazy."

We carried some ten boxes up to my room which didn't take as long with all three of us working together. Philip at the front desk passed by ever so often watching me bring my stuff in. I wondered if he had a girlfriend. I bet he did. He was all too cute to be single.

The next day I was trying to find a reason to go back down to the front office to see Philip. Luckily, the elevator was down for repairs and he was walking down the stairs as I was walking up—probably making his rounds. In order to make my move I had to be slick, smooth, sexy—so I pretended to trip right in front of him.

"Oops." I purposely slipped on nothing and tumbled into his chest. Philip valiantly caught me as I planned.

"You okay?" he asked and helped me to my feet. I know, it was helpless and I, as a woman, should be ashamed for stooping so low to get a guy's attention, but what guy doesn't like the female in distress game?

"Um, thanks, Philip." I didn't want to move out of his strong arms. I could tell he worked out.

"We wouldn't want our new resident to get hurt now would we?" Philip smiled. The blushing in my face was almost automatic when I saw that smile and those dreamy eyes. I looked away to hide my response. Philip helped me get my balance and walked away. And let me tell you, I enjoyed watching him walk away.

"Um, Andrea." I was startled to see Karen behind me, "Girl, I saw the whole thing. You are pitiful. If that wasn't the most blatant flirting I have ever seen, then I don't know what it was." She laughed and walked down the stairs to get eye to eye with me.

"I have no idea what you're talking about. I tripped." I

said innocently, leaning up against the wall. She looked at me crazy and stuck forty cents in the soda machine in the hall and got a can of *New Coke*.

"Yeah, you trippin' all right. Andrea, that boy is fine, but every girl in the dormitory is after him, and unless you want to be the most hated girl on campus, I would leave him alone," Karen said sipping her soda.

"Karen, I don't care about these heifers on this campus." She laughed at my comment and we hopped up the stairs to our floor.

"Okay, so you don't care, but any guy with that many options ain't no good."

"It's not like I don't have options too." I took the time to spy my reflection in a hall mirror. I swung my hair a bit—I was fine. I had to remind myself of that sometimes because I didn't hear it often. And sometimes, a girl would start feeling as if she wasn't fine if she didn't hear it enough. I could see the flaws that maybe other people couldn't; or least I hoped they couldn't. Like that little red zit on the side of my face by my ear.

Karen and I found our way back to the room and Dewayne was sprawled out on her bed looking as tired as could be. I looked at her and smirked. Karen walked by him and kicked his foot that was hanging over the bed.

"What are you looking so tired about?" Karen said with her hands on her hips.

"Just taking a catnap, you know that gloomy weather makes me sleepy." He yawned, which made me yawn for some reason. I went to the window and peeked through the blinds. The sun was completely hidden behind the clouds and it appeared to be evening, but it was only about maybe three in the afternoon. I heard a roll of thunder.

"It looks like it's just about ready to rain." I pulled the blinds up and opened the window. I could smell the moisture in the air and the wind was catching up slightly, causing my hair to blow wildly around my face. I turned around because Karen squealed when Dewayne grabbed her and pulled her on the bed with him. I had to get me a boyfriend; I wasn't sure how much more of this I could take.

"Hey, I'm gonna go down to the lobby to watch some television." Karen looked at me and raised her eyebrow. Dewayne had his arms and a leg wrapped around her and was nibbling her earlobe. This was way too much for me to see, so I thought that I'd give them some privacy.

"Mmmhmm, don't fall down the stairs thinking about Phiiiliip." She sang his name like we were little kids.

I gave her a glare. "No, I'm not going down to see Philip." And I left the room for them to do their canoodling.

I went down to the lobby area and I could see some of the girls still coming in. Small raindrops were speckling the windows. Philip was running from outside just as the rain released itself from the clouds. His white t-shirt was only slightly wet, but it was enough so that I could notice his body shape hiding underneath. I glanced away.

"Hey, Andrea. So we run into each other again."

"Yep, so we do. Where are you coming from? Aren't you supposed to be working?"

"Yeah, there's something in the working world called a break." He laughed. "I was about to walk to the cafeteria to get some food, but looks like the rain is going to keep me in."

"Well, would you like me to drive you there in my truck? Don't waste your break sitting here hungry." *That's right, Andrea, work that magic. The way to a man's heart is through his stomach.* What was I thinking? I had to calm my thoughts down. I was merely doing the man a favor, nothing more, nothing less. Philip accepted my offer and we both ran through the rain to my truck. My best bet was to find something in common with him. I mean we had to have at least one thing in common.

Being in the close proximity of my truck, I could smell the dampened aroma of his cologne. He wiped down the water off his arms, checked himself out in the passenger-side mirror and grabbed the seatbelt and snapped it in place. My first thought was that he was vain to do that. I pulled mine over also and clicked it in place, noticing his muscular legs in those khaki shorts. I glanced, unnoticed by him. However, I did notice that he was checking me out as well. I wasn't sure to be offended or flattered. Men didn't know how to glance—they gawked. Gawking was a more than obvious stare that tended to get most men in trouble as they shifted into staring to slightly fantasizing. I cleared my throat and pretended not to notice. He straightened himself up and looked out the window.

"Sure is raining hard ain't it?" he said, tapping the passenger window with his index finger.

I nodded, "My mom used to tell me stories of the rain to keep me from being scared." I smiled and started the truck, backing it up out the parking space that I was in.

"Really, like what?"

"Aww, you don't wanna know all those crazy stories."

"Sure I do, come on . . . tell me." He looked at me with those puppy dog eyes and how could a girl resist? Plus I really did want to tell him, glad that I had this little tidbit of my life to break the uncomfortable silence.

"Well, all right, if you really want to know. I had to have been about eight back then and it would rain so hard that it sounded like it was about to tear through the roof. Our house was a small wood framed house so if you can imagine, it sounded like a thousand drummers beating continuously on the roof. I thought that maybe the roof would fall in. I remember not being able to see the ground because it was covered with water."

"Yeah, I can see how that can be scary for a little kid."

"Yeah, the winds were pretty bad. I ran into my parents'

room and jumped in their bed . . . and I remember she would tell me that the rain was just the angels. She would tell me that the angels were just crying all at the same time."

"Really, wow angels, huh? Why did she say the angels were crying?" He seemed to be really interested as I could see that he was intently staring at me through my peripheral vision.

"I don't know why . . . oh wait, I remember now. Momma used to say the angels would cry for the sins of the world."

"The sins of the world, huh? No wonder it rains so much." He laughed.

I smiled at his comment. I didn't want to seem pious. My family had a strong church background and it was all I really knew. I wanted to get outside that country church circle. I was more than Sister Wallace's daughter. I was Andrea, and Andrea had a life outside of Greater Holy First Baptist Church of Heaven. Be that our town was called Heaven, it was full of very religious people who thought that if you dared to wear pierced earrings, you were going to hell. Fortunately, there were a few people slowly getting out of that, but the old folks still held to tradition. For some reason, something in me totally rejected their ideals, their religion. So I felt the only true way to learn about the world was to leave Heaven and find out for myself; take a part of the tree of knowledge of good and evil. All people were guilty in eating in the forbidden fruit in some way or another. To the good saints of Heaven, Dallas was like Babylon, but I didn't care. Moving out of Heaven, Texas was my forbidden fruit and I was determined to find out what existed outside of my town.

"So are you very religious?" Philip asked.

I hated when people asked me that. I didn't want to be one of those church ladies at the front of the church that would shout and pray out loud all Sunday morning and then after church gossip about who did what and where. I didn't want to be that type of person nor did I want to have those folks talking about me.

"I'm not religious per se," I told Philip. "I'm just taking a hiatus from all the church life for awhile to find myself, but I do believe in God."

"Well, uh, I believe in God too, heh," he giggled. It sounded awkward to say that. "But I guess that everyone believes in God right?"

"Not atheists." Here I was being overtly smart. Leave it to me to mess everything up by intimidating a guy that I like by being intellectually superior. Oh well, if he couldn't hang with me mentally, he didn't deserve me, right? I was about fed up with dating another dumb jock and repressing my intellect so that he could look good.

"Oh yeah, I forgot about them. To be from a town called Heaven, I figured that you would know a lot about God."

"Yeah, well, we have a few devils in Heaven I assure you." My window wipers squeaked and the lightning lit up the sky. It had become awfully dark for daytime. I stopped my truck in the parking lot in front of the cafeteria and it seemed the rain got a little heavier.

"Maybe I should wait until you're done eating; you might need a ride back. It looks like the rain isn't going to let up for awhile." Philip smiled that pretty smile and I knew that he was glad I made the suggestion.

"Yeah, I would like that. I tell you what, come on in and I'll pay for you to eat in the cafeteria." Now if that wasn't sweet, I don't what it was. But I couldn't let on that I was impressed.

"Good, that will pay me back for the gas it took for me to get here." He laughed again. I was really amusing this guy.

"You're funny, Andrea. Most girls on this campus can

act real stuck up, especially ones as pretty as yourself." The compliment caught me totally off-guard. I couldn't help but smile. I attempted to hide my reaction by leaning my head down to turn off the truck when I parked. Oh he was good, real good. But I had to keep my eye on him. It was guys like Philip that would make girls melt with their pretty faces and wonderful compliments and break their hearts, and I wasn't the one to be played with.

"I bet you think I'm a player, don't you?" He smiled at me with one arm stretched over the back side of the seat, his fingertips just millimeters from my shoulder. We were parked and already the car windows were starting to fog up.

"What? No!!!" I lied. "I think . . . I think you're a really nice guy."

"Aw, don't say nice. Nice guys finish last."

"What are you talking about, Philip? I know plenty of nice guys"

"Did you date them?"

"What?"

"I asked if you dated any of those nice guys?"

"Well, no, they are like my brothers."

"Well, what do you want from me? Do you want me to be your brother or your . . ." He smiled and leaned in a little closer. My God that smile was so irresistible.

"My what? I didn't ask you to be my anything." I reared my neck back. If he thought he was getting a kiss, he was definitely wrong—even though I did consider it for a second.

"Well, maybe, I'm asking . . ." Hmm, there were those games again and I had to keep my senses because I could feel my face flushing and I didn't want to be one of those floozy freshmen I heard so much about. I had numerous friends tell me about college life and what to expect.

"Okay, hey, I'm sorry. Don't mean to pressure you since

you just got on campus. I'm a big flirt. You have to excuse me." Well at least he was honest.

"Thank you." I looked away.

"We still on for our lunch date?" He smirked. I had to make it difficult for him.

I rolled my eyes, "Yes, and it's not a date." I was trying to be stern, but cracked a smile.

The rain didn't seem to be letting up. "You ready to make a run for it?" He didn't wait for my answer. He jumped out the truck and ran to my side, trying to open my door, but I had locked it. He crossed his arms, looking cold and wet. I laughed.

"I didn't tell you to get out in the rain!" I put my sweater over my head and unlocked the door. He swung it open and pulled me out into the rain, holding me up in his arms so that my feet wouldn't touch the ground. I squealed, not because of the rain, but because it surprised me that he volunteered to carry me to the door. It was sweet. I kicked my door closed. I was hoping I wasn't too heavy for him, but then again, it wasn't like I weighed all that much anyways.

"Come, princess, let me rescue you from this storm."

"Boy, you better rescue me faster—I'm getting wet!" Please God don't let this Negro slip and fall in the rain while he is holding me. But I must say, Philip was romantic and just plain ol' silly. The rain poured down drenching us both. I was wet.

CHAPTER THREE

Back at the dorm Karen was still with Dewayne "She sure has been gone a long time," Karen said as she looked up at the clock and situated her skirt back on while buttoning her blouse back. Dewayne smiled, half-dressed in his boxers laying across her bed.

"Then maybe we should've took our time then." He walked his fingers up her back.

"Stop, Dewayne, put your pants back on. She may be back any minute."

"A minute is all I need!" He joked and Karen gave him a look. She got up from the bed and looked out the window.

"Hmm, her truck is not out there. She must have gone to go get something to eat." Dewayne hopped out the bed and tried to sneak up behind Karen, but his flat feet smacking the cold tiled floor made her turn around. He still managed to steal himself a hug as he wrapped his strong arms around her, slightly lifting her off the ground. She popped his bare chest.

"Boy, put me down."

"Come on, Karen. Just real quick." Her eyebrows curved up and inward and she pushed herself out his arms.

"Real quick? Nuh-uh. What do I look like? I'm not your ho'."

"I didn't say you were."

"The way you acting I wouldn't know the difference and actions speak louder than words." Dewayne stood there looking confused, not really sure how to respond. He felt his inner male warning alarm going off. The inner male warning alarm was a little signal that went off in a guys head when he was about to get in trouble with a female. His next words would mean whether or not he would be in the doghouse or not. Once a boyfriend got in the dog-house, it was heck to get out of it.

"You know I love you." *I love you. I love you works some-times . . .*

"You always say I love you when you want some." *Not this time.* Karen crossed her arms and bucked her eyes at De-wayne, pushing him aside as she walked past. He looked slightly hurt trying to figure out exactly what he had done wrong.

"You need to be focused on college and not sex. That's not why we're here. Everybody can't be lucky like you and get a special scholarship."

"Yeah, I know, and I'm really grateful. It's not too often black folks get full scholarships without even applying."

"Exactly," Karen said, reinforcing her point by caressing his face. "I don't want you to lose it either."

Dewayne sighed. "I won't. We're going do this thing right. Get through college, get married, have Dewayne Jr."

"Dewayne Jr.?"

"But of course. We're going to have two handsome boys, Dewayne II, and Dewayne III."

"We are not having two sons both named after you. And

besides, what if we have a girl?" Karen gave him a look up and down like he was crazy.

He thought for a second, "Dewaynisha?"

Karen looked as if she was going to be sick. "How 'bout, no?"

"Okay, um, Courtney after my granddaddy."

"Yo' granddaddy was named Courtney?" Karen asked raising her left eyebrow.

"Yeah, what's wrong with that? But the boys must be named Dewayne." He eased up on her and grabbed himself a kiss. She kissed back, creating that smacking sound as their lips stuck together. Karen wanted to have Dewayne as a husband so bad, that she could literally see it in her mind as if he was as she closed her eyes. But pretending wasn't enough, she knew how the mind played tricks. She had needed certainty. What seemed so easy and well planned out for Dewayne didn't come easy for her. She wanted a perfect life and that alone made her worry about everything. She pushed him away again.

Dewayne eased up and looked in her eyes trying to figure what was wrong and she looked away. He could sense there was something bothering her even if she didn't say anything and she didn't want to. She was upset and just as confused as she was making him. Through her actions, possibly she was simply trying to communicate her frustration. She walked over to the window and looked out. He walked up behind her and wrapped his arms around her waist. She sniffed, trying to hide that she was about to cry. Her mood had jumped like a frog in hot grease. He put his chin on her shoulder.

"Karen, what's da' matter?" She wiped her face with her wrist and turned around, placing her head on his chest.

"I just get so scared, Dewayne."

"Why?"

"I'm scared because I've never had sex with anyone but

you and I love you so much." She buried her face in his chest more. He rubbed her hair with his hand.

"Well, I love you too. I'm not going anywhere."

"It just seems that everyone that I know that gets sexually active ends up breaking up. The sex gets old or the guy finds a new girl. Are you going to do that with me?"

"I'm too ugly to find another girl. I was happy when you started dating me." She giggled and playfully hit him in his arm.

"It's just that . . . Wayne, I was raised to wait, and since I didn't, I realize that maybe we should've waited."

"Uh oh, what are you saying? Are you saying that maybe you wanna chill?"

"I mean is our relationship based purely on sex?" Trick question. Dewayne needed to answer this right. Truthfully, he could say yes, because all they did was have sex. He did love her, there was no doubt.

"Of course not!"

"Okay," Karen stood back and let go of him, "let's take a fast."

"Is that like a quickie?" Dewayne joked but straightened up at her look of disapproval, "You mean no . . . nookie?" Dewayne had that hurt look again. The thunder clashed and the timing gave Dewayne's dumb founded look a little comedic flavor. She giggled.

"Not a bit. Come on it can't be that hard. Let's just find something else to do."

"Like what?"

"Television or play a board game?"

"Okay, let's play twister."

"No."

"Strip poker?"

"Okay, television it is." Karen sighed and clicked the TV on and sat on the bed. Dewayne slowly and awkwardly sat next to her with his hands in his lap. The rain tapped on the window harder and harder. Karen attempted to keep her wits because to her, rain was so romantic and was the perfect atmosphere for love making. Dewayne couldn't concentrate on the TV from trying to plot on how to accidentally brush against Karen.

"What time is it?" He stretched back behind her to the other side of the bed to look at the clock. His leg rubbed against her arm. She took a breath. He continued to lean back, rubbing his stomach, allowing his six-pack to only slightly peek through. She attempted to ignore him. She crossed her legs and Dewayne bit his lip to see her thigh, so smooth asking him to touch—well in his own little world. Alas, he couldn't resist, and when he sat back up he rubbed his nose on her earlobe. Karen took a breath.

"Well . . ." whispered Karen.

"Yeah?" whispered Dewayne.

"We'll start tomorrow." When it rains it pours. Love was in the air and young hormones were overriding the desire to be chaste. College was full of hot-blooded young people, with only one thing on their mind.

CHAPTER FOUR

"I heard that a lot of girls on campus really like you. Word on the street is that you get around." Philip and I were eating in the cafeteria. He looked up surprised. I confronted him with the info I had been given because I had to figure out what type of guy he was. I didn't want to be just another girl.

"That doesn't mean I like them," he responded.

"Do you have sex with them?" I pointed my little plastic fork at him, and continued to rake my casserole, waiting for a response.

"I thought you said you weren't churchy."

"I'm not, I mean I know I got things I need to work on, but there are some things I don't do just because."

"Like not have sex? I don't get it. What's wrong with sex? God made sex. When you love someone you should show them that you love them."

"And you really loved all those girls you had sex with?" I raised my eyebrow and gave him a skeptic look.

"I cared about them."

"Whatever. Sex bonds you mentally, spiritually, and physically with a person. The Bible—"

"Uh oh, here goes the little preacher."

I gave him another look. He had the nerve to comment. "The Bible says that when man and woman join they become one. When you have sex with a person you get everything they are physically. If they have a disease you can sexually get it from them. The same goes with the mental and spiritual. Mentally, you may start acting like them and spiritually you have a bond that can't be broken." Philip seemed intrigued and yet spooked. My best bet was to ease up or suffer the wrath of loneliness, plus I did think I was acting like my mother.

"Hmm, you ready to head back?" Philip looked at his watch. All my Bible talk had surely turned him off.

"I don't know. My roommate is probably engaging in what we're talking about right now. They're awfully touchy-feely."

"Really? And what's wrong with that?" Philips caressed my hand with his index finger and I pulled it back.

"I just prefer not to advertise." I got up from the table and threw my plate away.

"Well, since they like to spend quality time, maybe you can chill at the front desk with me for awhile." I looked back at him and he stood there with his head tilted, waiting for a response. He grinned.

"So I haven't scared you away with all my church talk?"

"Naw, you're smart. I find that sexy." I blushed. I hadn't had a guy tell me that before. I turned around quickly. This guy was a big flirt and I was going to have to be prepared at all times. I resituated myself because I wasn't going to be the one to be taken so easily. I didn't want him to know he was winning me over so well. In fact, in all my life of dating, I never felt so at ease. It was as if Philip really knew me.

"So, you're single because . . ." I asked nonchalantly. He glanced back at me as he threw his plate away.

He giggled. "You're asking me because . . . maybe you're interested?" I looked flabbergasted at his comment and gave him a face to let him know that his statement was all but appropriate.

"Why would I be interested in you?" I grabbed my keys and my backpack. He giggled and gave a smirk that I intentionally ignored. We walked outside and the rain was beginning to subside. It was still slightly sprinkling.

"You know you still haven't answered my question." We got back in the truck.

Philip checked his teeth out in the mirror. "What was your question again? I forgot." I started the truck. Philip wasn't slick. He was playing games and sooner or later he was going to realize . . . I had the dice.

"You want to walk back to the dorm don't you?"

"Ahh man, you would do me like that?" His eyes twinkled like little stars. I cleared my throat. Philip was hiding something and I wasn't going to be caught up in his little web of deceit. I cracked the window to let a little cool air in. In any case, I would be his friend first. From what I already know, he has plenty of girls already filling his head up with nonsense. All I needed to do was pop that little ego and maybe he would be a decent guy. Every dog needed to be trained, and maybe I was the girl to train this one.

"Philip."

"Yes, Andrea."

"Put your seatbelt on."

We made it back to the dorm and Philip had managed to not really give me a clear answer to any question I had directed toward him. But that was cool—sooner or later it would be my turn. The more disinterest I would show, maybe he would become more interested. I wasn't the type of girl that threw her panties at people's face. Brotha man was going to have to work for me.

As we entered the lobby I continued to walk up to my room, paying him very little mind.

"Hey, I thought you were going to chill with me downstairs."

"You know I just thought that maybe I should finish unpacking. Just call me later, okay?" I wouldn't give him my number. He worked at the dorm; I'm sure he could find it if he really wanted it. I walked towards the stairs hoping that when I got to the room that Karen and Dewayne would be done with whatever they were doing. Once I made it to the door I my ear against it. I didn't hear anything. I knocked.

"Karen, I left my key; open up!" I knocked again. I heard some movement and feet rummaging on the floor.

"Hold on, girl," Karen said and something else inaudible that I couldn't decipher. Dewayne answered the door and smiled.

"Sup?" he said, half out of breath. I looked at him suspiciously.

"Hey, Dewayne." He had his shoes in his hand but he was fully clothed.

"You leaving?"

"Yeah. I have to . . . get some stuff done." I nodded at him and he hopped out the door trying to put his shoes on. I closed the door behind me. Karen fixed her hair in the mirror.

"So . . . how was your little rendezvous with Philip?" She had to ask. I didn't know what to tell her. I wasn't quite sure what to think about him.

"He seems okay. But I can tell he is a player."

"I told you, Andrea. You better watch out."

"He's nothing I can't handle. Don't worry about me."

Karen put her hands on her hip facing toward me. She swayed in my direction. "Well, I am scared of you. Just remember what I said. These boys are nothing to be playing with." I knew that Karen was right, but I couldn't resist the challenge to see if she was wrong, to see if I could possibly tame the dog out of Philip. I went to open one of my boxes and pulled a clean sheet out and spread it on my bed, tucking in the corners and throwing some pillows on it to give it some sense of comfort. Not at all as dainty and cute as Karen's side of the room, but being prissy wasn't at all my style. I flopped down on the bed, and resting back on my elbows, I kicked my shoes off.

"So, tell me more about yourself, Karen."

"What do you want to know?"

"I don't know. Anything about yourself." I felt kind of guilty. She probably had told me a lot about herself when I was ignoring her. It's just something about long uninterrupted talking that tends to make me daydream.

"Yeah, well I think you're the one that needs to talk. I mean, what are you about small town girl?"

"I'm just tired of my town. It's way too small. If I stayed there, then I could almost predict who was going to ask me to marry them."

Karen eyes widened. "Are you serious?"

"Yeah, almost half the girls in my senior class got engaged after graduation. I just didn't want to be another Heaven statistic."

"That sounds funny. But I'm sure you've heard all the jokes," Karen said.

"Yeah, well I've come here," I stood up and spread my arms out like wings, "to be free and to find myself. To figure out who I am outside of Heaven. God knows I'm more than some small country girl. I mean, I grew up there just like everybody else, but I could never understand why I didn't have the same mentality as they did. Why didn't I grow with that same slow settled country behavior?"

"God has something already predestined for you to do."

"God and destiny are things I really have problems with though." I walked over to the window and looked through the blinds.

"Why is that? Everyone has a destiny. I mean some people have small destinies and some have very large ones. We need the presidents and world leaders as much as we need people to pick up trash. It doesn't mean that any particular destiny is greater than the other."

I hated to hear the word destiny. After my daddy died I remember how mama would try to comfort me; telling me that it was just meant to be. That God wanted Daddy to be with him, wanted him to be one of His angels. I hated when she said that. I hated when she spiritualized what happened. And for a while I hated her for what she said. Why would God steal my daddy from me when I needed him most? I was way closer to him than I was my mom, and now he was gone . . . forever.

"I don't know, Karen, it just seems that life doesn't seem fair no matter what you do or what you plan, it really doesn't matter. What if God is playing our lives like little game pieces and it really doesn't matter how we act or how much we love Him; whatever is going to happen is going to happen?"

"I think that what we do has to have something to do with what happens to us. I mean, sure there are things that are destined for us no matter what we choose. I do believe that some things happen based on a series of decisions that we make." I was disturbed, but my thoughts continued to swim in my mind like the clouds outside. My fingers rubbed down the window. I could see my transparent reflection in the window.

I sighed. "What about love?"

"What about love?" she asked back.

"Do you think that there is one person destined for us and that if we don't do the right thing we will miss them?"

"Well Andrea, if you are talking about destiny then

there is no way you will miss them, because any decision you make will ultimately lead you back to them. I think when it comes to destiny, there are many people you will date or love that you may be meant to meet because they will help you learn a lesson or something out of that relationship will benefit you for the future. Ultimately, I believe, there is that one person you are supposed to be with." Karen was bias. Sure she wanted to believe that Dewayne was her one and only. But who was I to slap her with a dose of reality that things just happen? I listened intently to what she was saying and sat down on the floor.

"But what if," I interjected, "we say that our destiny is affected by our choices we make? Then maybe we have more than one destiny meaning that we may have more than one person in life to love. Maybe what makes God so omniscient is that He knows all the decisions we can make that can ultimately destroy us and he knows all the decisions that can ultimately make us great. I mean, how do you explain people that get stuck in relationships that are abusive? Are they destined for that? Is that woman destined to be with an abusive man or did she make the wrong decisions that ultimately led her to that?" I pulled my hair out of its pony tail because it was beginning to bother me, and let my long hair fall to my shoulders. "What if, God has many possible people that could be destined for us?"

"Why would you say that?" Karen said, sitting on the edge of her bed with her legs crossed as lady-like as possible.

"Well, I hate to think that if only one person was destined for me that he could die before me meeting him and then I would never have loved. I'm saying that what if God has many people that could be compatible with me that he would be very please if I married; and that any one of those people would help me in different ways to reach my ultimate destiny."

"What if your ultimate destiny was just to be married?"

"Well, that would suck. Anyhow, isn't it also true that when you reach your destiny, that you die?" I replied.

"Well, it's like this. What if the man you married got in a car accident and he was so injured that you had to take care of him even though he was so crippled and disfigured that he couldn't have sex, speak, or do anything on his own?"

That was a good question that Karen presented and I seriously had to think about it. "Well, if I married him because I truly loved him then it wouldn't be a problem. I would stick with him and take care of him."

"Then that would be your destiny."

"Yeah, I guess so. I don't think most men would do the same. It just seems to me when a woman needs a man to be there for her, he leaves."

Karen rubbed her feet and laid down on her side on her plush looking comforter. "Well they aren't men, they're boys. But Dewayne is way different. I think he really loves me."

I didn't know Dewayne, so I didn't want to accuse him of something that maybe he wasn't guilty of. "Well, Karen, from what I know, guys can be really bad at leaving when times get rough."

It was all too real to me. In Heaven there was this girl that all the guys thought was so hot. Her name was Brandi Benningfield. Brandi was a cheerleader, and like most cheerleaders, dated the star football player, Martin Korwenski.

"Move it nigger," Brandi said as she pushed my books out my hand onto the floor of the school hallway. I would have slapped that redneck silly had my mother not taught me any better. She told me time and time again that I should let the Lord handle such ignorance. Besides, she had her click with her and there was

no breaking that circle. It was because of Brandi that I wasn't on the cheerleading squad. Dang, it was the twentieth century. You would think that people would stop being so ignorant. So I waited for the Lord, and I just felt like evidently He didn't see what was going on so I prayed that something bad would happen to Brandi. I prayed that she would get what she had coming for doing me wrong. Vengeance is the Lord's right?

"Hey, baby," she said to Martin who was conversing with his fans. She snuck up behind him and hugged his neck laying her head on his back. Her blonde hair blanketed his shoulders and he turned his head to see who had attached themselves to him.

"Brandi!" He smiled and pulled her around to his front. They engaged in a very intimate kiss that would be considered totally inappropriate. I was never one for public displays of affection. It was just plain gross and all Martin was doing was trying to show the whole school that he had the finest girl in school. His trophy wasn't all those gold footballs in the school display case, it was Brandi with all that golden hair. It was a story book relationship with all the fixings. She wore his class ring. They were voted homecoming king and queen and went to the playoffs. They must have celebrated too hard over that victory because Brandi stopped cheerleading. The rumors went around quickly and soon everyone knew . . .

"What do you mean you're pregnant?" Martin yelled at her in the middle of the hall. She was crying and scared. Maybe she thought he wouldn't kill her if she told him at school. He slammed the locker door by her head and she jumped.

"Please, Martin, I don't know what to do."

"Well, I don't know what you expect me to do." She tried to hug him, but he jerked back and walked away, leaving her huddled on the ground by the locker. I saw the whole thing and went to see if I could help but she glared at me.

"What are you looking at nigger?" Reminded me to not be so helpful to the racist whore. She jumped up and walked off swaying her hips. But those hips got bigger and her belly began to swell

*and she decided to keep the baby. Maybe she thought that after the
baby was born Martin would have a change of heart. That maybe
after he saw that beautiful little girl, that would put his priorities
in line and that he would step up and be a man. But he didn't.*

"Martin please," Brandi pleaded.

*"What do you want Brandi?" He was in the gym after school
lifting weights and clearly more concerned with his outward
physique than the offspring he had created. She stood there holding the baby in her now chubby arms. The pregnancy had not
done her body well and she had gained a considerable amount of
weight. It was hard to believe that just nine months ago she was
the captain of the cheerleading squad.*

*"I want you to be responsible, Martin. What happened to us?
What did I do?" He reset the barbell on its stand, sitting back up
and wiping his mouth with a towel. He looked at her and stood
up flexing his pectorals and bent down to whisper in her ear.*

*"You got fat. I don't want you. Get that through your stupid
head." He left her. He left her crying with a crying baby in her
arms.*

It was horrible, even for Brandi. But from then on I saw
that men could be cold and heartless to girls that they pro-
fessed love to. I saw that to some men, if you changed just
a little, he would leave you. I didn't want a man leaving me
because I gained a little weight or if something worse happened. But were these really men at all? No—these were
boys who were scared of change. Just like Karen had said;
little boys afraid of becoming men and everything that
came with it. It also scared me to think I prayed that something bad would happen to her. Did I have something to
do with what happened? Would God answer a prayer that
would hurt someone else? It made me feel slightly responsible and guilty and I didn't know how to get rid of the
feeling.

"No, Dewayne wouldn't treat me bad," Karen said. "If
he did, I would kick his butt." I smiled at Karen's confi-

dence in Dewayne. I didn't want to be prejudice of all men.

"I'm sure Dewayne is a good man." I picked myself off the floor and unpacked some remaining boxes from yesterday.

"Hey, I'm sure God has somebody for you; when you're not looking you'll find him." I looked at her with a box in my hand, pulling more books out and stacking them on each other.

"No, Karen, I won't find him," she looked muzzy and I smirked at her finishing my comment, "he is going to find me."

CHAPTER FIVE

Dewayne unlocked the door of his room and threw his shoes down in a corner. "Hey! Hey! You don't have a live-in maid. Pick those shoes up!" A voice said in the darkness. Dewayne squinted and felt around for the light switch.

"I'm sorry, Anthony." Dewayne flicked the light on and picked up his shoes and placed them next to his bed.

"Chill out with that cussing, too," Anthony said. "I'm trying to have a little Bible study. I have a theology test already at the end of the week." Anthony Turner was Dewayne's roommate who was majoring in Divinity. Anthony wanted to be a preacher and he had thought about going to seminary school but wanted to get some life experience from the real world as well. Besides, he figured that he could take his masters at a Christian school.

Anthony was an average black man, bald-head fade, coal black skin, with piercing dark almond-shaped, almost Asian like eyes and high cheek bones. His nose was keen unlike a black man, but his facial features were very strong, as if he was straight from Africa. He wasn't very tall, as his legs bowed at the knees. He was a die-hard Christian, the type that probably went to vacation Bible school every summer and highly educated on anything spiritual. That's what he was, pure book knowledge.

He laid on his stomach reading his Bible and taking notes with nothing but the reading lamp propped on the edge of his bedpost.

"Is that all you do is read your Bible?" Dewayne asked and Anthony flashed his bed lamp in Dewayne's eyes. Dewayne hissed like a vampire when the light hit his eyes.

"I knew it! Where's my holy oil at?" Anthony laughed.

Dewayne threw a pillow at Anthony. "Shut up!" The pillow hit Anthony in the face knocking his notes to the floor and he tossed the pillow back at Dewayne.

"I can't believe you already know about your tests."

"I grabbed the class syllabus and checked out when the tests were. This way I will be ahead and will ace this first test with no problem. The rest of those jokers will be caught off-guard." Anthony sat up and picked his notes up off the floor. Dewayne just grinned and shook his head. He was amazed at how nerdy his roommate was.

Both Dewayne and Anthony had taken summer school courses, so they pretty much had the dorm to themselves with the exception of a few others scattered sporadically down the hall. There wasn't much to do on campus throughout the summer but study, sleep or play video games. Dewayne usually chose the video game option, while Anthony was always in the books. It was amazing how Dewayne managed to ace summer school between playing Metroid on his Nintendo and spending time with Karen. Anthony had a strong work ethic and was expected by his parents to do well. He was from Baltimore so he had no one to really depend on down south. But he knew that he had not come to school to mess around and mess up.

Dewayne was from the hood—sunny South Dallas. And

even though he was just from around the corner, his mama didn't play when it came to his grades. When both guys found themselves completely bored, Dewayne would take Anthony around the hood and show him where all the best little eating places were. The hardest part was just getting Anthony to put his books down long enough get out and enjoy everything. Dewayne would laugh to see Anthony trailing behind him with a humongous book bag of textbooks.

Dewayne and Anthony were two opposite ends of the spectrum. Dewayne was the natural procrastinator, living every day for the moment, and Anthony was the business man using all his time to maximize his studies but yet missing the enjoyable things in life. As friends, they learned from each other when the other was truly willing to step beyond his comfort zone.

"What class is your test for?" Dewayne asked, changing out of his clothes and looking for a towel.

"My theology class. You taking a shower kinda early aren't ya? You must've got busy with Karen."

"Yeah, so?"

"Don't get yourself in trouble. Ya'll are kind of hot and bothered lately."

"Yeah, well, we decided to chill for awhile, Dad." Anthony looked at Dewayne who was good at finding a sarcastic remark at the right time. Anthony pitched a nearby towel that was tucked underneath the desk at Dewayne.

"Man, I'm not trying to be daddy for you, man, it's just I don't want you messing up. You have a scholarship and everything and it just seems crazy that you would come to school and just goof off."

"I'm not goofing off!" Dewayne was tired of hearing that he might mess his chances up. "And who said that you could just judge me, Anthony? I'm not like you. I'm still trying to get my life together. Karen thought that maybe

we need to concentrate on God a little more. God under-
stands me and knows I like sex."

"And you're cool with that? You're cool with chilling
without sex for awhile?"

"We just started adding sex to our relationship just recently so we did it before and we can do it again." Dewayne
wrapped himself in a towel and kicked his jeans off from
underneath the towel and tossed them on the floor with his
foot. Anthony just stared down at the jeans. Anthony had
this neat freak thing going on and every time Dewayne
came in—well a mess followed. Anthony found himself
constantly picking up after Dewayne. If he didn't, there
would be stacks of soda cans, fast food wrappers, and pizza
boxes everywhere. Anthony often wondered had Dewayne
ever learned the concept of trash bags.

Now to Dewayne this chaos did have a particular order.
There was a pile for clean clothes, dirty clothes, trash, trash
that you use over (like maybe a cool plastic cup), and of
course school books. But to Anthony this chaotic mess was
just one big pile. Anthony, on the contrary, was organized
down to his socks.

"Uh, Dewayne." Dewayne looked down at his pants which
had in no particular order stretched across the floor like a
throw rug.

"Oh sorry. I keep forgetting, Mom." He picked up his
pants and threw them on his bed. Dewayne reached under
the bed and grabbed his flip flop sandals and proceeded
out the door.

"I'm not your mother either!" Anthony yelled through
the thin door that shook when Dewayne closed it behind
him.

Dewayne's flip-flops rhythmically popped the hard hallway floor and went down the hall to the shower. The hall
was still empty and there were only about eighty residents
total in the entire three-story dorm. There were only six

other guys on Anthony and Dewayne's floor, but the students were slowly but surely moving in. The shower room was dark and had one flickering light; clearly something out of b-rated horror movies. The only other shower was upstairs on the third floor and that shower room had issues with the water staying hot. So, second floor shower room it was. He flicked the light on and off to maybe help the light to stop flickering to no avail. He simply entered the shower room under the continuous blinking bulb.

"They need to fix that thing." His voice echoed through the shower room. He turned on a shower head and put his towel in eyesight view—he knew how some guys would steal towels as a prank. The water blast felt like a fire hose and knocked Dewayne back a little.

"Ah man, I forgot my soap . . . oh well, I'll just rinse off." Dewayne splashed around in the shower. He closed his eyes, allowing the hot water to massage his neck and then the water suddenly went cold. Dewayne hollered and jumped to the side out of the blast of the water. Holding his shoulders, he put his foot back in the stream to see if the water had warmed up.

"Man, what's wrong with the water?" he spat.

"*Dewayne.*"

Dewayne stopped—silent. He reached for his towel, but suddenly, the flickering light blew out, creating a pitch-black darkness. Dewayne backed up against the shower wall covering his nakedness with his arms even though he could no longer see himself clearly. The towel was out of reach and he had failed to grab it before the light bulb popped out.

"Hello?" His voice resonance was followed up by an empty eerie silence that made his heart slightly thump harder in his chest. He wondered if he had imagined the voice.

"Anthony? Anthony, man, stop playing. Turn the light

back on." He wasn't sure, but it felt like someone was in the shower room with him. Goosebumps formed on his arms. *Find the towel* was the only thought that was going through Dewayne's mind. Through the darkness he felt along the wall slowly. But the closer his hand was against the dark wall, the closer he felt he was getting to, something. He could feel the presence of something. It was that feeling that you get when you know someone is pointing or looking at you even when you have your eyes closed.

He tried to focus his eyes but all he could see was darkness. The thought that someone whispered his name echoed through his mind like his voice did in the shower room. But who knew he was there other than Anthony? He closed his eyes, felt against the wall and reached forward. Grabbing his towel, he felt something brushing his shoulder. He didn't wait another minute. He turned around and started running, slipping down onto the wet floor. In a panic he pulled himself up and looked for the light of the hallway. Wrapping his towel around him, he ran back down the hall not looking back. He burst through his dorm door, disturbing Anthony once more in his studies.

"Very funny, man!" he yelled. His chest was heaving up and down trying to catch his breath.

"What's wrong with you?" Anthony said, closing his notebook.

"What's wrong with me? What's wrong with you, trying to scare me in the shower?"

"Man, I have been here the whole time. What happened?"

Dewayne leaned against the door clutching his towel with his balled-up fist. He was trying to figure out what had just happened. Some one was in there with him but if that was possible, then it couldn't have been Anthony.

"Man, I am trippin'," Dewayne said. Anthony laughed and sat up.

"Dewayne, what happened to you man?"

Dewayne went to his bed and threw his boxers on and to Anthony's disgust an old t-shirt that had already been worn. Dewayne sat there for a second with his towel whipped over his neck. He rubbed over his own hands to keep them from shaking and he didn't want to give Anthony the impression that he had been spooked, but he was. "Man, don't think I'm crazy or anything . . . but I could've sworn I heard someone call my name in the shower room. The voice I heard wasn't really audible. It was airy and misty like I really didn't hear it, but I did. And then, then the lights went off and—" Dewayne was interrupted by his roommate's laughter. "Come on, man, I'm serious!"

Anthony regained his composure. "Wayne, I'm sorry. What are you thinking, that the dorm may be haunted?" Dewayne wanted to write that idea off immediately. He never liked watching horror movies and he didn't want to live one."

"Probably just some guys from the other hall playing a trick."

"But, Dewayne, you said they said your name. Who else knows you around here?" Nightfall was coming fast and it was still lightning outside, giving the room an eerie effect. The only light in the room was Anthony's bed lamp, which casted a spooky look on his face.

"Ya know, people get killed in dorms all the time and the campus covers it up . . . ship the bodies out real quiet so the enrollment doesn't go down. You probably ran into an unrested spirit that wants vindication."

"Shut up, man!" Dewayne said, looking freaked out. "Don't tell me that. That sounds like a scary movie or something and you know black folks don't last long in those kind of movies."

Anthony fell back on his bed laughing. He couldn't help it. Playing with Dewayne's mind was too easy.

"Do you believe in ghosts?" Dewayne asked. He took his towel and balled it up using it like a pillow to lay his head on as he laid down on his bed. He assumed the fetal position and his eyes were wide when he asked his question, much like a child at a campfire story. Anthony couldn't resist teasing Dewayne some more.

"Ghosts? I'm not sure. I mean that would mean like a dead person who couldn't find his way. I have found that in different cultures everyone believes in spirits. Do I believe in spirits?" He leaned in, "Yes, I'm sure they are quite common in our day to day lives. I have read about other spirits that can assume human form and even pretend to be other people."

"Like what? Never mind, I don't wanna know. I'm getting scared."

Anthony continued despite Dewayne getting scared. "Angels for one example. I think people just assume they look like men, but I think they are spiritual beings that make themselves look like people for our own benefit."

"What do you think they really look like?" Dewayne asked. His curiosity in the unknown had been aroused.

"Who knows? If I look into history and reference what type of 'angelic' spirits other cultures have seen that had the 'ability' to look like men, and if I assume that these are the same creatures, angels can look like animals, half animals, unexplainable beasts, or something as simple as sounding like a voice, but . . ."

"But? But what?" Dewayne demanded to Anthony's silent thought.

"It was probably just another resident playing a prank."

"Yeah." Dewayne tried laughing it off. "Maybe so." They both sat there in silence as Dewayne still tried to process in his mind what had just happened. He was slowly convincing himself it was just a prank because that was what he wanted to believe. It is amazing how when we want to believe in something we can make it true.

"Where did you learn all this?" he asked Anthony slowly.

"In my mythology class. You should take the class. It's pretty cool."

"I'm a bio-chemistry major. I study genetics."

"You still need an elective. I think you will learn something."

"Well, since you put it that way." The thunder crashed and Dewayne jumped a bit.

Anthony pretended to not notice. "Mythology consists of centuries of stories of other people's cultures. It brings people, culture, life, and religion together. How can people really know about God if they don't know about the people he created?"

Still in the fetal position Dewayne wrapped himself in a blanket. "I don't know. What do you mean?"

"Well, what I'm saying is that in religion, mainly Christianity now, since that's what I am and I know so well, some people choose to be pious and not even look into other cultures and know why others do the things they do."

"Can you still be Christian and study other religions?" Dewayne asked. "Doesn't that show a lack of faith? I mean people can take this and that from other religions until they create their own. They can do whatever they want without any problem or issue. Is that what you're doing, Anthony?"

Anthony shook his head, "My faith is still in God and Jesus Christ, Dewayne. But I just have an inner desire to know more about God. God may have given the secret to eternal life and salvation to the nation of Israel, but I believe God has revealed himself to every culture and every nation in some way. You have to read for yourself." Anthony excitedly flipped through the pages of his book as the momentum of his words increased. "Do you realize how many accounts of the creation exist? True enough, there are differences but if we," He stuttered over his words trying to get the right words out, "look at what's the same and we may find the truth. In-in-in most accounts of creation, people believe that a-a-uh God or spirit that wasn't created by anything created t-the uh world from darkness, or uh-uh-uh-uh water and even in-in some stories he created man in either a clay like form or in-in uh a clay like manner." Anthony always got excited talking about things related to God. And when he got excited he talked fast. And when he talked fast he stuttered. And when he stuttered Dewayne got lost between his words.

"Anthony, have you thought about taking a speech class?" Anthony stopped mid-stream and glowered at Dewayne. He had the notion that Dewayne wasn't listening, so he just rolled over in his bed and moved his lamp so that only he could see it. Dewayne was in the darkness of the room.

"Go to bed, Dewayne. And I hope the ghost don't try to crawl in bed with you."

"Hey, that's not funny."

CHAPTER SIX

"Hello?" my voice echoes down the hall. "Karen?" I yell looking for my key. "Open the door."

"Who are you?" Karen speaks from the other side.

"It's me, Andrea."

"No, I asked, who are you?" she says again.

I'm confused and I knock harder. "Girl open this door and quit playing. Is Dewayne in there?"

"I can't let you in. It's out there and I don't want to let it in," I hear Karen say and she walks away.

"Karen!" I slam on the door with my fist. The lights in the hallway go out. I look behind me holding my breath. I hear nothing but the beat of my heart. I jiggle the knob once more and the thought that "it" is out where I am haunts me.

Footsteps. I don't hesitate and I walk in the opposite direction. I hear them walking and then slowly speeding up in my direction. I run down the hall—the endless hall. The footsteps keep a steady pace behind me.

"Who's there? Philip? Dewayne? Who's following me?" I keep running, knocking on doors as I pass by, trying doors to see if they're unlocked.

"Oh God! Somebody help me !" I run to the stairway exit at the end of the hall.

The door's locked and the only thing lighting the hall is the red glow of the exit sign. I stand with my back against the door as the foot steps get closer, waiting to see what will walk into the light and reveal itself. Waiting. Closer and closer until a dark silhouette begins to emerge and I feel my own breath leave.

"Andrea."

I woke up suddenly. It was a dream. College jitters I guess. I wiped the sweat from my brow and sat up in bed. Other than that freaky dream, I had slept well with the exception of some growling from a dog outside my window. I thought I had gotten away from the wilds of the country.

Karen was still under the covers snuggled tight within her comforter. I sat on the edge of the bed. My feet were cold on the hard linoleum floor. I thought that maybe it would be a good idea to go to the store and find some things to decorate my room. It would probably be good to get one of those small throw rugs to put down by the bed.

The bed creaked as I sat up from it and stretched. I took my hair and gave it one big braided pony tail and threw on some jeans. I threw on my t-shirt from the previous day because I hadn't had the chance to sort all my clothes yet. The rays of sunlight peeked through the mini-blinds, revealing the dust particles in the air. I grabbed my wallet from the desk and stuck it in my mouth to hold it as I put on my shoes and laced them up. I went to the mirror and looked at myself. Sure I was rough looking, but hopefully I wouldn't run into anybody this early in the day.

I quietly left the slumbering beauty to her dreams and went out the door into the hall. When I made it into the lobby I peeked into the hallway to see if Philip was working this early. He wasn't there. I was a little disappointed as I had wished to see him again. But I knew that I would have plenty of time to see and get to know Philip.

I walked some ways and spotted a little furry pile near the bushes on the outside of the building where my window is adjacent. Curious, I walked across the cool damp lawn and discovered the mutilated body of some animal. I wasn't sure if it was a dog or cat. The face and most of the body had been ripped to shreds and all that was left of it was pieces of fur and some blood-stained bones. I knelt down to see closer and noticed that there wasn't much blood around it at all. Whatever attacked this animal last night had its fill. I must write myself a mental note—call animal control when I get back.

I got in my truck and drove it down to a nearby shopping center. The day was cooler than before but the sun was still behind a few clouds. There was a nice feeling about getting my day started before everyone else was up and about. The shopping center was open twenty-four hours so I figured that this would be the college hang out if I needed anything at the spur of the moment. Who knew when one might need an emergency bag of cheese puffs or a roll of toilet paper. But this was college so I'm sure that most students were only interested in getting emergency contraceptives late at night.

I had avoided letting Philip know I was a virgin. I didn't know if I wanted to stay that way or not. It was just that basically I was scared. I had heard so many horrible stories about how sex hurt. Besides, I had so many home girls in high school lose their virginity in the most awful ways that I just didn't want to be known as the local town whore for the rest of my life. Kelly Fernando was my friend freshmen year. We had known each other all through junior high school and everything. I had known Kelly to be a fairly nice girl, smart as a computer and pretty too. But I guess every good thing has it's imperfections because Kelly's self esteem was horrible. She always talked down about herself and never really believed in who she was. I can remember how she would constantly put on tons of makeup just to feel pretty.

"Do I look ugly, Andrea?" Kelly asked me the question a lot. She was insecure and put on makeup like she was auditioning to be a mime. I was walking on eggshells not to destroy what she had tried so hard to build up. I searched my mind for the right words to say, deterring myself from the truth. Those all-so-innocent eyes covered with heavy spider-like eye mascara and outlined like a caricature with eyeliner were looking to me for some sort of approval.

"You're pretty, Kelly," I managed. "Very pretty. Do you really need to hide all that?"

"Hide what?" Kelly's expression was magnified by the way the makeup-drawn eyebrows arched and the dark clown-like ruby red lipstick gave her this Elvira, mistress of the dark look. Her dark hair was hair sprayed stiff so that if a hurricane came and killed her, at least her hair would still look good. Shawn Jenkins, one of the upper classmen, walked by and looked our way, but didn't say a word. Kelly grabbed my arm so hard I would have hit her, but I knew why she was so under Shawn's spell. Shawn was on the basketball team and I had to admit that he was all of that and a bag of chips. After seeing him though, Kelly went to painting herself again.

"Kelly come on, that's enough makeup," I said, grabbing her hand with the makeup.

"Yeah, but I gotta zit and I'm trying to cover it up." I'm thinking she got the zit from the make up but I didn't want to say that out loud. I just sighed to myself and leaned against the locker.

Now that I think about it, knowing Kelly's family I thought that maybe her problem started there. Her father wasn't the best man in the world. He was there in her life physically, but he might as well have been like those other deadbeat dads because he wasn't there emotionally. Kelly was always trying to get her father's approval in so many things, but he just didn't seem to care at all. Kelly's dad never hugged her, never told her she was pretty, and never spent more than two minutes in the same room with her. She complained about her dad often but never told him how she felt.

What Kelly didn't verbally say, she expressed, and that's when the makeup piled on. Slowly Kelly's face disappeared underneath this face that she had drawn on. Like a clown, she put a happy face on when deep down inside she was hurting.

She had met Shawn just a few days after school had started and there was something about an upper classmen speaking to freshmen that put Kelly into the very presence of God. I was beginning to worry because when Kelly was into a guy, she ceased to remember that she had friends anymore and my phone stopped ringing. But I tried not to let that bother me. She later called me up frantic.

"Andrea, oh my gawd!" I was half sleep and was still trying to figure out who was on the phone.

"Who is this?" I asked.

"It's me, Kelly." It took some time for the voice to register in my mind because I hadn't heard from her in two weeks.

"What time is it? Why are you calling me so late?"

"I did it," Kelly stated as if I was supposed to know what she had done.

"Did what?"

"IT." She emphasized more and in the language of teenagers I caught on emphatically. But as we continued to talk about Kelly's first time I grew more and more repulsed as I realized that it wasn't the same fantasy that I had built up for myself of losing my virginity. No, not in the least. There were no bottles of champagne and roses on the bed. There was no soft music by Luther Vandross playing in the background or burning incense in the air.

Kelly had given up her virginity at school. Somewhere between periods she and Shawn had met up and he and all his raging hormones had convinced her to go back behind the gym where the dumpsters were. Somewhere outside, against the wall of the gym, hidden behind a dumpster smelling of spoiled milk and surrounded by maggots and flies, Kelly Fernando had exposed her naked body and given up her virginity to Shawn Jenkins. The whole experience had taken less than two minutes to complete and by the time the bell had rung he didn't even give her a kiss goodbye. He just ran off to his next class leaving her against the wall in between the dumpster and the gym with nothing to show for it except a used condom at her feet.

This is why Kelly was upset that Shawn wasn't talking to her. This is why Shawn went around the school talking about Kelly. This is why Kelly eventually gave in to the negative attention around her. This is why I eventually stopped hanging around Kelly or she just stopped hanging around me.

Heaven's whore as they called her back then.

"Everyone is calling you names, Kelly!" I pulled her aside trying to get her attention.

She rolled her eyes. "It's none of your business, Andrea."

"I'm your friend. I'm trying to help."

Kelly exploded in rage, "Well uh, I don't think you can begin to imagine what I go through. You're so—"

"What . . . I'm what?"

"You're so perfect," Kelly said in a way that appeared to disgust her.

"What are you talking about? I'm not."

She interrupted me. "Oh please, don't even try to be humble. Andrea, you can't even see. All my life you have been the pretty girl. Just for once I want some attention!" She held back her tears and recomposed herself. "I want guys to like me. I'm so tired of being alone. You'll never have to worry about that. You're not like me. You can't understand me. So go back to being perfect and mind your business."

Perfect. That's what she called me. Befriending other girls seemed to always end up being some drama because in some fashion other girls were intimidated by me. I had something they didn't and the problem was I didn't know what it was.

My friendship convicted Kelly. It made her feel less than perfect. When Kelly told me that, I felt so alone. It made me feel like I was an outsider. I downplayed myself after that. I didn't want to appear like I was trying to be better than anyone. I just wanted to have someone, a true friend I could relate to who accepted me as me.

"Welcome to K-mart," the front store host said as I walked through the sliding doors. Sliding doors could make you feel powerful. Walking through them was an act of pure faith. I mean, people would confidently walk up to these doors knowing that they should open, and like clockwork, they would slide open as if to say "welcome master".

I grabbed my couple of items and went to the checkout line. Another girl was ahead of me and she smiled politely. She was an average looking black girl, slightly taller than me with short ashy brown hair all combed back and pulled into a knobby little stub of a pony tail. She was delightfully chubby, but not exactly fat, and her lips gave her a pouty look. She wore a sweatshirt and some shorts with some house shoes and she rested her weight on one hip. She had the school mascot, a zebra, on her shirt so I assumed she was attending the same college. She looked back at me again

and smiled. Her hands were full of little products and she
sat them down on the checkout stand as the elderly woman
at the checkout stand slowly picked the items up and
searched for the bar code.

"Hi, I'm Tamela. Do you go to Texas state college too?"
She asked me.

I was surprised that she had taken the initiative to introduce herself and ashamed that I had not.

"Um, yes. My name is Andrea." I extended my hand to
shake hers, but I could see that she still had an armful of
things and I waited until she was through setting them
down.

"You a freshmen?"

"Yeah, just trying to get used to everything." I was wondering if I had the essence of freshmen on me and if there
was a possibility that I could wash it off like removing dead
skin.

"So how do you like the campus so far?" Tamela seemed
like the type of girl that was more my style. Not too girly at
all. We could be good friends.

"The campus seems nice so far, but I haven't seen much
of it," I truthfully admitted.

"Oh wow, really? I can show you the ins and outs and
show you who to watch out for." Tamela's volunteering to
help me out was appreciated. The elderly cashier picked
up another item and Tamela sighed. "Looks like it's gonna
be awhile." she said.

I loved her assortment of jewelry. Her fingers were each
covered with little silver rings and she had beaded bracelets
on each arm.

"So do you like this school?" I asked.

Tamela shifted her weight on her other hip and thought
for a second. "I think that this school is okay. It's small and
quaint. There are little things that happen here and there
but for the most part, it's a pretty quiet campus."

Wonderful. I sighed. I went to a campus version of my town.

"So are you from Dallas?"

"No, I'm from a town called Heaven," I said attempting to smile.

She turned around and looked at me just as I thought she would. "Heaven huh? Are you an angel or something?" She smiled and squinted her eye at me as to examine me.

"No, just your every day average girl." My habitual attempt to play down myself again.

The elderly woman was about through with Tamela's items so I sat my two things down.

"That's going to be $14.05," the elderly woman said in a deep baritone voice, as if all vocal cords had been burnt by too much nicotine. I bit my lip trying not to laugh as I knew it would be very rude of me. Tamela glanced at me and I knew she was thinking the same thing I was. Why is it that people always found other people's misfortunes amusing? Maybe there was some dark evil side of us all that just couldn't help it.

"There's nothing average about you, Andrea. I can tell. Your aura is powerful. I felt you even before you walked up," Tamela said.

"My aura? What are you talking about?"

Tamela smiled and grabbed her bag of groceries once she had finally completed her transactions. "Nothing . . . don't worry about it. I just mean that I can tell you are a nice person and anybody nice like you isn't average. This world is filled with people who just want to use other people." The elderly woman proceeded to check my items out, slowly gripping them in her wrinkled and spotted hand.

"I guess so. But just because I am from the country doesn't mean that I'm naïve."

"Of course not. I just see things in people sometimes and . . . well I see things in you."

"Really?" She roused my curiosity, "Are you psychic or something?"

Tamela giggled. "Something like that. Hey did you drive up here?"

I nodded in reply.

Tamela looked outside at the sky through the windows of the store, "Look girl, I'm scared that I might get rained on. Can you give me a ride back to the dorm?"

"That's going to be $4.52," the dark voice came out of the woman. I handed her the money from my wallet.

"Sure, Tamela, no problem." I was beginning to wonder if anyone on this campus had a car. After paying for my things, Tamela silently walked behind me as I walked to my truck. She was silent and all I could hear were her house shoes sliding behind me. It made me uneasy and yet flattered me to have someone say that they saw something in me. Especially when I couldn't see anything. We got in the truck and headed back to the dorm.

"So has your roommate come yet?" she asked me. She rolled down the window and stuck her elbow out.

"Yeah. Her name is Karen. She seems real nice." She didn't really respond, but continued as if she had her train of thought going already.

"You should meet my roommate. Her name is Valerie. She is real cool, too. Valerie is from a small town like you so I bet you two would have a lot in common."

I smiled. "Yeah, I would like that."

"Good, well you should come up to the room later on today. We're not doing anything. Do you have any plans?"

Here was my problem: the inability to say no to people. I felt if I said no I would lose my chance at meeting new friends. I just didn't want to be the reason my friendships were killed before they could be started. "I guess that's cool," I finally said. "I mean all I have to do is register then

I can come to your room." We pulled into the parking lot of the dorm and Tamela opened the door.

"Good, I will see you later then. My room is 323," Tamela said as she hopped out the door and walked inside without waiting for me. I thought that I shouldn't think the worst. Meeting Tamela was good and she seemed to like me too. I think having a single friend would be beneficial versus hanging around Karen who was bound to depress me with her smooching with Dewayne so much. I grabbed my things and walked in the lobby and up to the second floor.

I opened the door and Karen was up and about spraying her hair down and sprinkling herself with perfume. I coughed walking past her.

"Girl, you are so dramatic," she smiled, pushing me aside.

"Is your boyfriend coming over?" I asked, thinking that maybe I should tidy up the place a bit. The boxes I had unpacked were still in the corner and there were a couple more I still needed to sort through. I didn't really attempt to decorate with the few posters that I had bought.

"No, I am going to go over there for a second. You want to come along? He has a really cute roommate."

"Maybe next time. I already planned on doing something this afternoon." Being the third wheel was one thing, but being intentionally set up was another. Plus, my focus was Philip.

"Oh, I get it." She puffed her hair out with a comb and smirked a bit, "You made plans with Philip. Girl, you work fast."

I threw my grocery bag down on the bed. "Uh no, Miss Thang, I did not hook up with Philip today. I just have other plans. I had a nice conversation with Philip yesterday and I find him to be a perfect gentleman."

"Uh huh. Which means you got the hots for him for real. But you have to watch out, girl, cause you know men can't be trusted." Karen put her comb down and fixed her lipgloss on her bottom lip with her pinky stroking left to right.

"I know you don't trust Philip and I don't know if I can either. But I just don't think he's a player like you make him out to be." Karen looked at me out of the corner of her eye and continued to rub her lipgloss on. It smelled like the wild spring strawberries that my mama would pick in the front of the house. Just watching Karen reminded me of how my mama would get ready for church in the morning. I needed to call her.

"I just heard from Dewayne that Philip has a lot of women who like him. You date a guy like Philip, you asking to get your heart broke. All men want is sex. And . . . well I hate the say this, but you are one of those girls that are naïve and so innocent. Most guys look at a pretty girl like you and they figure that you're easy game."

I felt insulted that Karen thought I was easy game. And what did my looks have to do with me being easy? My anger built up and I was simply tired of this prejudice. I figured Karen was like that cheerleader Brandi, who thought she was too good. I mean she had a boyfriend, why couldn't I? And what made her boyfriend so great? What made him the exception?

"What makes your boyfriend so great?"

"Who, Dewayne?" she asked as if Dewayne was immune from the subject matter.

"Dewayne is a good man."

"And Philip isn't? Maybe the issue is," I stood up behind Karen and looked at her through the reflection in the mirror, "maybe you saw Philip and you wished that you had him instead of Dewayne." Karen blotted her lips and rolled her eyes at me. "Maybe," I continued, "you wished that Dewayne was like Philip. Maybe you wonder what it would be like to have sex with—" She slammed down her lipgloss on the counter.

"You are out of line, Andrea. I love my man."

I had made her mad and it made me feel good. It made me feel good that I had gotten her just as upset as she had gotten me. I must have said something right because I pushed a button. There was something in her soul she couldn't hide. I could almost hear it loud screaming in my ears. She had a frustration that was so undeniable I could almost smell it.

"Whatever, Andrea. You do what you want to do. I'm sorry that I tried to warn you ahead of time."

"Well, maybe it's not Philip that you're worried about. Maybe, it's Dewayne." She looked at me through the mirror shocked and grabbed her purse, stuffing all her things into it. This time, I knew I was out of line. Dewayne was a cutie, but I didn't honestly feel that Dewayne would do anything bad to Karen. I had planted a seed wrongfully into her mind. But before I could say another word she had left out the door.

I felt like I had been a real idiot. Good going Andrea, messing up your friendships already. I haven't been on the campus a full week and already I was changing. I couldn't let my own fears control me. I laid down on the bed and covered my head with a pillow. Maybe I could wake up again and this would have been all a dream.

"Andrea," a muffled voice called. It wasn't in the room, yet it felt close by. I turned to look. I thought maybe it was Karen out in the hall. She probably left her key or something. I opened the door. Nothing out in the hall but a cold draft on the floor. I closed the door.

"That was weird," I said to myself. I looked at myself in the mirror and let my hair down. I examined my shape and posed, attempting to see myself in a more mature lady-like manner. I looked on the counter and I saw the lip gloss that had been forgotten by Karen. I grabbed the lipgloss and dabbed it on like I had seen Karen do. I was impressed at how it looked on me. The gloss not only smelled like strawberries, but had a strawberry taste too. If I wanted to, I could be so much more, I knew that. I flipped my hair to one side. I was beautiful.

"Andrea." I heard my name whispered again. The whisper was so soft and faint like autumn leaves being blown around the grass on a windy day. I turned around quickly as I felt the voice in the room. But that was impossible. I was the only one in the room. A knock was at the door. I looked at the knob as it slowly turned.

"Who's there? Karen is that you?" I held my breath thinking about the dream I had last night. I walked slowly to the door but could hear no one answer. I could, however, see the shadow of someone in the crack underneath the door. My heart thumped.

"Who is it?" I placed my ear to the door; nothing. I wished that these doors had peep holes. I unlocked the door and slowly opened it. I didn't open it wide; just enough so that I could peek out. As I looked in the hallway, it was as barren as before. I went back in and closed the door and looked back underneath to see if the shadow under the door had been given off by something else. I was practically laying on the floor. I didn't see anything. Maybe it was just my imagination. I picked myself up off the floor.

In the mirror a man stood behind me. I screamed and jerked around ready to swing. Nothing—no one at all. In my panic I knocked everything off the counter. The lip gloss had fallen to the floor and rolled under the door. I thought I saw a man in the reflection behind me—no, *I know* I saw a man; a tall pale white man, with dark long hair. But when I looked around I saw nothing. There was a knock on the door again, only this time

I woke up. I was still on my bed with the pillow over my face and my hair was still in a braided pony tail. I got up and the lipgloss was still on the counter top.

"Weird." And yet I was relieved. It was all a dream but it felt way too real. More real than any dream I had and how did I fall asleep so fast? Someone knocked at the door. I had a sickening déjà vu feeling that was trying to overcome me. I sat on the edge of the bed and walked hesitant toward the door. For a small room it seemed far away and I wondered if possibly I was still dreaming. I grabbed the doorknob and turned it slowly. I opened the door.

"Hey, Andrea. Is Karen here?" I sighed in relief.

"No, she left a few moments ago, I think. Dewayne, what are you doing here?"

CHAPTER SEVEN

"Where's Dewayne?" Karen asked, standing in the hallway of the men's dorm in front of a sleepy Anthony. There were a few men walking back and forth moving in. He had spent a good majority of the night reading.

"I don't know. I think he went to go register for classes. He might be back later on," Anthony said, rubbing the crust out of his eyes. He still wore the same clothes that he had worn the night before.

"I'm sorry, did I wake you?" she asked, walking into the room. Karen had her way of inviting herself into situations and Anthony had a way of being overly polite.

"No-no I was already about to wake up."

Karen sat down on Dewayne's bed, placing her purse next to her. "Did he say how long he was going to be?"

"I don't know. I was asleep when he left." Karen seemed upset and Anthony could tell slightly.

Anthony turned some lights on in the room. "Well I guess you can wait here until he gets back." He commented reluctantly as if he had a choice in the matter. Karen was an emotional bomb waiting to explode.

"What were you reading?" she said, making small talk.

"Just some theology books for my class. You want some pop?"

She nodded. "You, trying to be a preacher or a teacher?" He grabbed a soda out the small fridge sitting on the countertop by the sink and handed it to Karen. She tapped the top of it with her nail.

"I want to eventually go to seminary school. I just wanted to come here to get some life experience." Anthony grabbed a soda for himself and leaned against the sink. Karen flipped open hers, almost waiting for it to fizz upward but it didn't.

"I have a feeling that if you want life experience, then you are at the right school." She giggled and took a sip.

"Why do you say that?"

"I don't, Anthony. It's just that," she took a pause and it looked about time for that emotional bomb to explode. "Me and Dewayne." Boom! There it went and Anthony was about to get hit with the shrapnel.

"What about Dewayne?"

She wanted to keep it to herself but her mind was still simmering. "You're a preacher boy and, well, we are having some issues."

"Well, technically I'm not a—"

"I've been concerned that we aren't where we need to be spiritually. Anthony, I grew up in the church. I love God, I really do. But, well, since me and Dewayne started having sex things have changed."

Anthony took another sip of his soda to swallow the information that was being force-fed into his ears. "Well, Karen, Dewayne's a nice guy and you should make sure that God is the center of your relationship and not sex." He laughed.

"I guess I see who Dewayne can be and I know he's not

perfect and he jokes about everything. Anthony, I don't want him to mess up. I get so worried about him . . ."

Anthony halted her with his hand. "Karen, you can't be the man's mother. I know." He laughed to himself. "Look," he stared her square in the eyes, "Dewayne is smart, a little spontaneous, but smart. He's going to be okay."

"But my goal in life is to get closer to the Lord and I was thinking that since you're so into your word and he respects you so much—"

"That maybe I could pray him into Jesus Jr.?" Anthony said with a raised eyebrow. "Karen, you care for him and you want to help him, but he's not perfect; he's gonna make mistakes. Just let him be and support him."

"I don't have a problem supporting Dewayne through thick and thin. That's the type of person I am, Anthony. I just get scared."

"Why do you get scared?"

"Because I don't know what's going to happen. Sometimes I feel like he's going to mess up and I'm going to be the reason. I'd rather leave than be the reason he messes up his scholarship or his walk with the Lord."

Karen's emotions and worry were felt with Anthony and he walked closer to her, offering his words of advice. "God hasn't given us a spirit of fear, but of love and a sound mind. Everything you're talking about is your insecurity. Insecurity is fear, and when we let that take hold of our minds, bad things can happen. There's this quote my grandmamma used to tell me," Anthony held Karen's hand and patted it, "Let go and let God. You can't control what's going to happen with Dewayne, good or bad."

"Easier said than done, Anthony." She took her hand back and sighed, "I mean, I know I have my control issues, but it's still a lot to take in."

"Yeah, well, breaking up isn't the answer. You'd kill that

boy if you did that. He loves the ground you walk on." She blushed to have Anthony confirm that, "Have you talked to Dewayne about it?" He sat down on the bed across from Karen.

"Yeah, we talked and he is willing to do whatever is possible to get our lives back together, but then," she sipped the soda, "well we had sex again and I just don't want him to start getting tired of me or wanting someone else." She didn't give Anthony any eye contact but he knew what she was thinking.

"That's fear talking. I'm telling you that fear is a spirit and you can't feed into it or it will grow. Talk to Dewayne again about the issue or maybe I can talk to him."

"No, no don't talk to him. Don't tell him that I talked to you about this at all. I'll figure something out. But I just want to thank you."

"For what?"

"For listening. You're a good friend." Anthony smiled showing his dimple.

"I have a question for you. Now will you be totally honest with me?" Karen asked, giving Anthony this stern look. Anthony swallowed and tried to prepare himself for the question at hand. He wasn't sure what she was going to ask but he had some idea. Most of the time he had been asked, he was always presented with the option to be totally honest.

"Why aren't you with anybody?" she asked with a straight face, not breaking her eye contact with him at all. This was the usual question that he had been given, and being that his life was mainly down the straight and narrow, the answer was obvious.

"Well, I've been so busy with my studies and all."

She smiled and gave him a look of skepticism. "Fear of rejection?"

"Ha. Are you analyzing me now?" he sarcastically remarked. "When it's time I will date." He added, "In the Lord's time. My parents raised me to live a strict life."

"You better watch out. You may go wild if you get too close to a girl." She giggled. He shook his head and smiled. Karen noticed the quiet, cute, and innocent charm that he now possessed that seemed to magnify his devout stand with God. She admired that.

"Naw, it's not that serious. I mean, I just concentrate on my studies and what not." She still seemed amazed at Anthony. "What's the matter? Why do you keep looking at me like you're planning something?"

Karen was contemplating a plan with Anthony involved. "I know this girl that would be perfect for you!" Here Karen was, playing match maker. Karen had this way of prying in things that didn't concern her, knowing good and well if someone did the same to her she would not accept it all too willingly. Anthony was the type of guy who simply didn't respond well to being "hooked up" with anybody because for the most part, the person in question ended up being someone totally incompatible with him. So Anthony's initial reaction was not a good one when she brought up this subject. His nose curled up and a mental wall immediately went up.

"Anthony, don't look like that! No, really she is really nice. She is my roommate. Her name is Andrea." Red lights went off in Anthony's head.

"When girls say another girl is nice, they usually mean they are fat or ugly."

"No she isn't ugly or fat. And if she was fat, what's wrong with that?" Red lights were going off in everyone's head.

"Nothing. I just like my women nice and slim."

"Well, every girl can't be that way."

Anthony seemed to be confused because at the present moment he couldn't see why Karen was so upset. "Why are you even concerned, Karen? You are a fox." Anthony caught himself off-guard with his own mouth and even Karen had to regain her composure when he complimented her.

"Thank you, but women change. We have babies and gain weight. I just think that it's not right for men to love us just for our bodies. Then when we change you get all crazy when we love ya'll for all ya'll funky selves through thick and thin."

Now to Anthony, it appeared that she was venting for the entire female gender. It was as if for that moment in time she had linked with every woman in the world and they had all decided to cry their anguish through Karen and use him as their link into the entire male gender.

"Have you had a baby?" he asked her.

"No."

"Then why are you talking about this?" His question was quite logical actually.

"It's the principles behind the thing, Anthony. My daddy left my momma for a skinny white girl." Now everything was making sense. Anthony was very good at getting to the root of the problem and bringing a rational approach to what maybe he lacked emotionally to other people's problems. All Karen's pent up frustration and insecurities about Dewayne leaving her were coming to the surface.

"Is your mama fat?"

She looked like she didn't want to answer the question but she slowly spoke, "Yes . . . she is." Her mother's pain had become her own.

"So, it's safe to assume you're afraid that you're going to be fat after a while and that Dewayne is going to leave you?" Anthony asked.

"I'm not going to get fat."

"But you're still scared that you're going to lose Dewayne and maybe that's because of what your parents went through. I mean, sometimes we repeat our parent's insecurities. It's called a generational curse because we pass down the things to our children that we won't deal with."

"Yeah, well, maybe *you* have a sheltered life because *your* parents had a fear of you going buck wild." Karen had gone on the defensive and turned the tables on Anthony, hitting a sore spot. He knew his life was more sheltered than he desired, which was the very reason he decided to venture out more, but his intent wasn't to lose the moral strength and his faith in God that he developed up to that point. But in any matter, her comment had hurt.

"Why are you turning this on me? I'm trying to help you!" She saw his eyes flare a bit from his average calm look so she decided to step down a bit. He did help her and it was purely ungrateful to speak in such a way after he listened and shared so much. "People change, that's a reality I understand that most men—you're right—don't accept change. Men get with women expecting them not to change while women get with men trying to change everything about them."

Karen gasped and held her hand to her chest. "We do not. I love Dewayne for everything he is."

Anthony didn't really believe any of this and looked around the room. "You know that all this mess in this room is because of him right?" She gave a sheepish smile knowing that she was giving herself away. Anthony would make a good lawyer.

"Okay, maybe a few things should change about him, but generally, I love him for everything he is."

"Except that he doesn't have a strong relationship with God right now."

"Well, I don't either. We don't. And what woman doesn't want a praying man, Anthony? What do you want me to do? Be complacent with him when I know there's so much more inside of him? Just the other night I had this dream and it was like there was this halo around his head and I kept trying to draw his attention to it but he couldn't see it. And I kept saying, 'Dewayne there is something on your head,' but he couldn't hear me and then there was this dark shadow or something like smoke coming in from under the door like there was a fire and I couldn't see him anymore, but I could see that halo around his head so I used that to find him again in the smoke."

"Wow, that's deep. So you think that means that he has an anointing on his life to be a preacher or something?"

"I don't know what it means," she gathered her stuff and stood up knowing that the time had passed and that she needed to find Dewayne. "But he needs to get closer to God. I feel bad that he isn't, like it's partly my fault."

She began walking out the door and Anthony followed her. "It's not your fault. Ultimately, we make our own decisions. Do your part, deal with your issues and fears, and get your life right with God. If Dewayne wants to, he'll get his life right too. God is something you can't make a man do. He has to realize his own personal need for the Lord." She looked back at Anthony and hugged him. "Thank you."

"No problem. Hey, and don't go around campus trying to hook me up, I've been down that road before and it wasn't pretty," Anthony said, feeling the effect of Karen's control issues. Karen laughed not really taking him seriously and walked to the door.

She grabbed the doorknob and took another last look at him. "You really need to meet my roommate."

CHAPTER EIGHT

"Where's Karen?" Dewayne asked me, walking into the room. I was slightly relieved it was him and not something else.

"You didn't see her? She went looking for you."

He snapped his fingers in frustration. "Dang, I must've just missed her."

I stretched a bit and tried to calm my heart that was still slightly beating. I didn't want Dewayne to know that I had a childish nightmare. "You're welcome to stay and wait for her if you want," I said, cordially.

"Nah, I gotta go register for classes. I was just coming here to wait until the front office opened so I could."

"I have to go register too, maybe I could go with you."

Dewayne smiled. "Well let's walk. That way by the time we get over there it should be open."

"What if it rains?" I asked. I wasn't sure if I wanted to be sporting the wet look quite yet.

"You afraid of a little water?"

"Noooo," I said, not about to let on that I was too dainty

to hang with him. I was not going to be labeled as a girl that couldn't hang.

"I guess," he laughed. "I tell you what, we can buy an umbrella when we get to the student center okay?"

"Sounds like a plan." I prayed that it wouldn't rain. I grabbed my sweater and Dewayne and I walked down to the lobby. Karen was still not in the vicinity. I wondered how she could have missed him.

Dewayne was the perfect gentleman. He opened the door for me and we headed out toward the school main office. It would be quite a walk. We had to walk across the football field next to the dorms and cross the highway that ran through the campus. After that, we would have to walk around the school pond and then walk some distance until we got to the student center. Behind the center there was this magnificent building by the pond with all these stairs that students sat on and doors all across the front. Behind the student center was the main office. That was the building that we would go to register for classes. Driving, it would take us two minutes, walking would take us a good twenty.

Walking was far different. It allowed me to notice things that I would normally just speed pass. For instance, I didn't notice the snow cone shop cattycornered in the shopping center down the road. I hadn't even noticed the blossoming magnolia trees all over the campus and how pretty they smelled. I was glad Dewayne had suggested walking. It nearly took my mind off my dream.

"What are you thinking about?" Dewayne asked.

I guess my thoughts had manifested in my face. I shrugged my shoulders. "Nothing really, just had a crazy dream," I said, picking a leaf from a nearby tree.

"About what? You already having nightmares about professors and exam papers?"

I laughed at his wittiness but, it didn't take away the

eeriness the dream had given me. It was all too real. I had dreams before, but not like that one. I could almost feel that man behind me breathing on my neck. I shook my head. "You ever dream of something that seemed like it was so real? Like someone was watching you?"

Dewayne's adams apple moved down and up. His eyes didn't blink as we kept walking on the large football field. The lawn was freshly cut and there were a few sprinklers on various ends of the field.

"Yeah, I felt like that before." He mumbled his words under his breath. He seemed spooked. It concerned me and even scared me the more.

I grabbed him by the arm because he had walked ahead of me some two steps. "What's wrong with you? Are you okay?"

He looked back and his eyes had given him away. "Last night, while I was in the shower." He stopped. His face was so serious and he asked me to promise I wouldn't laugh at what he was about to tell me.

"Okay, Dewayne I won't laugh." We stood there on the fifty-yard line staring at each other.

"Tell me what you saw in your dream first," Dewayne said and I sighed. My heart fluttered because I felt silly, yet scared. Scared slightly, because he was scared about something and what I said had stirred him. I went over the eerie details of the dream I had. I thought Dewayne would have made fun of me, but what scared me more was that he just stood there, staring.

"Dewayne, what's wrong?" He blinked to break his shocked stare and walked down the field. "You told me you were going to tell me what you saw if I told you my dream." I chased behind him as fast as my little legs would go. One if his long strides took three of my steps.

"Technically, I never said that, Andrea."

"Dewayne! What was your dream?"

"Nothing!" He kept walking and I kept chasing. I could feel strongly that he had been spooked and my heart raced. A chill ran up my spine.

The shower . . . I didn't see anything—too dark . . . I didn't see anything," he said faintly.

"Why? Was it too dark in the shower?" I yelled. He stopped.

"How did you know that it was dark?" He turned and looked at me. His face was frowned up.

"Because you just said it was, Dewayne."

"No I didn't. I said I was in the shower. I didn't say anything about it being dark." His voice was exasperated.

"I just heard you say it, Dewayne. What's wrong with you?" I was starting to think that something was wrong with Dewayne, but he was looking at me with the same suspicion.

"Were you there? Were you and Karen playing a trick on me?"

"What are you talking about, Dewayne?" He stopped and collected his thoughts. His eyes searched for the words, searched endlessly for an explanation and I wondered what he was thinking. I could almost feel his thoughts like radio waves penetrating my head because he was thinking so hard , but it sounded like static. I needed him to clear it up. I needed him to speak. Once again I grabbed him firmly by the shoulders and looked him in the eyes. He snapped out his trance and looked as if I was hurting him.

"Dewayne, I know I haven't known you long, but you can talk to me, okay?"

"Okay, Andrea, loosen the death grip."

I let go quickly, not intending on pulling him so hard. He rubbed his arm. "You are pretty strong for a little chick." He laughed a bit and continued to walk at a decent pace. "I was in the shower," he continued, "and I heard something call my name. Then lights went off in the shower room and I felt like somebody was in there with me. When you said that something called your name and then you saw some guy behind you it made me think. Then my roommate was talking about spirits and ghosts last night, so he kind of freaked me out."

"Ghosts? " I wasn't sure what to think.

"Well we kept talking and he said it could've been an angel, like the one that came to Mary, to tell me I'm going to bear a child or something."

He snickered to lighten me up. I smiled. "Angels now? Well, maybe you need to go get a pregnancy test."

"Funny girl but for real, I did feel like something was in there with me." Between ghosts or angelic visits, I wasn't sure what to think.

"Aren't angels supposed to be all holy and happy-like? Since when do they scare the mess out of you?"

"I don't know. My roommate knows more about that than me. He's studying theology."

"What's your major?"

"I want to study Genetics. You know blood and DNA are the code of life. The classes I've taken so far this summer have really got me going. I think that by breaking the code of DNA we can explain why people have some of the special gifts that they have." We crossed the highway like two little kids, Dewayne, holding my hand and pulling me along so that I wouldn't fall. When we crossed it, he stopped to take a breath and continued to speak.

"My belief is that everyone has a portion of their DNA that is repressed and only through the right combinations they can activate it. Just like in livestock, when you breed for best results, I think, humans are pretty much the same way." I was attentively listening as he continued, "Let's take ESP for example and twins. People that do have ESP tend to be mixed up. And not all ESP is the same just like how genes are expressed, no two people look exactly the same. The whole fact that twins always have some psychic bond as well to me is that they are on the same channel."

"So we're cows now? Is that how you see me, like a cow?" He laughed at me but he really didn't answer so I wasn't sure if I should take that as a yes or a no. But I decided to laugh along anyways. The pond was beautiful and little ducklings followed their mother into the water. I couldn't help but get that warm fuzzy feeling.

Dewayne and I continued to walk and I was quite impressed at his ambition. I felt this strong emotion overwhelm me all at once. Intelligence was quite sexy and I was beginning to understand why Karen loved his dirty bath water so much. It hurt me a little. I wished that I had someone so funny, so attractive and so intelligent. I couldn't admit it to myself or would I ever admit to Karen, but deep down I wished that Dewayne was single. He was different from Philip. There was something in Dewayne I clicked with. When it came to having a broken heart, I was less likely to get that from Dewayne I was sure. I had fallen into my thoughts and once again failed to listen to what Dewayne was saying. I just enjoyed watching his beautiful lips move as he spoke forming each word with such finesse. At that moment and at that second I wasn't caring about anything but what I wanted and desired.

"Andrea?" he asked, waving his hands in front of my face.

I shook the fantasy out my head. Why was I having these thoughts? "Hmm?"

I could not let on that I had not been paying attention. "Dewayne, I totally agree with what you are saying," I said not, really knowing if that was appropriate to say or not. He frowned up and got really silent. I knew I had messed up.

We walked through the grass and around the pond and he was so quiet that all I could hear was the crunching of the grass beneath our feet. My sneakers were getting wet and I could feel the water seep into them and soaking into my socks.

"You weren't listening were you?" he said in a dry tone. He was really serious and that in itself was attractive.

"I'm sorry, I was daydreaming. It's a bad habit. Please repeat what you said."

"Nothing really. I mean I was just talkin' about school. I guess I've been hanging around Anthony too much. His nerdiness is rubbing off on me."

"Anthony?"

"My roommate." A horrible guilt weighed in the pit of my stomach as if I had gas and constipation after a large chili cook-off.

"I'm really sorry, Dewayne."

"No biggie. I'm used to it. Karen doesn't listen to me either, she just talks and tells me what she wants too." I felt a yellow warning light coming on. I wasn't sure that after knowing him so little time if I should be discussing his relationship matters. I mean there was a slight attraction to him and I didn't want to be out of line in giving him advice.

"Ya'll don't seem like ya'll have problems to me." We approached the student center and decided to walk around the side of the building to the main offices behind it. Dewayne sighed as he rubbed his hand along the side wall of the building. He glanced at me and I could see his eye twinkle from a ray of light that reflected from the sun. He was a nice looking black man. Stop—listen to him. That's what he needs, a woman who listens. But then—if I did listen and he was not getting that from the woman he was with, would that not make him like me or even want to hang around me more? What if, in turn, by giving him what he emotionally desired so much, I was subconsciously interfering with his relationship?

"She's unhappy with me. I try to make her happy. I try so hard. I don't know what to do anymore, Andrea. Maybe you can help me. Tell me from a woman's point of view."

These were the words of a man who was really in love and desperate to work his relationship out. All my silly fancies were vain and I should have known that Dewayne, being the good man he is, would do his best to work his relationship out. And here he was calling on me (Miss Super Single) for advice. I didn't want to let on that Karen had already spoken to me. But I could use what she had told me to help Dewayne to what his problem was. In truth, I had heard both sides of the story and both Karen and Dewayne had called on me to deliberate.

"Well, why are you upset with the relationship?" I asked, playing psychologist for the moment.

"Well, I was fine. We make love like out of this world," which is also the reason Karen, I might add, was upset, "And Karen is so beautiful but . . ." uh oh here it comes, the big but, "well sometimes there are some things I feel like I can't even talk to her about. There are some things that . . ." He paused gathering his thoughts and motioning with his hands as if that would make the thought develop quicker, "like when I was talking to you about the shower. Karen would have thought I was crazy and changed the subject but you—you listened. You even pressed on to hear what I had to say." Some how this conversation had gone back to me and I was getting worried. I had to protect Dewayne from walking down the wrong road (despite my own desires).

I gave him a friendly pat on the shoulder. "Tell her that. She'll listen if you tell her just like you told me. All women love a man who can express his feelings." Yes lord, this is the truth. I was loving Dewayne right now and wishing he was single. He nodded and I felt his attention off me as he went inward in his thoughts. I knew he was thinking of her and how he could work it out. When he had done that, I yearned for that attention to come back to me. But I knew it wouldn't be right.

"It's weird huh," he said.

"What?"

"That we both could hear our names being called. Do you think that maybe . . . it was God?" I had to admit. I was glad I could talk to Dewayne about this.

"Well, God is scaring the heck out of me."

He laughed at me and I giggled, but I was serious. We walked up into the offices and Dewayne grabbed a catalog and told me that taking his summer classes had almost qualified him to be a sophomore. He flipped through the book.

"Hey why don't you take this mythology class with me?" I hadn't really decided yet on what classes I was going to take, but mythology wasn't really my idea of classes.

"Why mythology? That has nothing to do with psychology," I asked, grabbing a catalog and looking for the class description.

"Well, Anthony suggested I take it, and since we were talking about all this scary stuff, discussing the unknown maybe, we could study about what has been scaring people for centuries."

"Myths?" I said.

"Yeah, I mean why not? People have tried to explain God and creation through myths. They have tried to explain why things happen, who they are, and why they are."

"So maybe you can figure out why you are through mythology." I was trying to make a joke, but evidently he didn't catch it. He just kept on writing his classes on his schedule. So I decided I would take this mythology class for the fall and see what it was about. I mean—I already had a study buddy so that was a plus. I put the paper in my lap and tried keeping it in place while I wrote, but my hair got all in my face. I swept it behind my ear and out of my eyesight.

I looked at the clock on the wall and it was thirty minutes before noon. I wrote faster. Students were crowding the halls and the campus was getting livelier every minute.

"Let's get in line and get registered before this line gets long," I suggested. Dewayne agreed and followed alongside of me.

"So are you taking the class or not?"

"I am. Maybe I can learn a little more about how people think if I know what they believe in."

"Cool, now I got someone to cheat off of." I looked at him crazy.

"You cheat off me, then you really want to fail this class because I don't know nothing about Mythology."

"I'm just playing."

We got lucky and had gotten in line with only about two students sitting in the waiting room before us. I signed the waiting list and Dewayne signed after me. I was happy too that he was going to be in my class.

"We better hurry back. I'm sure Karen will be back any minute looking for you."

CHAPTER NINE

A round eleven thirty, Karen stepped into the lobby of the girl's dorm. She thought that maybe she had just missed Dewayne. She was so deep in thought about him that she didn't notice Philip coming around the corner and she slammed right into his chest. She ricocheted off and fell to the floor.

"Whoa, are you okay?" Philip said, picking her up.

"Thank you. I wasn't watching where I was going."

"What's the rush?"

"I was heading back to my room to see if my boyfriend was up there."

He shrugged his shoulders. "I just came from up there to see Andrea and when I knocked no one answered."

"Where else would he go?" Philip dusted Karen off and continued to hold her hand to make sure she was okay.

"Probably to register for class."

She took her hand back, "Just wait around. He'll probably come on through this way. Why are you so frantic? Is everything okay?" Philip had his counseling frequency on high and Karen didn't want to worry him about anything.

She sat down in the lobby and shook her head, not looking him in the eye.

"Are you shaking your head yes or no?"

Karen was having difficulty resisting Philip's prying. She really didn't trust him and she didn't feel like expressing her feelings to the one guy she had bad mouthed so badly.

"Come on, Karen, I can tell something is wrong with you. I'm here to help."

"I know. Everything is fine." She smiled showing her little gap in between her teeth. Philip had an irresistible charm and there's a thin line between love and hate. Thoughts swam through her mind and she thought that maybe she *did* find him attractive. But just because she thought someone was attractive didn't mean she wanted to have sex with them. She crossed her legs and crossed her arms.

Philip noticed her body language, "You don't like me too much, huh?" she looked shocked knowing deep down he was right.

"Wh-what makes you think I don't like you?" Karen looked uncomfortable and this time she resituated herself in the lobby chair that she was sitting in.

"I just get this feeling sometimes." He squinted his eyes at her. He sat on the arm of her chair and she scooted as far to the opposite end of the chair as she could.

"Andrea had a lot of thoughts about me and I thought to myself where she could have gotten them from since she hasn't been here that long. Maybe she was warned by you to stay away from me."

Karen crossed her legs the other way and turned to look at Philip. "Philip I barely know you, why would I talk about you?"

"Yeah, that's what I was asking myself. Dewayne has been here over the summer and I thought that maybe he told you something and you were spreading things around."

"Well, maybe if you didn't have something to hide, you wouldn't have to worry about all these rumors, Philip."

He laughed this loud echoing laugh and rubbed Karen's shoulder abrasively which caused her to retract her arm back. "You have a sharp tongue don't you? Look, whatever you may have against me I assure you, I'm no harm. I'm really a nice a guy."

He was all in Karen's personal space and she wasn't quite sure how to react. She could feel the heat rising from her skin or it could have been his body heat, he was so close. Karen knew that she should shy away from his advances. It was fight or flight and she was not one to run very often.

"Well, Karen, as I told you, I don't know what you're talking about. Now if I intimidate you or if *you* are threatened by my friendship with Andrea then I think that's your own personal problem." He tilted his head and pulled back. "What was it that you were so upset about? I know when someone is upset; it's my job and it's got something to do with your boyfriend." Karen rolled her eyes sighing in sequence to her frustration with Philip, "You act as if you're not interested, but I can feel that you really want to talk."

"I've already talked to someone, thank you very much."

"So there is a problem?" Dang, he was good—too good. Karen stood up and walked to the front lobby and looked out the glass doors. She could still hear thunder rolling, although the rain had subsided.

"Okay, seriously. I'm not trying to be your enemy here, I just want to be your friend." He placed his hands on her shoulders. Karen glared at him instantly. He removed his hands and stuck them in his pocket. Karen sighed. Maybe she had been wrong about Philip. He was trying to help her and she kept putting up a wall. Maybe Andrea had been right. Maybe she had been insecure about her own

personal feelings and to protect herself she had decided
to be as mean as possible to Philip.

"Okay, have it your way." Philip said turning around to
walk off.

"No, wait. Philip, I'm sorry. I'm being—"

"A wench?" Well not exactly the words that Karen would
have chosen but once again, Philip was reading her cards.
There was something about how Philip approached her
with this gentle bluntness. But Andrea was wrong. Here
she was staring into Philip's eyes and not even once feeling an inkling of a feeling to cheat on Dewayne. Dewayne
was her bread and butter, the reason for the season. Karen
loved her some Dewayne but then . . . why was she still
staring into Philip's eyes? She blinked and looked down.

"Well, I was just being mean. Look, honestly, you seem
like a good guy and just to let you know, I think that Andrea really likes you."

"You think so?" His eyes brightened up with some glim-
mer of hope.

"Yeah, just some advice for you though."

"What's that?"

"If you mess with her heart, I got her back," Karen said,
staring outside the window. Tamela walked into the lobby
and stopped for a moment. Karen saw her reflection and
turned around not sure how long she had been there listening.

"Sorry, I didn't want to interrupt," Tamela said, easing
into the conversation, "I just wanted to ask Philip about
when the hall meeting was." Philip opened the conversation up by extending his hand to her.

"Tamela, this is Karen. Karen, this is Tamela." Tamela
shook Karen's hand firmly, but Karen only smiled cordially and turned back to look out the window.

Tamela shifted her weight on her left hip and looked at Philip who just shook his head for her not to even comment. Tamela's intuition interpreted her silence and she backed away a little.

"It's later this week," Philip answered her, "I'll put the poster's up."

"Okay, well nice meeting you, Karen. Hey, aren't you Andrea's roommate?"

Karen's eyes shifted toward Tamela. She thought to herself how nice it was to have a stalker. "Yeah, that's my roommate. How did you know?"

"I met her at the store this morning. She gave me a ride back to the dorm—I saw you helping her move in too." Tamela was nosiness at its finest and other people's business was her life energy. Tamela stumbled over her words trying to avoid the icy cold stare Karen was giving off. Karen caught herself once again. She didn't intentionally want to be rude, but her mind was on too many different things, like Dewayne. She was contemplating leaving Dewayne to grow spiritually, but she still loved Dewayne and she was afraid that she might break his heart and that was the last thing she wanted. Would Dewayne take it the right way? Was there another way to get his attention?

"My black sista, you have some negative energy in your aura. You need to release that and let it go. I have some tea that could help you."

Karen gave another icy stare to Tamela. "My what? That's okay, my areola is fine thank you," Karen said and Philip smirked to Tamela's dismay.

"Well, it was nice meeting you, maybe we can chat again . . . you, me, and Andrea. I live in room 323."

"Uh huh, good meeting you." She didn't even turn her head. Karen was unconcerned. Tamela shrugged and walked off confused, and Philip stood there in Karen's wrath

ready for round two. She looked over her shoulder surprised that he hadn't left. Oh he liked to take punishment—
must be one of those sadomasochist, she thought.

"That's sad," he said, standing behind her with his arms
crossed.

"What are you talking about?"

"I'm talking about how mean you are to some people.
Here Tamela, a perfectly nice person, is trying to befriend
you. But you can't see that because you are too stuck in
the mud with your own problems. Problems about a man
at that."

Karen turned around and looked up at Philip who she
noticed was incredibly tall now that she was standing face
to chest with him. "I'm not worried about that blippy."

"Blippy?"

"Yeah, she's a black hippy . . . a blippy. I mean what was
that about tea solving my problems. I need more than
that. If I'm gonna drink I'm gonna *drink*."

Philip smiled and his eyes looked cunning. "Well, I got
some Crown Royal in my room if you want some."

She pushed him aside, noticing once more how firm his
chest was. "No thank you. I'm under 21." She walked back
over to the couch and grabbed a magazine fanning herself.

"You hot?"

"Just a little flustered. Where is Dewayne?"

"What's the matter? You think he's cheating on you?"
he asked.

Karen stopped fanning and her mouth dropped. "Dewayne wouldn't do that to me."

"Oh come on, all people cheat every once in awhile.
Men do and women do it too."

"Well, Dewayne doesn't want to cheat and I wouldn't
cheat on him. That's not my style. That would be mean."

He walked over to her slowly. "Really, you would never cheat?"

"Nope." Philip didn't believe her. His face was full of cynicism.

"Why are you looking at me like that?" She darted her eyes at him and folded her arms. It was beginning to get hot again, but she didn't want to give off the impression that she was uncomfortable. Philip had his mental lie detector on overdrive.

"We all cheat . . . sooner or later. You see what happens is, first you get frustrated. Maybe because the person doesn't give you what you feel you deserve like time, energy, attention . . . love. Or then, maybe you get scared because you've been with the person so long . . ." Philip made his way around and sat on the coffee table in front of Karen, "That they are all you know, so you wonder if you're really in love at all or if you've found the best possible person for you. Have you ever wondered if there was someone better out there for you than your man?" he asked her, pulling the magazine out of her face so she couldn't distract herself anymore. "Someone who could do things better?" Philip spoke so gently and his words seduced her to contemplate the unthinkable. She bit her lip and gave him no answer but he continued to speak to her, watering in her soul the deep inhibitions and insecurities that she had long held inside of her heart. "Technically, there's nothing wrong with it, as long as you don't tell."

"What are you talking about? Cheating? That's wrong and I wouldn't hurt Dewayne like that."

"How can you hurt him unless he finds out? Would you rather break his heart and lose him forever because you're not sure and then try to get him back? No wait, you would rather spend your whole life with him and realize that he's not the one and then break his heart like that. Heartbreak is almost inevitable if you tell him everything. But if you love him and you care for him you won't tell him everything. That is why you should do your thing. Experiment. Keep your man and keep his heart safe at the same time."

"I'm not going to cheat on Dewayne." She tried to repeat it for herself this time.

"Don't cheat on him. Cheating is what you do to people to intentionally hurt them. Cheating is when you are trying to beat a person at a game. Are you trying to beat Dewayne at something? No. You are exploring your feelings. I can tell you have things on your mind that is bothering you and I can tell that you are about to let it go on that poor guy." She laughed because she knew he was right, "All I'm saying is before you let this bomb go, you relax for a minute. Breathe, and explore your feelings before you be selfish and hurt someone's feelings."

"I'm not going to hurt his feelings." Her argument was to no avail—Philip was ready with his rebuttal.

"You've had to hurt everyone's feelings today because you're upset and you're about to hurt someone's heart that's closest to you. So before you do that," he stepped closer and grabbed her chin and stared her directly in the eyes, "Look within yourself and fix that person. You're young, give yourself time." She had nothing to say and his sexy wisdom had melted the ice fortress that she had built around herself. She felt a drop of sweat roll down her back and she jumped forward arching her back and thrusting her breast forward, almost losing her balance in Philips arms.

"You all right?" he asked.

"Yeah, umm." She regained her balance and composure, "Just some sweat. Is the air on?"

"It's probably on the blitz again. I'll call maintenance." Philip walked to the office and Karen watched as he glanced at himself in the hall mirror and fixed his shirt.

That was a fine brother if she had ever seen one, but she didn't feel comfortable confessing that to him or herself. She thought there may be some truth to what he said . . . maybe. He made it sound so simple, so right. What if Dewayne was exploring his options? She didn't like that idea. That was way different. Her needs were emotional. She knew his were sexual. His exploring would be nothing more that hoeing around.

Karen looked up and just as if she had summoned him telepathically, Dewayne entered in the lobby laughing and carrying on with Andrea. Karen's eyes burned but she tried not to think the worst. Karen tried to clear her thoughts but it seemed there was that overbearing negative voice hovering over her now and it just wouldn't shut up.

Philip walked back in the lobby and scoped the situation. Like a deer in a cross-fire, he could detect that there was trouble. He walked over behind Karen, squeezing her shoulder gently.

"Breathe," he whispered. She sighed and complied to his advice. Dewayne looked surprised to see that Karen was waiting for him in the lobby.

CHAPTER TEN

Tamela walked up to door 323 and took her keys out. Her bracelets jingled down and made it difficult for her to situate the key into its lock. After fiddling with it for some minutes, the door opened. Valerie was holding the door rubbing her eyes.

"I know you're still not sleep." Tamela said, sliding into the room. Valerie mumbled, "I was just taking a cat nap," and closed the door behind Tamela.

To Valerie, Tamela was like a second mother. Their whole freshmen year, Valerie had stuck close to Tamela and they were inseparable. Even when rumors went around campus that they were lesbians Valerie didn't care. Even when Valerie's other white friends disowned her and called her a nigger lover, Valerie disowned them and kept Tamela as her friend. Tamela was the only one who'd stayed by her side and Valerie was willing to be loyal to that.

Valerie watched silently as Tamela went through the room rummaging through drawers. In the process Valerie's photo album hit the floor and a single photo of a bleach blonde woman with heavy makeup fell out. Valerie went over to retrieve it and put the photo of her mother back in its place. She came to college from her white trash life in the small town of Simon City (a town east of Heaven). Her mother abused her verbally and physically to the point where she really had no self-esteem in herself.

"Move, Valerie, you're in my way!" Tamela said, stepping over Valerie as she sat on the floor securing the picture. Their friendship was definitely not normal. Tamela told Valerie what to do all the time and really wasn't concerned with how Valerie felt on issues unless they outright affected her directly. But Valerie was content with this type of friendship. She took orders from Tamela like a flunky should. Tamela had become her idol and Tamela was creating Valerie in her image.

"Get my candle, Val." Tamela said, unfolding her knit quilt and placing it nicely in the middle of the floor. Valerie went into the closet and pulled a large brown box from the shelf and set it on her bed. There were several colored candles; some were fat, some were skinny. Valerie rummaged through, not sure which one she wanted.

"Which one do you want?" Valerie asked naively. Tamela opened her desk and grabbed a skinny leather bound book with a locket on it and sat down on the quilt on the floor.

"Give me the blue one." She pulled a small key that was attached to one of the many bracelets that she had on. It looked like it was one of the many charms. She used the little gold designed key and unlocked the book. Valerie grabbed the candle and a few matches and sat across from Tamela with the candle in the middle. She handed Tamela the matches as was their custom in room 323.

"What are we praying for now?" Valerie asked. Tamela struck the match and let it flicker for a second.

"I am going to put a spell on Karen to be nice to me."

"Who is Karen?" Valerie asked, sitting on the quilt.

"Andrea's roommate. The last thing I need is her trying to ruin my relationship with my new friend."

"Your new friend? Who is Andrea?" Valerie inquired again. Valerie was suddenly scared she would lose her position.

"She's real nice. She's from Heaven, Texas."

"Oh, I have family there."

Tamela didn't seem too concerned. "I think you would like her. I want you to meet her. Besides, she would make a nice addition to our group."

"I guess so," Valerie said, twisting her hair in between her index and thumb. Tamela wrote Karen's name down on some paper and placed the candle on it.

"Grab my hands," Tamela commanded Valerie, and without question, she did as she was told.

Tamela's cultic past-time both intrigued and scared her. Tamela made a racist professor stop harassing her by taking a graded test paper he had wrote on and using it in one of her spells. Once, Valerie had even asked Tamela to find a way for her to stay in college after applying for financial aid over and over and being denied. Tamela did one spell and suddenly Valerie was eligible for a special scholarship. Valerie had asked for Tamela to curse on this guy who spoke negatively to her all the time, but Tamela refused, saying that it would be wrong to do harm to another human and she didn't want to receive back the karma for her actions. Tamela told Valerie that every spell cast was for good and that she would hurt no one.

"Spirits of the north and south, hear the words that I speak from my mouth. Read this name and grant my request, let her words to me always be the best," Tamela chanted, then closed her eyes and repeated it.

Valerie often wondered where she found such beautiful poetry, maybe she wrote it herself. Soon Valerie had caught the rhyme and began to chant it herself. They would chant until Tamela deemed it right to stop. Without warning, Tamela ungripped her hands and took the paper and burned it. Instantly it was consumed in a blue flame as if it was made of tissue paper. It startled both the girls. The light on the candle flickered as if there was a breeze in the room but there was none.

"Valerie . . ." A voice whispered and Valerie fell back on her elbows.

"Wh-what was that?" Valerie asked.

"What was what? The paper burned fast that's all," Tamela said.

"No, the voice. You didn't hear that?"

"Hear what?" Tamela looked at Valerie like she was crazy.

"Nothing," Valeria blew out the candle and stood up quickly, "I guess it was my imagination."

Valerie situated her glasses on her face and pulled her long brown hair behind her ears. She knew it wasn't her imagination. She had heard a voice and that she couldn't deny. The voice was masculine, deep, and vibrated her very soul when it said her name. Her hairs, her skin, every cell reacted in her body when it spoke to her. Every time Tamela tinkered with these spells she found Valerie was shook by it. Valerie wasn't brave enough to tell her. Never had anything spoke to her; not while she was awake.

"So do you think it worked?" Valerie asked.

Tamela responded with a sarcastic look at her question. She took her notebook and bound it back and placed it in the drawer.

"I want to know what you heard," Tamela said with her back to Valerie.

"Nothing."

"You're lying and you don't do it well." Tamela turned around and stared her directly in the eyes.

Valerie held her head down and crossed her arms. She wasn't the confrontational type.

"Now Valerie, be honest with me."

"A voice."

"What kind of voice?" Tamela asked curiously as she stepped a little closer.

"I don't know. Look, let's just drop it. I don't know what it was." Tamela grew suspicious of Valerie's encounter. She had never known Valerie to have a personal experience like that before but she had been scared before. Her experimenting had started in high school. She was only sixteen and she had a horrible shyness around her other classmates. Her teacher, Ms. Rosemont, would call on her to do speeches and every speech would end the same way: Brian Brown, a boy who was mean beyond words, mocking her about her timidity.

Ms. Rosemont took Tamela home one day and explained that she could help her with her shyness and Brian, with certain limitations. She gave her a candle and some words. Tamela skeptically took them home and at first did nothing. But when she felt she could take no more of Brian's ridicule she did it. The following week, when it came time to do speeches, the tables turned on Brian Brown, who ended up peeing on himself during his presentation. Ms. Rosemont escorted Brian out and looked back at Tamela, who suddenly realized in a grip of fear that her spell had returned Brian's negativity back to him.

Now, as she sat in the dorm with her roommate, that fear had gripped her once again, the fear of the unknown. All the magic she had learned in the past four years and nothing had spoken to her. And now Valerie was hearing voices. Valerie was too scared to realize that she had been privileged to hear such a thing. Tamela tried to rationalize what Valerie must have experienced.

"Come on Val, tell me what did the voice tell you that it wanted?" Valerie stood at the sink and looked at Tamela frustrated. She opened the door preparing to leave. "Valerie, where are you going?" Tamela asked.

Valerie walked into the hallway not even turning around. "It didn't tell me anything. I don't know what it wants. I don't know what it wants at all!"

CHAPTER ELEVEN

When Dewayne and I went in the lobby, Karen was standing there with a perplexed look on her face. She didn't say anything; she just stood there. Philip came in from the office and looked around. I felt as if I had walked in on the end of a conversation. Philip walked behind Karen and whispered something to her, which evidently calmed her down. I looked at Philip suspiciously but he hadn't given me eye contact. He was still focused on Karen. I felt a bit of jealousy overcome me and I was slightly confused. Wasn't this the same guy she didn't want me to talk to? And now here they were—whispering amongst each other.

Dewayne walked up to Karen. "Hey baby." He kissed her cheek and she just stood there.

"Where have you been?" Karen said, looking at me shortly and then glancing back at him.

"At the office registering. why? Were you looking for me? Where have you been?"

"I've been here . . . waiting for you." There was this iciness to her stare. I could tell that something was wrong by her tone, but it seemed that she was holding her true feelings back. Philip stood a few steps behind her and I couldn't help but feel he had some influence in the matter and I thought it be better to ask him what was going on before I talk to her. Dewayne suggested they talk upstairs, leaving Philip and me to our thoughts. Philip stood there rocking on his heels, looking like he was hiding something.

"So, what were you two down here talking about?" I interrogated, walking up to Philip, who towered at least three feet over me. Awkwardly, he tried looking at me by hunching his back over. I stood back some so I could see his eyes and not up his nose. He smiled his charming smile to throw me off, but I knew there was more.

"What are you hiding, Philip?"

He tilted his head, "Why I gotta be hiding something?"

"Because one minute Karen is telling me that she doesn't like you and the next minute ya'll over here whispering." I waved my hands in his face to show my frustration.

"So she did say something . . . that's what I thought." Philip nodded.

"Excuse me?"

"Well, we've made a mends. I thought she didn't like me because I was talking to you, and after confronting her about it, we are friends now."

"Really." I stood back on my right leg and put my hand on my hip, "Is that so?"

"Yeah, you can ask her. Look, you don't have to be jealous."

I wanted to laugh that he thought I might be thinking they were together. "Jealous? You can be with whoever you want to be with. But I must warn you, Dewayne won't be happy." Philip's exotic shimmering eyes snatched my eyes like UFO beams abducting an unsuspecting country bumpkin in a field. He knew the affect his eyes had because it seemed as if he wouldn't even blink. I blinked a few times then looked away, attempting to not let him off the hook so easily. His attractiveness had a way of making me forget my thoughts, so I closed me eyes to regain my composure.

"Dewayne is not my problem unless he is dating you," Philip said.

Philip was the player poster boy and I had no will power to resist. "And *what* is that supposed to mean?" I tried to cock an attitude, but he chuckled and touched my hand. A warm fuzzy feeling was filling my soul and I did my best to repress the feeling because I so badly wanted to express my discontent to him. But I was fighting a losing battle.

"What do you think that is supposed to mean?" He coiled some of my hair in his fingers like a spool. I was the hair around his little finger. He must have noticed the sigh I released because he smiled slightly, revealing his perfectly straight teeth. He pulled me closer and I assumed that he must be referring to the fact that he liked me. At least that's what I wanted to believe, but once again he never really said it. Last thing I would want is to be assuming something and then he pull a fast one on me.

I pushed away, "Nuh-uh, Philip, don't play with my emotions. That's not even cool." I tried to pull away from his grip and walk off, but he grabbed my forearm and firmly pulled me back. It was slightly arousing.

"I'm not playing, Andrea. What do you want me to say?" I wanted him to say a lot, probably more than I was ready to hear. My fantasies ran away with me. That feeling I had when I was with Dewayne was taking over again, I couldn't understand it. I wanted him to like me and only me. That was the truth. Philip wasn't going to give up easily and invaded my entire personal space. He pulled me even closer as he unfolded my arms and slid his hands into mine.

"I really like you, Andrea. For real, you are an exceptional girl." Those are the words I wanted to hear.

"Exceptional you say?"

"Yeah."

"Well, thank you." I had difficulty taking his compliments, "But, Philip, you don't even know me. You're . . .
you're just in lust." I pulled away once again and walked
pass him. What else could I say? I didn't want to appear to
be a ho', although in my mind, I sure was considering it,
my head was spinning.

Philip did as I was hoping he would and didn't give up,
"I'm sure you've heard a lot about what I've done, and
well, you can judge me by rumors and past experience or
you can give me a chance and go with your heart." I wasn't
sure what my heart was saying. It was racing and left me
behind minutes ago. Philip did deserve a chance, however. He genuinely was interested in me and I had done
nothing but judge him from the first day. I realized that I
was being a hypocrite.

"A chance? A chance for what exactly?"

"I just," he took a breath, and then let it out like he was
growing weary of my doubt in him, "want to get to know
you better."

My heart said yes, "I'm cool with that." I kept my speech
short and to the point. I didn't want to give him the advantage of knowing what I was feeling and yet I didn't
want to have him think I was uninterested. I didn't know a
lot about men, but I do know the male ego is fragile and
must be validated constantly. So I gave him a tender pat
with my hand on his rock hard pecs. I felt them jump up
under my touch and I jerked my hand back. He giggled.

"Okay, well maybe we can go out. You have my number
I'm sure."

Philip looked pleased that I was willing to spend some
extra time with him. "It's on your file." I nodded and

thought that I was doing the wrong thing by dating the Assistant Hall Director; there's got to be a rule against that.

"Well then," I started walking back to my room, "I will talk to you later, Philip. I look forward to getting to know who you are."

"And I look forward to getting to know you as well." He winked and blew me a kiss.

I pretended to grab it in the air and stick it in my pocket. "I will save that for another rainy day." He giggled again. I flipped my hair when I turned to leave and thought about him on my way back to the room. I was daydreaming so much I ran into a white girl with brown stringy hair and glasses.

"Sorry, I didn't mean to run into you," she said humbly, fixing her glasses back into place.

"It's cool, no problem." I smiled back but she just looked back down and continued on her way. She reminded me of those hippies or those Amish women.

I leaned up against the wall and thought about Philip again. What was I getting myself into? I hadn't been in school too long and already I was pairing up with the finest boy in school. I must be asking for trouble.

I had completely forgot about Dewayne and Karen, but as I walked to my dorm room I could over hear their argument through the door. I sat outside the door and decided to wait it out. As I closed my eyes an image of the whole room flashed in my mind. I opened my eyes and shook my head. I rested my head back on the door and closed my eyes and it was as if I could see, feel, and hear what they were doing in the room.

"What's wrong with you? Why are you so quiet?" Dewayne said as he sat on floor next to Karen while she sat on the bed. He felt like he was in trouble and a fight was coming on. He really didn't want to fight again and he couldn't possibly think of what he had done wrong this time. Karen was trying to find the right words to express herself, and instead, she was coming off completely stand-offish.

"Will you please talk to me?" he begged.

"Do you have feelings for Andrea?" There, she said it. She felt better too.

The comment left Dewayne with his mouth completely open and he really didn't know what to say. "What makes you think that? We were just walking together. Surely you can't be that insecure, Karen." He had gone on the defense because she had attacked him on his whereabouts and he wasn't about to be controlled.

"Are you calling me insecure? Maybe I wouldn't be if I knew where you were!" Dewayne shook his head because he remembered he didn't want to fight and tried to embrace her to apologize, but for whatever reason, she moved away.

"Please calm down." His voice quivered and he didn't want it to be obvious, but it was. Dewayne wanted to ease whatever pain there was because he felt her heart leaving him and Dewayne couldn't stand rejection. Dewayne had experienced rejection his whole life.

When he was eight his father had left his mother and he never knew how to handle it. Dewayne's dad would never come around, and before long, when Dewayne was about fourteen he went to go find him. After asking neighbors and relatives he tracked his drunken father down at an old apartment complex in the middle of the ghetto.

He saw him sitting on the stoop smoking a cigarette and at first he wasn't going to say anything but he did anyways. He was angry because his father had not been around, so maybe his tone was angry. He couldn't really remember because the whole conversation was a blur. He attempted to vent all the years of hurt in one conversation, but his tears drowned his words. The old man couldn't handle all the questions because he had questions about his own life. Dewayne was reaching out for the one man in his life that he should relate to the most, and that man rejected him. With a flick of the cigarette, Dewayne's dad stood up and walked back inside his old raggedy apartment and locked the screen door. He spoke silently once he was on the other side and the words that he said would kill the little boy who so wanted his father's admiration.

"You are a thorn in my flesh that I wish I could remove," his father said. And in that instant, Dewayne was crushed. He didn't know whether to scream or laugh. All of his efforts to find acceptance were over. He was left out there in the summer heat in the middle of the ghetto with tears and sweat running down his cheek and he had heard all that he needed to hear. In his anger he cursed his daddy out and turned to go home. He ran the entire way—didn't stop once. No matter how tired he was, he just kept running. He ran away from the pain and the hurt and the sorrow. He ran away from the rejection. But somehow rejection had found him again. Here he was reaching out to Karen, but she was hiding behind the screen door of her mind.

"Karen, please, I love you," Dewayne said. She paused. He was almost in tears because all those old feelings came back. She could hear it in his voice and she remembered what Philip had advised her. She had to be mindful of others' feelings despite her own. She turned to face him and his eyes were swelling up with tears. She didn't like to see him cry because then she knew she had hurt him. Karen loved Dewayne—she was just having a difficult time. All relationships go through things like that. The question was, would Karen make the right decision?

"Am I disturbing you guys?" I asked as I peeked through the door to see Karen and Dewayne embraced in an emotional hug. He wiped his eyes dry on her shoulder to not let me see that he was crying. "No Andrea, we're done, come on in."

CHAPTER TWELVE

A couple of weeks of classes had gone by and everyone was getting into the routine of pop quizzes, study groups, and most importantly, study breaks. Philip and I were quickly warming up to each other while attempting to keep our personal and his professional life separate. Dewayne and Karen were as tight as ever, and although Karen really never discussed anything with me, she had begun to treat me differently. We would sit in the room and not even speak to each other. Two women insecure about the men they wanted all to themselves; two women unsure about the others' motives. When I came in the dorm room, she left. She wouldn't return until I was asleep. She didn't say much, but her communication was understood.

I usually reserved my communication with Dewayne until we got to Mythology class. I sat next to him so there was frequent note passing at times.

One day before class, he was writing some notes from the board and I was going to ask him what he thought I could do about Karen, but the professor started to speak.

"Everyone, have a seat and take notice of the notes on the board, please." Professor Yancy said.

The students frantically wrote notes down. I wasn't the note taker, which is the very reason I brought my tape recorder. This was the prime way to learn.

Dr. Yancy was an older woman maybe about fifty. She wore jeans and cowboy boots and spoke with a distinct southern dialect different from the average Texas accent; I thought maybe Alabama or some area like that. I glanced periodically at Dewayne, and tried to see if he would look at me, but he continued like the regular class to race his pencil lead across his paper to keep up with the words of the professor.

"All mythology is based on truth," she began her lecture. "At one point history was passed down by word of mouth. History eventually becomes legend and legend becomes myth. If we look at the mythology pattern of different cultures, we will find that the mythological stories of the Greeks, Romans, Sumerians, Egyptians and even some Native American and African cultures are very much the same." It wasn't profound or anything I hadn't heard before. I'd studied a little Greek mythology in high school English class. But if I knew everything I wouldn't be here. It was creepy to think that mythical creatures like Zeus and Hera might be real though.

"I don't claim to present answers in this class," Dr. Yancy continued, gesturing with a number two pencil in her fingers like a cigarette, "but to present questions in your mind instead. For at the time that we ask questions is the time that we begin to grow. You are in this class," she made eye contact with me and made me uncomfortable, "because you want to see the truth in knowledge. But we must ask ourselves: where do these stories of deities and gods come from? Does it make sense for people to create stories for pure entertainment? And if they did create these stories, how is it that so many people have stories so similar? For our Bible believing students, even Noah's flood is accounted in different cultures as an event that really happened. The Moses of the Bible, who wrote the first five books of the text, was himself raised an Egyptian. So does his upbringing from the Egyptian culture have an influence on what he wrote?"

A student raised his hand and the professor pointed to him. "But Dr. Yancy aren't the Egyptians polytheistic?"

"True, but in Genesis, the Bible uses the word Elohim, which is a pluristic word for God. And it even goes on to say, Let *us* make man in *our* own image. Many cultures speak of several deities working together to create the universe and being ran by a head deity. Christians don't see the creation story as mythology but as truth. But if this creation is truth and is so similar to the other creations, then could maybe these creations be just as true? Perspective and cultural language may change names and importance to certain deities, but the general creation may be the same.

"And perhaps a belief in deities means that all cultures agree that we are not alone in the universe. That perhaps somewhere, there are beings that had some hand in our creation. The Sumerians even believed that these beings came down from the heavens and taught them many things. The Sumerians are the first people to have a written history."

She continued to ramble on and I continued to find her conversation more and more interesting. I just had only known of God in my upbringing in church, but no one really went into depth about God. God seemed to me this untouchable, invisible, all-knowing being who was ready to strike you down and send you to hell the very minute you did something bad. It never occurred that maybe there were other "things" up there.

And where was up anyways? Where was heaven? Was it

far in the outreaches of space? Or was it in some other dimension? Where was hell? As a kid, I used to think it was underground but I've never tried to dig to find it. Maybe hell was some other dimension. Maybe the entire spiritual realm is just a parallel dimension walking along side of ours. It just seemed intangible to us because we had no way of getting into it and getting back. I guess that's why death was so scary. When you died and you crossed into that other dimension, you were stuck there. It's safe to say that the dimensional door for the spiritual realm is a one way door for humans.

"What about the devil?" the same kid who asked the previous question blurted out.

Dr Yancy didn't miss a beat, "Although every culture doesn't believe in the devil per se, they do have stories of a spirit or a god of some sort that used to be with the first deity family that caused trouble for mankind; an adversary, one who simply objected or had a different opinion about the creation of mankind. This story crosses cultures as well, but he is called many names. Some cultures believe that he works with God and it is his job to test man as part of a divine plan, so therefore he is not evil at all, while others, like Christians, believe that this spirit is totally against God. But like I said before, maybe they are both true." The class looked confused and I had to admit that she had lost me too for a second.

"If God creates all, then he knows everything and how it functions. It all comes from God. So then if we believe that God is omniscient, then even evil things happen according to His plans. With every bad thing there is a good thing. For example, with every death there is a birth. With every tragedy there is a blessing. In other words, everything happens for a reason; there is a cause and an effect. With out the Ying, there can be no Yang. If there are no shadows then that means there is no light. "

"So what are you saying professor?" I asked, "Are you saying that evil and good work together for a common goal?"

"Like I told you, I have no answers, but I want to produce questions. Good and evil may have different motives to what and why they do what they do, but for some reason all things work together for balance and harmony. Does not the Bible say that, *All things work together for the good of them that love the Lord?* For Christians these are encouraging words that keep them motivated because they know that even through bad times, it's happening for a reason. But the question is who, is the Lord?" I wasn't sure if I were in class or in church and I wasn't sure if Dr. Yancy was a Christian or not but she sure knew a lot of the Bible.

After class, Dewayne met back up with me in the corridor on the way to the library. I was still in deep thought from the class and new ideas were being stimulated in my mind. I had to thank Dewayne for suggesting this class to me.

"Now what were your thoughts about what Dr. Yancy was talking about?" I asked him.

"Man I don't know. Just the little bit she went over was mind-blowing."

We went inside the library and walked around the shelves. I wanted to see if I could find any books that could help me get ahead. Sometimes instead of buying my textbook, I would just get it from the library and copy the chapter from the textbook. It saved a little money, but no doubt it was the ghetto way of studying.

"I was with her until she was like God was pluristic or something." Dewayne shook his head and browsed through some books on the shelf.

"Well, what do we really know about the spirit realm Dewayne? There is probably tons of information that we don't even know about. I feel that sometimes church only gives us the top layer of information."

"Well I know that God is a triune being. So that's why He said, 'Let us create.' and when it comes to God and church, well the church gives the basics to spirituality."

"Yeah, salvation."

"But that's all you need to live right? With all there is to know about God I don't think everybody could handle that type of information. I think that a lot of crazy people in the insane asylum found out too much and probably lost they mind."

I laughed 'cause now he was being silly. He played it up even more by acting like he was having spasms. "You better stop, your face may stick like that." He corrected his posture at my motherly advice. I still wasn't convinced. "If we are going to worship God then why don't we go even further to know Him? We know what He does, but do we really know Him?"

"But Andrea, the important issue isn't whether we know Him, but if He knows us. It's a sad thing for the omniscient God to say He doesn't know you. It's as if you never existed."

"Point taken. But I'm talking after salvation." I looked up in the sky dreamingly, "Haven't you ever wanted to know more? Haven't you ever wanted to know why?"

"Why what?"

"Exactly!" I yelled so loud a neighboring person in the library shushed me.

"Okay . . . Andrea. You're scaring me," Dewayne said, lowering his voice.

"Why things are the way they are. Why the stars and the planets move, why does astrology know so much about our psyche, why mythology speaks of things and creatures we have never seen, and how does the Bible confirm or dispute these things? I mean, the Bible has been around for millennia. Who is to say its true?"

"Gosh, you sound as deep as my roommate," he chuckled. "But in the words of Anthony Turner, if the Bible were written by one person then it would be very bias. And things like astrology are not Christian-based nor is it Godly to participate in."

"Okay, I want to know what you think. You have to admit there is some truth to astrology."

"Yeah, but is it completely true? A half-truth is still a lie. I can tell you a lot of things about you and slip one thing that's wrong and direct your life the wrong way. Maybe it's that God wants us to rely on him and not the stars. God created everything and I'm sure that because of that code He has created everything in—like DNA, then everything he has created says something about him."

"What do you mean DNA? You're losing me now."

Dewayne looked energized to talk about something he was an expert at. "Well, if we compare what you're talking about to genetics, God has a DNA that is ultimate. His DNA is in everything and everyone. You can study nature and even man himself and learn something new about God. Look at the flowers, they only bloom when the sun is out. At night they close. Jesus uses parables constantly with nature to describe himself. But even though you can discover a lot about God through nature I don't think it's his intent for us to rely on the creations for answers and not the creator. That would become something like idol worship and God desires a one on one relationship with people."

"That makes sense, Dewayne. It's kinda cool how you can relate God to your studies."

"That's how I learn, Andrea, but you're pretty deep and I'm not the God professional you need to talk to. Anthony, my roommate, is the guy you need to talk to if you like talking deep spirituality. He took the class; maybe he could tutor you."

This Anthony was sounding more interesting, and studying was better reason in meeting him than Karen's motivation. Everyone speaks so highly of him and I was wondering if this man does no wrong at all.

Dewayne looked at his watch and his eyes grew big. "As much fun as I'm having talking with you, Karen will be getting out of class real soon and I don't want her to well— you know." I nodded in agreement with him. This Karen issue was craziness and I couldn't understand why there was a problem or why she was acting weird.

"How is Karen?"

He looked up surprised. "Isn't she your roommate?" he joked, but he knew the situation. "She's okay." I didn't believe him. He was just throwing me an answer to keep me in the dark. But being the girl that I was, I was still going to dig deeper.

"She hasn't been talking to me lately. Is she upset about something?"

"I don't know. I," he paused to think about what he was going to say. "Andrea, I don't want to lose her and she's been acting really weird about every thing lately." I had to respect that he didn't want to lose his girlfriend. It was sweet. The way he said it—it was so sincere. Dewayne was a genuine brotha. Karen needed to realize what type of guy she had.

"I understand. I'm sure she'll be okay." A slight bit of disappointment filled my soul as I knew that the issues with Karen were not done, but I had to admire how respectfully Dewayne composed himself. He walked down the shelves and turned around quickly to say one last thing,

"Hey, Anthony is having a college Bible study and I would love to introduce you to him, so if you could find the time, then maybe we can go."

I stood glad that he had asked me to go and I nodded again happily. "Yeah, I'll see if Philip will join me. Sounds like a lot of fun." He smiled.

"Yeah . . . Philip." He cleared his throat. I felt like he wanted to say something more but he wouldn't. His mouth just hung there open. I had to save him.

"Well, I'll see you later then?"

"Yeah, I'll talk to you later." He turned around to leave. I rested my head on the book shelf. I could still feel the tension between our friendship and I had to keep it down. I was trying to figure things out with Philip and the last thing I needed was any problems with that. I flipped around and rested my back against the shelf and slid down the side to the floor. I dislodged a book on the way down and it popped me dead center on the head. I looked to see if anyone had seen my blunder and rubbed my wound to see if I was bleeding. I examined the large book and it was big enough to have knocked me out. It's old leather bound cover had no title on the front and resembled a large en-cyclopedia. It hadn't been checked out much cause it didn't have numerous checkout stickers like some books had. I opened the cover.

"No wonder; it's a Bible." I chuckled to myself. Was God trying to enlighten me in some roundabout way? Perhaps I should focus on him and not my situation at hand. I flipped to see if there were any scripture that would pop out at me, and as I flipped I saw books I had never heard of before. I reexamined the cover page.

"The Holy Bible with complete Apocrypha. What is that?" Well, I figured it was worth checking out. Evidently I had missed out on some books of the Bible and I was al-ways willing to find out more. I lugged the heavy book to the front desk and began my process in checking it out.

"Andrea, my sistah. How are you?" Tamela walked up behind me and I moved my hair aside to see her better.

"Oh, hey Tamela. How are things with you?"

"Good. Hey, what are you checking out there?" I felt slightly embarrassed to reveal that I was checking out a Bible. If anything sounded more southern Baptist country, it was checking out a Bible from a library.

"It's a Bible."

She smiled and I knew she wanted to laugh. "Oh that's nice. So, girl, when are you coming by the room? I really want you to meet my roommate. You need some friends in your life. Isolation is never good."

She was speaking so much truth it was ridiculous. Hanging around guys seemed easier, less drama. But my socialization skills with my own gender were suffering. I had no real girl friends. I needed a female or females on my side, especially if this Karen situation never got resolved and she started talking bad about me. The last thing I needed was a reputation of being a ho' just because one female was insecure of me having an easy time with getting along with guys. But if I started hanging with Tamela, maybe I could have a female friend to vouch for me. That is, if Tamela wasn't a ho' herself, then . . . I would be a ho' by association and that would really suck. I had to get to know her better. Besides, I hadn't known any guy long enough for them to get comfortable in talking about what they thought about other females around me.

I was still on a potential target list and until they realized that I was just a little sister type and not a girlfriend, they wouldn't reveal all their manly secrets in front of me. That's how guys worked. I had more male friends in high school than girls. When cheerleading was thwarted because of a jealous female, I took a sports medicine class and helped the injured football boys out on the field. I actually enjoyed that and found that men gossiped worse than women at times. Men are far more outlandish with their gossip, blatantly stretching the truth about certain details of who they slept with (if they did at all). It was quite sad really how when they did that, their peers worshipped them. It was sad how they all believed whatever mumbo jumbo the alpha male of the group told them. In a nutshell, I can safely assume that men are very gullible. I guess it's in their nature to be easily swayed.

"Well girl, are you gonna come by or not? You just sitting there seriously thinking. I'm gonna cook and everything tonight," Tamela said.

"Oh um, is it going to be later because I just got invited to a Bible study tonight."

"Oh hence the big coffee table Bible rental, I see. Yeah, girl, come on over afterwards." She waved and left me to carry my Bible home. It wouldn't fit in my backpack and my little arms barely could keep a grip on it. Plus, I had to find Philip and talk to him to see if he would join me for this Bible study. I hoped he would enjoy something like that.

The book was sliding down my arms and I kicked it back up with my knees. Breathing out a little I began to have second thoughts about checking this big book out. I was going to stay optimistic about this school semester. I had made several new friends all who seemed to add something to my life. I was feeling real good about everything so far. Nothing could go wrong. Or so I hoped.

CHAPTER THIRTEEN

Anthony was in the cafeteria writing down notes for his upcoming Bible study later that night. This would be the first one he'd facilitate and he wanted it to be good. He had been attending the campus ministry and they had found him to be a very astute young man and were very impressed at his insight into the word of God. Sure Anthony was still young and his thoughts were probably his worse enemy, but he humbly took the challenge when they offered him the chance to lead his peers in biblical studies. After much prayer he decided to simply start with Genesis; the very beginning. In his eyes, if you don't know where you come from then you don't know where you are going. He sat there engrossed in his books writing notes.

Karen walked over to his table and sat down across from him. Anthony didn't even look up; he was way too engrossed in his book and she was amazed that his eyes never even swayed away from the words on the page. His eyes jerked left and right in their sockets, absorbing every word on the page.

"That book must be really good," she said, chewing a

French fry and then realizing it had no salt. He finally looked up and smiled.

"Oh hey, Karen, I didn't see you there."

Karen grabbed the salt-shaker from the center of the table and sprinkled her burger and fries accordingly. She thought to herself that they paid way too much in student fees for bland food. "What are you studying?"

"Oh, just some things for the Bible study tonight. Are you coming along?" Anthony's eyes lit up in anticipation and Karen didn't want to let her friend down. She knew how important it was, but her initial thought was say no because the new fall season of the *Cosby show* had begun and she didn't want to miss that. She enjoyed that show. It was the perfect family; the family she wished she had.

"Yes, I'm going to be there." She knew she needed to be there; both her and Dewayne needed to be there. Wasn't that the whole reason why they were having problems in the first place? They had fallen away from incorporating God in their relationship and now they needed to re-commit their relationship to the Lord. Maybe then would all her confusion stop.

Anthony marked his page, closed the book and slid his plate over so he could enjoy his lunch—a plate of fried okra and potato chips.

"So how's the situation coming along?" Anthony asked Karen.

She sighed a bit. "I'm still having issues—let's put it like that. I really don't know why, but I just get upset at Dewayne, and then my roommate Andrea, I think she likes him a little or maybe that he may like her."

"Did he say he liked her or did he show signs that he likes her?"

"Remember when I was looking for him a couple of weeks ago? Well all that time he was with her." Anthony shook his head and was quite surprised at Karen's jealousy.

"And that makes you think he was cheating. Karen, don't you think you jumping the gun a bit? I don't think Dewayne would cheat on you."

"I'm starting to believe that. I mean, we talked and he was so sincere to me. Anthony, he had tears in his eyes and everything. Sometimes I feel bad 'cause it's like I'm hurting him. What if I'm not the best thing for him?"

"So now you feel you don't deserve him?"

Karen looked away and she wasn't sure what was in her head. She had no strong thought in her mind at that moment and any thought that tried to be strong was broken down by her fears. She didn't want to be afraid but she was. Deep down she didn't want to be in a situation like her mother's. Deep down she didn't want to become her mother. But she was more like her mother than she knew.

"Anthony, I sometimes don't know what to think." She paused and Dewayne walked into the cafeteria. He had a smile on his face and didn't hesitate to sit down next to Anthony and eat his fried okra. Anthony glared at Dewayne, who was focused on Karen. Karen smiled, hiding her previous thoughts from him.

"Hey, Dewayne, how is the class coming along?" Anthony asked.

Dewayne thought about the right words to say, because he hadn't told Karen that Andrea was in the class too and he thought that maybe that information would be detrimental to the situation at hand. So he opted to leave that minor detail out.

"Oh the class is fine." Dewayne answered. "It's everything you said it would be. Dr. Yancy is very interesting." Anthony was at a lost for words himself because he hadn't told Dewayne that Karen had been discussing his personal business with him, so there were these pauses in social time that gave them nothing more to do than to put some more food in their mouths.

"So," Anthony said to break the silence, plus he was running out of fried okra that Dewayne seemed to be inhaling.

"So, Anthony asked if I was going to go to his Bible study tonight; are you going to come along?" Karen said to Dewayne.

"Oh Yeah, I was already planning to go." Once again, the information that he had also invited Andrea to come was going to be left out. It was a Bible study, surely Karen wouldn't be jealous. But who knew with Karen? She was an emotional rollercoaster these past few days for no apparent reason. She looked somewhat calm that he was coming to Bible study. Dewayne hid his secrets with his smile that his eyes could not disguise.

"Are you going to clue us in to what the lesson is going to be about?" Karen said.

"Ahh, you'll have to come to find out, but I assure you that you will like it. I've been studying a lot and I hope to take you deeper in the word of God. I, for one, understand how it feels to get the same old sermons day in and day out and I don't want to do that to people."

"Sounds like you really have something cooking in that oven you call a brain." Dewayne said with his mouth full.

"Well, like I said, I am metaphorically pregnant with the word of God and there's so much I want to share, but sometimes I'm nervous to how people will respond to it."

"Well maybe you should hold back. Everybody may not be ready," Karen commented.

"Why should he hold back because a few people aren't ready? There is always going to be someone that isn't ready. There are so many that need to *get* ready. And we can't really do that if we keep getting fed milk," Dewayne said to Karen. He was cool with the flow of the conversation as it was getting the spotlight off his secrets.

"I feel you Dewayne, I'm still waiting for God to direct me on what I should present to the people tonight."

"How do you know when God is really talking to you?" Karen asked. She asked the question but she really didn't direct it to anyone but to herself out loud.

"God speaks to us in many ways, Karen, you just have to be sensitive to his spirit. Read his word for the logos, his written word, and look for his rhema, his divine word which can come through inspiration of a pastor or even a friend. When people give a word from God though, just be on guard. Usually God gives word to people to confirm what he has already told you—watch out for wanna be prophets or as they say, false prophets."

"Then how do you really know what is God and what isn't?" Karen questioned.

"Karen, the Bible says *'my sheep know my voice'*. When you get a daily walk with God and you talk to him often, you get familiar with the way he talks to you. And he talks to people differently and in different ways so you can't let people dictate how God will talk to you."

"What do you mean, Anthony? You don't mind if you give me a pre-sermon to do you?" Dewayne jokingly said.

Anthony smiled and leaned forward to make his point clear. He focused so that he wouldn't stutter. "I knew this guy at my old church in Baltimore who was, for lack of a better word, highly pious. He was what they call in the clouds. So holy that he couldn't relate to anybody but God himself. Nothing was really wrong with him, but he was an extremist. He felt nothing wrong with this extremity and, in truth, he was a die hard Christian to the point that he would be very condescending to everyone he met, even other Christians. His associates would be constantly disconnected to this brother. Not that anything was wrong with him, but he was so holy that in his mind he was already in heaven and nobody on earth could touch him. I remember that he used to say that the Bible said God would rather you be hot or cold and that if you were lukewarm he would spew you out of his mouth. But I read that the Bible says to be not overly righteous or overly wise but to avoid all extremes. I asked myself would the Bible contradict itself, so I thought why would he use the hot and cold water as an illustration."

"Well, you tell me reverend." Dewayne said.

"Well, think about it . . . hot water is used for cleaning and sanitizing things. Cold water is used for drinking, and quenching a thirst. Warm water isn't useful for drinking or sanitizing. This scripture is not talking about extremities, it's talking about being useful to God. It's about if we are at a point where we can be used by God. This particular guy was not reaching people, he was pushing people away with his religiosity—is that a word? Well I made it one . . . religiosity.

"He was so high up in the clouds that no one felt that they could talk to him. He was next to Jesus. Now answer this. How can you lead people to Christ who feel they can not talk to you? How can you lead a person to Christ who can't talk to you and doesn't trust you? Trust and love go hand in hand. We need to trust and love people enough to let them see our real selves. We are not so holy that we haven't done anything wrong and that people can't relate to us and our experience. We have become Christians because we were weak and we needed God. It's that weakness that will relate to other people and be a testimony to guide them to the very strength which is Jesus Christ. That was my only concern with the extreme holier than thou attitude that this brother had."

"So was he wrong?" asked Karen, feeling slightly convicted.

"No, we all have different experiences and relationships with God. No two relationships with God are the same. For example, if two girls date the same guy they will have a different relationship and find that even though the guy is the same, he relates to the two girls differently. The same is with God. He is so diverse and so omnipresent that he has such a multidimensional relationship with each individual person. Maybe that particular brother's faith is not mature enough to handle the freedom that God gives without feeling that he has done God some wrong. We all have a different measure of faith. Your faith may allow you to listen to secular music but to another that may hinder his walk with Christ. To each his own. Our relationships are all different and who are we to put rules on our individual relationships with Christ? No more than you could tell your friends how they should run their relationship when you know nothing about how they interact with their beloved?"

"Well, what is church for then?" asked Dewayne.

"To strengthen us. To edify. To remind us what we are living for. Christ set the foundation, we don't need to make any new rules. Plus, we have a screwed up idea of church. I am the church, you are the church. We are church. The church is us. Church is an entity not an event. We must change the way we think. I am edifying you right now so right now . . . you are at church."

Karen giggled to herself at the revelation that Anthony was giving. He was deep and she couldn't deny that. Dewayne was getting more and more intrigued at what he was talking about. He thought to himself that he wanted to get as serious about the Lord as Anthony was. If God was no respect of persons, then surely He could give him as much insight into his word that he had given Anthony. And he had to admit Anthony had been blessed with an eye and an ear to understand and comprehend God's word in a way that was way different than he had ever heard.

It baffled Dewayne why Anthony didn't have tons of people listening to him. But the real men of God were never popular. They were controversial because they went against the system. Jesus himself set the pace by standing up against the Pharisees, the religious people during his time. It was those same religious people that led him to his death on the cross. Dewayne thought of all the times he had been discouraged about church because of church folks. He then realized that after two thousand years nothing had changed with mankind that much.

"I'm gonna see you at Bible study tonight Anthony . . . and Anthony do me a favor."

"What's that, Dewayne?" he replied.

"Don't hold back."

CHAPTER FOURTEEN

I wasn't sure what I should wear to a Bible study. I mean, it wasn't really church, yet I still didn't want to be too casual. If this was a party, I would have tried to put on my best apparel. But then again, I didn't want to be overly dressed in a manner that made me look as if I hadn't been to church in a long time. That's how people dressed on holidays like Christmas and Easter. It was weird how church would be so crowded on days like that. I would rather not even go to church on those days because of the peacock way that people dressed on those days. If there wasn't anything more grotesquely distracting than how overdressed people adorned themselves, it was how that equaled to looking holy. I laughed to myself at the thought. Sinners hid behind Christian masks to avoid attention to their spirit, but yet drew attention to their outward appearance. It was quite ironic.

I chose to be simple and cute—well being cute wouldn't be difficult. I looked in the mirror and wrapped my hair in a pony tail. I looked at the book that I got from the library.

"Well, at least I got a Bible to study with," I laughed to myself. I grabbed the big Bible that I got from the library and flipped through the pages and noticed books in the Old Testament portion that I had not seen before. I stood in a state of bewilderment.

"Never seen these books." I wondered what they could have different in them. I wondered why they were not in the other versions of the Bible. I needed to talk to someone who knew a lot about the Bible. Maybe this Anthony guy knew something about that. Dewayne spoke so highly about him and he sounded very intelligent. I wanted to take this book to show him, but it seemed way too big to carry to a Bible study. I placed it to the side and thought maybe I shouldn't take it. Big Bibles were the same as dressing up too much. It was too flamboyant and overkill. I would rather not carry one at all. There was a knock at the door. I opened the door.

"Hey, Andrea . . . how are you?" It was Philip, looking handsome in a tank top, jeans and flip-flops. I glanced at the clock. I reached up and hugged his neck as best as my short self could.

"I'm fine. You off work tonight?"

"Yeah, I'm off work." He smiled and pulled me closer to him, holding my waist as my feet were lifted slightly off the ground.

"So, do you have any plans tonight, Philip?"

"No plans in particular, unless they are with you." A smooth line indeed, and even a smoother way for me to invite him to Bible study.

"Great! Because Anthony, Dewayne's roommate, is having a Bible study and I really want to support him tonight, so I was wondering if you wanted to come along." There was a blank stare on Philip's face and he stood there motionless.

"Philip, say something." I waited.

He looked away. "You want me to go to Bible study with you?"

"Yeah, what's wrong with that?"

"Nothing, It's just."

"Just what?" What could be the problem? There were some issues that were hindering Philip and I couldn't put my finger on it.

"I don't like Dewayne and I don't like his hypocritical Christian friend, Anthony."

"Hypocritical? What's so hypocritical about him?"

With a sigh, Philip continued, "When he first got here this summer, Anthony was talking to this girl named Tamela, one of the residents. Everything seemed cool until they got in a spiritual debate. Just because she didn't agree with his beliefs, he broke up with her and broke her heart. Was that really Christian-like? I mean, he is so self-righteous."

He looked disgusted as he walked past me and further into the room. I really didn't know Anthony, but now I didn't like what I was hearing. On one hand, Dewayne was praising him, and on the other, Philip was tearing the man down. I didn't have a problem with anybody and yet everybody had a problem with each other. I was torn between friends. I had just gotten here and had seemed to already fallen in the middle of an ongoing drama.

"I've met Tamela and she seems really nice, weird, but nice. I haven't met Anthony and I don't want to have any preconceived notions about him because I don't know him. Philip, please, Dewayne invited me and I really want you to go."

"Dewayne, huh? You two are getting awfully close."

"We're just friends, Philip, and he has a girlfriend."

"Guys can have girlfriends and still like other girls. Men have wives and cheat all the time. And women have hus-

bands and leave them for their, quote un-quote, 'friends'."
I had the feeling that Philip had insecurities about relationships.

"Is that what you think I'm going to do to you, Philip? Is
that why you are a player? Because you don't trust
women?" I looked in his eyes and it was like I was watching
a movie.

"You are trying to figure me out, Andrea."

"I wouldn't have to figure you out if you would just talk
to me and let me understand you. I have given you no reason to not trust me so I need you to talk to me."

Philip sighed and sat down on my bed. I was feeling like
he was at the midst of a break through.

"Philip, please, I don't know anything about you. You
want to trust me and I want to trust you but I don't know
anything about you."

"Fine, you want to know me? What do you want to
know? I'm not hiding anything from you." It felt good to
hear him say that. "My mother was a simple woman and
very beautiful. You remind me of her, just very down to
earth. She always wanted more from life. She was always
chasing the wind. She met this guy who she became totally
smitten with. They fell in love and had this mad affair and
she later got pregnant with me. She told me that he left
her after the pregnancy and that he never spoke to her
again."

"I'm sorry, Philip. I'm sorry that your mother had to go
through something like that."

"That wasn't the problem. When I was about twelve, I
got this . . . call. It was from my dad. He said he wanted to
see me and not to tell my mother. I went to go meet up
with him at this church. I thought it would be safe to meet
him there and he agreed. So we met at this Catholic
church that he had suggested. He was this tall white guy,
looked like he had a lot of money. He seemed really nice

and I asked him why he had left. I figured it was maybe because he was a racist or something. I thought that maybe my mother was just a black fetish of his and he didn't want to be with her because he knew his family wouldn't approve. I was half right. He told me that his family was totally against him marrying my mother but he didn't care and that he wanted to be with her. He told me that when she found out about how his family felt . . . she left him."

"Oh my gawd," I covered my mouth with my hands, "did you talk to your mother?"

"I went to my mother to confirm this information and she was in shock that I found out. Her guilty look was enough. She told me that he had lied to her about who he was, but I told her that she lied to me. She wasn't any better than him!" He glanced at me and looked away to hide his emotion. "She denied me the right to get to know my father. She denied me the right to make my own decisions about him because of her own personal feelings. So I ran away. I ran away and moved in with him. My dad was able to teach me everything about being the man I am today."

"So you just left? You left your mother and went to live with your dad?" I was amazed at how he could just emotionally cut her off so easily. He rubbed his forehead and I could tell that he had not completely dealt with his decisions, but his stubbornness would not permit him to reflect on himself.

"I don't have any regrets. My father moved me to England and I lived there with him. My mother . . . she killed herself."

My mouth dropped open, amazed at how unfazed he was at saying that. "Doesn't that make you feel anything?" He stood up from the bed and looked away from me into the mirror.

"Should I feel anything? She was a liar and a coward." There was an iciness in his voice that I had never heard before. I didn't want to comment. Something was wrong with the whole situation but I wasn't sure what to think.

"Don't think bad about me, Andrea. Imagine if you couldn't trust your parents. If everything you knew about your parents was a lie. I came back to the states to start over. To begin again. My life isn't perfect but you wanted to know."

He was right. I had asked to know something about him. I had asked to get a peek in his life and it wasn't picture perfect; but whose life was? Who was I to judge him because of his parents? I walked up behind him and laid my head on his back and rubbed his arm.

"It's okay, Philip. I'm not judging you. Look, I really need to go to Bible study and maybe if you go it can help you with your—"

"Problems? You think I need help? You think God can help me? It would seem to me that God is the one who gave me my screwed up parents who couldn't seem to get along. No, I don't have time for that. Look, can we just do something else?"

"But I promised Dewayne."

"Dewayne again!" He snapped at me. "It would seem that you have so much loyalty to him."

"Look, I'm not going to lie to you. He is just my friend."

"Yeah, he's your friend like I'm your friend." He pushed me away and walked to the mirror, sighed, and in frustration fixed his hair and shirt. "Look, I'll talk to you later." He walked out slamming the door.

I was hurt to say the least. I wanted to reach out but I figured that I should give him some time. I had opened up a wound and now I had to deal with all the emotional baggage that he had to offer. I really cared about Philip and I wanted to deal with his heart as carefully as possible. It said a lot that he had shared such a painful memory with me. I just needed to give him time.

I closed the door and took a sigh. Maybe now I could

really get some help from this Bible study. I needed some guidance and a way to deal with it. Mental note: don't forget Tamela's invitation. I wasn't a liar and didn't want to lose my integrity with my new friends. One of which was Dewayne, so I headed out for Bible study. It didn't take me long to get there. It was in the student center and most of the students were already there by the time I arrived. I felt like I was late, but it appeared that everyone was just socializing. I searched around for familiar faces. I guess that Dewayne hadn't arrived yet. I searched for the ring leader— Anthony. Surely he had to already be there. A couple of people were congregating around one guy at this table. He was handsome and had a nice smile. He nodded as the three students demanding his attention like a celebrity. He had a nice energy about himself and he reminded me of Dewayne.

"I see you made it." I jumped in surprise. Dewayne had snuck up behind me.

"Boy, don't do that." I hit him in his arm and he looked as if I hurt him, but I think he was just being overly dramatic.

"Andrea, I didn't know you were coming along!" Karen came up behind Dewayne and grabbed his arm and snuggled her head on his shoulder. I was surprised that Dewayne had not mentioned to Karen that he invited me. I looked at him and he gave me the strangest eye contact. He looked guilty and I felt that he had not told her for a reason. I understood.

"Yeah, I just decided at the last minute." I smiled at her and Dewayne took a sigh of relief. He was my friend and I didn't want to be the cause of anymore confusion.

"Let me introduce you to Anthony," Karen said and I shook my head and tried to see if the one I had picked out was Anthony. She pointed and I was right. Anthony was the handsome gentleman at the front table.

"Hey, Anthony, com'ere. I want you to meet some-body!" Dewayne yelled.

I was so embarrassed and I felt like I was on the spot. I tugged on my skirt and I was hoping that it wasn't too short. Goodness, he was a preacher boy and I didn't want his first impression of me to be negative. He walked over and gave that gentle smile that I noticed when I walked into the room. He extended his hand and I gave him mine.

"Wow, nice grip. I'm Anthony and you are?"

"Andrea," I responded very professionally like I was on a job interview. "Nice to meet you." For the life of me I couldn't understand why I was so self-conscious.

"Yes, I've heard a lot about you. Are you going to be staying for the Bible study?" He still held my hand with his large thumb gently on the top of my hand. I was surprised to know that he had heard about me. I hope he hadn't heard anything bad, especially with me and Karen being not so cool. Looking at him he didn't seem like the bad person that Philip described, but then again . . . Philip had issues when it came to Dewayne and his circle of friends, and somewhere I was caught in the middle trying to be cool with both groups.

"Yeah, I really want to hear what you have to say. I heard a lot about you as well. Dewayne speaks so highly of you." Anthony looked over to Dewayne and Dewayne patted him on the back.

"This nut right here? I hope it wasn't anything crazy that he told you."

"No, I didn't tell her that you were a spy for the govern-ment . . . oops great now we'll have to kill her," Dewayne joked. Anthony laughed silently, revealing more of his cute smile. I couldn't help but stare at him. But there was something just nice about his spirit. He looked like a prince, but he wore no gold or fancy apparel. All he wore was a simple sweater and some jeans.

"Okay, well let's get started," Anthony said clapping his hands to commence the Bible study. "You guys get your Bibles and you can have a seat close to the front."

Oh, I didn't want to sit near the front, but since Anthony invited us to the front I didn't want to be rude. Karen and Dewayne sat in the front row. I sat in the one behind them. I was trying my best to not violate Karen's space. I really wanted to be her friend; I mean she *was* my roommate. I felt naked sitting with these people I didn't know because I didn't have a Bible. I didn't know what to do with my hands. Everyone else was flipping through their Bibles, pulling out highlighters, writing on notepads with pens, and placing bookmarks in certain places. I was tugging on my skirt; it slid up a little bit more when I sat down and now I was even more self-conscious.

Anthony started his sermon and everyone was into it. He had a charismatic way of speaking. He wasn't boring in the least. His voice was as animated as his actions and he wouldn't stop smiling as he spoke. In truth, I don't think he could stop smiling. His smile, it seemed, was embedded on his face and I wondered why this man was so happy. He was talking about the power of prayer.

"The Bible tells us in Ephesians that we fight not against flesh and blood, but against spirits, principalities, and powers in high places. We have to know what we are fighting against. Your enemy is in the spiritual realm and they are of an immortal nature. They have been around for centuries and they know a lot about you. They study you, and your family. All your problems are not because of people. It may seem to you that people have done things to you. It may seem that people are against you but these people are just being used. These people who think they are doing their own will are being manipulated by the spiritual realm to do the will of the enemy. Man has free will, true, and that free will only decides to which universal force will you submit to—God or the principalities and powers.

"Principalities are a type of angel. God is King and within are the angels who are different Princes. You didn't know that there were angels who want you to go against God's will did you? Well there are. Lucifer is the main angel we focus on as going against God, but in fact, a third of the angels in heaven were fallen. Man was given dominion over the earth in the beginning and when he went into his fallen state he lost his position much like the angels. The angels then took over the previous position of man, having dominion over the earth. That's where we get principalities. There is a principality over every country, every state, and every city. If you are not in Christ, you are submitting not to the will of God. You are submitting to the will of these principalities who are headed by their leader, Lucifer, better known as Satan."

Anthony paced back and forth getting eye contact with different people. The crowd was silent. "These fallen angels do not love man and do not understand man, but they manipulate man to do their will. We know that the devil comes to kill, steal, and destroy and those under this umbrella of manipulation have no other desire than to obey that same precept no matter how good their morals are. Without God, man will do what is right in his own eyes because the angels they are submitting under have done what was right in their own eyes. It is the spirit of rebellion." Anthony continued and my mind was moved and intrigued. I wanted to know more but I was pressed to daydream. I focused to keep my mind on what he was talking about.

"You see, when we start to pray we cause things to happen in the spiritual realm. We empower the angels of heaven to battle with the principalities, the angels bound here on earth. With God's help, you don't have to be controlled by these invisible forces. You don't have to be confused, depressed, apathetic, or uncontrolled. You can be free. Without Christ, you are a slave to these forces. The forces have created a system for this world to go by and they want to keep you blind to what's really going on."

Anthony took a sip of water from a water bottle, and although I wanted to take notes, I didn't want to miss anything, "The Bible says that when two or three people of God gather together, we cast 10,000 demons to flight. When we pray and praise God we 1) empower the angels on our team and 2) energize our spirits because we connect ourselves with God and 3) overpower the demons that are set out by the fallen angels to distract and destroy us. Make no mistake, demons and angels are different. There are different entities in the spiritual realm just as there are different races in mankind. The Bible makes clear distinction. You can't fight your enemy if you don't know who he is. But don't focus on the spiritual war; focus on doing God's will. In the process of doing His will, we will have to stand against the devil and his forces. That is where prayer comes in. That is why we need good Christian friends. We are a body. We work together. Together we can do more. Do not let the invisible forces create things to bring dissension."

I looked at Karen and she looked at me. I felt like I wanted to cry and she bit her lip and turned back around. I thought about all the drama that we had been experiencing that had been separating us. I wondered if the devil was trying to keep us apart. I felt the tears well up in my eyes. I needed to know what was going on in my life.

I didn't want to cry there and I didn't want to make a scene. Something was making me uncomfortable and I felt like I needed to go. As I got up to leave, I noticed Anthony's eyes follow me out but he continued to talk. I just couldn't focus in my mind on what was going on. He was saying a lot.

A cold feeling overwhelmed me like a breeze when I got into the hall. I stopped and looked around. No doors were open. I was scared and disappointed in myself to think my emotions could have been manipulated in some way. I walked out the building and walked back to the dorm, holding my arms close to my chest. The chill wouldn't go away but I figured the autumn nip was hitting. I stopped. I turned around feeling as if someone was walking behind me but I didn't see anyone. I continued, putting a little more pep in my step. I thought about going to share what I had heard with Philip. He may not have wanted to go, but that didn't mean I couldn't share what I had heard.

Tamela was down in the lobby. "Hey girl, wassup. Where you been?"

"Um, Bible study," I said to her and I could tell she wasn't pleased. I recalled on what Philip had told me about Tamela and Anthony over the summer.

"Anthony, huh?"

"Yeah, look, Philip told me that you and Anthony were dating for a second and that ya'll broke up because of your beliefs."

"Yeah, well let's not talk about that. You still coming to my room to hang out?"

"Yeah, I was just—" She grabbed my arm and pulled me along side with her down the hall and to the elevators.

"Girl, you gonna love what I cooked. I got some jambalaya in the crock pot that you are gonna love!" She didn't let me finish talking and before I knew it we were on the third floor headed to room 323. She opened the door and her room smelled like incense.

"Smells nice in here," I told her.

A skinny long-haired white girl with glasses sat in the corner reading over some book. She looked up and placed the book down and sat silently in the same chair, waiting for Tamela to introduce us. I remembered the girl from the hallway.

"Andrea, this is Valerie, my roommate. She is from East Texas as well."

I perked up a bit. It was good to hear that I wasn't the only one who was a country girl. Valerie seemed to be far more sheltered though from my perception. I watched as she couldn't even give me direct eye contact and I thought to myself that this girl had some major issues—some serious issues. But no matter, it wasn't my place to judge. I needed to give her a chance; see what she had to talk about—if she could talk at all.

"Hi, Andrea. What city are you from?" I strained to hear Valerie's bashful whisper.

"Heaven, Texas."

"Really, my brother moved there not too long ago." She seemed to light up a little when she heard me mention Heaven and realized how small of a world we really lived in. Tamela went to her crock pot and scooped out some of her jambalaya and gave me a hot heaping bowl. I held it with both hands and I looked around for a spoon. Valerie, sensing my desire, gave me a spoon like the good little servant she appeared to be, never once looking me in the eye. This girl had no identity.

"Does it taste good?" Tamela asked, her eyes staring hard at me evidently making up for the lack of attention I was getting from Valerie.

I took a bite and let the combination of spices, rice, and sausage work its magic on my taste buds. For lack of better words, it was an orgasm in my mouth. Tamela stuck her foot in this jambalaya, as the old folks would say. I gave her no verbal appreciation, but I'm sure the look on my face was plenty. She smiled accordingly and took my hand.

"Andrea, my sista', we should hang out more. You need some girls that you can relate too. You don't need to join a sorority to have friends."

"I wasn't thinking about joining a sorority."

"Good, you're already in the right frame of mind." She took my hand and led me to the throw pillows on the floor. Valerie took a pillow as if it was assigned to her. Tamela lit some more candles.

"What's up with the ambiance that you're trying to create here? You trying to seduce me?" I joked, but seriously, I was starting to get nervous and I wasn't sure if I was down with the lesbian thing—no let me make that clear in my mind, I wasn't cool with it at all. I had to plan my escape just in case Tamela tried to make a move on me. I thought of reasons to leave.

Tamela laughed and slapped my arm playfully and led me down to the pillow between her and Valerie. "You funny, girl. Ain't nobody trying to seduce you. I just wanna, ya know girl talk. No men, no drama," she leaned forward. "I can tell you need that in your life."

Slightly offended that my life was becoming obvious, I had to admit Tamela was right. I did need some girls that I could talk to. I thought that maybe Karen would be that. I guess I was wrong.

"Andrea, earlier you asked me about Anthony." Tamela got comfortable with a throw pillow, "We met over the summer semester. Anthony seemed like a really nice guy, but in truth, he is just another hypocritical Christian." She turned her head maybe to hide the tears in her eyes but yet I couldn't feel any sadness in her words. "Anthony and I met and he seemed like the type of guy that I could talk to about anything. He seemed real opened-minded and that he would accept me for me. I would never expect that he would betray me because of my upbringing. I mean everyone isn't the same, right?"

"Right." I was trying to stay on track with what Tamela was trying to tell me, but it seemed she was going to beat around the bush several times before revealing the whole story. Valerie rubbed her hands nervously and switched to twisting a strand of hair.

"Andrea, I like you because you're not like him. I see you as a very open-minded person. When I started to date Anthony we clicked a lot because I must admit, he knows a lot about spirituality and I do as well. But he began to tell me that if I didn't believe in Jesus, that I was endangering my life."

"What exactly do you believe in?"

"Well, I don't want you to get scared or anything." I nodded in agreement but I wasn't sure what to think of what she was trying to say. "Look, Andrea, I think it would be easier if I just show you." Tamela said as she lit another big candle and closed her eyes.

Tamela took a breath and raised her hands with her palms directed up, and as she sat there, she mumbled something under her breath. I couldn't make it out, but as I sat there in the dim room I saw that the candle she had just lit began to lift into the air. I held my breath and stood frozen in shock as I watched her do this.

Valerie touched my arm knowing my fear and whispered as to not disturb Tamela in her concentration. "It's okay. Don't worry."

I looked over and took a breath. I didn't want Tamela to think ill of me as she did about Anthony. But once more, I wasn't quite sure what I was getting myself into. The candle sat in between us, center circle, for about thirty seconds and slowly lowered itself back to the ground. Tamela smiled and opened her eyes.

"I can do things, Andrea. I practice magic," Tamela spoke to me; her voice so soft now.

"You're a magician? Anthony was upset that you're a magician?" I tried to give her the benefit of the doubt, but she just looked at me and shook her head giggling just a little.

"No, not quite. I am a witch. But please don't get scared. It's not like what you see in the movies. I practice magic for good. I don't do bad things. I just find that it empowers me to control my life."

"Okay, to control your life." I was still trying to let it sink in a bit, "So why are you telling me all this?" This was information that really was making me uncomfortable and seeing what I saw would freak anyone out.

"Andrea, I see a natural power inside of you. There's this energy that I feel around you and think that if we were friends, I could help you tap into that. Please just try to understand, I'm not trying to convert you or anything, I just want you to see that what I do is not some dark thing. I don't go around flying around on some broom or anything. It's my religion."

"Do you worship the devil?"

"I don't believe in the devil. I believe in angels. I pray to the angels and they hear my requests. Everyone has a guardian and I can help you find yours. There are spirits everywhere that just want to help you and if you let them they can help you empower yourself."

"Empower me to do what? Raise candles in the air? Why would I need to raise a candle in the air?" Tamela laughed, but I was dead serious. But she took my hand and grabbed Valerie's hand who in turn grabbed my other hand.

"Empower you as a woman, as our sister. When we came here we were just like you. With our help you can know things that only God herself knows, but we must help you get there. I know it sounds like a lot but I promise you that I can show you more about yourself that you didn't even know."

"Like what?" I was curious to know what I didn't know about myself. This curiosity left me open like a book. Valerie gripped my hand tighter and looked into my eyes.

"Your father is looking for you." Valerie spoke so somberly and distinctly.

"My father is dead." I was almost through with these girls for speaking such things. If they thought I was about to sit here and let them talk about my dead father, then they were completely wrong.

"Andrea, your father is alive and he is looking for you. Your mother has kept a secret in her heart about your father."

I ungripped her hands and looked at Valerie crazy. "What are you talking about? What would my mother be keeping a secret about? I went to my father's funeral. He is dead and I don't like you talking about him like that."

"Please, Andrea, calm down." Tamela said. "Valerie only speaks what she hears in her head. She is rarely wrong. I've helped her develop her gift. For the longest she and everyone she knew thought she was crazy. Maybe, you can relate? Maybe, you just need to discover these truths for yourself."

I stood up and my heart raced at the offenses my ears were taking in. I could understand now how Anthony could break up with this girl. Who was she to dip into my home life like it was just open territory?

"You don't know what I've been through." I pointed at Tamela and confidently stood up.

"I apologize for stepping over my boundaries, Andrea. I just want you to understand."

"Yeah, Tamela, I understand. I understand that you two

are crazy. How dare you tell me that my mother is lying to me and that my father isn't dead. Who do you think you are?" I kicked the pillow over and left the room.

I ran down the hall not looking back and took the stairs to my room because I didn't want to wait for the elevator. Valerie's haunting words stuck in my head and it only made me madder that I could not exorcise her words from inside me. I fumbled with my keys and busted into my room, glad that Karen had not made it home from Bible study. I didn't want to have to explain what I had just been through. That same cold feeling overwhelmed me. There seemed to be more shadows in the room other than mine and I paused before turning on the lights. I closed my eyes to clear my head.

Call your mother, talk to her. I couldn't control my own thoughts. I needed to prove to myself that Valerie's words couldn't be true. I needed to know the truth. If she was lying, if Tamela was lying, then I would know who was trying to lead me astray. But what would I do if my mother was truly keeping a secret? There was no way my father was alive. I knew he was dead. Maybe possibly Valerie meant something else. I had stormed out so quickly that I didn't give her a chance to explain. I picked up the phone and dialed slowly, not sure how to say what was on my mind.

"Hello?"

"Hey mama."

"Hey baby, how's school?" Her sweet voice eased my mind and I found true comfort in who she was. I despised myself for allowing these people in college to make me doubt what I had grown to know what was true for so long. But wasn't that what college was about? College was there to challenge not only your academic knowledge, but everything you held as truth socially as well.

"School is cool, I'm just having so many issues with these people here."

"Awe, baby, is it da' classes?"

"No, it's my friends, Ma'. All the guys like me so they are cool, but they don't like each other, so they don't like me hanging around the other guy, like I'm their property."

"Baby that's how mens do."

"Yeah, but the females here are acting stupid too. They are jealous of me over stupid stuff that I'm not even doing. And other females want me solely to be their friends and act like I've known them for years when I've just me them. I've never felt so wanted and yet so split."

"Well, Andrea, it seems you are blessed to have so many people love to be around you. Just be careful because everyone who says they are your friends really ain't."

"I know. Everybody believes in so many things too. I don't know who to believe right now."

"Andrea, we raised you to understand what the Bible says and our faith is in Jesus, but you have to know God for yourself. You can't get to God using my faith baby."

My mama was going into preaching mode. If I was there I knew she would be ready to sit me down and rub some holy oil all over my head and I wasn't in the mood for that. I didn't want to talk about Jesus, I wanted to talk about Daddy.

"Mama, I have a lot of questions in my head. I'm so unsure about so many things. This girl here at school, I guess she is a psychic or something," Mamma grunted when I said that followed by a "Jesus" under her breath. I continued. "She told me Daddy was looking for me and that you were keeping a secret from me." I laughed to myself at how silly it sounded, but my laughter was not accompanied with my mother's laughter at all. In fact, her silence made me wonder if the connection had been lost. Maybe I needed to call her back. Possibly I had accidentally hung up with her.

"Hello, mama?"

"Yes, baby." I took a breath.

Her failure to respond filled my heart with fear. All I could hear was her breathing. "Mama, are you okay?"

"Who told you these things?" My mama sounded sterner than I had ever heard her before.

"Just some girl I met. She was being silly and knew what she said couldn't be true. I'm so tired of people acting like they're my friends and they keep feeding me lies."

"Andrea, baby, you know that when your daddy died, I was the only one there for you."

"Yeah, Mama, I know. I was there for you too. We pulled each other through that time."

"Yes, I know. You are a special child. I've always known that. I didn't want you to hurt or be hurt. I've never wanted you to suffer more than you had to. I remember your daddy would tell me that you were tougher than I thought you were. He used to tell me that there was nothing you couldn't handle, that you were his little angel."

"Yes, I remember. He used to tell me that I was tough as nails." Mama laughed and I could tell from her voice that she was holding back tears.

"He used to tell me that we should tell you some things about . . . us that you should know. I didn't think you would be able to handle it but he thought it was time. We got in an argument about the whole thing and well that's when he—"

"When he what, Mama?" I could feel my heart beating and I wasn't sure what to think. My mother was telling me something new that I hadn't known before.

"Yo' daddy had a heart attack right there. I felt so guilty about the whole thang. I never forgave myself. I didn't even wanna talk about it. I didn't want you to know I felt it was my fault."

"Wait, oh my gawd, so you and daddy were arguing over me and that's how he had a heart attack and died?"

"Yes, baby, I'm sorry."

"But what could have upset him so much? Why were ya'll arguing over me?"

"We were arguing whether or not to tell you that," she was breathing so hard that my breath was in sync with hers. My heart was pounding in my chest and my ear was burning because it was pressed so hard on the receiver of the phone. "You're adopted."

I dropped the phone. I wanted to scream but I refused. I wanted to curse but I didn't. Valerie was right. I could still hear her voice on the phone but I didn't pick it up. I was in a state of shock. I grabbed my room keys and walked out the room. I don't know what my mother thought I was going to say. I couldn't formulate my mouth to say anything. At that moment I didn't know who I was anymore.

I felt rejection overcome me and in my mind. If she wasn't my real mother then my real mother didn't want me. What could my real mother have gone through that possibly caused her to give me up? I felt like my parents that I knew for so long were strangers. My whole idea of who I thought I was, who I thought I was going to be like, and who I thought I looked like was gone.

Why had she kept this from me? My mind was stunned as I walked down the hall, to the stairwell. If there were people in the hall I was oblivious to their presence. In one short moment I had found a new reality. What else was there that I didn't know? Who else was not what they appeared to be? I did know one thing, I had found the truth. I had discovered a newfound truth that was going to take me down a road that I was quite unsure of. I wasn't even sure if this truth bothered me. In fact, I was relieved. I took a breath and knocked on room 323. Tamela opened the door and stood shocked that I had returned. Valerie stood behind her silent, watching me from the pillow she apparently didn't move from. The candles were still lit and the incense still burning. I entered the room.

"I want to know more," I said. Tamela took my hand and with out hesitation she gave me a hug.

"Come, my sister. Let our journey begin."

CHAPTER FIFTEEN

Anthony shook hands, making his way to his smiling friends who so patiently waited for him to thank his guests for attending Bible study. Dewayne held Karen close and kissed her hand and she smiled. She felt better and yet worse for how she had treated Andrea. "Dewayne, I have to tell you that I have treated Andrea so bad these past days." Dewayne looked at her in the eyes while Karen got sympathetic with him.

"It's okay. I know that I haven't been all that receptive to you."

"It's not just you. I'm not sure why I've been so jealous with you. It's been so bad that I've pushed you away and I've pushed a very good friend away."

"Maybe you shouldn't be talking to me . . . maybe you need to tell this to Andrea."

Anthony walked over and he got that warm feeling from how close Dewayne and Karen looked. "Now look at you two. You guys make me wanna get a girl myself."

"Yeah, you need a girl with your single self, but next

time we'll screen her to make sure she isn't all weird like Tamela."

"What? You used to date that weird, spacy girl?" Karen said. "What did you have in common with her?" Anthony looked around to make sure no one over heard because Karen was talking awfully loud.

"We didn't really date, we just went out a few times over a two week time span."

"Yeah, but he was really into her for a good minute." Dewayne joked as he nudged his friend in the stomach.

"No, it wasn't even that serious. She was really into me. Tamela had major issues. She was the first girl that I met here on campus and since there weren't many people here on campus during that time, we spent a lot of time together. But I never openly told her that we were girl-friend and boyfriend so I can't see how she can say that I broke up with her.

"As I got to know her she tried to get me into this witch-craft stuff. She would tell me that she put a love spell on me so that I would love her forever and that she could summon the spirits to help me in school with my grades if need be. I told her that I was just fine and the Holy spirit was the only spirit I needed to do anything for me. I told her that through Christ I could do all things. Not through anything else. Well, she would get awfully mad when I would bring up Jesus and she accused me of judging her. I told her that judges give verdicts. I was advocating on her behalf. I was stating the facts and only the facts. She stormed out and next thing I knew I found out she was sleeping with that Philip guy so I told her that maybe we shouldn't talk anymore."

"Wait, Andrea is talking to Philip. I knew he was a ho'," Karen said and Anthony looked confused when she told him this.

"Philip is talking to your friend that I just met?" Anthony asked.

"Yeah, but he has issues too. Don't let me get started on him," Karen said not really looking at Dewayne. Dewayne didn't want to even touch that issue but he didn't like Philip for obvious reasons. Anthony had a disappointed look on his face.

"So do you think she could really do all those things?" Karen asked.

"Man, that stuff is real. I had a great aunt that used to do stuff. My momma used to tell me that she was a gypsy. You can't play around with that type of thing," Dewayne replied. Anthony place his study guides in his book bag and led his friends outside as the custodian began to lock up.

"Yeah, Dewayne's right. All that stuff is real. But the deeper you go the more spirits you have to invoke to get power. The Bible tells us that once the holy spirit comes upon us, we shall receive power and also says that greater is He that is in us than he that is in the world. You see what may take a hundred spirits to empower a witch to do, the holy spirit can do in one person who believes in Jesus."

"If you ask me, I don't want a hundred spirits trying to occupy my body—that would get awfully crowded," Dewayne joked.

"Yeah, seriously, it would. Besides, they may have power, but none of those spells can give them eternal life. None of those spells will save their soul from hell. Even the witches have to understand that they need Jesus."

"That's scary to think that witches are real," Karen said, huddling up under Dewayne. Anthony shook his head as he walked across the grass and looked up in the sky at the bright twinkling stars.

"Why be afraid? Are you scared because you don't know

what they can do or are you afraid because you don't know what God can do? If you are a Christian you have nothing to be afraid of because we are children of God, the Father of all spirits. Whatever they do to you they have to answer to Him. Besides, witches are just people too. Most don't see what they do as an evil thing, they are just misled and need to be guided toward the right path. Some, in fact, want to get out and are so deep into it that they are either scared or trapped under demonic influence. Demons are a serious force to reckon with. So don't fear them. Have compassion for them. You can't lead anyone to Jesus that you don't have compassion for and you definitely can't lead them to Christ if you are afraid of them."

Anthony had a way of getting his point across in the most gently way that made a person want to love everybody they came across. He made it sound really easy. Karen thought to herself that it took a special person to do such things. Karen had to learn to be more compassionate toward people. Dewayne himself simply avoided people that he had problems with, which is why he simply did not associate himself with the likes of Philip or Tamela.

"Where did your friend go anyways? I saw her leave early." Anthony asked.

"I don't know. Maybe something you said hit home," Karen replied to Anthony.

"Is she a Christian?"

"I think she is," Dewayne said, "I mean she's real curious about spiritual stuff." Anthony gave a low moan indicating that he was thinking about something in his mind that he wouldn't reveal into the open. Karen was once more beating her conscious up knowing that she had treated Andrea so wrong and all she could think about was how she was going to make a mends with her.

"Remember what I talked about today, about the power

of prayer? There may seem to be a lot of issues going on at the time but God can solve all of it if we involve him in our situations." They all stopped walking because Karen watched the ducks passing by in the pond.

"They are so carefree. They don't worry about a thing," she said, watching the ducks one by one follow each other into the pond. "I wish my life could be like that."

"You don't have to worry, Karen, God can take care of everything. Why are you worried?" Anthony asked. Dewayne leaned against the tree unable to watch his girl in so much anguish. She turned around and she had tears in her eyes and Anthony motioned his hand to Dewayne to do something. Dewayne looked up and embraced her.

"Baby what's wrong?"

"I don't know . . . I'm sorry."

Anthony took the initiative to take both their hands. "Hey, can we pray? I mean for real. The school year has only begun and already the devil is attacking my friends. I've been really feeling in my spirit too that God wants us to get ready for something."

Dewayne perked up when he heard Anthony say this. "Get ready for what?"

"I don't know. But can't you feel it? It's in the air. I can feel it every time I pray. Something is over this campus." Anthony wasn't quite sure what he was feeling himself. "Just because we love God, let's not be naïve that the devil exists and that he is always planning a method for our demise." Karen looked scared and Dewayne gripped her hand tightly to let her know that she would be okay.

"Anthony, man, I've been hearing things too. It's been scaring me. Maybe God is trying to warn us about something. I'm ready to get serious and pray against whatever is out there." So that's what they did.

The triad of believers stood by the pond and offered a prayer up to the Lord. Not sure what to pray about, they went back and forth asking God to do His will, to bind them together in love. Dewayne seemed to pray the hardest to Karen's surprise. He had a fire within him that she had underestimated. Maybe she had prejudged her man wrongly. In fact she knew she had. She didn't know him like she thought she did. He was already a man of God. All this time she was trying to push and make him one, and he already was one. All she had to do was let him be. Karen herself was overcome with emotion, allowing her tears to flow as they chose. She had to release; she was so burdened in her soul. And then it came . . . her peace. As the Bible would say, the peace that passes all understanding.

CHAPTER SIXTEEN

"Amen." Anthony ended the prayer and exhaled. Dewayne looked at his watch and broke loose his hands noticing how late the time was.

"Man, I have to really get to writing this paper for class or I'm going to be really messed up. It's the first paper ya know."

Karen hugged Dewayne's neck and kissed him on the lips. "Get to the library and get to writing. I'll talk to you later."

"Okay, I love you." He kissed her back and ran back toward the campus.

"Well, would you like me to walk you back to the dorm?" Anthony offered her.

"Thank you, sir. I would appreciate that." Karen replied.

"I'm glad to see things are way better and that you are expressing yourself Karen," he said as they walked across the now quiet road.

"You know so much, Anthony. You were right when you were skeptical of how people would receive what you had to say. But I want to tell you that you really helped me tonight and that God has really given you a gift. People walk through life choosing not to see reality. People would rather escape reality."

"You're right." Anthony stuck his hands in his pockets and jiggled his change as he strolled. "Some guys I know here on campus drink alcohol every day. I remember one of those guys came to my room, and when I answered the door he smelled like weed and alcohol. I'm thinking to myself, he's looking for some way to numb his pain, his pain from life. Looking for some type of joy, constantly through physical means and not spiritual."

"Sooner or later he's going to need his body to work right and it's not going to because of all the drugs he's used to alter it." Karen added.

Anthony nodded in agreement. "Yeah, even if I weren't a Christian I wouldn't indulge in all that because I do love my body. I thought to myself that this guy must not love who God has made him to be or he doesn't understand who he is. If he did, he wouldn't destroy his body like that." Anthony said, "I think that if we get in the mindset that we are renting these bodies out and that we have to return these bodies back to God, we would treat them better. It's like when you rent a suit or a car. I'm sure God wants it in just as good of condition as he gave it." Anthony walked her up the steps of the dorm and gave Karen a hug. "Let me know how things go with you and Andrea."

"I will. Oh yeah, just for the record. I think that Andrea needs a guy like you in her life, not Philip." Anthony smirked and looked down at his shoes and then back up. Karen watched him as he silently took the comment and walked into the distance. She thought that he was way too good of guy to be alone. It almost angered her that no girl had scooped him up yet. She turned around and walked into the lobby.

"Looks like someone took my advice." Philip sat at the front desk studying his books and spying on Karen at the same time.

"What do you mean your advice?" Karen said as she walked past the desk and flopped onto the lobby couch.

"Aw come on, Karen, I saw you two. Talking so intimately to Dewayne's room-mate, and all in public too. You're far bolder than I thought."

"Anthony is just my friend. Dewayne was just with us."

"Yeah, yeah, sure. And Dewayne is just friends with Andrea right?" She felt that old anger rise up and then she shook herself. Why would she let Philip get her mad? He was just instigating because he had no life of his own.

"Philip, I don't need you telling me what I should be thinking. Don't you have some work to do or something?"

"I'm not telling you what to think. I'm just going by what I see. And it looks like you and Anthony are pretty close."

Karen glared at Philip and walked up to the desk as calmly as she could. "You are so demented in your mind, you can never understand how a man and a woman can be truly brother and sister and not have sex."

"Oh come on now!" Philip laughed, "I see church folks say they brothers and sisters as a smoke screen to have sex without people knowing. You may not admit it but look around Karen, a lot of people are having sex secretly. They keep them around as friends just in case they need them for a special moment if you get my drift."

"No, I don't. Are you insinuating that I would sleep with Anthony?" Karen was appalled at Philip's way of thinking.

"Hey, we already talked about this before so why be redundant?"

"Yeah, but I didn't know that you saw all your female friends as potential sex partners."

Philip smiled and raised his hands, "You say that like it's a bad thing." Karen couldn't even look at Philip, she was so disgusted.

"Everybody that you love, you don't have to have sex with, Philip. It's a sad person that feels that every time they get close to someone, they have to sleep with them."

"Sex to me is just a way of expressing myself, and not only that, but a very natural need, like being hungry. We all need sex and it's better when we can help each other with that need. Who else's business is it but the person who is hungry and the person willing to feed that need? What does it matter between consenting adults?" He curled his lip at her.

"You're trying to confuse me by asking valid questions, but the issue at hand is that you're comparing sex to like going to the bathroom or eating. Philip you can live without sex believe it or not." He looked shocked when she said this. "And I do believe that sex is sacred."

"If it's so sacred, then why are you and Dewayne so sexually active?" Karen once again was struck hard by his words and she didn't know what to say. How dare he bring up her personal sex life with Dewayne. She knew that biblically they had done wrong and he had no right to discuss such things.

"You know what Philip. I'm through talking with you." She turned to leave but not before he could reach over the desk and grab her arm.

"Hey wait. I'm sorry I was out of line."

"Yes you were." He hopped his legs over the desk top and pulled her closer.

"It's just that, well, Karen, I find you incredibly attractive and I wanted to see where your mind was at." Karen pushed away from Philip with both her hands, but he still gripped her shoulders and kept her in close proximity.

"Excuse me. Aren't you dating my roommate? Hello, re-member Andrea?"

"Yeah, I know. But that doesn't mean I'm married. Look, we don't have to tell her. I really care about her and I don't want to hurt her, but I have needs and she doesn't seem sexually active and I know you have needs and you don't want sex to ruin your relationship, so how about we help each other out?" His crafty logic was more than seductive, it was plain immoral. If she listened long enough she would be caught like a bug in his Venus flytrap.

"Let me go, Philip." She struggled some more but his arms were too strong to budge.

"Come on, you're being unreasonable."

"Philip, I said let me go!" She pushed again and once more he didn't even flinch. A feeling of panic entered her heart as she knew that she was helpless against him.

"Is there a problem?" another voice asked from the front of the lobby. They both turned to see that Anthony had come back. Philip let go and turned to go back in the front office. Karen went to Anthony trying to compose herself.

"You okay? I came back through because I had your notes from the Bible study and I'm sure you would want them."

"Thank you, Anthony." Karen took the notes in her hand and grabbed his hand. "I'm okay now. Can you walk me to my room please?" Her eyes were on Philip, who de-cided not to pay either of the two any mind now that An-thony had come into the picture. Anthony was aware that something wasn't right with how Karen was acting, and since he already knew Philip's profile, he wasn't about to leave her alone to deal with him.

"Yeah, I'll walk you to your room." They went down the corridor into the elevator and onto her floor.

"What happened back there? Are you going to fill me in?"

Anthony questioned Karen who was tired from all the emotional roller coasters she was experiencing today.

"Philip was being a jerk as usual. He was coming on to me and he is still talking to Andrea."

"Sounds like drama to me."

Karen rubbed her head. It was throbbing and she thought maybe she was getting a migraine. "You have no idea. I'm so tired of negative people. I'm tired of going around the corner and someone feeding me mess and expecting me to take it. Anthony all I want," she paused because it seemed that if she spoke it she would jinx her chances of ever obtaining what she truly desired from life.

Anthony pressed on, refusing to let her not proclaim what she wanted because in his view, you had to verbally speak what you desired in order for it to become manifested. It was a spiritual principle he had obtained by studying the Bible. If men were created in the image of God, and God merely spoke the universe into being, then as his creations made after his own likeness there is a power in our words, whether they were negative or positive.

"Say it, what do you want, Karen?" He was totally absorbed in what she wanted to say and she felt like an over-shaken soda bottle about to burst with one twist of the cap. She looked at him like she was a child, and with glazed eyes she spoke.

"I just want some peace in my life, Anthony. Is that too much to ask? I know maybe the problems I have are self afflicted, but I'm tired."

Anthony was slightly surprised to know how college was already affecting her negatively and bringing her down, but it was no abnormal thing for students to get that way. It did however bother him that she was already tired and he didn't want to crucify her for that. His heart went out to her and so he did what any guy would do—he hugged her. She jerked back. Subconsciously she reacted to Philip's words and now she was rejecting Anthony.

"What's wrong?" he asked her. She looked shaken and she wasn't sure how she was feeling. Scared and insecure, she walked away from him and down to her door.

"I'm sorry, Anthony I know you're trying to help, but um . . . right now I just need to be alone." She slipped inside the room and closed the door.

With a sigh Anthony turned and went back to the stairs. "Maybe being alone is what you don't need."

CHAPTER SEVENTEEN

I went to the pillow that I had left earlier and sat down. "I want to know all there is to know."

Tamela smiled and looked at Valerie and Valerie gave her the book. "And you will. Close your eyes and repeat after me." I heard Tamela open the book and the smell of incense grew stronger. I was scared and I knew I was dabbling in something that I knew nothing about. I had found my fruit of the knowledge of good and evil, and like Eve, I was falling. But I didn't care. I wanted to know no matter what the cost. I didn't care anymore because the mother—the good Christian mother that I grew to know had lied to me my whole life and was thinking about holding the truth from me even now. I couldn't understand how someone could love you and lie to you at the same time. So I did what I wanted to do. I turned my back on my past and sought to find my own truth.

"Angel spirit over me," Tamela said and I repeated, "remove the curtains that blind, and reveal to me what I can't see. Bring power to my mind."

Her words electrified my soul as I repeated them and

we continued to chant. Each time I felt myself falling deeper and deeper, like I was inside some neverending hole. I felt light-headed and the hairs on my arms stood on end. I felt cold and hot at the same time and a draft blew through the room. The candles went out.

"Andrea." I heard a whisper. Valerie screamed. I opened my eyes and I could see them scurrying around in the darkness, but apparently they couldn't see a thing.

"Oh my God," Tamela said in the darkness. I felt around in the darkness and I felt something breeze by my face and go toward the ceiling. I doubled back and fell on my elbows looking for the wall or anything to help me get to my feet. I looked up and something was there. It turned and looked in my direction.

"Turn the light on!" Tamela screamed and I crawled in her direction. I could see Valerie's silhouette reaching for the lamp on the desk. Click. Click! No light.

"The power's out!" Valerie said just before a shadowing figure swooped down and grabbed her by the throat and hemmed her up against the wall.

"Oh sh—" Tamela cried as numerous roaches scurried out of cracks and crevasses of the room and crawled over her body. She was frantically trying to get them off. I needed to help Valerie but I didn't know what that large dark thing was holding her. It was almost like smoke but shaped like a human.

"What's going on? Andrea! What's going!" Another figure grabbed Tamela and pinned her up against the wall with no effort at all, gagging her mouth with its smoky essence. I could hear nothing but her gurgling. I panicked not sure what to do.

"Let them go!" I screamed and my words rippled the air, vibrating their fragile looking bodies. They turned and looked at me in the darkness. It was evident that they too could see. Their faces were like men but their eyes were dark or gone all together. Their whole essence had no solidity about it. Like static on a television, these apparitions phased in and out of reality. Sunken holes took the place of where I thought I should see eyes. They released Valerie and Tamela at my command as if they were at my beckon call.

"Demons, Andrea! Run!" Tamela weakly coughed holding her throat.

"Demons?" I said. Valerie tried to grab the book they were reading from, but a third smaller one that resembled a child ran from out of the wall, grabbed the book and climbed to the top of the shelf. She laughed as she did so. But no mistake, this was no child at all. I was scared. I ran for the door but it wouldn't budge. I turned and I could see my reflection, and in it behind me was a man, white like a pearl and his long black hair floating around him.

"My child," he said, "my special child." And he wrapped his long snowy fingers around my shoulders. He was so tall and thin. His face was so beautiful and feminine, yet strong and distinct. His grip on me calmed me remarkably and he told me that everything was going to be all right without saying anything at all. His presence lit the room like I remember the moon would light the fields back home at midnight. It wasn't bright but just enough so that you could see. Valerie gasped and fell back on her bed.

"Blessed be, it's an angel," Tamela said. He paid her no mind but waved his hands and both girls fell prostrate on the floor unconscious. I pulled from his grip which he did not resist.

"What are you?" I asked him.

"Your friend has identified me correctly." I stood in awe. He was beautiful and I couldn't fathom in any way that he was an angel. Something I had heard so often about was actually standing before me with his arms outstretched hungry for my embrace.

"That's impossible."

"All things are possible, Andrea. You just have to believe." His voice was so strong and yet his lips barely moved. It was almost like he was speaking another language and my ears were translating.

"Who are you?"

"Maybe the question you should ask yourself, Andrea, is who are you?" He smirked and I grabbed a pair of scissors from the floor and pointed them at him. I heard giggles around me in the air. I jumped back from the figures who turned their heads down when I looked at them.

"Don't be afraid of them, they are mere kindred at your service. They need you as much as you need them."

"Don't play with me, buster!" I wanted to be tough, but I was truly scared again.

"I am called Donyel. I am your father." I shook my head because he looked no older than me.

I am not affected by time, I am eternal. He pushed his thoughts into my mind as quickly as I thought them and dropped the scissors.

"How did you do that?"

"You are mine; I know your thoughts."

"So you are what she said. . . . you're an angel?" I swallowed my words and my knees shook, but I managed to stay standing. He nodded in reply.

"But then what am I?" I blinked and he was in one instant directly in front of me.

"You are like us."

I shook my head in denial. "Impossible . . . it can't be."

"Oh yes, I've watched over you since you were a child. Remember when you prayed about Brandi? It was I who answered you. It was I who protected you from her evil.

You are created in my image, you are my princess—powerful in every way. You are like God." He kissed me on my lips, causing this fire to shoot down my neck and through my spine. I felt weak and empowered simultaneously. I closed my eyes, and when I awoke, I was sitting on the pillow and Tamela and Valerie were chanting the same rhyme as before.

I let go of their hands and stood up. The candles were still lit, the book still in place, and no sign of Donyel or his demon minions.

"What's wrong?" Tamela asked. Valerie looked at me with a long stare and I think I was almost as pale as she already naturally was.

"You don't remember do you?" I asked. I looked at the clock and an hour had gone by, but it seemed like only seconds had transpired. Valerie said nothing and walked out the room.

"Valerie, where are you . . . what are you talking about, Andrea? Did you see a vision? Did my spell work?" Tamela went on.

"Your spell?" I thought to myself maybe my mind was playing tricks on me and maybe—just maybe I was hallucinating.

"Let me call you later, okay?" I grabbed my keys and ran out the room. I could hear Tamela calling after me, but she was confused and I didn't want her state to affect mine. Everything about me was tingling and I felt like my skin was on fire. I was dizzy and I couldn't focus on where I was going as my vision blurred in and out. There were several other girls walking in the hall, coming out the laundry room, socializing and studying. I ran into one girl, and like hacking into a phone line, I could hear all this random talking; something about her boyfriend. But her mouth wasn't moving. I backed up and bumped into another girl and she said all these mean and hateful things to me, but once again, her mouth wasn't moving. Yet another girl brushed up on me and all this depression entered my soul that I knew could not be my own.

What was happening? Could I hear all these thoughts? More and more thoughts poured into my soul and I could not control what was entering and leaving. I covered my ears but the thoughts continued. I felt as if I was going crazy. I closed my eyes and visions of other people and their memories filled my mind. I couldn't stop it. No matter what I did, I couldn't stop it.

"Stop it! Stop it!" I screamed, and suddenly . . . there was silence. An eerie silence. I opened my eyes and everyone in the hallway was frozen still. They were all inanimate like I had stopped time itself. I looked at my watch. Time still appeared to be going as usual. Whatever I did though, they weren't moving. Had I killed them? They looked alive and as I looked further down the hall I could see Valerie, frozen in position about to descend the stairs.

"Valerie," I said to myself, and in an instant I was directly in front of her. I scared myself and tried to regain my wits. What was going on? I stood on my guard. What if someone walked into the hallway and saw all these people standing still? What would they say? I saw Valerie and she looked so scared. I touched her face and she blinked. When she saw me in front of her she shrieked and fell back on the floor.

"Calm down! Calm down. It's okay." I tried to calm her down but when she looked around and saw that no one was moving, it didn't make the situation better. Panic over took her and she scooted back against the wall in a corner all huddled up.

"Oh my God what are you?" She was crying. I walked closer and her eyes quivered back and forth. I could feel her fear. I could smell her fear. Smelled like old stagnant dirty water like if you hadn't drained your sink of dishwater in about two weeks. I never knew the smell of fear before and I wasn't sure how I knew that it was fear. But I just knew. I reached my hand out to her and suddenly visions popped in and out my mind—her thoughts.

Valerie remembered the whole ordeal. Donyel had succeeded in erasing Tamela's memory, but not Valerie's. Her perception of what had just transcended was totally different however. She could not see the demon minions but she could feel them choking her. The darkness was not the reason. They had not manifested physically, but somehow I could see their spiritual bodies. She had seen Donyel. He was all glowing like I remember but to her I was glowing just the same. I was floating on air alongside him and in her eyes I looked just as angelic as he did.

I did not remember floating or glowing. But her memories confirmed what I had seen. Donyel was real and all these powers were real. I pulled my hand back and her thoughts left my mind. I looked at my hand and it was shaking.

"Look, I don't know what's going on," I told her, but I wasn't sure if she was receptive to my words. "Please, Valerie, listen to me. I know you remember everything that just happened and I promise you I won't let anything happen to you. We are going to figure this out."

"What is there to figure out? He is an angel and he is your father." Her comment surprised me. I hadn't even gotten that far in my mind to think about that. Valerie scooted away as my mind wandered. I thought to go after her, but I figured that it would be to no avail. I looked back at the hallway of living statues. I had to figure something out. I no longer knew who or what I was.

I wasn't sure how to get things back to normal. I wanted to have a nervous break down but I didn't want to lose any more of my sanity. And in a flash, as if it was a part of me, I raised my hand to the frozen crowd.

"Continue," I whispered and everyone began to move as before. One curly-haired girl looked confused because she was walking behind me when I froze the hallway so now, to her perception, I had just disappeared. I made my way down the hall and touched her on the shoulder.

She jerked back. "How did you?"

"Shhhh," I said and placed my fingers on her lips. She went into a trance-like stare. *You never saw me* I said in my mind and she blinked and turned the other direction without another word to me. I had just given her a hypnotic suggestion using only my mind. I wasn't sure how much power was at my fingertips, but I had to be careful. What scared me most, it felt so natural—almost instinctive.

The voices of everyone's thoughts still filled my head and I closed my eyes to push them out. I had to gain control. I quieted my mind and their thoughts became whispers. Ten minutes later they faded to an almost inaudible sound. But I knew they were still there. When I lost focus and got too close to someone, their thoughts would enter me again.

Philip. I opened my eyes and he was walking toward me. I must have felt him coming. I ran up to him and hugged his neck.

"What was that for?" he asked.

"I'm just so glad to see you. So much has happened to me."

"What's wrong?" he said, looking so concerned. He grabbed my shoulders and held me close.

"Can we be alone? I don't even know where to begin." He nodded and led me down to his apartment in the dorm. It was on the first floor and was decked out. I needed to get away from the distractions of other people's emotions. I was like a piece of silly puddy, everything was sticking to me emotionally. I could even feel Philip's attraction, but I managed to block it out. I needed to talk to

him. I knew I could talk to him, I knew he would understand. He had been lied to by his parents too and he had
learned to start over.

He made me some green tea that was very soothing. I
held it with both hands and tried to calm the whirlwind of
thoughts in my head.

"You okay? You seem to be anxious."

"I don't know what I am right now, Philip. I don't know
why I came to you, but I was just hoping that—"

"Look, you can talk to me. I'm here for you." He rubbed
my back and I felt like I could tell him anything, but I
knew I couldn't. He wouldn't understand the Donyel part.
I didn't understand myself. What had Donyel done to me?

"I talked to my mother and she revealed to me that I was
adopted." I smiled. I wasn't happy, but I smiled. I smiled to
cover up how deeply hurt I was and I think that he could
see right through me.

"Oh, Andrea, I'm sorry. What made her tell you now?"

"That's the thing." I stood up and paced because all this
nervous energy was building up in me again and I felt as if
I would explode. "She wasn't going to tell me. She was going
to keep it a secret. I found out . . . um on my own."

"On your own?"

"Yeah, I . . . someone I knew found out some info and I
went and asked my mom about it and she pretty much
gave herself away. Look, what I found out is besides the
point. The point is that she lied to me and would have
continued if I hadn't said anything."

"I understand." He walked up to me and took my tea
out my hand and placed it on the table. "I understand you
completely." He hugged me firmly and I let myself com-
fortably relax in his embrace. So much passion was inside
him. I felt his pain from his parents as well as my own and
I couldn't help but cry. I sniffed to keep from getting his

shirt wet. He rubbed my hair with his hand and kissed the top of my head.

"I'm here for you, Andrea," he whispered. And I wanted to believe him. I so much wanted to trust him. I knew he could relate to what I was going through. If that was good or bad I wasn't sure. But at the moment it felt good.

"I need to find answers now. I need to find out who my parents are for real."

"Are you sure you want to find that out?"

"I don't think I have a choice."

"What do you mean?" he said, looking confused. He pulled back and looked at me. I smiled, covering up once again what I was thinking. I didn't want Philip to get hurt so it was best just to leave him out of this.

"Look, Philip, it's just something I have to do."

"If you need me to do anything, I am here."

I shook my head. "No, I'm fine."

"Are you sure there isn't anything I can do for you?" He drew his face closer to mine. I could feel his breath on my skin and I felt my skin burn with desire. I closed my eyes and bit my lip.

"I-I have everything under control." His sexual vibe was so strong and with my new gift to sense this, it was overwhelming me. It coupled with my own emotions and deceived me. I rubbed my head on his cheek like a finicky cat.

"I know you have it controlled. But I just . . . want—" He rubbed his lips on my neck as he whispered in my ear. His arms pulled me up higher and closer to his torso.

"What do you want?" I whispered back. I felt myself losing control once again of my reality.

"I want . . . I want you." He placed his lips on my lips. My heart played hopscotch in my chest. Gently and softly he rubbed his lips around the outside of mine without kissing them—teasing me so nicely. I titled my head left and he tilted right and our lips embraced and danced to a song that was unheard. Was it love? No—it was misery. I knew it was. I was trying to rationalize what I was doing. This wasn't the time to be kissing. Why was I being such an idiot? His hand lowered to my hip and I pulled his hand up. I tilted my head back as he tried to slip his tongue in my mouth. I didn't want to be one of those girls who ran to a man every time she was in distress and I didn't want to do anything I would regret.

"We need to stop, Philip," I whispered. His skin was so hot and when I let go of his lips, his mouth fell to my neck and picked me slightly off the floor.

"Oh, Andrea. Don't worry . . . just relax." I wanted to relax, but this was going too fast. It felt good, but I didn't want to have sex, not like this. I pushed against his shoulders and he pulled harder on my body squeezing my waist harder on his pelvic region. I couldn't move. I couldn't breathe.

"Philip, stop . . . you're hurting me." I freed one of my hands and tried to release one of his hands that was groping my posterior, but he simply grabbed that hand and held it behind me.

"Ow, Philip! Stop!" I screamed and I could feel my adrenaline pumping. He wouldn't stop. He acted like he couldn't even hear me. I felt my back slam against the wall as he used it as leverage to prop me up.

"Shhhh just relax." he said, gnawing at my cleavage.

"Philip, stop!"

"Mmmm, Andrea." He propped my right leg up with his arm and I began to panic. He groped his hand under my thigh, pulling at my underwear. Was he going to rape me? Did he not hear me or see me resisting? Did he even care at all?

"I said STOP!" In one quick motion, I kicked him in the

head with my right elevated foot and I pressed my left foot up against his thigh and with my right hand against his chest, I pushed with all my might. I felt his grip loosen and watched him fly across the room against his bookshelf. I sat against the wall, shocked. Did I do that? I looked at my hands and cried. I fixed my shirt. Donyel had unleashed something horrible in me. Philip sat at the foot of the bookshelf knocked out. I walked over to him nervously.

"Philip, wake up." I hoped I hadn't killed him. He moaned. I felt relieved he wasn't dead. I couldn't get my hands to stop shaking. I grabbed him by his ankles and dragged him to the couch and placed him there with little effort. I had gotten stronger no doubt.

I left the room and went to my own.

"Come on, Andrea, don't panic," I said to myself. I couldn't let these powers get the best of me.

Shadowy apparitions kept appearing in the corner of my eye. *Andrea.* I turned to look and they would be gone. I could feel their presence as well. I was scared—so scared I ran down the hall. As I stormed through the door, Karen jumped up from the bed.

"Girl, what's wrong with you? Running in here like you the police." She held her hand on her chest and stood against the door breathing hard. Beads of sweat rolled down my face.

I swallowed to catch my breath and wiped a lone tear from my eye. "Sorry. I was just—jogging."

"Joggin' huh. . . . in those clothes?" I looked at my outfit and thought that maybe I was wrong for trying to lie to Karen. I was very upset about Philip but I felt embarrassed and ashamed. Karen had warned me about him and she had been right.

"Hey, I'm glad to see you though, Andrea. Look I'm so sorry for how I've been treating you lately and I was just wondering if we could . . . you know start over." Our petty problems were far from my mind at the moment. "Oh yeah, Karen, I mean I'm cool if you're cool." I took a breath. I squinted my eye and tried to focus as I saw another shadowy figure following behind every step of Karen.

"Quit hiding," I told it.

"Hiding? What do you mean? My feelings? Yeah, . . . I know I need to express myself more. I shouldn't take things out on you. It's just that I've been going back and forth about all these things in my mind."

I wasn't talking to her, but I was glad she thought I was. I inched closer and the figure unwillingly began to materialize. It was like I was forcing it to do so. Karen couldn't see it at all. It looked like the others, ghostly in appearance and very human-looking except her eyes were dark. When I say human-looking, I say it very loosely because the skin was so scaled and burned looking. She, this demon, spoke without moving her lips. All I could hear was this buzzing noise like a fly that she made. But I understood when she spoke.

Daughter of Donyel, I am at your mercy! Please do not banish me.

I stood speechless and this apparition phased in and out of reality. I looked back at Karen who was attempting to regain my attention.

"Girl what's wrong with you?" she asked.

"Nothing. I just want to clear the air like you. I have my own demons I need to conquer and get out of my life." I aimed the last part of my phrase toward the apparition who bowed and flew out through the window.

"Wow, well I feel like a load of bricks has been taken off my shoulders. I don't know about you," Karen said. If only she knew how true that statement was. I gave her a hug and she hugged me back. Suddenly my hairs stood on end again.

My mind flashed and I saw a vision. *I saw Karen, she was in the hospital giving birth.* I pulled back.

"What's wrong?" she asked me.

I looked at her and then I looked at her stomach. I placed my hand near that area and I could feel another life resting within her; not demonic—a human spirit. "Karen you're . . . pregnant."

"What are you talking about?" She shook her head but I'm sure she was thinking this through. The mood swings, her feeling ill, all of those things had gone together.

"I think—you're pregnant. Have you had your period?"

"I can't be. I mean, no. I mean . . . what makes you think I'm pregnant?" She began to get scared and I didn't want to push her into panic. I could see that the thought was worrying her.

Karen was way too young and she had enough on her plate. She didn't need to be worrying about a pregnancy. But I know what I sensed inside of her. The human spirit has a vibe about it. It gives off a rhythm like a note in a song. But it's only one single note. A pregnant woman has another spirit within her, a child, so the vibe coming from her is more like that of two harmonious notes playing together. The spiritual vibe of a pregnant woman is just as beautiful as the physical attributes. So that's what I could sense—I could feel these harmonious rhythms emitting from her. But how could I explain that to her?

"Look, Karen, I really don't know how I know, I just think that maybe you are."

She sat down and thought for a second, almost trying to deny the thoughts that were now in her mind but unable to resist the fact that she had been feeling weird lately. "I can't be," she laughed. "I mean really, look, to prove it to you I will go to the clinic tomorrow and get a test." She said it to supposedly calm me down but I know that she was really trying to convince herself.

I gave her a hug and agreed to go with her tomorrow. She grabbed my hand and looked into my eyes and I do believe that was the closest that we had been since we met. I understood her nonverbal thoughts and everything in her was good. She had been insecure and jealous on account of her condition. I think that maybe had I tried to talk to her more, maybe my basic female intuition would have picked up on this without the assistance of my new found gifts.

"Hey why are you crying?" Karen asked me. She wiped my tears from my eyes but I saw her eyes were beginning to water too.

"You know. You were right about Philip. He tried pushing himself on me."

"What? Are you all right? Do you want me to call Dewayne?" I grabbed her arm to calm her down.

"No, no I'm fine. You should be more worried about *him*." I giggled as I thought about how hard I pushed Philip off me. "It's just that I gave you such a hard time about who he was and you were right all the time."

"He's just a jerk that keeps his brain below his belt." I smiled that she didn't judge me. She didn't even say "I told you so." She just hugged me.

CHAPTER EIGHTEEN

A week had gone by and for a good majority of us, life would never be the same. I had no one but Valerie to talk to about what had happened in her dorm room and she was reluctant to talk to me. Every time I saw her on campus she would walk in the other direction, scared to even look at me. I thought maybe I could get be back to normal, but I kept feeling people's vibes, hearing their thoughts and I even developed a new ability—I sneezed and teleported myself from the bathroom to the bedroom. I didn't have time to freak out; I had to learn to control these gifts.

I kept seeing demons. They knew I could see them and I think they knew who I was. They were embedded in the faces of people or hovering over them like shadows. There were even some that I thought were actual people. It made me not even want to leave my dorm but I couldn't stop life. Besides I had power over them. I needed to find out more about angels. The more I knew about what they could do, then maybe I could figure out what I could do.

"Dewayne, I need to talk to you." I stopped him on the

way to the cafeteria. He was all bundled up with his hooded sweatshirt tightly fashioned. "What's wrong with you? You look like you've seen a ghost." I tried to hold my expression. It wasn't exactly a ghost I had seen. I pulled him over to the bench by his arm.

"Whoa..Andrea, why are you rough housing me? Girl, you got some kinda death grip there too by the way." He rubbed his arm and pulled his hood down to give me my attention.

"Dewayne, I need you to be serious. I've been seeing some things and experiencing some things that I can't quite explain."

"What kinda things?" I wasn't sure where to start. Dewayne had been the one I had come to because he was so open-minded about things, but this was even more than I could handle and I still second guessed myself as to whether it was all really actually happening.

"Remember when we talked about angels and stuff a while back?" I said.

"Yeah, and you thought that maybe I had an enunciation experience." He giggled and I popped his arm again for not taking me seriously.

"Seriously, Dewayne. I think that maybe I saw an angel." He looked at me all confused.

"Are you sure? I mean maybe it was just your imagination."

"No, Valerie saw it too."

"Who is Valerie?"

"Tamela's roommate."

"Oh that little quiet white girl . . . oh yeah, I've seen her around. Uhh, she's sorta weird; she's probably been abducted by aliens or something." I gave Dewayne a look and guarded his arm that was beginning to get sore from me popping it so much. "Sorry . . . so do you really think an angel came to you? I mean how and why?"

I was about to tell him everything that went down in

Tamela's room but Anthony walked up coming from his class. "What's up, guys? What are ya'll talking about over here?" Dewayne looked and gave Anthony a handshake.

"Andrea thinks she may have seen an angel," Dewayne was quick to say. I popped his arm for revealing my secret without me telling him to do so. "Ow! Wow you hit hard," he said rubbing his arm. I didn't intend on getting too many people involved.

"Angels? What makes you think you saw an angel?" Anthony asked. I really didn't want to say anything but Dewayne nudged me to continue talking. I wanted this to be a private matter.

Dewayne looked at me. "Andrea, look you can trust Anthony. He knows more about this stuff than I do. I trust him and you should too."

"Yeah, you can trust me." Anthony smiled. I was such a sucker for these charming smiles these men beheld. Anthony was a nice cool guy and there wasn't any reason that I shouldn't trust him, so I don't know why I was being so evasive toward him. I was positive that he could feel that.

I sighed. "Valerie saw it too. She can be my witness that he came to us in the room last week."

"Who's room?" Anthony asked.

"Uhh, Tamela's room," I said, watching Anthony's eyes roll in his head with disappointment.

"And what were you doing there? You know she is into a lot of cultic stuff." Anthony asked.

"That's besides the point—"

"No that is the point. Did she summon this angel?" The look Anthony gave me reminded me of how my dad would look at me when I did something that I knew I shouldn't be doing.

"Look, we were just messing around. I didn't really think what she was doing was going to work. I was just looking for answers."

"Yeah, that's how it happens. Folks play around with the devil and then they get surprised when the devil gets the dice in his hand. What did you guys use, a Ouiji board?"

Okay, now he was getting on my nerves. I didn't need him making me feel bad—I was already scared. "No, I didn't use a ouiji board! We had a . . . spell."

"A spell!" Anthony threw his hands up in the air. Dewayne grabbed Anthony's shoulder to calm him down.

"Okay ya'll, let's focus. What's done is done. Everybody calm down, okay? Andrea, what answers were you looking for?" Dewayne mediated.

"I found out that I was . . . adopted. So I went to Tamela for answers," I said.

"Why Tamela?" Dewayne asked.

"She was the one who told me that my mother was lying to me and that my dad was looking for me. But my dad is dead."

"So you tried to conjure the dead!" Anthony asked.

"No, Mr. Preacher, not the dead. She did a spell for me to see the truth and then he came."

"Who?" Dewayne asked. They were both interested in what I was saying now and I could hear nothing but the wind. I kept getting an icy feeling and was scared to say his name out loud. What if he heard me? I looked around at things that were moving. Was it the wind or was it those shadowy apparitions?

I paused and reflected on that night. "I don't want to say his name. All I know is that afterwards, I could see a lot of things. These people, I guess are demons."

"What do you mean you guess? They either are or they aren't," Anthony said. He acted as if I should know without out a shadow of a doubt what I was going through.

"Look, Anthony, I don't know squat about what I'm seeing. Before I got here my life was fine, and now I'm seeing some freaky angel who I think is following me around with his demons. I can hear people's thoughts, I'm stronger than I was before, and worst of all, this angel says I'm his daughter."

"His what?!" They both said, shocked. I had blurted it out so fast that I wasn't even sure what I said. I was so upset and Anthony wasn't making me feel better. He was just making me mad.

"Did you say that he's your dad?" Anthony asked.

"Did you say you can read my thoughts?" Dewayne replied.

Too many questions and I was so frustrated. Anthony wasn't sure himself if he could believe me. Dewayne, for some strange reason, received everything I had just said. I really didn't want to say anymore because of Anthony.

"It doesn't matter. Anthony doesn't believe me."

Anthony rolled his tongue over his teeth in frustration. "Did you read my mind to figure that out?" I gave him a sarcastic glare.

"You know what Anthony? You're a real . . . Lord help me because I know you're a preacher boy. . . . you're a butt hole." He looked shocked that I gave him such a comment.

Dewayne stood in the middle, mediating and holding the peace but it was all falling apart in his hands. "Come on, let's cool out for a second."

"No, I'm through, Dewayne. This was a waste of my time. He doesn't believe me and I find that quite amazing. Maybe it's because everything he knows is finally being put to the test. Maybe what he doesn't believe is himself." I walked away without another thought.

Dewayne looked at Anthony with a disappointed look.

"Why you looking at me? She's the one summoning angels." Anthony justified himself. Anthony walked off in the opposite direction. Dewayne was wondering why he seemed so upset. He ran off after Anthony, thinking that maybe if he could get Anthony to understand more then he could help.

"Anthony, as your friend," Dewayne said as he grabbed

Anthony's arm and turned him around before he could walk further, "I think you were wrong on how you treated Andrea a second ago."

"She made her bed now she has to lie in it."

"This is not Tamela, Anthony."

"I never said it was!"

"Well, to me it's like you're treating her like she is. Look, the girl made a mistake. People do that, even Christians. How are you ever going to lead anyone to know the love of Christ when every time you see them down you stomp on them?" Dewayne's words permeated through his heart and mind. Anthony looked away and stuck his hands in his coat.

"I didn't stomp on her. It's just . . ."

"Don't justify this, Anthony. If I recall, you were the one who said how can you lead people to Christ when they can't talk to you, Remember? You asked me how you can you lead a person to Christ who can't talk to you and doesn't trust you. Trust and love go hand in hand, Anthony. We shouldn't be so holy that we act like we haven't done anything wrong and that people can't relate to us and our experience." Dewayne fumed. "Or maybe, you were just being hypocritical."

Anthony tried to save face. "I know what I said. Look man, I can sense that she is a good person. When I first saw her I saw something different about her. Then when I find out that she is hanging with Tamela doing the same things, I was—"

"Hurt? Anthony, there is something different about her. I can witness that there's something weird happening on this campus, even you said it. Maybe she's a part of this and that's why you're attracted to her." Dewayne grinned and playfully pushed on Anthony.

"What? No . . . I don't like her. What are you talking

about? You and Karen are always trying to hook me up."
He crunched his face all up like he was a little boy eating
brussel sprouts.

"I didn't say you had the cooties, Anthony. I just asked if
you liked the girl. There's nothing wrong with liking her.
She's pretty and she's nice."

"She doesn't like guys like me. She likes guys like
Philip." Anthony was trying to convince himself otherwise
but Dewayne knew his friend all too well.

"Philip . . . that blue-eyed gigolo? Yeah, Philip may be the
pretty boy mixture of perfection, and sure he is all buffed
and all, and yeah, well, maybe he has a lot of money . . ."

"Dewayne, are you trying to make me feel better?"

"My point is, Anthony, that maybe girls get distracted by
these outward things but when it comes down to it . . . the
man they need is you. You have a good heart, you're a
man of God, and dark brothers are bound to come back
in style." Anthony laughed to think his melanin was as fad-
dish to women as stripes or plaid in the fall season. Dewayne gave him a brotherly hug to reassure Anthony's
confidence.

"So . . . you like her don't ya?" Dewayne looked eye to
eye with Anthony who simply looked away.

"Have you nothing better to do with your time than
worry about who I do and don't like?"

"Actually, no."

"How's that class coming along?" Anthony asked attempting to change the subject.

"Man, I made an F on my first paper."

"See, that's what you get for waiting 'til the last minute
to write it."

"Naw buddy, that paper was good. I'm supposed to have
a meeting with the professor later tonight to discuss my
grade. Matter of fact, she pretty much insisted on it."

"Well, if you never question anything . . . you never get answers," Anthony replied. "This weekend, I'm flying back home so you have the room to yourself, okay?"

"Cool. No problem, and don't worry, Anthony, I will keep it clean."

Anthony looked skeptical at this very empty promise from Dewayne. He never knew the word clean to come out of Dewayne's mouth, ever. Anthony was about to walk off when Dewayne caught his arm again.

"Hey, Anthony, please try to get along with Andrea, for real. I know you like her," Anthony was about to object, but Dewayne raised his hand. "Ah-ah! Don't say anything . . . I know you do. Be patient with her, okay? She is really cool."

"Okay, Dewayne. Thanks man for . . . well, putting me in my place. I guess only a real friend would do that. You're right, I need to practice what I preach." Anthony's sentiment made Dewayne feel good, but he tried to cover it up.

"Cool man, be careful on the way back to Baltimore. Call me when you get back." They gripped each other's hands and patted backs. Anthony walked on to the cafeteria and Dewayne went to look for Andrea. She was awfully upset, and if what she said was true, then Dewayne wanted to be there for her. He thought about his own experience in the shower. Maybe there was more truth to what he had felt that night. If so, and if Andrea saw something, then maybe they could help each other figure out this mystery. Dewayne made his way to Hugh Hall and went up to the fifth floor to Andrea and Karen's dorm and knocked on the door.

"Hey, Wayne, baby," Karen answered, half sleep.

"Were you 'sleep? I'm sorry," he said.

"I've just been tired lately." She led him in and closed the door. Dewayne looked around and noticed that Andrea had not been there recently. Her bed was still made and the lights were off. Karen didn't have classes on Tuesdays and Thursdays in the afternoon, so it was up to her on how she spent that time. Dewayne felt her forehead to make sure she wasn't sick.

"You want me to pray for you?"

"Um, thanks, but I'm okay . . . but uh. . . ." Karen took Dewayne by the hand and led him to the bed. Dewayne's man alarm went off because he knew what she was about to say next.

"We need to talk Dewayne."

He swallowed, thinking that he was in trouble again. "What I do?"

"It's what we did, Dewayne . . ." He got a creepy feeling but he sat there silent. "You know that I've been real upset with you lately and I'm sorry. So many things have been going on with me. I don't want you to be mad, but . . ."

Dewayne was thinking the worst. "Yeah, what is it?" His heart stood at the breaking point and he held her hand. She squeezed it, scared to reveal what was deep down inside.

"I'm pregnant."

Dewayne's eyes got big. He didn't expect that. Karen was scared to know what he thought. She didn't want him to change his feelings about her. He just sat there quiet for a second. The silence was killing her, so she kept talking.

"I don't know when it happened. I guess when we last decided to stop and I started having mood swings and feeling sick. Andrea got this feeling and she told me that I should go to the doctor so I did and—"

He places his fingers on her lips. "Shhhh. Baby, I love you." He hugged her. A tear came out her eye. All the fears that stirred in her mind about being alone with this baby were silly.

"Are you cool with this?"

"Yes, Karen. I'll just get a job and we'll do the best we can. I love you. We'll figure something out. Did you think I would be mad at you because you're having my baby? Sure it's a little early, but God has a reason for everything. We'll figure it out."

She hugged him. "I love you, Dewayne." Dewayne laid back as Karen laid on his chest, listening to him breathe in and out. He rubbed through her hair and stared aimlessly at the ceiling. He was about to be a daddy. It was as scary as it was exciting but, he wasn't the one to run away from a challenge. He wouldn't be the kind of father that was absent from his child's life.

"Did you say that Andrea told you that you were pregnant?" he asked, thinking back at what she had blurted out.

"Yeah, she said she just knew. It was really weird." Dewayne remembered what Andrea said about all the gifts that she said she had gained. He knew he needed to talk to her. If she wasn't here, he worried where she could be.

CHAPTER NINETEEN

Valerie sat in the library at a study table. She often liked to go there to get away from the hustle and bustle. There were wall to wall books. Valerie just needed to take her pick as to which genre she would take refuge in. It was one place she could get away from Tamela, but Tamela was not sure why she was hiding. She was afraid of Andrea. It wasn't what she *saw* that scared her so much, but it was what she *felt*. Angel or not, there was something cold and dark about Donyel. The name gave her shivers. She could hear whispers when she slept that kept her up all night and when Tamela wasn't around, the demons would throw her off the bed.

One night she could have sworn she felt somebody walking around her bed when she was sleeping and sit by her face, breathing on her. She was too scared to open her eyes, but when she finally stirred enough courage to do so, she saw nothing. The night after that it was like somebody was sitting on her chest and she couldn't move or scream. She just laid there stunned. It felt as if her spirit was being stripped from her body. She wasn't sure what to do and all she could hear was this buzzing sound. She felt very awake and very asleep at the same time. She knew it was a demon tormenting her. She searched through book after book to get an answer; Any spell or something to remedy these spirits. Nothing was working. So here was her refuge—the school library.

She leaned her head against the wall wondering why she could remember these horrible thoughts. She wondered why she had been chosen to be tormented. Maybe if she got rid of Andrea then all this would end. It seemed logical. She was the reason why all this had started in the first place. Why had Tamela decided to add her to their friendship? They were just fine without her. Maybe if she just left school, or even better, died, things would go back to normal. Yes, that was the only way. So she thought that would be the perfect solution, she would kill Andrea.

Valerie searched her book bag and pulled out her scissors. Pulling them apart, she created two very lethal knives. All she had to do was catch Andrea off guard and do what she had to do.

"I'll kill her and all this will be over."

Valerie, she heard whispered in her mind and the familiarity of the voice made her jump out of her chair. She looked around and there was no one else on the floor but her. Holding the two blades in each hand she stood up and peaked around the shelves.

"Hello? Where are you? I'm not scared of you."

Oh, you're scared . . . now what are you planning to do with those knives? She skipped down the aisle and hid behind a shelf. It frustrated her because the voice came from within, so it sounded like he was all around her. She covered her ears thinking that would help, but it was futile.

"Leave me alone! I promise I won't tell anybody, just leave me alone," Valerie whimpered out loud on the floor.

"I'm not worried about who you will tell. It's what you're

trying to do." She looked up, and before her was a young man dressed in normal collegiate clothing with long black hair pulled back. He reached out his hand and the knives flew out her hand. Unarmed, Valerie felt so scared that she thought she would have a heart attack.

"Are you Donyel?"

"I am." He opened his arms vainly. "My, I'm getting quite popular around here." He walked closer to her and knelt in front of her, tracing her jaw line with his long fingers. "What I want to know is, why do you still have your memory?" He let his lips graze her forehead. "What secrets lie within, Valerie?"

"Are you going to kill me?"

"I'm bound by certain laws but that's never stopped me from finding a loophole. But as of yet, the answer is no."

Valerie was confused in the way he spoke. It was almost teasing. Was he playing with her? She scooted to the side to inch away from him. He placed his arm to block her movement.

"I don't have any secrets. I promise." Her heart almost stopped. Donyel wasn't concerned with her babbling. His focus was deep in her eyes. His own eyes were so still and so un-human.

"I don't care how many of you people I see. I am still amazed at how you function; so fragile and so dispensable. Why does Father love you so much? I do not know. It's like loving toilet paper really." He laughed to himself.

"Father? Who's father?" Valerie asked.

"Naïve little witch," he laughed. "That's okay, Valerie. I'll be your father if you don't know." He patronized her with a pat on the head.

"Unwelcome spirit before me, be ye banished and let me be," Valerie chanted nervously over and over quickly, closing her eyes. All was quiet. She opened her eyes. Donyel was gone.

"Boo!" He reappeared in front of her. "If you haven't noticed, Valerie, I'm not a demon. You can't cast me out. In fact, I rule over you. You belong to me."

Valerie stuttered nervously, "I belong to no one."

He pulled her up by the hand. "Oh, but you do. But I don't want to hurt you."

"You want to use me," Valerie cut him off. He was shocked that she knew his intentions.

"Oh yes, you're special and I think I know why. It's very faint but now I understand your strength." He sniffed her neck and licked her cheek. She cringed at the feeling of his touch. His saliva sizzled on her neck and she wiped it immediately, fearing that it would burn. She tried to push him away, but he was solid as stone.

"Your ancestors have crossed my path before." Valerie felt stunned as she felt her feet not touching the ground. He had elevated and taken her with him. "You are gifted, Valerie. I don't want you to be afraid. You are one of the strong, but I won't tell you if you don't want to know."

She was scared, but she was wondering why she had been able to know things and feel things that Tamela was unable to sense. But to her it seemed that even Donyel didn't know; he was only guessing. But he sensed something within her, and if she allowed him to enter her soul, she was scared that he would kill her.

"What if I say no?" Valerie asked.

He smiled, but in his eyes he was determined. "You have a toughness you normally don't show. I have underestimated your strength. I guess they are right when they say watch out for the quiet ones. Valerie, you know that Andrea needs your help. I'm not trying to hurt her. I'm her angel."

"You said you were her father."

He levitated and orbited around her slowly. "You're

right. I am." He grinned slyly. "It happened a long time ago."

"Angels having children? I've never heard of such of thing."

He drifted behind her and grabbed her by the shoulders. "There's a lot you haven't heard of but has happened in this world. You couldn't see. But I can help you see. I can help you understand." His whispering was seductive and Valerie began to get hungry for knowledge. It upset her that she was always the one being taught.

"Aren't you tired of Tamela ruling over you like she is queen?" he asked. "The things I can tell you will make Tamela sit down and learn from you. Once you know who you are, you will be empowered as the beautiful woman you should be." He waved his hand in front of the window and in the reflection of the window Valerie saw herself more beautiful than she had ever been. With just the breath of the whisper in her ear she felt wisdom and understanding filling her head about every issue in her life. Her breathing increased as she yearned for more. She wanted more. She felt him ease away from her, leaving her cold and wanting.

Mid-air, she turned and faced him with a hungry look in her eyes. Donyel took her into his arms.

"I want to know," she said, looking up into his eyes. His long hair had unbound itself and wrapped around them both. He was illuminated again like she had seen before, but she wasn't afraid.

"So you shall." He pulled her close and embraced his lips to hers. She closed her eyes and arched her neck back allowing his electric vibe to shoot through her being with his touch. She felt dizzy and she saw either a vision or a dream. His voice guided her.

"Valerie . . . Valerie. Don't be scared. I'm here. Relax and go

with me into your bloodline; into your past. Hear the voice of your ancestors speak to you. Follow those voices to me. Follow those voices to me . . ." Everything was dark and then blurry and she found herself outside. Her dress was old and ragged. She looked around and she was no where near the campus. Where was she? She walked on in this dream-like state until she saw a sign: *Heaven, Texas population 400.*

"Heaven, Texas? How did I get here?" she said to herself. Looking around she saw Negro slaves picking cotton all around her. It appeared that she was looking at the past, about one hundred years before. Their songs were slow and haunting. They didn't notice her there. She walked among them and they paid her no mind. She tried touching them, but her hand passed through them like clouds.

"Where am I? Donyel! Where are you?" She felt panic as she thought she had been tricked. Had he thrown her into some alternate universe and trapped her there to keep her quiet? She turned around and found herself on the porch of a large house. She felt disoriented for a second, but then decided to open the door. Inside was a well furnished home with what she thought to be antique furniture. Candles lit the room and more Negro slaves walked around cleaning things up. One woman carried a child and put her down to clean the house. She was a mulatto child. Her hair was curly and she wore a nicer dress than the other slaves. Valerie looked at her noticing her remarkable beauty for such a young child. It seemed as though her eyes lit the room up. The Negro mother was so protective over her, keeping a close eye even as she was cleaning. Valerie felt weird as the child turned her head in her direction. There was no way she saw her. The other people couldn't see her. The child smiled. Valerie gasped. Could she see her? Valerie walked up slowly to the girl.

"Hello, my lady," the girl said as she bowed to Valerie who now was convinced that the little girl could see her. She looked at her mother who obviously could not see her, otherwise she would have *done something by now. The child whispered to not alarm her mother.*

"Hi, what's your name?" Valerie asked. The little girl smiled and giggled.

"My name is Isabella and yours is Valerie." Valerie looked in awe at the little girl who seemed to have a gift of knowing things.

"How did you know that?"

"I don't know. I just do. My mammy says that I have the eyes of God." In truth, Isabella had pretty light hazel eyes.

"Chil'e, who's you talkin' to?" The slave woman turned around and pulled the child by the arm. "You's seein' devils?"

"No, mammy, I don't see devils. I's just talkin' to myself." The mother let Isabella go and looked around cautiously as Valerie sat still and quiet for no reason at all. The woman couldn't see her no matter what she did. Valerie was still trying to figure things out. Why had she been brought here?

"Where am I? What is this place?" Valerie asked. Isabella waited till her mother was some distance and began to answer.

"This is Miller Manor. My pappy sent you didn't he?"

"Your pappy? Who is your pappy?" She pointed at a large painted portrait and Valerie almost screamed to see the image of Donyel in timed clothing on the fire place mantel. The same white skin and long black hair except he had it curled in several locks.

"That's your daddy?" Valerie asked. The little girl nodded.

"I don't have too many friends. Everybody says I'm the devil's child, so my mammy don't let me play outside. My brother, Paul, don't like my pappy. But Pappy scare him so he don't say nothing no more."

"You have a brother too?" Valerie asked Isabella.

"He my mammy first son. But we's got different pappies." She covered her mouth and giggled, then ran to catch up with her mother who called her from the other room.

"Wait!" Valerie yelled. She ran to the other room to catch up with Isabella, but when she did, like a dream, she moved into a

whole new setting. She was no longer in the manor, she was in slave quarters on the same plantation.

"Paul, you's can't fight mastah on yo' own. He's gonna kill you!" *One slave told another young robust slave who sat in the corner holding a book in his hand. Valerie assumed he was Paul.*

Paul stared ahead with no fear in his eyes at the other slave. "Mastah Donyel is a devil and tha Lawd God ah'mighty gon'a free us. This angel came ta me and told me his se'f."

Valerie sat confused trying to put this puzzle of history together. Before she knew it she saw Paul leading a rebellion against the manor. Valerie saw a woman run out to Paul begging him to stop. She had long dark hair and she was elegantly dressed.

"Paul, I beg of you, stop. You know he can kill you," *the woman said.*

"Isabella, you have power to stop him as well but you's just sit here and watch all this evil go on and on and on." *Valerie watched the vision take place and assumed that some time had elapsed because Isabella was older.*

"Paul, he's my pappy!" *Isabella exclaimed.*

"Well, he's ain't mine!" *He pushed her aside and she fell on the steps.*

I saw Donyel in his fury charge through the front door. "What is this outrage?" *he said staring at the slaves. Some cowered in fear just to see him, but Paul held his ground. Some slaves looked as if they were being attacked by unseen forces and then even Paul fell to the ground holding his throat. Something was choking them and Valerie had an all too familiar moment. Donyel sat there watching as the slaves fell to the ground fighting for their lives against these invisible forces.*

"The Lo'd rebuke you!" *Paul said weakly as he held his throat.*

Donyel aimed his attention at Paul. "My little stepson, who taught you how to read? And the Bible at that?" *Paul managed to get back to his feet long enough, but not before Donyel levitated him into the air, choking him once more.*

"Stop it!" Isabella waved her hand creating a sound wave of energy that formed a ball of fire and knocked Donyel back against the pillars of the house.

"Isabella, my daughter . . ." Donyel said, looking quite betrayed. *"Have you sided with these slaves? If that's your choice, you two will die as one!"* He raised his hand and a whirlwind knocked her off her feet onto the ground.

"No, I can't let you do this!" Isabella screamed. Slaves were running everywhere screaming that the devil had come. Paul had dropped to the ground because Donyel was no longer focused on him. Isabella used everything in her and threw all types of fire balls from the air at Donyel, flinging him through wall after wall.

Isabella looked at the weary Paul, her beloved brother, with tears in her eyes. *"I's sorry, Paul. Go,"* she hugged him. *"You's free now."*

"What about you, Bella? I's can't leave without you!" The wind picked up and evidently she controlled even that.

"I said go!" Paul looked into the house and saw Donyel rising from the flames. He didn't waste any time waiting to see the outcome of the fight. Valerie watched as Paul ran toward the slave quarters. A young slave woman who looked pregnant peeked out and he grabbed her hand. They both fled together into the darkness of the woods. Valerie wanted to help, but sat there watching the manor burn and everything around it. Soon the flames were so blinding, Valerie could see nothing else. She closed her eyes and when she blinked she was in a den.

"This is getting confusing," Valerie said to herself. There at the end of the room an old woman sat in a large chair by a fireplace. Valerie walked into the room and it looked well furnished like the other house, but she could tell that she was some place completely different. It was modestly decorated and had a warm homely feel about it. It reminded her of the cabins that she went to during summer camp as a child.

"Well, what are you so confused about, child?" The old woman

*said. Caught off-guard once again, Valerie eased up to the old
woman. Looking at her, the old woman appeared to have lost her
sight. Her eyes were covered with a white coat.*

*"How did you know I was here?" Valerie asked. Maybe the
woman had a sixth sense because she was blind.*

*"It's been too long, Valerie. You don't recognize me? Well, I guess
I've gotten all wrinkled and feeble in my Years." Valerie looked at
the old woman once more and then again. The old woman smiled.*

"Isabella?" Valerie asked. The old woman nodded.

"Now the question is, what're you doing here, Valerie?"

"I don't know. I'm looking for answers."

*Isabella held out her old wrinkled hand and waited. Valerie
slowly placed her hand in Isabella's.*

*"Baby, we's all look fo' answers, the mo' you get the mo' ques-
tions that arise. Find the questions 'cause the answers are merely
a goal. The questions are the road you take."*

*Valerie shook her head; she didn't want riddles. "Who am I, Is-
abella?"*

*Isabella groaned deeply and patted Valerie's hand. "When I
was younger I was all alone. Donyel disappeared and continued
to torment me with his demons and Paul had left to start a new
life with his wife. I met a man, a white man. He took care of me,
though, and gave me plenty of money, which I saved up, and
back then I had nowhere else to go. I's thought I loved him. I had
two girls, twins, named Hannah and Wilma. Them both were as
fair as snow. I prayed that God would not pass on this curse I
had inherited from Donyel. I prayed that He take away from them
po' babies what I had been given. I felt ashamed of who I was; of
what he had done to my family. I was strong to fight the demons,
but I wasn't sure if my kids be.*

*"A French boy from Louisiana married Wilma, unsuspecting
that she was a child of a slave. Hannah married herself a nice
negro freedman and they took care of me on this here farm." She
rubbed her wrinkled face with her bony hand. "I's watch my grand-*

babies and they seem normal, but I gets scared for them. They normal, but ev'ry now and then, they be hearin' thangs."

In frustration Valerie threw her hands up. She didn't know what any of this had to do with her. She never felt so lost and confused.

"Child, you must calm down. I've told you ev'ry thang I know." Valerie took off her glasses and wiped her face that was tearing up. She wanted to get out this limbo of existence. She wondered how much more she could take.

Isabella stood up with her cane and wobbled over to Valerie and took her into her arms. "Po' baby. You've lost your way. Let your bloodline be the map, you'll find your way home."

"My bloodline?" Valerie asked, looking back at Isabella. Was Isabella implying that Valerie was her descendent? Isabella winked at her and walked away, fading into the shadows.

"Isabella, wait! Tell me more, Isabella. Don't go!" Valerie ran but the room faded away like night on the brink of dawn. She played back everything she had seen. If what she thought was true then she was a descendant from Wilma, Isabella's daughter. She knew her family had some strong French roots, she just didn't know they had strong African roots as well. Who would have thought that this small town, country white girl had a black heritage like any other black person? Now she saw Donyel as Isabella saw him.

"Isabella was a fool, Valerie," Donyel said, appearing out the darkness. Valerie turned to face him.

"A fool? You are a supposed to be an angel. Who gave you the right to act like a human and take slaves and even have children by them?"

"It was my little experiment. I was only participating to get to know the human psyche better. Even God wrapped himself in flesh and became the Almighty Yeshua to understand and have compassion on you. I was doing nothing more than what God did Himself." He opened his arms in a crucified position, mimicking Jesus.

"Who is Yeshua?" Valerie asked.

"That is the one you call Jesus, but the Hebrews know Him as Yeshua. That is the name of the Son in their native tongue. Lucky he is omnipotent so he knows to whom you are speaking." This was Valerie's first time hearing about these things. Her church background was practically null and void.

"Enough about the Chosen One, I have chosen you for this time." He pointed at her, beckoning her to come closer but she resisted.

"Me? For what?"

"I need my bloodline redeemed. My children, my anointed ones, have gone astray and I want you all back."

"Back for what?" He paused at her question and smiled.

"To empower you of course. That's all I ever wanted to do." Valerie looked even more stumped as she still felt he was not telling her something. Isabella outright resisted Donyel up to her old age. Not to mention, she can't forget how quickly he rejected her when she did leave. She hadn't seen the full battle, so who knows who won that bout?

"What does Andrea have to do with this?"

"Andrea is of Paul's bloodline. That was a special bloodline. I have a special job for her. That's why I brought all three of you to this school." Valerie thought back once more. What did he mean all three? He must be looking for the descendent of Hannah, Isabella's other daughter who married the black man.

"Any daughter born to me has all my gifts and none of my seed. Isabella's children were gifted with my powers, but were the seed of mere men. They are made in His likeness not mine. They must come back to me. That is why I wanted to keep Isabella close. I needed to keep the blood pure but she left. That is why I need Andrea, and that is why I need you so I can make a new covenant." Valerie wasn't sure what to think. His speech was smooth and convincing. But yet Isabella's face kept warning her otherwise.

"Isabella and Paul said you were the devil."

"They are slaves! Would you believe the words of superstitious slaves?" He tried reaching out to her but she backed up.

"Yes, they were your slaves! And that's what you want to have again . . . human slaves." Valerie ran in the opposite direction. To what, she didn't know. She just ran. There was a void of nothingness but all she knew was that she wanted to get out.

She awoke with a jerk in the library with her head on the desk, gasping for air. She looked around and everything appeared normal. A hand grabbed her shoulder and she shrieked.

"Whoa, calm down. I need to talk to you." It was Anthony and he had just come from class.

"I saw you laying here and I need to ask you some questions. Andrea came to me earlier today. She said she saw an . . . angel. She says that you . . ."

"His name is Donyel," she said not even looking up. Sweat dropped from her brow. Unable to comment, Anthony stood perplexed to the way she spoke. She looked like she had been running, but when he saw her she was just sleeping.

"Are you okay?" he asked as he reached out to her.

Valerie pulled back, "No I'm not. I'm not okay. It's Donyel, he brought me and Andrea to this campus for a reason. We're part of some plan of his!" She looked at Anthony and he could see her paranoia. "Andrea is going to need help. I don't know how she can do this by herself."

"Do what? What are you talking about?" Valerie wasn't very good with putting her words together and she got more frustrated when people didn't understand.

"Andrea needs help! Donyel is trying to get her."

"This angel is named Donyel and he is trying to get her . . . for what?"

"I don't know. He said to purify his bloodline, but I don't believe him. He wants to do something else." She went on to tell him what she saw in her vision and Anthony was trying to process what he was hearing because she was unloading a lot of information. He recalled how Andrea had reacted the same way. He didn't want to turn Valerie off the way he did Andrea.

"How do you know all this?"

"The vision. It was all in the vision." Valerie was shaking but her eyes looked stronger. Anthony was overwhelmed at how real this was becoming. He wasn't sure what plan of action to take. Valerie jumped up from the chair and grabbed her book bag and headed to the elevator. She held her head high and there was a new strength in her stride.

"Where are you going . . . hey wait!"

"I'm going to help Andrea. Are you coming?" Unsure whether he was on the good side or the bad side, he contemplated her offer. She waited for a second and without anymore patience, she pushed the button for the elevator and went in.

"Hey, wait!" Anthony ran to the elevator and placed his hands in it before the door could close, halting it's process down.

"You're wasting my time, Anthony."

"No, I want to help. I want to help Andrea, but I don't know what I can do."

Valerie sighed and looked around the elevator. "You act like I do. You're a preacher, right?"

"Right, well, sort of." He walked in the elevator.

"Well, maybe you should have a little faith." Valerie gave Anthony a big reality check and she wasn't even Christian. The doors closed and the elevator proceeded down. They were silent as it slowly trekked downward.

"He said some things," Valerie said out of the blue. "He said things about Yeshua wrapping himself in flesh."

"Who?" Anthony asked.

"Yeshua," she sighed. "He called Jesus by his Hebrew name like he knew him. What did he mean by that?"

"Well, the Bible says that God sent his only begotten son to earth. That Jesus is God incarnate. That He is both the Father and the Son."

"He said that he did that to understand us better."

"Well, yes and no. By experiencing humanity God could have more compassion with us because he bore all the temptations and He still was able to stand as a sinless man. But his main reason was to be the sacrifice for all sins so that through Him, we could have eternal life. No one can be in the presence of a perfect God with sin in your life. And the Bible says that the wages of sin is death, so by principle if we sin, then we must pay by death. But when Jesus died on the cross he bore all the sins of man. Then he rose from the dead to show that God has all power over death and he went to heaven in the presence of God to bear witness to Him anyone that accepts his gift of salvation."

"What is sin?" she asked so simply. And that was the question that Anthony had to think about.

"Sin is . . . .anytime our will gets in the way or contradicts God's will."

"How do you know God's will?"

"That's what this is for." Anthony pulled his Bible out his backpack. "Much like a will and testament of a person who dies is the will of God. A will is a legal document and doesn't go into play until a death happens. After that, anyone in that will gets an inheritance. In the same respect, If you are in the will of Christ, meaning you've followed every precept He has for you to do, then you get the inheritance he has left for you, which is not only eternal life in heaven, but blessings here on earth as well. But if you follow your own will, you will have to die because no one has died for your will and only you can die from your will. As a result, other people will inherit what you have."

"That's very interesting," Valerie said as the elevator door flung open. Anthony smiled and decided not to preach anymore. He saw how what he said hit a special place and he prayed within that it was good ground. He never had taken the time to talk to Valerie, and even though she believed in something else, he realized that God had brought them together for a reason.

"Can you tell me more about this Donyel?" Anthony asked and Valerie smiled. For her, it was different to have anybody consult her for anything. She had a new confidence in who she was now that she knew where she came from, and with that, a sense of connection with Andrea. She looked at Anthony and situated her glasses.

"I'll tell you everything you need to know on the way to the dorm."

CHAPTER TWENTY

I felt like a dried up autumn leaf blowing aimlessly in the wind. I was totally disconnected and dead to the world. I had nowhere to go and no one to depend on. Those who did know acted as if I was some kind of outcast—and maybe I was. The many times I had been to school or church had not prepared me for this. I thought I would cry, but the wind dried my eyes as I walked against it. The only indication that I was crying was that my nose was running continuously. In any case, I normally enjoyed this time of year. All the leaves changing color to different types of gold and red. It was quite beautiful if anyone actually took the time to look at them. But the leaves would just fall and when they were gone, no one would miss them. They would crumble and disappear; blown away by the incoming winter winds.

I wanted to scream, but I couldn't. I had all these gifts and so little answers. Every time I learned something new there was yet another question. I looked up in the sky staring as far as I could.

"Where are you God! Where are you? I demand answers

now!" The tears came down. I didn't know who or what I was. I had all these gifts and if I was part angel, surely I could concentrate and talk to God himself. If I could see angels and demons, God couldn't be too far away. If I could just think and accidentally transport myself from one place to another, then surely I could . . .

I closed my eyes. "Heaven. I want to go to Heaven! Take me to Heaven now!" I felt weird for a second, and slightly dizzy and I knew that I was moving. The wind circled around me, and soon I felt and smelled different air around me and a feeling of stillness. I opened my eyes.

"No! Are you mocking me!" I screamed in disappointment. I was in Heaven, Texas in the middle of Main Street by the corner gas station. I ran to the side of the building hoping no one saw me. I hit the brick wall with my hand over and over but it didn't hurt. But I saw the bricks slowly giving away and it made me feel even more like a monster. "Come to me God! I need answers! Come to me right—"

"Andrea."

I turned around and a young man tanned with brown hair stood next to me touching my shoulder. His skin was golden and shiny. His hair was wavy and just a shade darker than his skin. It was medium in length and his eyes were bright and like fire. It scared me to see his eyes. For a moment I couldn't look into them because they were almost burning mine like if I were looking into the sun. I looked away. Immediately I knew he was an angel, but not like Donyel. Donyel had a jewel-like essence in his eyes, but not the fire. Donyel's eyes were like diamonds in the dark—just as beautiful but reflecting nothing. But this angel was reflecting some glorious light from his eyes.

"Who are you?" I said facing the wall. He put on some sun glasses and turned me around. I saw his face without the flare from his eyes.

"I am called Arquel. You are not to summon the Father,

but I was sent to you to give you what you ask for." He was forceful in what he said.

I leaned my back against the wall and looked at Arquel who looked almost younger than me. His voice echoed and made my heart shudder, but I kept my composure. He was beautiful. He wore a rusty denim jacket and jeans with a v-neck white t-shirt. He looked like one of those Calvin Klein models. He was attractive without a doubt.

"Keep your thoughts pure for I am sent by the Lord," he told me and I felt convicted of my thoughts. He was so serious and so focused.

"So you were sent? Sent to give me answers? Why can't I talk to the Lord? Is he afraid to confront me?"

"You must calm yourself, Andrea. You are forbidden to see him. You are of the Nephilim."

I almost choked. "Excuse me? What the heck did you just call me?" This angel was about to get hurt.

"Forgive me if I offend you. Let me explain. You are a child of Donyel. Many centuries ago the Fallen Ones left their home in heaven and had half-breeds like yourself, and brought much evil into the world. The world was in an age of innocence. The Fallen Ones sinned against God for which there was no mercy or no redemption. Their hybrid children were the powerful ones that stories are written about. Some people thought they were gods themselves and worshipped them and made statues of them. Soon, these children thought they were gods and demanded worship from men. These stories were passed down and soon became myths or forgotten entirely. They were the catalyst for magic and sorcery in the world. They were more than human and their heart was bent on evil and domination. From the different families and sects came much division. Many great wars were fought between them and much blood was on the earth. At that time they began to overpopulate and it would seem that man was the endangered species. They were created in the image of the Fallen ones, but man was created in the image of God and man was losing.

"The prophet Enoch wrote about it and saw the coming of the first righteous man, Noah, his descendant. So the Father brought the Great flood to wipe them out and used Noah to preserve the human race. Yet some Nephilim survived using their powers. Their descendants were evil like their fathers before them and they brought war against God's chosen people and their ancestor's disembodied spirits, forbidden to reach the realm of heaven, were bound in the realm below heaven and warred with mankind as well." Arquel looked into the sky. "The Nephilim were the giants in the land and they had no heart to serve the Lord. But they were defeated.

"The Fallen Ones were forbidden to rebel again but they have not given up. The ones that haven't been bound have mastered their art. Their children were at first too obvious, too big, too hybrid looking, but now they have genetically controlled their seed to create more human looking ones who are just as powerful. Andrea, you are that product. That is why you cannot be allowed in the presence of the Almighty."

I didn't know what to say. I was mad and very upset. I felt that I had been dealt a set of cards that was not good and I had no choice but to keep playing the game.

"That's not fair. I–I can't be evil. Look at me! I'm a good person." I pushed against his chest and he didn't budge. He wasn't reacting to any of my comments.

"I am not speaking on morality, I am speaking of your fate. Your spirit, that which drives you, is a product of the Fallen Ones. The seed of evil is within you and when it grows it will bloom. Inside of you are many seeds of evil and as you ripen you will become more evil. As of now,

you are but a bud so you cannot see what I speak of. Soon
you will not be able to control what is about to overcome
you."

I shook my head in disbelief. "I can control it."

"If you consummate with another fallen seed, you will
give birth to children who are twice as evil and twice as
powerful."

"Donyel, he is one of the Fallen? Is that what he wants
from me? He wants me to continue this line of children?"
I felt sick. I felt like giving up. I mean, what was the point?
What was the point of anything I did?

Arquel touched my face. "There is a purpose for all
things, Andrea—even you. The universe is created for balance. God created Lucifer and all the Fallen Ones knowing what they would do. They are created for a purpose
and their destruction is already predestined. It is Father's
will that darkness will finally have an end. Everything is
being orchestrated and the Father is the conductor."

"What are you trying to say? That you want to use me to
fight, even though I can't be with God? Haha you have to
be kidding."

"There are certain principles in the universe that cannot be broken. Your redemption is one of them. The Mes-
siah came to redeem man, not the Fallen Ones or their
children. There is no savior for your sins and there are
none of your kind that is pure to redeem your sins. All
there is—is evil with yours. But your children may be redeemed if you don't pass the seed to them. Your destiny has
already been prophesied. Your children will war with Donyel
if you follow my commands and stop his army."

"What do you mean my destiny?"

"Donyel tried this once before." Arquel looked as if he
was reminiscing,

"It was 1858 and your people were slaves like the Israelites
were once. Isabella was the first daughter and Donyel's

plan was to start a generation with her. Isabella revolted and later had twins by a man named Uriah. Because he was a son of Adam, his seed redeemed her children's blood. Isabella was later killed by Donyel's demons when she could fight no more. She exists in constant war with these demons in the nether realm." Arquel looked solemnly at me. "That is your curse and your fate. Donyel was forbidden to interfere in human affairs any longer and it was ordered that the son of Adam would take his powers and imprison him once and for all. Donyel sought to kill off all the slaves that had any connection with him and his power to avoid this prophesy. It was Paul, Isabella's half-brother, who later joined with his nieces, Wilma and Hannah. When the demonic attacks became too much, they prayed that what be bound on earth be bound in heaven in the name of the Lord Yeshua. Committed to be their guardian, I fought with Donyel a thousand days and finally bound him in the nether realm below the heavens."

"What is this nether realm?"

"The nether realm exists in the third of the seven heavens. It is the place for demons and bound Fallen Ones. They war constantly, fighting each other as they did in life—there is no peace. Those who are tormented there, seek people to pull them out or to pull people in."

I was scared because I didn't know what was going to happen to me. My mind stirred. "What happened to Paul?"

"Paul was killed in the final battle with Donyel. His children were warned about the Fallen Ones but the human flaw came into play. The more you tell one to stay away, the more interested they become. It is the human flaw. This unhealthy interest led to Donyel's escape. This was the case with your mother, Maggie, Paul's descendant."

My heart must have stopped when he said that. My eyes widened and my jaw dropped. He knew who my real mother was. He knew my history. This angel had watched my family for some time and the answers lied with him.

"Tell me about her please." I pulled on his jacket and stared him directly in his dark shades. I saw my own determination in my reflection. "Tell me about my mother."

"I can do better than that. . . . I can show you." He took my hand and everything began to shimmer around me. I had that floating feeling and I felt warm wind surrounding me. A bright light blinded my eyes for only a second.

When I opened my eyes everything was dreamy looking. I was in a bedroom and Arquel was standing next to me.

"Where are we?" I asked Arquel. He looked at me and touched the air. It rippled like the water.

"We are in the past. The past is like a shadow cast by the present. As the sun sets the shadow gets longer and longer as does history. The shadow is not tangible but can be seen. Only the Eternal Ones seen can turn to see these shadows and men cast their shadow." He was right. My hand passed through everything around me. Well there goes that idea that I could change the past by time traveling.

"If the past could be changed, then there would be no beauty in the present. What makes the present so virginal is that no decision has been made until the present. Each moment is a gift and the past is not cast to give you regret, but it is cast so you can remember and keep moving. Life is like the rising sun and death is the night. When it rises you are a child. If you walk from east to west, that is your life span.

"When you enter the world your back is to the sun. It is written that all are born into sin. You walk in the darkness of your shadow. You enter a world that has a history defined already, a long history that you don't know of. You must know where you came from to know where you are going. You must follow your shadow to know which way is west. As life progresses, the history already paved becomes less pertinent to your progress and you hit

a noon day in your life. In the noon, the sun is directly on you. The shadow is still there but doesn't give direction; this may be the hottest time of one's life. At this time it is hard to know which direction to go. It is good to be still and revive. At that point you decide to follow the sun or your shadow.

"The afternoon is the final phase as you walk toward the sun for direction. Your steps are followed by your shadow. Your shadow is the effect of you walking toward the sun. Those you leave behind see the length of your shadow, your past, your history, but you may never see it. Those who run after the sun never see night. But some don't follow the sun. They continue to follow their shadow. If they follow their shadow in the afternoon phase of their life, then their back is always to the sun and they simply return to the place where they started, always walking in darkness and never in light. To those that walk in the night, it would seem that chasing the sun has caused you to disappear over the horizon. They walk in the night and soon have no shadow at all and all they have for direction are the stars above them. So they use the stars that never move as direction. As a result they never move— roaming the night waiting for their shadow to return."

Arquel's metaphors for life were like water to my soul. It sounded both hopeful and depressing, but I wanted him to continue to talk.

He just pointed outward. "Andrea, you were born in the shadow, but your children will chase the sun. You must end this curse."

"What curse?" I saw a woman lying on the bed and she was sleeping. She was a beautiful girl. Her hair was flipped and she wore this pale pink lipstick. She looked like something out of the late sixties or early seventies. A young man snuck in the room and laid on the bed next to her snuggling behind her and kissing her on the earlobes.

"Stop Thomas I'm trying to get a nap," she said slapping his thigh behind her.

"Awe, Maggie, you know we're going to be married soon," he said to her and she sat up.

"Yes, I know, Mr. Francis, but I want this to be done right."

I looked at Arquel and grabbed his sleeve about to lose my balance when I heard what he said.

"Is that . . . is that my mother?" I asked and he nodded.

"These are the shadows. She can't see you." I began to cry. She was about my height. I walked up to her and I wanted to touch her, but like a shadow, my hand went right through her image. She laid on the bed looking so peaceful. I wanted so bad to hug or talk to her.

"Andrea!" I turned around and I was back on campus lying on a park bench. Philip was over me and he had a bandage on his head. I felt slightly bad for that bandage on his head because I knew it was my fault. I looked around for Arquel who was gone. I couldn't even feel his presence.

"How rude?" I said, thinking that he could've had the decency to say goodbye.

"Are you calling me rude after you knocked me out and then have been avoiding me for the past week?" Philip said. I sat up and looked at that negro crazy.

"Please, boy. I don't have time for you anymore. I got other things to worry about." I tried to get up, but he leaned in front of me. I raised my eyebrow and he got a defensive look in his eye. I think he was scared I was going to push him again.

"Look, I don't know how you pushed me like that, but that's not the issue."

"Oh, that is the issue, Philip, you tried to rape me."

"I did not try to rape you! Look, you got me totally misunderstood." He grabbed me by the arm and I glared back at him. I wanted to break his hand. "I was slightly buzzed because I was drinking before I saw you. Okay, maybe I came on a little strong, but no harm was done. The issue here, is what happened? Why are you avoiding me? I thought we were getting somewhere."

I stood up amazed that this boy was totally incoherent

to what I was telling him. "Have you heard anything I've been saying? Philip, I told you no and you kept going! I don't care if you had just drank gasoline, that doesn't give you the right to put your hands on me when I say no."

"Then why were you all in my room at night?"

"I was confiding in you about my mother. I thought you would understand, but obviously I was wrong." I tried to walk off and he grabbed my arm again and for the first time I was surprised at his strength. It seemed his rage made him slightly stronger.

"Oh, but you can confide in Dewayne, huh? Is that what it is? You like this Dewayne guy? Are you sleeping with him?"

"What are you talking about? Philip, let me go." This boy was talking outside of his head. I saw the shadowy apparitions hiding next to him. I knew demons had to have something to do with this.

"You know what, Philip? You seriously need to calm down. You don't know what you're doing and I think you may need to get some help."

"I need you, Andrea. But every time I look up, you're with him!"

I was so tired. I didn't have time to fight everyone's demons. I was not the demon slayer. I pulled away from him and backed up. He stood there staring at me and practically fuming.

"Philip. I . . . I don't want to talk to you. You have plenty of issues from what I can see and I don't want to deal with that. So if you would. . . . . excuse me." I walked away from him and I felt his anger burning as I walked off. I hated these gifts sometimes. I thought that maybe I could make him forget me altogether, but then I had to watch myself. I may erase something important and really get in trouble. I knew Arquel watched my every move.

My mother's face kept running through my mind. I had

to know more. Arquel had left me with more questions. She said she was about to marry that man; what was his name? Thomas Francis, that was it. If she married him, then her name would be Maggie Francis by now. Arquel didn't tell me I couldn't look for her. Looks like I was going to take me a little trip. I would take the weekend and pay them a little visit using my powers as the yellow pages. I ran into the dorm and walked into the bathroom, hiding in one of the stalls. I closed my eyes and pictured her in my head.

"Take me to Maggie Francis." As I said the words, I saw everything around me dissipate and winds whirled around me. I was traveling through the air in another dimension behind ours. I saw everything speeding past my face. I saw person after person passing by me at high speed. Soon nothing but women passed by me. I assumed my spirit was searching for different Maggie's and narrowing it down. Finally I saw her. She was older and still beautiful. She was talking to some people and shaking their hands. My spirit shot through the air and landed not too far from where she was. I re-entered normal time. I was back in my physical form and very dizzy. I laid down on the ground feeling slightly sick. There was so much pain in my stomach.

"You will only speed up the process of you falling to the evil side the more you use your powers." Arquel stood over me. I looked up. I should've known he would follow me.

"Don't you have something to do?" I pulled myself up.

He gave me a blank stare. "I am a recorder," he said slowly. "I don't interfere but my only job is to record all that happens to those I am assigned to."

"Sounds like you have a little attitude there, Mr. Arquel. Nevertheless, I have no choice but to find answers to who I am."

"Those who continue to chase their shadow will soon get lost in the night."

"You should seriously write fortune cookies." I walked off and Arquel faded away. I knew for sure I was going to hell for treating an angel of the Lord like that. I wasn't sure about anything that I ever learned religiously when it came to spirits and angels anymore. Every minute I looked up I learned something new.

I looked around and could see the Dallas skyline in the distance. I wasn't sure what part I was in, but I was still not too far from the city limits. I was behind a church building and it appeared that a church meeting was going on. I also noticed that it was night now. In my mind only seconds had gone by, but in actual time it seemed I had traveled for some hours. I guess traveling like that is the same as sleeping. You are unaware of how much time has gone by. It may seem that you've slept only an hour when you've slept over eight.

"It's now or never, Andrea." I tried to pep myself up to go inside the church. I looked at the sign in the front of it that read: Rev. Thomas Francis, senior pastor.

Oh my God. If he is the pastor, then my mother must be the first lady. This is wild. I had to be sure. No reason in embarrassing myself. But my spirit had brought me this far for some reason. But when I asked to go to heaven I found myself in Heaven, Texas. I was still able to make mistakes, evidently. An old lady wobbled past me.

"Excuse me, ma'am," I said to her.

"Yes, baby, how can I help you?" She was so elderly and shriveled. She hunched over and her eyes could barely be seen from under her thick fleshy eyelids. Her mouth was concaved from the lack of teeth in her mouth and she wore a shiny black wig that looked obviously unnatural on a woman her age. Nonetheless, she was stylish. Her body hid behind a very church-like green dress with matching heels. The heels had little embroidered crystals in them. She took my hand and I could feel every loose feeble bone through her wrinkled thin skin. I held it gently because I thought I'd break her hand if I held it too tight. She patted my hand with her free hand and looked at me, waiting for my question.

"Do you know what the first lady of the church's name is?"

"Sister Francis of course."

"No I mean her first name."

"Oh baby, I'm sorry. Her name is Margaret. Margaret Francis." I assumed that maybe Maggie was just her nick name. It was a safe assumption. Now I just had to develop the guts to walk up to her.

CHAPTER TWENTY-ONE

Valerie and Anthony knocked on Karen's door together.

"What do you guys want?" she asked, half sleep with the door still closed.

"I'm sorry, Karen, please answer the door. This is Anthony." Karen opened the door and let both of them in.

"Where's Dewayne?" he asked. "I had tried to call him in the room but there was no answer."

"He had a meeting with his professor about his grade." Anthony and Valerie sat in the room and no one knew what to say. Karen wiped her eyes and attempted to fix her hair.

"Why do ya'll look so secretive?" Karen asked.

Anthony shook his head not sure how to begin. Valerie crossed her arms and rubbed her shoulders, although it wasn't cold.

"I need to find Andrea right away. We have reason to believe that . . . she may be in a lot of danger." Anthony stared so intently in Karen's eyes that it worried her.

"Danger? Is it Philip? She told me that she was having problems with him." Valerie shook her head.

"No, this has nothing to do with Philip. It has something to do with—" Valerie started.

"We just need to find her," Anthony interrupted her. He wasn't sure if it was appropriate to involve too many people. From what he had studied about angels, they were very powerful and they were nothing to mess with. If Donyel wasn't on their side, then they would have a lot of problems ahead.

"We need to tell her Anthony," Valerie suggested.

"Tell me what?" Karen asked.

"Look, Dewayne is your boyfriend and Andrea's friend. Anybody close to Andrea needs to be careful because there is no telling what Donyel might do."

"Donyel? Who is Donyel?" Karen looked at Anthony. Anthony bit his lip not wanting to say anything, but Valerie left him no choice. In a way she was right. Ignorance and disbelief would not keep this angel from doing his will.

"Karen, do you believe in angels?" Anthony asked.

"Well yeah. I believe we all have a little angel watching over us," she replied.

"Well, the type of angel I'm about to tell you about isn't little and he is doing a little more than watching over us."

Karen looked back and forth at Valerie and Anthony confused. "What are you talking about?"

"Valerie says that she saw an angel named Donyel and that he is trying to get Andrea."

"What are you talking about? Wait a minute, I heard that you're a little weird. Don't you hang with Tamela? Anthony why are you believing this girl?"

Valerie looked offended and jumped up. "Look, Andrea, saw it too!"

Karen laughed at Valerie. "Look, little girl, you need to calm down. Why would an angel want to harm Andrea anyways? Aren't angels supposed to be good?"

"Actually, Karen, I heard Andrea say it too. Andrea saw an angel and she told me that the angel told her that she was his daughter. I later saw Valerie in the library and she confirmed her story. So Valerie isn't lying. And all angels aren't good. Remember, Lucifer is an angel himself. I've always studied this but I guess I never realized how real it is. If Andrea and Valerie are right, then Donyel is what the Bible calls a principality. The evil angels that fight the good ones."

Karen looked flabbergasted. She couldn't believe her ears. "Whoa slow down. Are you telling me that Andrea is an angel too?"

"No, she's only half angel. Look, we're wasting time," Valerie said. She was determined to get busy thinking up a plan. "There's gotta be a way to stop Donyel or kill him. I can check to see if there is some spell I can use . . ."

"No, we're not using spells. If there is an answer, it's gotta be in the Bible. We are going to depend on God to help us," Anthony interjected. Karen didn't know what to think at this point. She felt like she had been thrown out of a moving car, everything was just moving fast.

"Excuse me Anthony. Can you not be so preachy for one second and listen. I'm just thinking that if we conjured him with a spell, then we can send him back to wherever with one." Valerie reasoned.

"And how do you know you summoned him? What makes you think that he didn't summon you guys?" Anthony replied. Valerie looked insulted.

Karen acted as referee this time and pushed the two apart who were getting quite close. "Okay, hey! Time out! I'm having a hard time trying to follow you guys. Spells, angels, what else, demons?" Everyone got quiet and Karen didn't even want to know what they knew about demons.

"Okay, Anthony. If you are dead serious about this bad angel I. . . . I believe you. But why now? Why did he come to this campus?" Karen asked. Anthony stood up in between the girls and paced the floor. Karen sat on her bed and Valerie sat on Andrea's.

Anthony tapped his forehead. "We've all been experiencing strange things here. Dewayne said he felt something, Andrea, and now Valerie. According to Valerie, it's part of some new generation Donyel's creating and Andrea is a direct result of that. Angels having children hmmm."

Valerie looked at Karen while Anthony delved deeper. Karen shrugged her shoulders.

"It seems like I've read something in the Bible about this. I gotta go back and do some referencing. Look, I've got to leave town to go home this weekend. Your best protection is to stay prayed up."

"This is ridiculous! We need a better plan than prayer!" Valerie stood up. "You're not the one with demons attacking you. You're not the one getting choked at night! Anthony, I'm afraid for my life and I know Andrea is, and you guys are acting like this is some kind of fairy tale I'm telling you. Look, this is real!" She slammed her hand on the wall and a tear fell from her eye.

Karen sympathized, "This is kinda scary, Anthony. Maybe we need an exorcist or something. What are we to do if this Donyel just appears out of nowhere?" Anthony nodded. Karen was about to say something but Anthony discerned it was going to be inappropriate so he shook his head to her.

"Valerie, you pray to angels and they tell you that they will protect you. The Bible tells us that there are good angels and bad angels. It tells us that we should test the spirits to know if they are of God. The Bible says when two or three gather together, He is in the midst. God Himself will be with us and He will protect us. We don't have to be scared. Jesus loves you and he doesn't want you to be afraid of angels or demons because they are not greater than you if you are his. Donyel will want you to fear, he feeds off fear, remember what you told me? Have a little faith."

Valerie wasn't sure what to believe at that moment. "Anthony, I know you mean well, I just don't know anything about what you believe. All I know is that something is trying to get me and Andrea and God knows who else."

"Let's not freak out. We at least know that he needs you guys so he's not trying to kill you. There are some Christian references about the angels and I can check what I know. Maybe I can find something to stop him with. Valerie, fill Karen in with everything that you saw in your vision. I'll come back as early as I can. There's got to be something we're missing."

"Yeah, we're missing Andrea," Karen said with her hands on her hips. "I hope she's all right." Valerie started to share with Karen all that she saw. She told about how Isabella revolted and how she did all she could so that her descendants could be free—free from spiritual slavery. It gave Karen chills. There was a knock at the door.

"Maybe that's Andrea," Karen said as she walked to the door. Karen had a warm feeling from what Anthony was talking about and she felt this strong desire to pray. She opened the door.

"Hi, is Andrea here. . . . Oh hey, Valerie, what are you doing here?" It was Tamela at the door. Anthony thought her timing was impeccable. Karen rolled her eyes as Tamela let herself in.

"Uh hey, Tamela." Valerie lost all the strength in her

voice and put her head down, "It was nice talking to you, Anthony. I think that maybe I should go now."

"Hey Karen how are you doing?" Tamela said.

Karen rolled her eyes again, "Andrea isn't here, Tamela. I'll tell her you came by." It was obvious to Anthony that Karen didn't like her.

"Hi, Anthony. Long time no see." Tamela said to Anthony who was following Valerie out. Tamela put her hand on his chest and he pulled back removing her hand.

"I have to pack," Anthony said. "Karen, if you see Andrea, tell her I'm looking for her, and Valerie?"

"Yes?" Valerie responded to Anthony.

"Remember what we talked about." Anthony left and took the stairs downward. Valerie walked pass Tamela who was quick to pull her arm and jerk her back around.

Tamela eyed down Valerie suspiciously. "So what were you two talking about?"

"Nothing, Tamela."

"Nothing huh? But he doesn't want you to forget. What are all these secrets Valerie?" She backed Valerie up against the wall. Karen tapped Tamela on the shoulder.

"I think that you should probably back off, Tamela. She's been through a lot and if you were her real friend, you wouldn't bully her like that."

Tamela turned and Valerie swept off to the elevator. Tamela smiled and held her peace with Karen.

"Seems like my anti-skank spell didn't work," Tamela said. Karen counted to ten in her head, because at that point she was about to lose all the peace she could muster up.

"You know what? I'm a child of the most highest God. There is no spell you can do that can phase me. Matter of fact, I bind up every spell you do in the name of Jesus." Karen said with a smile.

Tamela's heart stopped for a second. Being a witch, she

was familiar with binding spells, but wasn't sure about how Jesus would affect her. All she knew was that she felt nervous.

"Well, it was nice seeing you again, Karen. We'll have to talk again later." Her attitude was catty and she left after Valerie.

Karen smiled again and laughed to herself. Anthony had pumped her up about being bolder in faith. She felt renewed and she didn't think anything could bring her down. She closed the door and looked out the window. She touched her belly and thought about her baby. She needed something to offer this child. She didn't have much, but if she could give it God, she could give it everything. She tapped on the window sill with her finger nail.

"God please protect Andrea . . . please God," she whispered to herself. A crazy angel was too much to think about. What if she was being watched now? She closed the shades and laid back down. She was so exhausted. She pulled a picture of Dewayne from her desk and held it close. Every time she blinked her eyes, they became heavier and heavier.

"Where are you Andrea?"

CHAPTER TWENTY-TWO

"Would you like a church fan?" the happy usher offered. I gave her a smile back.

"No thank you." It took me two days to do this. Two days
to walk through these doors. I took whatever money I had
and got me a room in this old inn down the street from
the church. It was run down but at least I had a good view
of the church from it. Every time I tried to walk to the
church, fear filled my heart and I would run back. I
should've told Karen or Dewayne where I was going. But
this was something I had to do on my own. I remembered
what Arquel told my about using me gifts. This evil must
be like a cancer in me. Every now and then a pain nipped
at my stomach. But I was confident that I was in control. I
saw many demons, especially in the inn. They walked
around like people but I saw some that were very much inhuman. As gruesome as it was, I tried not to be afraid,
holding my breath as I walked by them. They looked like
half human, half animal, as if someone genetically spliced
them with other creatures as an experiment. They knew I
could see them. The angels of the Lord floated above the

church and they were so large it was incredible. I was more frightened at the sight of them and what they might do than I was of the demons. This is why it took me so long to step up to the door. They watched my every move. I would notice that some demons couldn't even get inside the church. Others would have to hide in people's souls. Before I walked in, I saw the demons attach themselves to whoever they could. Some people were harder to attach to for some reason so they bounced from person to person.

When I got inside the church there were more demons inside than I thought was possible. I had difficulty differentiating between the people and the devils. Some demons were putting people to sleep, others were talking endlessly to people so that I knew there was no possible way these people could be focused on hearing the sermon. Others were merely aggravating children. From my perspective it resembled a circus. It was so sad. The praise and worship made many of the smaller unattached demons leave, but the larger ones were shaken but not stirred. These were tall, like giants and they held down the people they were attached to, resting their heavy long hands on the tops of their host's shoulder. One looked at me and smiled. I turned my head pretending not to see him. One was attached to the musician of the church himself playing the organ alongside him.

One brother sat next to me and I saw that the demon he had was holding tightly on his arm like a girlfriend. She looked slutty and her breasts were exposed. All she had on was a linen wrap around her waste and she looked and smelled dead. When he looked at me, his mouth move but she spoke like he was her puppet.

"Hello, my sister" the demon said through him. Their voices were in unison. I swallowed, scared to even say anything back to him. This was like a scene from the walking dead. If this brother knew what was attached to him, maybe he would want to get rid of her. She had much control over him. When she turned her head he turned his head. I wondered if this brother had any control of himself at all. I got up and waited the remainder of the church service in the bathroom.

I washed my face in the sink. I was so tired of seeing spirits. It was more than I could handle. I looked in the mirror and it looked funny. My reflection rippled back and forth. I took my finger and slowly touched the edge of the mirror and it penetrated the surface like it was water.

"You okay, ma'am?" I jerked around. A little girl stood at the door of the bathroom with a concerned look.

"Yeah, yeah, I'm okay." I looked back at the mirror and it was in its normal state. "Um, is church over?"

"Yes, ma'am." Why did this little girl call me ma'am? She had to be about seven but there was no reason to call me ma'am.

"Can you tell me where I can meet the pastor?" The little girl nodded and I followed her. I looked out the door of the sanctuary and there were demons outside hunched over like cats ready to pounce on unsuspecting people leaving the church.

"Over here ma'am" the little girl said and she went through the doors and pointed at the pastor and his wife who were still at the front of the pulpit shaking hands with people. I walked down the aisle to the front of the church like a bride in a wedding and they both looked at me and smiled.

"Are you a visitor?" asked Pastor Francis.

"Yes sir," I replied.

"I hoped you enjoyed the service," said Maggie as she shook my hand. I really didn't know what to say. I was scared and speechless and my heart was beating a mile a minute. I opened my mouth but nothing would come out. I just held her hand—I held it tight. That's when I saw everything in her eyes, like a flash, as if it were my own memory.

Maggie and Thomas were engaged. They were both very much in love and passionate. Thomas was a budding preacher and ready to give her the world. Maggie loved Thomas with all her heart but she was scared. She didn't want to lose love or be hurt. She had made so many mistakes before when it came to men and had been taken advantage of, and even though she knew Thomas would never do that, she needed some reassurance.

She sat on her porch swing one night looking up to the stars. Grandma used to tell her that the angels were always watching over her and that they would keep her safe through all things. Grandma also told her to watch out for some angels that would try to deceive her like men do some times. She couldn't remember the story, but grandma used to say that his name was Donyel and he was as wild as any man. He would have his way with women and that she should be careful and chaste and save herself 'til marriage.

Maggie often thought that her grandmother was crazy and that she was probably venting about some old boy friend she had back in the day. Maggie became very curious about the supernatural. She dabbled with tarot cards every now and then and was heavily into her horoscope, unknown to her fiancé. When she asked Thomas about angels, he told her not to worry about all that.

"Just read your word, that's all you need to do. Don't get caught up in all that." Thomas told her.

"Thomas I'm just asking a question."

"All your grandmama's babbling is crazy. We can't talk to angels. Angels are sent to do God's work and God's work only." She poked her lip out at how harsh he was with her. She snuggled up behind him and wrapped her arms around his waist.

"Remember the other night? I was thinking that maybe we didn't have to wait, I mean if you want to . . ." Maggie enticed.

"Maggie, now you know we can't do that. You were right, let's just wait till after the wedding."

She let go frustrated. He left it at that and refused to speak anymore on the subject. Frustrated, Maggie went home, still questioning in her head the superstitions she had heard and the doctrine that Thomas preached to her. Maybe it was a little of both. Maybe angels were there to help. She sat by her open window on the floor looking up at the moon.

"Donyel, are you my guardian angel? Donyel, Donyel who are you?" She laughed at herself. She laughed at her grandma, whose words echoed in her head.

"If you're real, Donyel, come to me. I wouldn't mind having a sexy angel by my side." She fell to the floor laughing about how her grandma talked about Donyel having his way with women.

"Maggie." She heard a whisper. She sat up. She heard a voice and looked around the room.

"Hello, is someone there?" She looked out the window and the wind was blowing. The trees waved back and forth through the summer night.

"Maggie," the voice said again. She slid some house shoes on, grabbed a flashlight and went out to the porch.

"Thomas, are you out there?" The screen door startled her as it slammed shut from the wind. Dust blew around her and she covered her face to keep it out her mouth. She didn't recognize the voice to be Thomas'. She heard rustling on the side of the house in the bushes. She hopped off the porch and walked around to the side of the house and turned on the flashlight. Nothing seemed to be there.

She heard another rustle in the trees behind her. She hurried back to the screen door and attempted to shine light on the trees where the sound came from. "Who's there? Come on, stop playing. I'm about to call the—" The phone rang and she screamed. She stepped inside and answered the phone which was by the door still peeking out into the darkness.

"Hey girl! You going out tonight? Can't have you getting married and you haven't partied." It was her friend Olivia on the phone.

She took a sigh of relief. "I don't have time to be foolin' in the streets with you." Maggie told Olivia. "I don't think that's proper for a future pastor's wife."

"You ain't one yet, so you need to live a little," Olivia joked, "or has the pastah told you to stay put?"

"No one tells me what to do, girl, and you know that!"

"Great, then meet me at the Candy Room." Olivia hung up and didn't wait on hearing any more talk of her not going.

Maggie and Olivia were running buddies but Maggie was trying to quietly stop hanging around Olivia as much by order of Thomas because it was bad for her image. Maggie had complied to this request, but she felt it was about time to reward herself, to do something fun for a change. Being holy twenty-four-seven was a difficult job.

"One last time," Maggie told herself. She'd go to the club, have a couple of drinks, dance and be back before Thomas even knew it. So she slipped on her tightest dress (which was put away in the garage) threw on a wig, fixed her makeup, and threw on her go-go boots. No one would recognize her anyhow if they did see her. She giggled to herself, feeling the bad girl come out. "Not too shabby if I have to say so myself."

When she made it to the club it was already crowded and smoky with several people dancing. She sat on a stool waiting for Olivia. Thirty minutes went by, an hour, then an hour and a half. Maggie considered going to a pay-phone to see what happened.

The Bartender leaned over. "Aye you Maggie?"

"Yeah?" Maggie looked startled that her cover had been blown and quickly, perhaps it was because she was sitting around looking like she was looking for someone to arrive.

"Your friend, Olivia, just called and said she couldn't make it. Her tire came up flat at her house. She said she'll make it up to you," the Bartender said, reading a note that he scribbled from the message.

"Oh." Maggie was relieved that was the reason the bartender

had spotted her out. "Thank you sir." Maggie got her purse to leave.

"Going so soon? The night is still young."

Standing before Maggie was the finest man she had ever seen; a white boy with strong shoulders and very keen features. His smile was perfect, his face was young, smooth, almost prettier than a girl and his hair was jet black flowing down to his shoulders. She couldn't see his eyes through his dark shades but she could feel them.

"Yeah, looks like I got stood up," Maggie giggled to herself.

"It's a Shame for you to get all dressed up and leave without one dance," he flirted to her. Maggie thought the same, and as much as she tried to think otherwise, something was infusing her thoughts to not resist.

"Well, I guess so . . ." She extended her hand and the mysterious gentleman took it. He danced her in circles around the floor and mesmerized her. She hadn't drank anything but it felt like it from dancing and the manly scent of her dance partner alone intoxicated her. She laid her head on his chest when some Al Green came on and he held her close.

"A girl like you should never be alone," he said.

"I must tell you the truth, I'm gonna be married soon."

"Now why would you want to do that?" He smiled. She liked his smile. "Are you in love with him?"

"Yes."

"Maybe you are. But there's love and then there's your destiny. Women give up so much of their life to be someone's wife. Are you ready to give up your life for him? Are you sure that he's yours?"

"You are quite the talker. Have you found your destiny Mr. . . . I'm sorry what was your name?"

"I believe I just found my destiny." He looked at her and she blushed. "But what does it matter what my name is, if I can't have it?"

He was all too tempting and it was like he knew what she

wanted to hear. Everything he said and did was just. . . . right.
"I think I need to go home now." *She patted his chest and headed through the crowd. Her head was dizzy and she almost tripped on her heel.*

"Whoa!" *He caught her and helped her get back on balance.* "You okay?" *She nodded.* "Here," *he continued,* "let me help you to your car at least. Some people we meet are for the moment. But some people we meet are for a lifetime. Maybe I was supposed to be here for this moment."

"That, they are." *She smiled at him, this man was simply irresistible. They went out the club exit and down the sidewalk until they got to her car.*

"So, I guess this is goodby . . ." *Before she could finish, he embraced her fully on the lips. Caught off guard, she received his kiss through pure animal attraction. His kiss was firey and it felt as if she was melting into him.*

She pulled back. "Wow, um, I think I should really go now."
"Are you sure?" *he asked. She nodded.*

"There are some things, Maggie, that you should allow yourself to feel. There's a world I can give you that you're not going to get from that man waiting for you. Go with how you feel." *He caressed her face and then it dawned on her. How did he know her name?*

"I never told you my name," *she said.*
"And I never told you mine." *He removed his shades, exposing his glimmering eyes.* "I am Donyel."

She froze in disbelief. "D-Donyel? That's impossible." *But there was no denying the inhuman glow from his eyes, so horribly beautiful.*

"You desire me. I know you do. Why do you deny yourself that which you seek the most, which is me?" *Donyel wooed her and caressed her face. She jerked back and tried to open her car door, but it locked automatically. She pulled at the handle and slammed on the glass to break it, but at Donyel's will the car slowly flipped on its side.*

"Nooo!" She screamed in defeat and ran down the street. "Help! Someone Help me!" Her scream echoed and everyone around her was frozen in place as if Donyel had stopped the pace of time. "What is going on?" She ran down the alley.

"Maggie! Don't deny me!" Donyel yelled through the air. She could no longer see him but this fiery cloud was behind her filling the alley like a fog. She coughed as she inhaled and she could feel the fog enter her. Orbs of fire surrounded them and lifted her into the air, ripping off her clothing and burning her skin at the same time. She was scared and in much pain. Donyel didn't care though. He laughed as she screamed. He was aroused that he was overcoming her; that he had once again begun his reign of human domination. He slapped her and she spun around in mid air, unable to control any of her movements. He grabbed her in her embrace and she struggled as much as she could, but it was use-less. Her feet no longer touched the ground.

"What are you?" she choked. She felt him everywhere on her body yet nowhere at all. His fiery presence burned through all her orfices. She screamed in agony, no longer feeling in control of her limbs. In the mist she saw his face form, she felt his hands claw at her back and he took his pleasure with her, killing her from inside out.

"You belong to me," Donyel said.

Then there was darkness, a quiet darkness.

When Maggie awoke, she was lying on her couch alone and in much pain. She was wrapped in her ripped clothes. She shivered because she thought that he might come back. She laid there all day but he never came. She showered; crying as the water fell over her face.

"Oh God I'm so sorry, I'm so sorry," she prayed, wondering what devil she had unleashed. But no amount of washing could make her feel pure again. Nothing could wash that cold darkness that she could still feel inside of her. Nothing could wash away the image of his face when she closed her eyes. She thought that he was just a nightmare, but the scars on her back proved other wise.

"God, help me." She looked in the mirror.

"I am your god now!" Donyel's image was in the mirror. She screamed.

I let go of her hand and all the pain and guilt fell right on me. I covered my mouth.

"You were raped," I said with barely a breath in my words. She stared at me intently and the pastor held his wife by the shoulders.

"Excuse me, young lady?"

I shook my head because I didn't want to believe it myself. "Donyel . . ." I whispered to myself but I didn't think she could hear me. Donyel had raped my mother. The secret of being adopted was one thing, being the daughter of an angel another, and now the child of not love, but rape, was all too much.

"Did you say Donyel? Who are you?" Fear grabbed hold of her and she panicked. She grabbed me by the arm and looked at me in the eyes. I could no longer see her clearly because my eyes were filled with tears. I was so tired of crying, so tired of hurting. I was the child of some monster.

"I'm your. . . . your daughter."

She let go of my arm and covered her mouth. "Oh my . . ."

"You need to leave and you need to leave now!" said Pastor Francis, overhearing the conversation. He stepped in front of his wife to protect her. "You are not her daughter you. . . . are the spawn of Satan." My heart dropped and I didn't think that I could take anymore rejection than this.

"I just wanted to talk . . ." I could tell that I was digging a hole that I could not get out of. Maggie ran out the sanctuary and Pastor Francis grabbed me by the arm. "Please I didn't mean to—"

"What did you mean to do, huh?" He threw me forward into the foyer, "Did you expect for her to welcome you into her open arms? Did you mean for her to accept you as her daughter? She labored in pain nine months with you when I told her to have an abortion. We hid her pregnancy from the church so that we could be married . . . told everyone that she was on a mission trip for the Lord. But she was afraid. . . . she was afraid he would come back if she had an abortion. And he did. He threatened my life and hers if you weren't born. So what do you want from us? You want my wife dead?"

"No, I just needed to know who she was!"

"Who she was?" Pastor Francis stepped closer in my face until I could feel his breath. "She was a bright and passionate young woman. Now she is hurt and terrified because of your father and because of what you are. Yes you look human, but deep down you're a devil like him. So devil, leave my church and never return in Jesus name!"

My heart dropped that he was casting me out like I was a demon; maybe I was. I turned my head. I tried so hard to hold the tears in, but I couldn't. Because he said to me what I already thought about myself to begin with. I couldn't argue with him at all. What was the point? I backed away without saying another word. He pointed like a statue with his eyes burning so much hate at me. I felt bad for bringing so many painful memories to her. I wanted to die. I wanted to kill myself. I walked down the street with my arms folded feeling lonelier than I had ever felt.

"Andrea, so you know the truth." Donyel appeared out of nowhere. I turned to look at him. I slapped his face with all of my might. His head barely turned.

"You raped my mother you monster!" He felt no remorse, no conviction, and I wasn't sure if he was able to.

"I am your savior. Your mother would have aborted you.

Who is the monster, Andrea? In time these human feel-ings of guilt will pass."

"You don't want me to have guilt so I can be like you? If guilt makes me human, then I will keep that."

"Why do you hold on to the things that bring you the most pain, Andrea? You love and you hurt. You give your-self to people and you feel pain when they betray you. I come to bring you a life where you have the power. I come not to hurt you, but to teach you how to not hurt. Don't you want to not hurt?" It sounded good but there was something just not right in his philosophy.

"Pain reminds me that I am alive. Those who don't hurt don't feel. I don't want to lose the ability to feel. You are a hypocrite. You lust after those who can feel because you want it for yourself. You want to feed off their need to feel, but you're jealous that they can. You're jealous that God gave them that ability so you want to destroy that which makes them most human. You've sinned against God for walking outside the purpose of your design. For those you can't destroy you give them so much rope to hang them-selves. You feed their feelings until they are overwhelmed and they can't maintain what they feel and they're feel-ings deter them away from reality."

He clapped sarcastically. "So you can predict your fa-ther now? You can read me? You know my plan? Yes, maybe you're half right, but my beautiful Andrea, it goes so much deeper. I could care less how you feel. I'm not Lucifer, I'm Donyel. I have my own agenda. People are so hung up on their desires that I just want to give you what you want. You want to be numb and void of this life. You hate to feel. I don't make you do anything you don't want to do. You want it, I give it to you. So does that make me evil? No, just a good father." He stepped closer but I backed away, "Peo-ple get high and drunk or have sex to forget. They feel best when they're getting high, having orgasms, or when they are drunk. I do the world a service by bringing relief from this world of pain. Okay, maybe they feel the pain after it's gone, but that's not my fault. Frankly, some suffer so much it's best for them to be put out of their misery. Sometimes death is the best thing for people. You choose death to solve the problem of the sick, the elderly, and children who are unwanted. Sometimes death allows the strong to live. It's like pruning a plant. I help prune the plant of mankind. It's your fault for being human and having that flaw of guilt."

"The flaw of guilt? The flaw of knowing right from wrong is known as sin. Yes that makes me human. The things you bring only make me forget about the sin or the guilt, but it's still there. You can't take it away. Only Jesus can take it away."

"Jesus?" he laughed, "Have you forgotten? You are of the Nephilim. There is no hope for you. So give up on this Jesus thing and join us. You have no idea how big this is. The Father, the angelic council under him, the fallen council on earth, the demon refugees looking for bodies and then poor blind mankind stuck in between unaware of what's going on or even who they are. Andrea, this is your destiny. Either way you will die. I've come to bring you truth so you will be empowered to change this world. This is a war, and if we must go out, then we will go out fighting. Yes God has his Bible, but together we will write our own with our own ending."

I looked at him like he was crazy. Did he seriously think he could change prophecy? The way he talked he justified it as if he were doing it for good. "This is God you are talking about Donyel. For such an eternal angel, you can not be that foolish."

"Foolish? Foolish is how God cares so much about something so weak and perishable," he said almost snarling at the smell of me. "I am insulted every time a man is accepted into his family. Why man? The angels are far more glorious and beautiful. Yes, we fell but man fell too. Man proved to be just as hungry for power as the angels. But did he die for us? No. He came to die for man to bring him back into the family of the Elyon." Donyel had a certain jealousy in his voice like when a parent favors the youngest over the eldest child.

"Every story in the Bible reminds me of this mockery; Cain and Abel, Jacob and Esau, The prodigal son. Always the second son greater than the first! Must God continually remind us angels of how he loves man more? And for what reason? What has man done to deserve any of it! Nothing. This is why you must join us. God has spit in your face. Join me, Andrea. You are my daughter."

My life was at the crossroads and both roads led to dead ends. No matter how much I tried in the past to be a part of the church, there was always something holding me back. And if all this time, all my belief in God was in vain, then what was the purpose? If there was no way of me getting into Heaven I should do whatever I wanted. But there was more to it. Through all the rejection, only one still wanted me in his life. That one was Donyel. I couldn't deny that he was my father, my real father. My very blood witnessed that. And maybe because my birth mother made me feel like a curse, maybe because I never understood church and what it stood for, maybe because I just wanted to feel like I belonged . . . I took his hand. He pulled me to his side and smiled.

"Good. I knew you would see the light." I did what I could to not feel. I didn't want to feel the guilt anymore. If I was a devil, then why should I deny my calling in life? I was born into this and into this I was going to live. I turned my head and a tear dropped. I didn't want Donyel to see it. "Andrea, remove the guilt from your soul. Accept who you are."

I wiped my face. This was about my survival and Donyel had the answer. It hurt me so bad to say it, but I gathered the thought and then the unction to say the words.

"I am your daughter."

CHAPTER TWENTY-THREE

The air in Baltimore was a dramatically different than that of Texas. Anthony was glad that he had brought his larger coat as the weather was near snow season. Although he was glad to be home, he wasted no time fraternizing with old high school friends or filling his stomach with mama's stew. He hit the street and did what he was best at—research. Hands in pocket and his scarf around his face, he walked down the harbor walkway downtown to a large book store. It was cattycornered by the aquarium so he had to weave his way through a crowd of tourists. He wondered to himself why there were so many tourists at this time of the year. I guess everyone was entitled to a vacation. With his mind focused on his goal, he stormed through the doors of the bookstore looking for anything to help him.

The smell of warm java and new books invited him and the soft world music playing overhead was inducing him into a relaxing trance. People were scattered throughout the bookstore on couches, study tables, even on floors engrossed in their choice of reading material. The environment was unbearably tempting to indulge in some sort of laid back position and lose the entire concept of time. That is what Anthony enjoyed most about reading. It was his way of escaping.

In a book, he lost the concept of time itself and fell into another time. It was a world that he controlled by the turning of a page; and the character's life would stop in time as he took his break, and proceed as he continued to read. It was like he was peeking into someone's life without their knowledge. Was it our God-like complex that made people enjoy reading? What if we are just a story in a book written by God himself? What character in a story doesn't feel like every decision being made isn't leading to some undetermined outcome when in reality the end of the story is already determined waiting for the reader to dictate that character's fate or destiny. If these character's lives existed within these books, then their existence survived on the reader's ability to imagine them in their heads. Anthony shivered at the thought that his life may be nothing but a book, then shrugged the idea off—he had such a wild imagination. He loved how characters took lives of their own in stories and he thought that one day he should take on writing himself.

But that wasn't the goal today. It wasn't time to find his favorite book and curl up on those inviting sofas with a mug of hot hazelnut expresso. No, now was the time to focus and research all he could find out about angels. He walked through the aisle and grabbed any and every book that had the word angel in it. His scanning was hopeless. All he could find were things that related to people writing about guardian angels and meaningless philosophies on angels through history.

Anthony threw book after book aside. With each book another hour passed with it. He wasn't interested in fat naked babies with tiny wings who couldn't possibly put them into flight. No. He was looking to find anything that came anywhere near to these fierce warrior angels that manifested at will. Being able to look human and being able to physically incarnate were two different things and he wanted to figure out if there were any accounts on this phenomenon. With so many books, Anthony felt like he was getting nowhere fast. It would take more than a weekend to read all these books. Aggravation was setting in and Anthony's head was taking it out on the table.

An employee passed hearing the banging on the table and noticed the stacks of books that Anthony was pulling out and got slightly concerned, giving Anthony a very practical look. Anthony grinned slightly knowing that if he didn't buy the books, the employee would have to put them back. The young man wore glasses and had a nappy little curl. He was incredibly skinny and lanky and he seemed like the type of guy that a lot of people bullied. Anthony related somewhat to this geeky kinsman and apologized for pulling so many books out.

"Man, I'm really sorry. Look, I can put these books back; it's no big deal."

The employee shook his head and smiled. "Don't worry about me. I'm just doing my job. What are you trying to find?" He picked up a book. "Angels, huh? It seems like a lot of people are getting into angels now days. It's one of my favorite topics. I love that TV show with Michael Landon."

"Yeah, but I'm looking for a little more than guardian angels and cherubs." Anthony rubbed the tightness out his neck.

"Well, maybe I can help you. My name is Shari. I know where a lot of books are and I happen to be a paranormal slash unexplained occurrences expert."

Anthony shook his hand that was extended and thought it couldn't hurt to have a little assistance. Two nerds were far better than one. Shari was probably one of those guys that went to Star Wars conventions and could analyze everything about the movie to a T.

"Hey, I'm Anthony. Well, I don't know how you can help me, but you're welcome to try. Do you know anything about angels having children?"

"Angels don't have children. Angels are spirits." He laughed. Anthony looked slightly disappointed.

"Unless . . ." He continued and Anthony's ears perked up.

"Unless what?"

"Well, the idea of angels having children is old." He walked over to the religion section and grabbed the Bible. Anthony was following and feeling more like he was the assistant.

"There is this debated scripture in Genesis 6 that speaks of the Sons of God taking the daughters of men and having children and what not." He turned to the scripture and showed Anthony. He had read the scripture many a day and it never really dawned on him what it was talking about.

"For centuries some Rabbis and Fathers of the Catholic church said that this spoke of the sons of Seth having children with the sinful children of Cain. But then again, why put so much emphasis on Seth's children? All through the Old testament, mortals aren't called Sons of God only angels are. Plus, the offspring produced from this union created giants which the Bible calls Anakim and the Raphaim." He flipped through the Bible to the book of Joshua. "The Anakim and Raphaim were descendents from these angels and these people were evil and occupied what the Israelites called the promise land. These people were giants as well and sought to destroy the children of Israel. Some theologians believe this is why God told them not to intermarry within theses nations because they had the blood of the angels. The Bible talks about the giants also in the book of Numbers . . . I think chapter 13 verse 33." Anthony took out some paper and started taking notes writing down the names of the groups.

"Wow you're pretty educated. You know your Bible," Anthony complimented.

"Yeah, well I go to church a lot," he laughed. "I know the Bible like I know my best friend."

What church was this? Anthony had been to church too and had never heard such things. His church experience was summarized into some popular scripture that the whole congregation knew. Anthony wondered why he hadn't been aware of so much knowledge of the word of God. Had he been too concerned about the basic things and not the mysteries of God and his universe? But here he was in the bookstore and a kid who looked slightly younger than him was teaching him—a student in divinity.

"So how is it possible that they had children if they are spirits?" Anthony asked.

"Well, Jesus is God incarnate right?"

"You're a Christian. Only a Christian believes that," Anthony said and Shari smiled at him.

"I follow Jesus, but I'm not the issue. I'm trying to help you out. Focus, Anthony. Jesus," he paused to think for a second, "was resurrected and his physical body still exists in heaven. So it's possible for physical beings to interact in the spiritual realm completely intact. Look at Elijah who was caught up and Enoch who walked," he stopped and went to another book shelf.

"What's wrong?"

Shari followed alongside the shelf with his finger and clapped when he found it. "Here ya go, The book of Enoch. It was supposedly a part of the Bible about 1600 years ago but several priests and rabbis took it out and said it wasn't canonical so the book was removed and lost. Some time in 1773 it was found buried in Ethiopia by some guy named James Bruce. Some theologians believe it was the fallen angels themselves trying to hide their existence in the physical world. I remember one preacher told me that the Devil's biggest accomplishment was making people not believe in him."

"But how do I know this was a part of the Bible?" Anthony questioned.

"Well, it was supposedly written after the flood, not during Enoch's life, but before Moses. Moses wrote the first five books of the Bible called the Pentateuch. The collaboration of those books, during time of Jesus, was called the Torah. It was the Bible the Hebrews used because basically they were still living the New Testament." He paused for a laugh that Anthony didn't give. "Well, um, Jesus and many other scriptures, including the book of Jude and Revelations, have scriptures that are almost exactly the same as scriptures in Enoch. Some theologians believe that Jesus was quoting these scriptures when he was talking to the Pharisees. But back to the subject of angels."

Anthony took the book and flipped through it and took a seat. "Yeah, back to the subject because you never really answered my question."

"Oh, so I'm the teacher now?" Shari smiled.

"Well it would seem."

"What was the question?"

Anthony rubbed his forehead trying to understand. "How can a spirit procreate? Mary was a virgin so her birth of Jesus was different. It just proves that it is possible. Looking at this scripture in Genesis it says these angels took wives. They actually married these women.

"And the Book of Enoch expands more into the subject by showing that these angels taught their wives and children magic and the secrets of the universe. Then the angels taught the men how to make weapons and swords. So now we see why witchcraft is a sin. It is also in that book that it says that angels taught men how to write, which is quite interesting because the Ancient Sumerians were the first ones to have a written history and they have many accounts of some type of large beings coming down from the sky teaching them how to do things and having children."

Anthony sighed because Shari was telling him far more than he could write down and he felt as if Shari had been waiting to show how smart he was. No doubt that this kid was smart, but Anthony needed something to help him.

"Sorry, Anthony, you're probably tired." He looked around. "And I have to go in a minute; but to make a long story short because there is no way I could tell you everything I know, The Bible says in Matthew 22:30 that the righteous will become like angels in heaven. Okay get this, don't let me lose you. Before Adam's fall, he was perfect and he could do anything. I mean anything. Anything Jesus did, Adam could do because Jesus came to earth in the perfect state of man. Adam could walk on water and even breath underwater because he had to name the fish, right?" Anthony nodded but was thinking that Shari was probably high because he sounded a little crazy, but he was trying to see where he was going with this conversation.

"Okay, so when Adam and Eve fell," Shari continued, "they're whole body structure changed states. They could no longer do the things they used to do. They began to get sick, they were vulnerable to death and the things that cause death. They became mortal. Mort is Latin for death. Get it? When we get back to that place in God we will be transformed into another state. So get this . . . when you fall, you change molecular states. My thought is that, and I'm just guessing here, that when the angels fell from heaven they knew that their bodies would change from spiritual to mortal. Although they lost their glory, they still retained their powers and abilities. So much so, that God had to ban them and their children from entering heaven and he bound the angels that took wives in an abyss and killed their offspring in Noah's flood. The fallen angels that are bound are waiting for their day of release as spoken of in Revelations. But there are others that weren't bound or escaped. Theses angels themselves just want to rule and have dominion and we stand in their way. They were the sons of God. When we accept Christ we become sons of God. That's like slapping them in the face when we take back our place in the kingdom of God over them."

A light went off in Anthony's head, "So they want to keep us blind and keep us under their rule and the demons want to drain us like batteries. Can we kill demons and angels? Is there a way?"

"Angels cannot be killed, but when they manifest bodies, it can make them vulnerable to damage but not like humans. Angels are like balls of energy that can change form at will. And remember, even science proves that energy is neither created or destroyed, it just changes form. As for demons, they have no bodies. If you kill one who is demon possessed, you kill only the body. The children of the angels can be killed, however. They heal very quickly and only by chopping off their head or burning them can you be sure they are really dead . . . like in David and Goliath. Demon and angel motivations may be different, but they pretty much work together. But God has given us power through his Holy Spirit. Whatever we bind on earth . . ."

"Will be bound in heaven," Anthony interrupted, nodding, "That scripture I am familiar with."

"Then I know you're familiar with Ephesians 6:10. Just remember that. But I'm gonna go. Remember, you have God's holy angels by you side. You're not alone in this

fight. This war has been going on for eons." Shari gave Anthony a handshake and walked off. "Good luck Anthony. I
hope I helped your situation." He waved and went to the
back of the store.

Anthony felt relieved that he found some information
that he could use. He walked downstairs to the front register. He had his notes and his two books, the Bible and the
book of Enoch, and he was all set. He had a better understanding, and when it came to Donyel, he would do what
he already knew how to do as a Christian—just keep on
praying. But when it came to Andrea, his mind was still
confused. She was that gray area that wasn't quite easy to
define. He had found her to be someone that needed
help. Yes , she was in a fallen state but there had to be
some way he could help her. He had to get to her before
Donyel got to her.

"That will be $39.05, sir." said the girl at the front regis-
ter.

"Yes, is there a manager around here?" Anthony asked.
The girl looked up and pointed out her badge.

"I am the manager. Is there a problem?"

"No, I just want to compliment you on your service
here. Your employee upstairs named Shari was superb and
I forgot to tell him thank you. So if you could, tell him
that he was such a great help to me."

"Sir, you must be mistaken. We have no employee
named Shari here."

"Sure you do, the little skinny black guy with a curl. He
wears glasses?" Anthony said, but the girl just shrugged
her shoulders.

"I'm telling you, sir, there is no one here by that name
or description."

A creepy feeling came over Anthony. He looked around
the store and the guy was nowhere to be found. If things
weren't already weird, this had to happen. He turned

back and looked at the girl at the register who continued with his transaction and handed him his change.

"Thank you, sir, and have a nice day."

Anthony took his change and looked at his books in his hand and chuckled within. This was so unreal it was ridiculous. Shari had a uniform on and everything. He couldn't have been a passing customer. But if he wasn't an employee, then who was he. . . . or what was he? Anthony took his change and took one last look back at the bookstore. "Thank you. I think I will have a nice day."

CHAPTER TWENTY-FOUR

Anthony got back to campus that Sunday evening. It was raining hard and he wished that he had brought his umbrella. The campus had a quiet resonance about itself.

"Stop right here, driver," he told the cab driver. He wanted to stop at Hughes Hall before he went home. Anthony got out the taxi cab and went to go look for Karen. He wanted to share everything he had learned, plus he wanted to know if she and Valerie had made any progress in finding Andrea. He was hoping that maybe he could talk to Andrea—no listen to Andrea. He made her so mad before and that wasn't his intention at all.

He walked into the dorm lobby and shook the rain off his jacket and wringed his drenched cap. He looked around and it was quiet in the lobby. Maybe the gloomy weather kept everyone in their rooms. He went up to see Karen, and knocked on her door. The door opened from the pressure of his knock. It was unlocked and the lights were off. He was hoping that he wasn't in one of Karen and Dewayne's "quality time" sessions.

"Karen . . . Andrea, are ya'll in here?" he whispered. He heard crying in the shadows and a small whimper in the corner of the room. "Karen?"

"Anthony . . ." Karen flicked the desk lamp on. She was all wrapped in a blanket and her eyes were sunken and glazed from crying.

"What's the matter?" He dashed to her side and she dropped her face into his arm. "Where's Andrea? Did something happen to Andrea?" Andrea's side of the room hadn't changed since he had left and he began to think the worst. Karen was trying to talk but she just kept crying. He wrapped his arm around her and tried to calm her down enough to get something out of her. "Come on, Karen, talk to me."

"It's Dewayne," she paused and shook her head, whispering, "he's dead."

Anthony stopped for a second and tried to retract what she had just told him. He thought she had said that Dewayne was dead, but that would have been completely preposterous. "Wha-what did you say?" This time he looked at her in her eyes to get a clear understanding. Perhaps she was joking with him.

"He's dead, Anthony. The day after you left, the police said they found his body in the pond. They said it looked like he committed suicide. There was a bottle of liquor and some kind of scribbled note saying goodbye."

"What!" Anthony stood up and really couldn't believe what he was hearing. This sounded like some type of bad dream. Everything was happening at once and he wasn't sure what to think. He had just spoken to Dewayne last week and he wasn't in any way looking suicidal.

"Dewayne wouldn't do that." Anthony said.

"I don't know."

"Dewayne wouldn't do that!" Anthony emphasized his point.

Karen's eyes watered up, "I told him I was pregnant and then he was flunking Dr. Yancy's class, so maybe the pressure got—"

Anthony grabbed her and lifted her to her feet causing her blanket to fall off. She had difficulty standing because she had been laying down so long.

"You're pregnant? That wouldn't make him kill himself. Dewayne is not that type of guy. Where's Valerie? How many people know?"

"Not that many. They didn't want to worry anybody or scare the campus. They called me that night you left. I already told Valerie and I haven't seen Andrea."

This was getting more and more confusing. Karen wasn't thinking straight and everything Valerie had told him before he left for the weekend and what he had experienced was starting to sink in. Anthony didn't want to think that this angel had gotten to his friend before he could warn him. He didn't want to believe this. He let go of Karen and left the room.

"Where are you going?" Karen screamed after him.

"I don't know!" He took the stairs to blow off steam. He didn't want to accept the idea that Dewayne was gone. No. This was completely and utterly an impossibility. To think that Valerie was right was too scary. Maybe he had been kidnapped. But drowned? Dewayne would not drown himself. Something was not right. He stopped on the third floor and went to Tamela and Valerie's room.

"Who is it?" Tamela asked when he knocked frantically.

"Where's Valerie? Open the door, Tamela." Tamela whispered behind the door and got real quiet. Anthony slammed on the door again. "Open the door, Tamela!" The door cracked open.

"What do you want?" She peeked through the door. Anthony pushed his way in.

"I need to talk to Valerie." He walked in the room and Philip was in Tamela's bed wearing nothing but a sheet. Anthony looked back at Tamela who was still at the door holding the knob, wearing a sweat shirt that came down to her knees.

"Excuse you, Anthony, Valerie isn't here," Tamela said as Philip sat up. He wrapped the sheet around his waist and stood up towering over Anthony by at least five inches.

"You know breaking in rooms is a violation of school code," Philip said.

Anthony looked up at Philip who had a cocky smile on his face and glare in his eye. "Yeah, well I'm sure there is some rule about sleeping with the residents . . . and is that weed I smell?"

Tamela walked in between the two who looked like two bulls getting ready to butt heads. "Look, Anthony . . . I'm a grown woman. Are you jealous?" She rubbed Philip's chest and Anthony was about to be nauseated by the image of these two, not to mention the smell of the room. He didn't want to be there any longer than he had to.

"Trust me, Tamela, I could care less who you sleep with. Matter of fact, you two make a perfect couple." Anthony left the room and went into the hall. Valerie was coming out the elevator. "Valerie!" He ran up to her and she looked away.

"Have you heard?" she said. The tone of her voice was confirmation that what Karen had said was true.

"Are you talking about Dewayne? That's impossible." She turned to Anthony and she had tears in her eyes. It was enough to pierce his heart. "No. I won't believe it."

"Anthony. There is no easy way to get through this. They said he committed suicide."

"Valerie you can't believe this. Too much has happened. What if it was Donyel?"

"So you believe now? You really believe everything?" She looked so deeply in his eyes that he had to look away.

"I don't believe that Dewayne . . . killed himself. Look, I think I saw an angel myself. A good one though. I think he tried to tell me how to get Donyel." Valerie walked past Anthony toward her room but he grabbed her arm. "I don't think you want to go in there right now. Philip's in there." She looked frustrated that Anthony had told her that. I don't think she liked Philip all too much either.

"I don't know what to think Anthony. The police told us about Dewayne but this school just goes on like nothing happened. There wasn't even anything in the school paper about it. They covered the whole thing up." Valerie took Anthony to the other side of the corner to whisper. "I was trying to figure it all out, what we all have in common. Yesterday when I was comforting Karen, she was going through his stuff that she had. He was awarded the same scholarship I was to be at this school. I went to the library to look at the scholarship and it's been awarded only to a handful of students in the past seventeen Years." Valerie was looking paranoid and breathing heavily.

Anthony looked confused trying to understand where she was going. "I don't get it, what's that got to do with anything?"

Valerie continued, "I got a friend of mine in the scholarship office to look up all the scholarship recipients this year and in the past. Only ten students have received it since it was introduced. Since there's never anything in the school paper, I went to the city newspaper archives on microfilm to see if there was anything on the whereabouts of these students. Counting Dewayne, all eight have died, three from a freak car accident, two suicides, one died with a strange health related illness, and two others, brother and sister, were in a plane crash when they were headed home from college." She crossed her arms and paced around Anthony.

"That only makes nine counting you?" Anthony said rationalizing what she was assuming.

Valerie face turned pale, "Andrea is the tenth." Anthony grabbed her to keep her still.

"This isn't the time to lose it. Where is Andrea?"

"I don't know. You don't think she is dead too?"

"No, from what you told me, Donyel wouldn't do that. But if you guys haven't found her yet . . . then Donyel must have her." Fear filled her eyes and she covered her mouth.

She remembered how fierce Andrea appeared when Donyel manifested in their room that night. "Anthony, he's exterminating the descendents of Isabella! He's going to kill me!" She pushed against his chest sniffing up her tears.

"Look, Valerie. Don't get scared. I need you now," he grabbed her and stared her directly in her eyes and she swallowed her tears that were trying to fall. "Go to Karen and try to get her together."

As he was talking Philip left Tamela's room. Anthony stopped talking to let Philip walk by but he wasn't about to walk past without giving his last two cents.

"Hello Valerie. Hey man, I heard about your friend committing suicide. Look, if you feel the need to go home you can, the school will allow you take a break."

"What are you talking about?"

"Your roommate, Dewayne. . . . he committed suicide this weekend. Look as a Resident Assistant I'm willing to set you up with any counseling sessions you may need."

"No thank you, Philip. I don't need your help and what do you mean that I can go home?"

"Well everyone knows that when your roommate dies you get an automatic A in all your classes for the semester. So there's no need for you to be here. You will be missed." Anthony was thinking that Philip personally wanted him gone.

"I'm so glad you're concerned about my well being, Philip." Anthony said sarcastically.

"I'm just doing my job." He grinned and looked at Valerie. Anthony didn't trust Philip at all and he didn't want to talk in front of him to Valerie.

"Valerie, I'll talk to you later." Anthony said. Valerie nodded and walked back to her room. Philip angered Anthony so much and Philip knew it.

"So . . . Anthony, I see that you and Valerie are getting a little close. That's cute."

"Is your life so boring that you have nothing better to do that live vicariously through other people's lives?" Anthony snapped.

"Hey I'm just making an observation brotha, no harm," Philip responded.

"Well for one I'm not your brother and two Valerie and I are not together. Why don't you worry about your relationship with Tamela? She's more than enough drama."

"I don't need Tamela. I've got the sexiest girl on campus." Anthony watched as he gloated on his conquests and thought that he couldn't possibly be referring to Andrea.

"You've gotta be kidding right? You can't be still with Andrea. You were sleeping with Tamela."

"Well what Andrea doesn't know won't hurt her." He was now invading Anthony's personal space but Anthony didn't waver, "I trust that you won't disclose that little situation between me and Tamela to Andrea. I love her and I don't want to see her hurt. If you were to tell her something like that, it would crush her. And if she gets crushed . . . well, I have to crush you." He smiled devilishly.

"Whatever happens, Philip, you are bringing it on yourself. And I don't think I have to tell Andrea anything. I think she is quite capable of finding out on her own." Anthony slid away from Philip and took the stairs down.

Philip fixed his clothes and checked himself out in the hallway mirror to make sure that everything was in its proper place. Perfection was his obsession and he wanted everything in his life to run smoothly. Anything interfering with that perfection was a problem in his world.

"*Philip.*" Philip looked around. His name was being whispered and he couldn't figure out where it was coming from.

"*Philip . . .*" After hearing it again he ran down the hall and into the janitor's closet down the hall. The voice was inside his head and there was no escaping it. But he wasn't trying to escape; he was trying to find a place of solitude. He closed himself in the janitor's closet and flicked the light on.

"I'm here."

"*My son. Listen to me. There are many around you that are evil. You are my son. You are made in my image.*"

Philip fell to his knees and bowed raising his hands in submission. "Speak to me and let me know your will."

"*You will carry my seed and purify our blood. Give me a perfect offspring that will strike fear with those that would try to contend with me. We are at war and there are many that will try to stop you from this.*"

"I will not allow them to stop me Father. I will do anything for you, I love you. Please come to me . . . please don't leave me."

"*I will come to you at a certain time Philip. Prove your love to me and carry out my will. Destroy the evil ones.*"

"Who are these evil ones?"

"*I will reveal these to you at a certain time.*" A light filled the small closet room and Philip fell on his face in fear. When he opened his eyes there was silence. Philip raised himself to his feet and dusted himself off. His heart was pounding and he stumbled out of the closet. He looked around the hall.

"Anything. . . . anything for you . . . my father, Lord Donyel."

CHAPTER TWENTY-FIVE

"**W**ell Valerie, you've been unusually quiet, even for you. Are you okay?" Tamela grew suspicious of Valerie's secrecy and the atmosphere in the room was very uncomfortable. Valerie sat on her bed sketching a flower pot for her class, trying to ignore Tamela. Tamela was burning incense waving it around the room. Valerie rubbed her nose because the strong smell was making it itch. Like a slithering snake, Tamela sat on the bed next to Valerie.

"I've noticed how close you and Anthony have been getting. Do we have a new love?"

"We're friends and nothing more." Valerie never once looked up, just continuously shaded the picture with a dark charcoal pencil. Tamela looked down at the picture and looked back at Valerie pulling the pencil out of her hand. "So what do you and your new friends talk about?"

Valerie sighed. "Give me my pencil back." Tamela sat up straight, surprised at how forward Valerie had become.

"My . . . where did we get this attitude from? You've changed a bit."

"That's what people do, we change. I have that right."
Tamela leaned in a little close to Valerie.

"Valerie, let's be real. All you are and all you ever will be
is white trash." Valerie lowered her eyes and Tamela nodded in her ability to tear her esteem so easily.

"You're so sad, Valerie. That's why guys don't want you.
Why would a guy want someone who doesn't even love
herself? You better be glad that you have a real friend like
me. I was there when you had nobody. These new friends
you have just want to change you. And you're so weak
about knowing who you are that you would follow in a
heartbeat." She snickered and patted Valerie's leg. Valerie
held her composure, but spoke with a strength she only
had when was about to blow.

"You know what Tamela," she said as she lifted her head,
"I know exactly who I am. I know where I'm from and unlike you I know what I need to do in this life." She took
her pencil back gently without breaking eye contact with
Tamela. "Now if that makes you feel uncomfortable, that
you don't have someone to pump your ego day in and day
out then, maybe you don't know who you are." With a smile
she looked back down and continued etching.

CHAPTER TWENTY-SIX

I had finally made it back to the dorm. I had decided to walk back after my confrontation with Donyel and it was a long walk. My mind was spent and I felt drained of all emotions. Donyel words stayed echoed in my head even though he wasn't present. Nothing was black and white anymore. No one was good. Everything was against me. Nature had rejected me and I felt ready to reject the world. I was zoned to my own thoughts as I walked in the street. One man must've thought I was whore. He kept walking behind me asking me to get with him. I tried to ignore him and walked faster but he pulled my arm and grabbed my booty. Without a second thought, I grabbed his chest and jolted a shock into his body causing him to convulse on the ground. I looked at my smoking hand and instead of being scared, I decided to enjoy it. I had power. It suddenly started raining again and I laughed insanely to myself.

I'm not sure how far I walked, but my feet didn't hurt. The rain poured down but I continued on. The deeper my anguish, the harder it fell. The more I thought about the lies and deceit I had been given all my life, the louder the thunder crashed. The wind blew when I thought about my papa that died so many years ago. I was his little girl, and he had looked me in the eyes and told me that. The lightning struck when I thought about how Philip claimed he loved me and he tried to rape me.

I blocked out the thoughts. I didn't want to reflect on them anymore. I didn't want to hurt anymore. I walked into the dorm and instantly I felt like something was not right. I was suddenly overcome with grief but I shook it off. I went up to see Tamela and Valerie. That's where it had started. You could say they helped me figure things out. I could hear them talking outside the door and thought not to go in at first. I could feel such strong vibes coming from the room. I knocked at the door and Valerie answered. She smiled to see me at the door.

"Andrea." She took me by the hand, "We've been looking for you," she whispered to me. Tamela stood up from the bed behind Valerie.

"Hey Andrea. How are things? I trust you had a good weekend?"

"Yes Tamela. I had an interesting weekend." Valerie looked back at Tamela and then at me. I could sense that she wanted to talk to me alone.

"What's wrong?" I asked. She pulled me into the hallway by my hand and she looked as if she would cry.

"It's Dewayne. I don't know how to say this, um, this weekend the police found him," she took a breath, "drowned in the pond." I stood there shocked because I could feel this void all around me as if I already knew. She hugged me but I didn't want to believe it.

"Where's Karen?" I thought about how she must be feeling. I could feel that Valerie felt guilty about the whole thing.

"I think she is in her room. She's been taking it hard. Anthony asked me to check on her later." I could only imagine what she was going through. She was expecting a child and now Dewayne was gone.

"Something isn't right Valerie, I can feel it."

"Dewayne's gone . . ."

"I know. I think—I think I always knew. I just didn't want to believe it." I didn't cry and didn't want to. Valerie pulled away from me.

"You're taking this awfully well, Andrea. Are you okay?" I had drowned my emotions away in my power. I could feel Valerie's pain and I wished she would stop because I didn't want to feel her pain or mine.

I pushed her aside. "Look, I don't have time for this Valerie."

"Andrea! What's wrong with you?" I looked back at her. There was such a pain in my heart. A pain like my soul was being torn in two. My insides were being pulled and squeezed.

"Leave me alone, Valerie!"

She persisted. "Anthony and I think it could've been Donyel."

"That's impossible. Donyel was with me this weekend." Valerie stood there shell shocked for a moment. She pulled her hair behind her ears and fixed her glasses.

"So. . . . you've been with Donyel? Why would you go after him?" I just wished Valerie would just go somewhere else and stop bothering me but she was like a little fly buzzing around.

"If you have forgotten, Donyel is my father. I am his." I don't think she was accepting my new found revelation but I couldn't care less. I could tell she had a new strength about herself.

"Valerie, why are you so concerned? This has nothing to

do with you." I was about to walk off but she caught up with me and stood in my way.

"This has a lot to do with me. Look, Donyel told me the same thing, but he's a liar. I was there to help you to connect with Donyel. I can remember what happened . . . I know about Isabella." I took a step forward. Valerie never ceased to amaze me.

"Who told you about Isabella?"

"Donyel came to me. He searched my soul. I am a long descendant of Isabella. I am an extension of that family that migrated and stayed her in Texas. My name is Valerie Larue, Andrea, I am connected to Donyel just like you. That's why he couldn't make me forget anything."

It all seemed to make so much sense and none at all. Had we been brought to one point in time for a reason? If what she was saying was true, then the reason she could hear Donyel's voice was because she was a distant cousin.

"So why are you telling me all this?"

"Isabella revolted against Donyel. She did it for a reason, Andrea. Donyel is evil." I turned my head because I wasn't sure what to believe. All I knew was what Donyel had told me and that he accepted me no matter what. Here Valerie was, telling me to turn my back on him now.

"You must be mistaken."

"Andrea, you must listen to me. He said he needed all three of the descendants. I am from Wilma's side of the family, you're from Paul's side of the family, and he said he needed a third person from . . ."

"Hannah's side?"

She stared at me speechless. "So you do know."

"Yes I know, Valerie. But I'm not sure what all this history has to do with us."

"If we don't know our history we are bound to repeat it.

I think that's what Donyel wants. He wants to rule over us again."

I laughed at her comment but I wasn't quite sure she was completely wrong. I remembered what Arquel told me but I still couldn't deny what Donyel wanted from me. With the feeble changing mind of human nature, why should I even trust Valerie? If there was one thing I knew about people was that one minute they liked you, and the next minute they didn't. Valerie had proven that. Wasn't this the same girl who didn't want to talk to me at all? Isn't this a girl who is a witch herself? If anyone should be evil it should be her. At least with Donyel he didn't change. His mind was made up with what he wanted. Now here I was, raised in the church and I was with lack of a better word . . . a child of a devil. I couldn't deny that the man that brought me into this world was a monster. And I reflected things about him that I couldn't change. What do I do when the curse of my father is passed on to me? If I must be damned why should I even resist?

Karen came into the hallway from the elevator. I turned to look at her and she was glad to see me but her eyes were still sad and dark. I felt the deepest void in her heart and I felt like someone had dropped tons of heavy sandbags on my shoulders. The human flaw, as Donyel called it.

"Hey, Andrea, we've been looking for you." Valerie gave Karen a hug and she broke down in tears.

"I already told her Karen." She whispered in her ear. Karen looked at me while she hugged Valerie.

"I know you guys were close friends." I didn't want to hear this. I didn't want to hurt and the closer she got to me the harder it was for me to control myself. Her emotions were too overwhelming. So I did what I knew how to . . . I left. In a flash of light I disappeared. I wanted to be gone. Karen shrieked that I had vanished before her eyes and Valerie tried to calm her down and explain things. Karen had been in the dark too long and now she was seeing the truth. I didn't mean to scare her. Even as I walked around them against the wall I think Valerie could still sense me. At one moment I think she looked me right in my eyes. I couldn't take this anymore so I left the hall all together and I went to the only place I knew to go.

CHAPTER TWENTY-SEVEN

Anthony sat in his room reading a note from Dewayne's mother. She would pick up his things later. No matter how much he heard people say it, it just wasn't clicking. Anthony didn't want to believe it. But just because you don't believe in something doesn't mean it doesn't exist.

He ran across a picture of him and Dewayne; a Polaroid they had taken over the summer. Dewayne's eyes were tiny slits because he was smiling so hard. Anthony was beside him doing a thug pose, which he laughed at because that was so unlike him. Dewayne helped Anthony to live. Dewayne was the type of guy who lived every day to the fullest. Even when he was sad, Anthony couldn't recall a time when he wouldn't try to smile or make someone smile. Anthony threw the picture down and held his breath. He was holding it in so hard. He didn't want to breath, he didn't want to blink because if he did—he would cry. It was like a pounding pressure in his chest and in his throat. He turned his back on Dewayne's side of the room.

He wanted Dewayne any minute to come into the room

and throw his smelly sneakers on the floor and tell him how his day went. That was supposed to happen. Not death. Dewayne shouldn't have died. When he could hold it no longer, a well of tears clouded his vision and Anthony fell to his knees. His cry was silent but painful. He thought that maybe if he had been quicker to figure things out, Dewayne would still be around. Anthony was the guy who always had an answer, the person people looked up to.

"If that angel has anything to do with this . . ." he whispered to himself clenching his fist.

Everywhere I went I could sense pain and hear thoughts. I went to Anthony's room for answers but I could sense he felt helpless. I stood at his door for a moment trying to compose myself before I knocked.

"Who is it?" I heard him on the other side of the door.

"It's me . . . Andrea." Anthony snatched the door open and had the same look as the others had when they had seen me.

"Are you okay?" he asked. I nodded and entered the room. I saw that Anthony was trying to pack his things up in boxes but there weren't near enough boxes to do that. I felt cold.

Anthony wiped his face and hugged me. I was shocked for a moment having never seen this side of him. "It's okay, Valerie told me the whole thing." I pulled back.

"Something is going on." Anthony said getting himself together. "I think Donyel may be involved."

"You think Donyel would kill Dewayne? Why? That makes no sense Anthony. He was with me."

"So you met with him again?" He looked very disappointed and I could feel his emotions hit the roof.

"I've already talked to Valerie and it seems you've convinced her that Donyel is the bad guy so that's probably what you think of me so I guess I should be leaving." He grabbed my forearm and stared me in my eyes like I had hurt his feelings.

"I didn't say that. Andrea, you're not evil."

"Who made you judge Anthony? I've already been told by an angel that I'm not welcome in heaven. I've been told by Donyel that God has spit me out like he did him."

"Donyel had a choice and he made it."

"His choice cursed me Anthony!"

"You have a choice! Yes you do! You have a choice whether you are going to live or die. You have a choice to have hope or lose hope all together. Andrea, just because Donyel's your father doesn't mean you have to be damned with him. My own dad isn't perfect, he's had affairs on my mom but that doesn't mean I have to follow his footsteps!"

"Your dad isn't a fallen angel, Anthony. There's a big difference."

"What I'm saying is that you may be under some curse but that doesn't mean you have to pass that curse on to the world. Andrea, maybe what God wants to do is end this curse. That curse can end with you. But you have to want it to end. Let me help you." He seemed so passionate about what he was saying and when I looked into his eyes I saw what he saw. He had seen an angel too.

"You were visited too?"

He nodded. "I have to admit, When you and Dewayne told me all that stuff I really doubted you. I don't know why, I learned all this stuff in church but I never thought it would actually become real. But now I'm seeing weird things."

"It's not weird, Anthony. It is real; Donyel is real, angels are real, and demons are real. They've been here longer than we know. The only weird thing is how we forgot but why do you care so much? Aren't you super Christian? I'm surprised that you were even hanging around Valerie." My sarcasm made Anthony flinch like I knew he would. I had hit him where it hurt but in my mind he deserved it. I didn't really want to run him off because deep down I didn't want to be alone. But everything was hitting me so hard and at that moment I didn't know what else to do. I was angry and I wanted him to be angry too.

Anthony just shook his head. "Andrea, I know I've done you and Valerie wrong. But I can't just sit back and lose you to Donyel." My senses started scrambling and I was feeling confused.

"What are you talking about Anthony? What do you mean 'lose me'?"

He held his tongue and relented to speak his mind. "Andrea, I see a good person in your eyes. I don't know what Donyel has told you but I know you can overcome him. I really," he chose his words carefully, "care about you Andrea."

"You care about me." I repeated. There was still some insecurity he had about me but there was also some connection he felt he had with me. It made me feel weird but I didn't want to assume anything and strange enough as he pulled on my humanity, my powers had difficulty tuning in correctly. I could feel this fire in his eyes that made me want to believe that he could do anything.

"This guy, who I think was an angel told me so much about these fallen angels and what they did so long ago." Anthony continued, "If Donyel is one them . . . he's dangerous."

"And so am I. I'm his daughter, I'm not human. I also saw an angel other than Donyel and he told me that the evil seed inside of me is growing. So when I die I will become . . ."

". . . a demon spirit." He finished. We stood silently. I could tell he didn't want to accept that revelation more than I didn't want to. All these things were new to me. I imagined those ghostly figures that walked around unknowingly to mankind just hungry for the warmth of a human soul like beetles to a fire. I didn't want to be one of those terrestrial spirits.

"We don't have a choice. My spirit inside me is evil. I can't change that."

"But what about your soul?"

"Excuse me?" He held my hand gently and all his passion was felt in one burst. It reminded me of the feeling of drinking hot chocolate when you have been in the icy coldness of the winter.

"You spirit may not change but your soul can. You may not have inherited a human spirit but your soul is very human."

I wasn't sure what he meant but I couldn't compose myself. I blinked constantly to keep my eyes dry. His hope was unbelievable and I couldn't understand how he believed so much in me when I couldn't do that for myself. I looked further within his soul and he was so pure and beautiful. His spirit was so strong. The light coming from him was glorious and so powerful, it reminded me of the angel Arquel I had seen. I closed my eyes and I could see Dewayne in his heart. I saw their friendship. I felt how much he loved Dewayne and how much Dewayne loved him. I cried to see Dewayne in his memories. I couldn't bare the thought of him being dead. I felt his desire for revenge and his power of restraint.

Andrea, come to me. I opened my eyes.

"Oh my God he's calling me." Anthony grabbed my other hand.

"Who, Donyel? Fight it, Andrea. Your spirit is what you are but you control *who* you are. Your soul is just that. Your soul is your will." I let go of his hands. It was too much for me to hope; because what was the point if we couldn't change anything? God designed the world to be changed by human will. I was something other than human.

"But it doesn't matter what my will is if God's will is for me to be damned!" I pushed him away and he fell on the bed. I scared myself because of my strength. A tear rolled down my cheek and dropped off my chin but I covered it with my hands because I didn't want Anthony to see me. I felt so ashamed of who I was.

"I'm sorry Anthony. I'm . . . so sorry." And so I faded from his sight.

"Andrea! Come back!" He jumped from the bed and felt in the darkness for me. I could hear him but I was already following the summon. Anthony's voice faded behind me. The winds whirling around me dried my tears. I wished I could stay in this form and never materialize again. My heart was so heavy and this weightless feeling seemed to ease that. But the longer I did this the less human I felt and the more painful it became. Imagine smiling for a long period of time. At first the smile is fresh and looks very real and happy. The longer you hold the form of that smile the less natural it becomes and you no longer smile inside. As it goes, your muscles ache from holding the smile too long and there is an instinctive feeling to release. This is how I felt.

Anthony knelt down on the floor. He felt so helpless. His life was changing and he knew that he could just leave. He could leave the campus and never return. The school would allow him to leave. Why should he wrestle in his mind with what other people did? He was saved and he was a Christian. His life was fine. But the people he had made friends with were not on that level. Could he turn his back on Karen, when he knew that she was still learning about the power of God and now pregnant? Could he turn his back on Valerie, a practicing witch, but on the brink of learning her true purpose in God? Could he turn his back on me? Anthony knew what Dewayne would want him to do.

"God, heavenly Father, I am so confused. My brother . . . oh God my brother is . . . dead. I don't know why you allowed this to happen and what exactly you want me to do but I need you to let me know. I know Andrea is Donyel's child. But there's got to be something more. I just can't let her give in to his will. I just can't let her give up. She's special . . . I know she is. I knew it when I first saw her. But she's just used to being so strong all the time that she won't let me in when she's weak. God have mercy. I'm asking as your child, to have mercy. Help me help her." Anthony was so lost for words that he just ended his prayer. His heart had filled with sorrow and he didn't cry but he just laid there weak and exhausted. He had forgotten to eat. A whole day and half had gone by and he hadn't even thought about it. So he slowly passed out on the floor.

". . . in Jesus name . . . amen."

Although I was already far on my journey I could hear the echo's of Anthony's prayer traveling behind me I couldn't get away from it. I followed the summon back to the campus. I looked around but I didn't see anyone. The rain had simmered down some to a light drizzle. It was so quiet that I could hear my footsteps echo on the pavement. I was walking through a breezeway between two buildings. It was dark and dreary like something you would see out of a horror movie. The rain had awoken the crickets from underneath the cracks and crevices and they hopped and chirped all on the sidewalk. I kicked them aside.

"Donyel, are you here?" It was so quiet that I thought that my breathing was too loud. I felt uncomfortable but I was unsure what I was so scared about. No one could do anything to me. But maybe Donyel could.

"Andrea." I turned and looked around and Philip was standing behind me. I hadn't even heard him come around. I took a breath.

"Philip you scared me." He's eyes reflected the little bit of moonlight coming out from the passing clouds.

"I'm sorry." He said.

"It's okay." I looked around. "I don't think this is a good time to talk."

"No I mean . . . I'm sorry. I'm sorry for what I did and I was wondering if maybe we could start over." I looked at him and he seemed to be sincere in his voice. He just stood there staring at me.

"What are you doing out here?" I asked.

"I was in the library studying and I saw you out here. I should ask you the same question." I didn't want him to know. But I wanted him to leave.

"Philip, we already talked about this. You have problems and you need to go find help." He grabbed my arm as rough as usual.

"I need you."

"Philip, let me . . ." I grabbed his arm and immediately I saw into his soul. It felt like a dream.

Philip was in his room and he was crying.

"What am I doing!" he screamed and tore his shirt. He was breathing heavily and pulling at his hair. I saw the demons around him slithering around his feet. They were females. They wrapped their arms around his leg and rubbed their faces on his thighs like cats in heat.

"I just want some peace! Oh God!"

"Calm yourself my son," Donyel spoke to him. I could see that Donyel was levitating behind him, but he couldn't see him at all nor could he see these demons.

"Why do you have me doing these things?" he cried as he dug his nails into his skin across his chest.

"Stop destroying your body. You have only one." At the wave of Donyel's hand Philip's chest was restored.

"What am I?" Philip fell to his knees and the demons embraced him little to his knowledge.

Donyel showed no concern for his despair. "You will obey what I tell you, Philip. You are my son and you will be strong!"

"I am not strong, Father. I can't do this anymore!"

"But you will. Do you love me?"

"Yes, I love you."

"Prove it! I grow weary of your crying. You are so much weaker than your sister. She is so powerful. She doesn't need the demons to empower her."

"Why do you make me feel worthless?"

"You are weak! I should kill you."

"No. Please . . . I'm your son. Please, Father."

"Produce me an heir. A powerful one. One of pure blood. One that will follow after my ways."

"I will follow your ways you don't need another." He raised his hands to Donyel much like a small child would. Donyel looked disgusted. Philip had not inherited great powers. But his soul was so dark and his spirit was so evil that there was nothing good in him. He didn't have that light like I had seen in Anthony.

Donyel waved his hand and slapped Philip across his face knocking him to the floor. "Don't tell me your will. You will follow mine and mine alone."

"Yes, Lord Donyel."

I let go of his arm. I jumped back because I didn't want to see anymore. He looked at me innocently and smiled.

"What's wrong, Andrea?" He tilted his head. His smile seemed fake now. His eyes seemed inhuman. I saw now how much he resembled Donyel.

"Look, Andrea . . . I love you."

I shook my head and jumped back. I didn't want him to touch me. "You tried to rape me. You tried to get me to love you and you're. . . . you're my brother?"

His smile dropped. He stepped forward, "I didn't intend on you growing so powerful so soon. That's amazing. Father was right when he said you were powerful." He grabbed my shoulders and I struggled with him for a second.

"Let me go." I touched his chest and blasted him with fire from my hand. He was thrust back against the wall of the building, but he got up unharmed. I had been thrown back from the force of the blast into the grass. I scooted up to my feet.

"Andrea, please, let me explain!"

I tried running but Donyel appeared from around a building. He was dressed in a dark trench coat and he wore a very nice pinstriped gray suit. His hair flowed behind him. "Playtime is over." His head was slightly bowed and his eyes locked on mine. I gasped for my breath. Philip clumsily stood to his feet and wiped his face. Donyel's gaze snapped quickly from me to Philip that knocked him back to the ground with some invisible force. "You can't do anything right." I was scared to see how he treated Philip. What made me any different? He turned my way and smiled. "Andrea, my princess, come here."

I shook my head. "Philip is your son? The whole reason he is trying to be with me is because of you?" It was so disgusting that I thought I would puke.

"This goes so much deeper, Andrea than incest. This is power. This is keeping that power centralized. We are the divine ones; the powers that be. What is one more arranged marriage?"

"I am not going to have a baby with Philip." He seemed to try to quiet his anger. I couldn't understand his patience that he seemed to have with me and not Philip.

"Andrea, remember this is a war. If I let you go, I lose my power to average mortals. It has been prophesied against me that a mortal, a son of man, would inherit my powers to defeat me. We can't let this happen, so together we can create another of pure blood, we can create an entire family, and no one will defeat us."

"You mean defeat you. The prophesy was against you not me. Maybe you shouldn't have started having children with mortals. Now it seems that you're afraid that your descendents will join the power of God to overcome you. are You afraid of the children of God?"

"We are the children of God! These mortals are just mud! How can a God so mighty and powerful adopt mud as his children? What sense does that make?"

"Is that what you thought of my mother when you raped her? She is just mud? Is that what you think of Philip too? Is that what you think of me? You say that God has rejected me but how do I know that you just don't want me for this baby and then I'm just another mud person?"

Donyel smiled wider, so much wider that it was unnatural. I could see his teeth were gritting. I felt I was angering him and thought to watch my tongue. After all, he was still an angel. "Andrea, I thought we came to an understanding." He rubbed over his hands.

"We did. But my friend Dewayne has come up dead. And my other friends think that you did it." He looked at me. Philip's eyes popped opened and he stood straight up.

"I can't believe you . . ." Philip started.

"We can't believe you would accuse me of such a crime." Donyel interrupted Philip and gestured him to stand back.

"Why else would Dewayne do such a thing? He wasn't suicidal," I asked.

"Evidently he was. You just met him, Andrea. What could you possibly know about him?"

What did I know about anybody as of right now? I was so confused and didn't know who to believe. I had to guard my thoughts. Donyel had a way with words and I didn't want him smooth talking me. I veiled my thoughts the best way I knew so that he couldn't intercept my doubt. But he was powerful. I smiled and pretended to not think ill of him.

"I guess I didn't know him." The breeze blew my dark hair around my face.

"These mortals are weak, Andrea. We are the strong. And we all know that only the strong survive." Donyel looked at Philip and took my hand, joining it with his. Philip smiled and grabbed me by the waist. I leaned back, resisting Philip trying to kiss me.

"Don't deny your destiny, Andrea." Donyel said. I disappeared out of Philip's arms and materialized behind them. Philip looked confused that he was no longer holding me.

"I make my own choices, Donyel."

Philip looked scared at how I stood up to him. I wasn't sure why Donyel treasured me so much but he didn't want to harm me. He just forced himself to smile.

"Who made you change your mind?" Donyel scanned my soul and I could feel his power intercepting through my mind. I tried to block him but it was futile.

"Anthony, the preacher boy?" He laughed at this. "Is he the little encourager of your soul now? That's quite some connection he has with you. Remember, these feelings you have for him will only bring you pain."

I looked away from Donyel to prevent him from intercepting my soul. "Feelings? I don't know what you're talking about. Why do even care about Anthony? Is there something that makes you fear him?"

"I fear no man, Andrea. I hope that you will see the truth about these mortals. You are not one of them and you will never be. Deep down you know this. You look at Anthony and he makes you feel more like a monster. God's glory shines on him like the sun but what does God do for you? Doesn't that make you a little jealous?"

I didn't want to hear anymore. Half of it was right but half of it was wrong. Anthony made me feel human as well. "Shut up!" I threw my hands up and flung fire at both Donyel and Philip. Philip was thrown into the bushes far off but Donyel barely budged. It tripped him up slightly, but I saw that it would take more than that to injure him.

Donyel looked back at Philip who was attempting to get up. With a wave of his hand he picked Philip up into the air and immediately restored his burns that I had given him. While he was distracted, I faded away into the darkness and escaped.

CHAPTER TWENTY-EIGHT

Karen and Valerie knocked continuously on Anthony's door. He was knocked out from fatigue. He could hear the knocking but he couldn't get his body to respond. He just laid there, drooling on his carpet. He hadn't locked the door so Karen walked in.

"Anthony? Are you okay?" She knelt beside him and felt his forehead. Valerie closed the door behind her and stood in the entrance.

"What's wrong with him? Is he sick?" Valerie asked. Karen's examining finally woke Anthony up, who gave a weak grin to show he was okay.

"I'm just . . . tired. That's all," he said.

Karen helped him up and sat him on the bed. "You're stressing yourself out, Anthony. Come . . . lay down."

"There's no time for me to sleep." He struggled to sit up. "Andrea needs us. I know she does. I was talking to her a while ago but she disappeared."

"I know. She did the same thing at the dorm. I didn't know she was powerful like that."

"She's Nephilim. I've done some studies on it and read

up on what's going on." Valerie walked forward, always interested in what Anthony had to say. "What's a Nephilim?"

"The Nephilim were the children of the Watchers. The Watchers were a group of Angels who fell during the days of Jared, Noah's great-great-grandfather."

Karen had sat next to him and she was still attending to his health. "You haven't eaten, Anthony. We need to get you something. That's why you're drained. You've been studying so much that you haven't taken the time to take care of yourself."

Anthony waved his hand to get Karen from mothering him. "I'm fine. I feel okay."

"No, you're not. Valerie, can you please order a pizza?" Karen asked her.

Valerie nodded. "I still want to hear what he has to say about these Nephilim, Karen."

Anthony obliged, "Well, they fell from their holy state to a carnal state because they were jealous that God had created women for men but had not created women for them. As the story goes, God had told them that they were eternal and that they had no need of wives. But their lust warred with them and they decided to take wives anyway. The children they had became giants. They enjoyed the taste of blood and they began to become cannibals. Soon the world was being overpopulated with these hybrid creatures. God had become displeased and that's when he told Enoch that he would use Noah to be the survivor of a new world. The death of all those people in the flood caused a catastrophic affect on our universe. God didn't accept the spirits of those dead Nephilim into the spirit realm so they became . . ."

"Demons." I had interjected my comment. "Good to see we're all on the same page." They all jumped up to see that I was in the room. Anthony looked relieved that I was okay and Karen looked slightly spooked.

Valerie took my hand to make sure I was okay. "Where did you go?"

"I was on campus walking by the library and found Philip. I talked to him . . ." I started.

"Are you okay? He didn't try to attack you again did he?" Karen asked.

"Again?" Anthony looked at me and I looked away.

"I'm okay. There's nothing he can do to me, trust me. But I did find out that Philip is my . . . well Philip is . . . Donyel's son." The long frozen stares in their eyes reminded me of this painting I had seen of Justinian and Theodora back when I took this art history class my senior year. I knew every moment there was something new and I didn't want to burden them anymore with anything else, but I was just as surprised if not disgusted as they were.

"You've got to be kidding," Karen said. I shook my head. Anthony rubbed his head trying to configure in his mind what Donyel was plotting.

"Philip is Nephilim?" Anthony asked.

"He must be the third one. You, me and Philip," Valerie said. "Donyel said he needed all three."

"You think that Philip is a descendent of Isabella?" I responded to Valerie.

"Could be. Donyel said he was trying to purify his blood line. But Anthony, you said that these children become demons upon death. Wouldn't that mean that . . ." Valerie looked at me, "What about other descendants? I mean I'm from that line of people."

"The children have a chance if their fathers are mortal. That's what an angel told me," I told her.

Anthony paced the floor, "But they still have that power that can draw them to evil. It's a hit and miss. I remember Dewayne was telling me something about genetics. When it comes to hybrids mixing with other hybrids you can produce a child that is totally good or the complete opposite and totally evil." Karen was getting scared and began to get faint.

"Are you okay?" I asked her.

"Yeah, I'm sorry. Look, I need to order that pizza." Karen picked the phone up and began to dial.

"So that's what he meant by purifying the line? He wants to use Philip who carries his seed to insure that a child is born that has his powers and follows his image? But why?" Valerie asked.

"That's why he wanted me to be with Philip. So if he wanted just us three, then maybe, he had nothing to do with Dewayne's death at all," I said.

Valerie shook her head in disagreement and went on to explain to me what she had found out about the scholarship coincidence. "Students before us have been dying, Andrea. That has to have something to do with it. If we don't do something, Donyel's just going to keep on coming after us, or someone else we don't know." Valerie was trying to convince me and I was in a mental tug of war.

Karen couldn't concentrate on the phone call long enough because she was listening to us. This was all too scary for her. "Wait a minute," she said, "we're talking about a dark angel, people. How are we going to fight an angel? How do we know he's not spying on us right now? How many of us have actually dealt with an angel with a plan of world domination?" Anthony looked at Karen and rubbed her shoulders. I felt weird watching him hold her.

"It's going to be okay, Karen," Anthony assured her. "We have God on our side. We'll use what the Bible tells us and fight on the spiritual plane. There is much power in prayer." I remembered how his prayer echoed through the sky.

"Here we go again with this prayer!" Valerie blurted

out. "Why won't you guys just let me make a spell . . ." I held my hand up because I knew where this conversation was going.

"Valerie, I think Anthony is right. Prayer is powerful." I looked at Anthony and then back at Valerie. "Fighting fire with fire will just cause more destruction. Magick is his way. If we use water to fight fire, we may be able to snuff this problem out for good. That water is the Spirit of God. If we have Him on our side, then we can get through this. For some reason I think that Donyel is intimidated by Anthony and if this powerful angel is intimidated by Anthony because he is a Christian, then I think it's worth looking into." Anthony was surprised that I had given him so much adoration. He smiled at me.

In some unofficial way, I had dubbed him our leader. If we were going to get through this, we were going to need a leader.

"So are you up for the job?" I asked him.

He looked at me confused. "What job?"

"Are you going to help me get rid of Donyel once and for all?" Anthony's eyes almost popped from their sockets. Karen felt reassured because Anthony was well informed on the spiritual realm. Valerie was willing to listen despite her disagreement on the passivity of prayer.

"I don't know, Andrea. I'm just one man," Anthony said.

"Yeah, but you're a man of God. There's power in that," I responded.

He shrugged his shoulders. "You have far more power than I have."

"I have different powers that I got from Donyel and as far as I can tell, it only slows him down a little. But what you have . . . you have received from God." I went and sat by him and looked him in the eyes ". . . and even Donyel has to recognize that." I gave him what he had given me—

hope. I wanted to believe in him just as he had believed in me. I think he realized what I was doing. At a point where we all felt helpless, we relied on each other's strength to get through.

"I'll do it. . . . if you're by my side, Andrea"

I smiled and there were sighs of relief all around us. I took his hand and gripped it tightly feeling, for the first time, safe. "I'm not going anywhere."

CHAPTER TWENTY-NINE

Tamela was in her room meditating deeply. The room smelled of frankincense and she repeated over and over a monotonous chant that pulled her deeper and deeper into a trance-like state. Philip must have knocked four times before she realized someone was at the door. She had to break herself from the folded up state of sitting down. She pulled her legs from the pretzel-like formation and hobbled to the door.

"What took you so long?" Philip asked. Tamela straightened her back and stretched her arms.

"What's wrong with you? You look like there's a fire in the building," she said.

Philip pushed his way into the room and looked around. "Where's Valerie?" he asked.

"I think she has new friends." Tamela folded her arms as she slammed the door looking slightly betrayed.

"These friends she has are evil." Philip commented.

Tamela perked up and walked up to Philip. "What are you talking about?" Philip sat down on the bed and tried to calm down.

"Tamela, I need your help. An angel came to me and told me that Valerie is making friends with evil people. Andrea is a demon. She's not human. She is some spawn of the devil and the angel told me that Valerie is under some type of spell. Do you believe me?" Tamela covered her mouth. She wasn't sure what to think. Donyel was in the room and Philip could sense it, but neither could see him. Every now and then when Philip glanced at the mirror he thought he saw Donyel's shadow.

"What? Philip, I didn't even know you knew about this kind of stuff. What makes you think that Andrea is a demon?"

Philip held her by the shoulders with a look of fear. "I told you, an angel came to me. It told me that Andrea is trying to destroy us all and that she is the one who killed Dewayne. Dewayne didn't commit suicide."

"This is crazy." Tamela shook her head in disbelief.

"The angel told me he protected you when all three of you were in the dorm together and Andrea ran out. She ran out because he cast her out to keep her from killing you that night." Tamela knew there was no way of Philip knowing what happened that night. She was very aware of spirits and didn't need to hear anymore. She grabbed her book of shadows and flipped through the pages.

"I knew I felt some type of different energy from Andrea, and even Valerie felt it. What do you want me to do, Philip? I mean I have a few spells, um, a vanquishing spell to send her to hell."

"No!" He stopped her from flipping the pages. "I don't want you to vanquish her. She knows things and we need to capture her in order to break the spell she has on Valerie. She is very dangerous; I don't want you to get hurt."

"You said she killed Dewayne. The police reports say it was suicide."

"That's what the campus said to cover up the incident

and to keep the police from getting too heavily involved. But in truth, he was murdered by something vicious." Tamela covered her mouth again in shock. She went to her drawer.

"If you don't want to kill her, then we can bind her powers until you can capture her." Philip smiled knowing that Tamela was playing right into his hands and that everything was going according to plan. Tamela grabbed a sheet of paper and was written on the top was: *Binding spell.*

"Are you sure it's going to work? This is a life or death situation," Philip pressured.

"It should work. I've never had to use it before, but it's worth a try. Can you get me something that belongs to her?"

"I have keys to all the rooms." Philip didn't count on having to do that, but he nodded and hoped he wouldn't run into Andrea since she was able to spontaneously pop up without warning. "I will need to you to go with me to keep watch and we'll go up to their room to see what we can find to use."

Tamela nodded but felt uneasy. "What if they come back and Andrea catches us? You said she killed Dewayne, what would she do to us?"

"I'm not sure. We have to be careful."

Tamela walked to Philip facing him and staring him in the eyes. "I feel safe knowing you are here. It's still hard for me to think that Andrea is a demon though. She seemed so cool, and why would she kill Dewayne? That makes no sense."

"Tamela, believe me, when a person is a demon spirit, everything is a lie. The angel told me that we need to capture her so that he can take her to where she needs to be. The people she has possessed we have to stop at all cost. They will try to protect her."

"Who? Anthony, Karen, and Valerie?"

"Yeah, she's possessed them all." He shook his head and walked over to the window.

Tamela came behind him and rubbed his neck and kissed his back. "Let's do it."

He turned around and hugged her and she felt confident for a moment that what they were doing was for the good. Donyel smiled in his hiding place unseen by the two. They went down to the office and grabbed Philip's set of master keys and proceeded back up in the elevator. Tamela held his hand firmly and Philip kept his eyes on the elevator's slow progression from floor to floor.

"What do you want to do with her after we bind her powers?" Tamela asked.

"The angel that came to me said he will reveal his plans after we are done." Tamela was feeling uneasy. Her hand shook slightly and Philip could sense it. "You're nervous?"

Tamela's mind was trying to make sense of what Philip had just told her. "It scares me a little. I mean, how do we know what we are doing is right at all? Are you sure Andrea is a demon? I don't want to . . ."

"Tammy, I have told you things that only an angel could know. Even this Dewayne thing. I wasn't sure what to believe either and don't know why he chose me to do this, but all I know is that I have a mission to do and I need your help." The elevator opened and Philip got off and held his hand out, beckoning for Tamela to get off the elevator. She looked at the buttons on the elevator and then back at Philip. Her mind was at some crossroad and she almost felt the need to stay inside the elevator.

"Are you coming or not?" he asked with his hand still out.

The elevator door began to close and Tamela watched as Philip's expression on his face dropped. Just before it closed completely though, she slid her hand in the crack and made it pop back open. With her hand still out, she grabbed his hand. She had made her decision and refused to rationalize anymore than she had to. She was obsessed with Philip, and if supporting him would make him want to be with her more, then she would do what she had to do. He smiled and led her to the dorm room and listened to see if anyone was in there.

Philip motioned to Tamela that the coast was clear and unlocked the door. "I want you to go in there and find what you need. I will stay out in the hall and let you know if anybody is coming and try to keep them away the best way I know how."

Tamela nodded and went inside the room. She looked around the room trying to decipher which stuff belonged to Karen and which stuff belonged to Andrea. There is some frantic movement one goes through when they are nervous. Somebody could walk in the room at any moment. In paranoia, she would stoop down and stop moving, thinking she had heard something in the hall but Philip made no sound and manned the door, every once in awhile peeking in to see how much progress she was making.

"Hurry up," he whispered inside the door. She scrounged for anything like hair, which would be ideal, or even a sanitary napkin which would be perfect considering the spell. Primarily, the more personal the item was, the more powerful the spell, but all Tamela found was a hair band that was on Andrea's side of the room. Remembering that Andrea was always tying up her hair, she grabbed it and ran.

"I got something, let's go." She grabbed Philip's hand and they ran to the elevator. When they got in, Tamela leaned against the door and took a breath of relief.

"Well, let me see it. What did you find?" Tamela raised her hand up and showed him the hair band. He took it in the tips of his fingers holding it very delicately. "Are you sure it's going to work with this?"

"Well, it's all I could find. Better that than nothing." Her heart was pounding and she tried to take a breath to calm herself. Philip handed it back to her and got off the elevator when it got to the third floor.

"What else do we need to do?" Tamela exited out the elevator, got her room key out and he followed her to her room. She checked to see if Valerie was there which she wasn't, so she motioned for Philip to come in.

"Well, it should be pretty simple from here. I'll bind her powers and then hopefully you can get her before she hurts anybody else." Tamela grabbed a small stick and wrapped the hair band around it. "Philip, you are positive an angel told you this?"

Philip touched her shoulder and looked her in the eye. "Why do you have so little faith?"

"Well, it's just so much to take in. I would never had thought you would believe in the things I believe in and now you are so receptive."

"I've always believed what you believe in. That's why I was so mad when Anthony broke up with you. You didn't deserve a man like that. You deserve a man like me." Tamela looked away but Philip knelt down so that he could be eye to eye to her. "I'm serious, Tammy. I don't want you to pull away from me now. I need you. The universe has brought us together."

"You really think so?"

"I know so." He grabbed her by the shoulders and kissed her firmly. It struck such a cord with her that she had a flash of Donyel and Andrea when they were in the room that night. It felt like déjà vu but she saw something. She pulled back and Philip looked at her to figure out what was the matter.

"I'm sorry, Philip. I just saw a vision of . . . the angel. You're not lying. I saw Andrea and the angel and you're right, she is different. She isn't human. If what you're saying is true we have to stop her."

He nodded. "Thank you, Tamela." She took his hand and commenced to doing her spell, which consisted of saying Andrea's name as she wrapped another cord around the item.

"So when are you going to try and capture her?"

Philip looked away and unknowingly was staring his father directly in the face. They each had the same blank icy stare on their face. "When she least expects me to, Tamela. When she least expects it we will take her together and bring balance back to the universe."

"Blessed be," Tamela said, bowing her head. Philip wrapped his arm around her and smiled cunningly to himself.

CHAPTER THIRTY

I really didn't want to do this. I didn't want to say good-bye. I waited in the lobby trying to wait out the funeral. Anthony stood in the back of the sanctuary all dressed in a nice suit and a white tie. Karen came out of the sanctuary apparently looking for me with her eyes all red from tears. Valerie had told us she'd meet up with us afterwards. I didn't know how to control myself and I didn't want to hear all those thoughts and feel all that pain.

Karen touched her belly and looked up. "It's time." She took me by the hand and we went back into the sanctuary. Anthony stood very still and when he saw me he smiled. I took his hand. When the usher directed us, all three of us walked down the aisle. Anthony was our cornerstone, standing in between putting his arms around us both. I could feel the intensity of Karen's heart filling with sorrow and I tried so hard to separate my feelings from it. The organ played softly and I couldn't help but notice the lovely white floral arrangement that surrounded his picture. I didn't want to look at the body in the casket, but when Karen broke down, I had no choice. Anthony tried pulling her up when her legs gave way from under her. I ran to her other side and picked her up gently. Her scream chilled my heart.

"Dewayne! No, baby! No!" An usher led her to a pew and fanned her there. Dewayne's momma went to comfort her. Anthony just stood there silently. He wouldn't scream, he wouldn't holler, he just stood there gripping his program tightly in his fist. One tear fell and then another. I didn't want to touch him. His sorrow was so intense that it made me dizzy. I looked over to Dewayne's body and turned my head quickly. I held my breath and touched his chest.

"Andrea," I heard Dewayne's voice. I saw time backing up in high speed. I saw this montage of faces. I saw Isabella then Hannah. Then I saw Donyel again.

"Andrea," Dewayne's voice whispered again.

"Dewayne? Where are you Dewayne?" I looked around but I couldn't make anything out. Time was out of control and then it continued as normal. I was walking on campus and I saw Dewayne walking in front of me.

"Dewayne!" I yelled for him but he didn't turn around. I ran to catch up just as he was turning a corner. When I turned the corner I saw that he was talking to Philip.

"What do you want?" Dewayne asked.

"I want Andrea," Philip said, stepping up to Dewayne and backing him up against a wall.

"Hey, man, you best get up off me!" Dewayne said, pushing Philip.

Dr. Yancy walked out of the building. "Is there a problem, boys?" Dr. Yancy asked.

Dewayne walked up to Dr. Yancy. "It's all settled now. I was just on my way to talk to you about my grades."

"Oh, I see. Well, Dewayne, looks like you're not doing too well," Dr. Yancy said, fixing her glasses. I was watching trying to figure why I was having this vision.

"I can do better, really, I've just been distracted," Dewayne said

right before Philip grabbed him in a headlock, choking him,
"What the . . ." he gagged.

Dr. Yancy walked forward a little more and morphed into
Donyel before his eyes.

"Like I said, Dewayne, looks like you're not doing too well."
Donyel smiled. I covered my mouth to keep from screaming.
Donyel was here all along! He slapped Dewayne and he fell to the
ground.

Philip kicked Dewayne in the stomach and laughed, "Andrea
belongs with me! She's not going to be with you now!" I shook my
head as they beat him some more.

"Stop it!" I cried. But they couldn't hear me. Just shadows, like
Arquel had said before. Dewayne grunted and tried picking him-
self up. Dewayne ran for the building and tried to open the door
but it was locked. Philip ran behind him.

"Catch him," Donyel commanded. Dewayne could hear Donyel's
laughter in his ear as if he was next to him. Dewayne waved it off
like flies in front of his face. He could feel his pulse in his throat
and his breath burning his chest as he ran. He tripped, turning a
corner around a building and fell into a thicket. Philip caught
up with him and Dewayne kicked his chest and threw a rock at
him. It hit Philip in the back. He was looking for something—
anything to fight with but couldn't find anything.

I felt useless watching. "Run!" I screamed, as I watched Philip
get to his feet. Dewayne limped through the vacant campus. No
one was around to hear him yell for help. "Someone, please, what's
going on?" he cried. The buildings seemed endless and Donyel
was doing something to Dewayne's mind to confuse him. He panted
for air and held his injured leg. Philip grabbed him around the
throat, choking him. I could hear him gagging and gasping for
air until it he was too weak to fight. Donyel told Philip to pick De-
wayne up and he did as he was told. I watched, helplessly, as
Philip took Dewayne's unconscious body to the pond and held his
head under the water. I cried silently as the bubbles slowly ceased
to rise to the top and he threw his limp body into the pond.

"Philip killed Dewayne? Philip killed Dewayne!" I was mad at myself. How was it that I could not have seen or forseen this? Had my infatuation for this idiot blinded me that much that I couldn't see the truth?

Donyel appeared from the shadows, "The last son of Hannah is gone. Now, go and . . ." He morphed back to Dr. Yancy, "I will cover for you, Philip. The last thing we need is you going away for murder." They laughed together and Philip ran off.

I jerked my hand back from Dewayne's body and looked around. Anthony was still standing there gripping the program and Karen was still hugging Dewayne's mom. There had been no apparent time lapse. I understood what Arquel said now. Philip wasn't one of the three that Donyel was looking for; it was Dewayne. I had believed a lie. I walked off and Anthony followed me. I ran outside.

"Andrea, wait up!" Anthony ran to my side. "Are you okay?"

"It's my fault, Anthony." I held my head down.

"It's no one's fault."

"No, you're wrong. Donyel used Philip to kill Dewayne."

"What?" Anthony shook his head. *I could feel his anger rising inside him.*

Karen walked down the steps, "He was afraid of you, Andrea. Donyel was afraid that Dewayne might give you a child so he got rid of him."

I looked behind me at Karen. "How did you kno . . ."

"I've been having dreams. This baby inside of me . . . she . . . I don't know. I see things in my dreams now. I wasn't quite sure, at first, but now, hearing what you just said I just know there's something more." I grabbed Karen and hugged her.

"Am I missing something?" Anthony asked. "Why Dewayne?"

"He was the last of Hannah's lineage. Not Philip. He could have been the one that Donyel was afraid of because if he was from that family, there was chance that he could produce a child that could defeat Donyel. Donyel is a deceptive devil and he's using Philip to get to us. Valerie was right," I said, still hugging Karen.

She looked at me scared. "Then my baby could be in danger."

"Not if we stop Donyel first. He will pay for what he did to Dewayne, I promise you," I told her. Anthony's eyes began to panic.

"What's wrong?" Karen asked him.

"If Donyel is trying to kill all of Isabella's descendants and start over with Andrea . . ." He took a breath and both Karen and I almost read his mind, ". . . then we need to find Valerie."

CHAPTER THIRTY-ONE

Valerie fixed her clothes while she observed herself in the mirror. She looked at the clock in the corner and felt relieved that she still had thirty minutes to spare. She told Karen that she was okay with driving herself to the funeral. She felt bad that Dewayne was gone and she wasn't sure that if he had been her boyfriend that she would be able to deal with the loss. Valerie had never really been in a loving relationship like what she had seen with Karen and Dewayne.

She brushed her hair and imagined the pain that Karen must be suffering. If Dewayne really loved her, why would he commit suicide? It just didn't make sense. So much had happened in the past that just thinking about it gave her a creepy feeling. Was she really sure she could trust Andrea? What about Anthony? Anthony had already had his preconceived prejudices and he barely knew her. When it came to friends she wasn't that good at judging them.

"Ah, Valerie just the girl I was looking for," Tamela said, walking through the door. Valerie didn't feel any better when Tamela walked through the door. Philip closed the door behind Tamela.

"Oh, hey Philip, what are you doing here?" Philip smiled that typical charming smile but through the mirror it looked different—evil even. Valerie gasped and turned around quickly.

"What's the matter?" Tamela asked.

"Nothing," Valerie said, regaining her composure. "I'm just really upset . . . about Dewayne's funeral today and sometimes it just hits me that he's gone."

"Funny." Philip smirked. "Wasn't like you guys were all that close."

"He's still human, Philip. Don't you have any regard for human life?" Valerie walked pass him. Tamela stood in front of her. "Excuse me."

"You know, Valerie, you sure have been changing." Tamela examined Valerie's eyes while holding her face. Valerie shrugged back because Tamela was disturbingly close. "Could it be, that these new friends of yours are brainwashing you?"

"Tamela, what are you talking about?"

"Valerie, Andrea is not who she seems to be!" Tamela yelled. Valerie moved around Tamela. She wondered if she was beginning to remember what happened that night. She grew nervous. If Tamela's memory had come back, what had she told Philip?

"You're crazy, Tamela."

"Tamela says you felt her powers, Valerie. She's more than just a gifted Witch like yourself. She's supernatural." Philip's voice was so deep and haunting. Valerie ignored the two and placed her heels on to leave.

"You know. Tamela, right now I'm not too sure this Wiccan stuff is all that it's cracked up to be." Tamela stood in front of her again. "Now, if you would please excuse me I have a funeral to go to."

Philip walked up behind Tamela and rubbed her shoulders not really giving Valerie eye contact. "Valerie, you are the one who is deceived. How do you really know that Andrea is telling you the truth? The truth is that she isn't human." He looked at her in her eyes and Valerie looked away. "But you already know that don't you? Do you know she is a devil? You are doing the devil's will, Valerie. She is responsible for Dewayne's murder!"

Valerie looked up shocked, "You are lying."

"Please, Valerie," Tamela said, grabbing her shoulders. "I don't want to bind your powers. Remember, we are to do no harm and here I find that you are consorting with demons!"

Valerie felt uneasy and her mind was spinning like a merry-go-round. She was confused. Philip was speaking the truth but also feeding into the doubts she already had about Andrea. "How do I know that you're not with Donyel?" Her mind focused.

Tamela looked at Philip, "Donyel? Who is that?" Philip looked around at some unseen force and anger built in his face. Valerie felt another chill over her skin and she knew that she needed to get out of there. Only she could see how his face changed back and forth as if demons were using his face like a mask.

"You . . . you're the one who isn't human!" Valerie screamed and pushed her way out of Tamela's arms. Tamela pulled her by the arm and swung her back on the bed. Valerie squealed as she plummeted on the mattress. She swung her hair from off her face and fixed her glasses.

"Looks like we'll have to do this the hard way," Philip said, pulling some rope from his pocket. Panic struck Valerie's heart. Tamela grabbed Valerie at Philip's command, trying to keep her still. Valerie kicked Philip's chin, which didn't make him any happier.

"Keep her still!" he shouted.

"I'm trying!" Tamela said and slapped Valerie to get her to behave. The two girls wrestled on the bed and on to the floor and knocked Philip back on the opposite bed.

Valerie pulled her protection amulet from around her neck and attempted to chant behind her tears, "Angel of the north protecting me, keep me from my enemies!" she screamed. It was all she could remember when it came to protection. She pulled at the carpet on the floor with her nails as Tamela used her body weight to hold her down. Philip attempted to regain control and pulled Tamela aside and socked Valerie with the back of his fist. Valerie laid on the floor stunned. She was hurt. Her spell had not worked. She looked up and saw the fuzzy images of Tamela and Philip standing over her.

"Tie her up," she heard Philip say as he threw the ropes at Tamela. Then she saw the fuzzy image of another materialize faintly behind them. It was Donyel.

"Lord Jesus," Valerie whispered.

Donyel smiled unseen by anybody else but Valerie. *"Should have thought of Him before,"* he said, and with no more strength to fight, Valerie blacked out.

CHAPTER THIRTY-TWO

We made it back to the dorm and ran to Valerie's room. Karen slammed on the door like a police officer.

"Valerie! Are you in there?" Anthony yelled. There was no answer.

"She may be gone," Karen said.

"We have to make sure," I said. I grabbed the doorknob and it broke off in my hand. "We'll worry about school security later." Anthony stood amazed at how strong I was getting and shied away from his stare by walking into the room. Karen looked around the room and shrugged her shoulders. There seemed to be no noticeable sign that anybody had been in the room. It was clean as a whistle.

"I guess you're right, Karen," Anthony said, looking into the room behind us. "Maybe she got stranded on the street."

"No wait." I halted him with my raised hand. "Something isn't right. This room is way too clean. The last time I was in here there was at least some clutter. This room looks like it's been cleaned."

"I think Tamela has a right to clean her room every

once in a while," Karen sarcastically remarked, but I ignored her. My attention was on this spot on the carpet.

I knelt down to get a closer look. "There's a drop of blood." I touched the spot.

I saw Valerie being tied up by Tamela and Philip, and then they picked her up and carried her away. Donyel levitated in the room, and with the wave of his hands, everything moved into order. I stood in the middle of this vision that seemed all too real. Donyel knelt down where I was (so close it was eerie) and noticed the same spot.

"Andrea," he said and I jumped back. There was no way he could see me; this was just a vision. "I know you will see these events. I can create many illusions but the stain of blood I can't erase. So, I will tell you this, if you want to see your friend, then you must agree to be with me and seal this covenant once and for all. I trust that you will find me with no problem.

I gasped for air and fell backwards like a jolt of electricity had hit me. Anthony pulled me up. "Andrea, come on, snap out of it!" But I couldn't. My mind was picking up signals from all over and I jerked in pain each time they infiltrated my thoughts.

I stood silent and stepped back.

"What the . . ." Was I dreaming again? I couldn't understand but it didn't feel like I was asleep. With eyes closed, I felt a cold sensation go over my body and then it stopped. It was followed by a floating sensation like when I would make myself fly. I opened my eyes and I was in the vortex of some kind of cyclone of mirrors. All the mirrors whirled slowly around me.

"This is going to make it difficult, remembering which one I came out of." I floated forward. I could see that this floating tunnel of mirrored portals ended at some point. I thought the wisest thing would be to go there.

"What are you doing here?" An old bearded man pulled my ankle and very easily swung me in the opposite direction. I man-

aged to control myself from floating too far away. He looked at me suspiciously. "You are of the Nephilim. Your kind is forbidden to go beyond these levels of heaven." He pointed viciously at me with his old finger.

"Who are you?" I floated back to him with the greatest of ease as I asked my question.

"I am Kefa. I watch the gates of Heaven." I stood in awe.

This floating mass of portals wasn't my first idea of the gate of heaven, but it seemed that this was exactly what this old man was doing. He nodded at me and folded his legs resembling Bhudda the way his belly popped out from his garment when he was all scrunched up. I began to realize that he was floating in the vortex but that the vortex was floating around him. I could see my destination directly behind him and he seemed to make the cyclone become even more narrower to keep me from shooting past him.

"And you are . . ." he waved his hand in front of him and closed his eyes. I could see the palm of his hand illuminate like it was heating up or on fire, "Andrea Wallace, the daughter of the fallen Donyel, from Heaven, Texas. Your time has not come and when it does you are still forbidden to surpass the third heaven."

"How did you . . ."

"I am Kefa. I know Heaven, Texas. I had been there at one point in time." His eyes smiled but his face did nothing.

"What do you mean that you've been there? Aren't you supposed to . . ." He waved his hand and I was jolted back.

"Silence!" I was about through with his rudeness. "At one point I took time on earth, on a mission. So I went to your town when it was first being settled."

"Why Heaven, Texas?"

"There is much you don't know about Heaven, Texas. There are many doors to the spirit realm throughout the world and several of them lie within . . ."

"Heaven?" How ironic. It was as if someone named the town knowing that the town itself was a gate.

I looked in his eyes and visions flashed through my mind. I wanted to know more and the visions of Lake Papa Pete skimmed through my thoughts. All my life I had been told legends about Lake Papa Pete. As the legend goes, some crazy old man jumped in the lake and was never seen again and so they named it after him.

"You are Papa Pete? The legend is about you."

He nodded. "But this is not why you have been brought here. You need answers, you seek knowledge. "He smirked and leaned forward, floating himself closer. "The secrets the earth has been given freely are still undiscovered or unread. Most men have no desire to know these things but rather make up in their own minds their own realities to satisfy their personal lives. The spirit realm has no walls or limitations. I have graduated from the school of life; it is you who is still learning. Who shall teach the children?" His hand graced my cheek and I backed up.

"This can't be real."

"What exactly is your question?" He threw me for a loop. I didn't prepare questions. "To know the answers, Andrea, you must know the right questions."

"And you have the answers I'm looking for?" Kefa shook his head and pointed behind me. I looked over my shoulder and two other angels startled me with their presence. I hadn't even heard them approach. "I summoned these angels to bring you back to your place. Otherwise you would be lost here forever. Shariel, Arquel, could you please escort our friend to her dimension?"

I looked over to Arquel, finally recognizing him in his angelic glory. He nodded at me.

"Wait. I need answers. Arquel, please I know you know Donyel. If there is any more to who he is, please tell me," I pleaded.

"There are things you must discover for yourself. There are things I can not reveal to you." I was upset that Arquel was still being just as aloof as before. Shariel, the other angel, convicted him with a look.

"Remember that Donyel is a rebel," Shariel explained. He spoke

*to me in a passionate way and was not as regimented as Arquel.
"He will do whatever he has to do to get what he wants, but yet he
must still follow certain universal laws or else the angelic council
will get more involved."*

"What is this council?" I asked.

*Shariel continued his lesson. "On earth as it is in Heaven,
there is a government. The Father is on top and below Him the
Powers and below them the hierarchy order of angels; they make
up the council. There are laws that govern the angels as there are
laws that govern man."*

*"Government?" I asked. "So if there's a law, then there's a con-
sequence?" Shariel nodded. This was highly interesting, but I
wish I had more time to go into it more with him.*

*Shariel continued. "Donyel committed his first crime when he fell
and his second when he had children. But his offense must be handled under the appropriate jurisdiction. The higher his crime however, the more involved the council gets. I would not think he would
do more to attract attention from the council."*

"What are you saying?"

*"Donyel may hurt people, but he won't use his hands to kill.
He will however . . ." Arquel raise his hand to Shariel to keep him
from speaking. Shariel bowed his head. I was really getting upset
at Arquel's attitude.*

"What? What can he do?" I asked.

*Arquel finished. "Donyel escaped bondage through permission
of mankind, your mother. He has avoided us long enough. With
your help we can bind him once again. You must return now."*

*"Wait! Can I see Dewayne? I know he must be here." Arquel
and Shariel took each others hands and directed their free hands
toward me and I was blast by some force from their hands back
into a vortex.*

"Andrea!" Anthony cradled me in his arms trying to get
me conscious again.

I sat up dazed. "I saw another vision. Donyel has Valerie. He wants me in exchange for her."

Karen grabbed a knife from the counter. "Then what are we waiting for? Let's go after him."

"It's not going to be that easy, Karen," Anthony said, looking up. "This is an angel we're talking about. He is immortal. He is very powerful and he can't be killed. We really don't know what we're up against. We need to have a plan." My dizzy spell was fading and I didn't want to keep using my powers frivolously, but I knew that I would be the only one who could face him.

"We can contain him though," I commented shaking off the dizziness. "That's how Paul did it in the past. I'm beginning to understand something that I saw in another vision. Donyel can't just kill people. He has to use another person to be his agent because that way his sin isn't held personally on him and he hasn't broken a law against the council."

"The council?" Anthony asked.

"It's a hierarchy of angels. I'll explain it later. He uses Philip to carry out his crimes but that doesn't mean he still can't play with our minds. We have to stay alert. I can handle Donyel, but we have to find a way to stop Philip." Karen threw the knife down and began to get emotional. The pregnancy was getting to her. I could feel her anguish and her confusion.

"It's okay, Karen." I tried to comfort her.

"No, it's not! This isn't real! This has to be some kind of dream," she replied. Anthony grabbed Karen and gave her a hug.

"Karen, we can get through this together. The angels said that we have to bind up Donyel. The only way they can find him is through me," I told her.

"And what if you die, Andrea? Huh? Have you thought

about that? What do we do then?" Karen screamed at me and I didn't know how to answer. I had thrown a big burden on my shoulders and maybe I had bitten off more than I could chew. Doubt attached itself to me from Karen's words.

"We're not going to think about that, Karen," Anthony said strongly. He looked dead in my eyes. "Andrea is strong, but our faith is in God, not in her strength. If he helped little David beat Goliath, he can help us with our giant." I was amazed at how powerful Anthony's faith was during this time. It was . . . attractive. I smiled and joined in on the hug. A warm feeling entered my heart. Anthony had strength and a power that was so inward and even more intense than what I had.

"What's wrong, Andrea?" Anthony asked. I guessed he noticed the tears coming from my eyes.

"Nothing."

"No, please, we need to be open right now." Anthony was pulling at my heart and I had no choice but to give in.

"Okay, I am scared. You are so strong Anthony. I admire you for that . . . I just wish I could have that confidence in God that you have."

"You just have to pray, Andrea. Give him your all and trust in Jesus. Jesus sent his Holy Spirit to help us and he said that once the Holy Spirit comes upon us we shall receive power." I pulled away and turned my back.

"I never could understand why I couldn't get into the Bible like I wanted. I never could understand why I couldn't relate. But now," I turned back around and wiped my tears, "I understand. Anthony, all that applies to people. He didn't die for me and he didn't give the Holy Spirit to Nephilim. He gave that to you. I thought about being scared and about saving myself, but then if I did that, I would lose everyone that I care about the most. I don't want to be mad at God because I'm mad at my father." I walked up to him and rubbed his face. I saw a beauty inside him that I wish he could see himself. "You are David. The Holy Spirit is with you. I am just what I am. I feel alone because just like Donyel said, I'm not a part of this."

"Andrea, we're all connected." He grabbed my hand. "God has a plan and whatever it is we're going to see this through to the end. Faith has nothing to do with religion, race, or . . . species." He chuckled a bit. "I believe that. I want you to believe that as well. Hear me. Faith comes by hearing and by hearing the word of God."

I smiled and nodded. "I hear you and I believe. I believe that Jesus is going to get us through this somehow." He smiled. Faith was scary. I had absolutely no idea what I intended on doing and sensed that Anthony didn't either.

He led us three in a prayer. I stayed silent while Karen interjected a "Yes Lord" here and there. While we prayed, I felt a sense of peace overcome me. I can't really explain it. But while we stood there in the middle of a witch's room (of all places) I believe that God met us. I felt a sudden surge of strength added on to the strength I already had (but only when I was closest to Anthony). Tears rolled down my eyes and I sniffled and snorted to keep my composure.

"In Jesus's name, Amen," he ended. I wiped my face and we walked out the room. I closed it the best that I could, considering I took the knob off. "I want you girls to meet me in my room later tonight to regroup. Get some rest."

"But what about Valerie?" Karen asked.

"I believe Andrea, that he's not going to hurt her. He wants you not her and this may be a trap. We need to rest and have a game plan." He walked us to the elevator and we all got in and didn't understand how he expected us to rest with so much on our minds. "With you being pregnant, I'm not sure if I want you to go."

"I'm going, Anthony, and that's it. He killed Dewayne, no matter if he used Philip or not, Donyel was responsible. One can chase a thousand demons and two can chase . . ."

"Ten thousand I know, Karen; but how many angels?" He asked jokingly.

I looked over at him. "I think we're going to have a few angels on our side as well." The elevator opened and I stepped out. Karen put her arm around me and for the first real time I felt sisterhood.

"Remember, ladies, rest and pray up. We have a battle ahead. And Andrea . . ."

"Yes?" I replied.

"I want you to read the second chapter of the book of Joshua in the Bible."

"Why, what is it?"

He smiled and I was wondering what he was up to. "Just read it. I think it will help you see that sometimes God takes those who may *seem* to be on the enemy's side for His will. All it takes is a little faith." The elevator closed. I was left with my own thoughts there were so many it was like shuffling a deck of cards.

We made it back to the room and Karen lied down immediately. I took the covers and tucked her in. I knew that this was a lot for her to handle. I really didn't want her to fight but this was her battle as much as anybody's. I sat by her bed until she fell asleep.

What scared me even more than dying was that if I did die, then what? I rolled over and hugged my pillow. I didn't want fear and doubt to overcome me. I needed to have faith. It was so much easier when Anthony was around. I could feel God all through him. Now, I was cold. I sat up and grabbed my Bible and flipped it open.

I took a long sigh and read to myself. "Joshua Chapter 2."

CHAPTER THIRTY-THREE

Valerie was still dazed and her face felt slightly swollen. She focused her eyes but couldn't see anything. She couldn't tell where she was or what time it was. Her glasses were not on her face. They must've fallen off at some point. Her wrists were sore and she couldn't move them. She pulled at them and that's when she realized that they were tied securely behind her. It was dark and damp.

"Hello?" She tried to yell but she heard her voice echo into the void. She tried to hop out of the old splintery wooden chair she was bound to but didn't accomplish anything but toppling herself over sideways. Her head hit the wooden floor with a thud.

"Help," she whispered as loud as she could. She saw a light in the darkness, and a shadow approaching her. She raised her head and attempted to move her hair from her view. She squinted her eyes but the glare from the flashlight the person was holding blinded her more.

"Andrea?" she weakly asked, "is that you?" She felt a large hand grab her by the hair and sit her upright in the chair. He wasn't concerned with her pain or her screams.

Philip flashed the light on his face and whispered in her ear menacingly. "When are you going to realize that she isn't your friend? She left you, Valerie. You know why? Because you're like us." Valerie shook her head.

"You are a liar, Philip. I'm not like you, I'm not a devil." He slapped her and her hair fell over her blood-stained face. She didn't want to doubt Andrea but she felt herself getting weak. All she held on to was that Philip was evil and maybe there was a chance that she could convince Tamela.

"Tamela?" Valerie whimpered. Tamela stood in the shadows unseen, but Valerie could hear her breathing in the corner.

"Philip, maybe she isn't that possessed. Maybe we should untie her," Tamela said.

"Tamela, listen to me." He took her by the shoulders. "If we untie this demon, she will try to kill us. Don't be deceived. Don't worry." He embraced her in a hug. "Once we get the source of this evil, she will be back to normal. You have to bear with me on this. If we are obedient, the angel will bless us both."

"Don't believe him, Tamela! Donyel is a fallen angel! He's evil . . ." Philip slapped Valerie to make her shut up. Tamela turned her back. Philip walked over and pulled Tamela closer and held her face gently in his hands.

"You trust me don't you?" he asked, staring into her eyes.

She slowly nodded. "Let's just find Andrea and get this over with."

"Stay here and watch Valerie." He handed her a gun. "If you hear anything unusual, call for me first before you use this. I will be upstairs."

"Philip, I don't how to use this gun."

"I'm not asking you to use it. If Andrea comes I don't want you to kill her. I will handle her. If she comes at you before I get back down, then shoot her anywhere but in the head. She can heal very fast but if a Nephilim has a fatal head injury or is decapitated, they will die."

"What's a Nephilim?"

"That's the type of devil she is. I can't go into detail. Just call me if she comes." And he walked off and ran up the creaky steps of the house. Philip squinted his eyes attempting to see in the darkness. It was cold and musty smelling as if something was rotten in every corner. The walls were singed with soot and the wooden planks of the floor ripped through the carpet. Philip guided himself along the wall shaking off the cobwebs that attached onto him. Down the hall was a dim light flashing underneath the door. He focused on that to direct him down the hall.

"Father," he whispered, "is that you?" A rat ran across his foot and Philip hollered, kicking the rat before it could get away.

"Are you okay up there?" Tamela yelled from downstairs.

"I'm fine. I just . . ." He thought for a second, "It's dark up here. Can't see," he said too embarrassed to admit the truth. He walked past a dingy mirror. The distorted image made him look like a monster. He backed up away from the mirror and ran down the hall.

"Donyel are you here?" Philip said, entering the door with the glowing light. Donyel's back was facing Philip as he looked out a half boarded up window. His long black hair was flowing as if a wind was hitting it, but Philip could feel no breeze.

"Do you sense them coming?" Philip asked. Donyel slowly turned around and placed his arms behind him. His eyes showed no emotion and his lips were tight. He looked Philip over carefully.

"Do you believe you can defeat her?" Donyel whispered into Philip's ear.

"She will be mine," Philip replied in determination.

"But she has friends now."

"We have Valerie, Father. Your plan will succeed."

Donyel looked at Philip. "It's not my plan I don't have faith in."

Philip looked disappointed. "I won't fail you."

"And your wannabe-witch girlfriend?"

"She won't fail."

"I must be sure of this." He floated back and lifted himself into the air. Philip's eyes filled with fear as he saw Donyel's eyes illuminate and he began speaking some ancient language. The room began to shake and Philip grabbed onto a large wooden wardrobe to keep his balance. Three orbs of fire broke through the windows and began revolving around Donyel. Donyel appeared to juggle them in a triangular formation and shot them to the floor burning the same triangle formation into the carpet. The flames burned and began manifesting into shapes.

"What is going on?" Philip screamed.

"They are my," Donyel smiled, "back up plan." The shapes first looked like horrid deformed burning monsters and then shaped into dead humanoid little figures.

"Demons," Philip whispered, horrified. One of them turned around and smiled at him with a jagged-toothed grin and Philip hid behind the wardrobe again. Donyel laughed and waved his hand over them as to bless them and they bowed before his presence.

"Not just any demons, my son; specialized demons, each for a specific purpose. They will weaken your adversary and confuse them."

"We will stop them completely," said one demon confidently.

Philip regained his courage and stepped forward. "What am I to do in the mean time? I'm . . ."

"Just wait," Donyel interjected. "If I can get Andrea here alone, then we have her. Otherwise . . ."

"Otherwise what?"

"Where two or three are gathered . . . he is in the midst."

"He who?" Philip asked. The demons became unsettled and even Donyel seemed slightly reluctant to speak anymore. "Why aren't you answering me?"

"Enough, Philip!" He waved his hand and Philip was thrust back slightly by an unseen force. He shook himself and left the room in a rage. But even as Philip ran down the dark hallway, Donyel continued to infiltrate his mind.

"If you do as I tell you without question, I will give you your reward." Philip stopped in the hallway and leaned against the wall. His heart at that moment felt unsure.

"My reward." He laughed at himself and looked at himself in the distorted mirror, "The only reward I wanted was you." But there was silence. No response from Donyel. No warm feeling. No love. "Father!" he screamed out.

"End your foolish mortal vanities and go see to the witch," Donyel responded with a piercing mental amorism that laid Philip prostrate to the floor in tears.

"Yes. Forgive me. I'll do as you say!" And he was relieved. Philip ran down the stairs.

"You are harsh with the boy. I can sense his pain," the first said, a demon of depression that was wrapped in a linen hood.

"He was my imperfection," Donyel stated. "So powerless to do my bidding, Avraxius, but Andrea is the perfect balance to mother his seed. Once that connection is made, I shall have a generation of children that are powerful and able create me an army."

"And are these not children of the most high that we attack? Who is to say that they will not be warned of our attack and send us into the Abyss?" The second demon in the formal gown rebutted.

"My dear, Sorra," Donyel answered, "they are far too young to even know what to do or how to do it. Most

Christians do not know how to fight on spiritual planes. By the time they do get warned, you will already be on your way. And you, Uziahath, do you have any concerns?" Donyel directed toward the final demon dressed in a warrior's garb.

"Unlike my companions, I am quite confident in my abilities, Lord Donyel. And when I am finished, I shall take a body as my spoil," Uziahath, the demon said in some ancient language.

"Do as you wish, but Andrea belongs to me. Now, Go!" Donyel waved his hand and the triad of demons faded into the shadows to their assignments. Donyel turned to the window and smiled.

"Come to me, Andrea," he laughed again. "Come to Donyel."

CHAPTER THIRTY-FOUR

"*. . . but Andrea is the perfect balance to mother his seed. Once that connection is made, I shall have a generation of children that are powerful and able create me an army.*"

Karen woke up with a shock. She wasn't sure what she had dreamt about.

"Army? What the . . ." She remembered that creepy face and it gave her shivers. She hadn't been sleeping all that long and she wondered if she should wake Andrea and tell her about the dream. She rubbed her stomach.

"This baby is giving me some crazy dreams lately." She looked over and Andrea was nowhere to be found.

"Must've gone for a walk," she said to herself and looked out the window. A chill came over her. Avraxius stood behind her listening to her breathe. She waved her hand around Karen.

"*Mmmm, I sense your pain, Karen. Let me in please.*" Karen bit her lip. She couldn't hear Sorra but she could feel her.

"*Why did Andrea leave you alone at a time like this? Doesn't she know what you've been through? Look, there on the table.*"

Karen took a picture of Dewayne and her cuddled together.

"Dewayne would've made a good father," Karen whispered to herself, rubbing the picture of Dewayne with her
finger.

"Too bad you'll never know for sure." A tear dropped from
Karen's eye when Avraxius said this.

"No," Karen wiped her face, "I don't have time for this."

"You are human. Allow yourself to mourn." He wrapped his
cloak around her and she felt the weight of it on her
shoulders. *"Andrea is always talking about what she needs, but
has anyone asked or even been concerned about yours? You're the
one who's pregnant. You need to think about that. You have no
one. Who are you going to run to? Your mother? How are you
going to pay for college? Then you'll have the baby and be fat and
no man will want you then."* Tears continued to fall down
Karen's cheeks.

"I don't know what to do," Karen said.

"I know. Accept me," Avraxius whispered in her ear.

In her tears she said it so simply, "I'm so . . . depressed."
And Avraxius entered her spirit.

Meanwhile, Anthony was back at his room. He was on
his bed reading about and looking for anything that could
help him. He had at least twenty books open to all types of
subjects from angels to myths. He was tired of reading and
he needed to take his own advice and get some rest. He
held his Bible on his lap and crossed his legs.

"Well, God, I don't know why you've brought me to this
point in my life, but here I am." He sighed. "I've never en-
countered the things that I'm facing and I'm not quite
sure what to do and I'm scared."

"Oh really? How scared are you?" Uziahath, a strong demon
of fear, said telepathically spying on Anthony's prayer. *"You
do realize that Dewayne died because of Donyel. Have you really
thought about this? Do you really want to die?"*

"I don't want to die," Anthony said. "But, God, I want you to protect me."

"God has a weird way of protecting people doesn't he? Have you ever really seen an angel face to face? Can you imagine how powerful Donyel may be? Can you even fathom in your mortal mind the things he can probably do to you? If you do die, he will rip your limbs from your body and bleed you out." Anthony's imagination envisioned the entire thing like illustrations in his books. *"He will torture you just enough to keep you alive. You will scream and nothing will happen. You don't know this Andrea girl from squat! I suggest you grab your stuff and head back to Baltimore and leave all this behind before you lose your life. Dewayne is dead you fool! And Valerie is dead! And you will die as well! The devil is nothing to play with!"*

Anthony's eyes grew big and his hand shook. He gripped his Bible even more but he couldn't seem to make the pictures Uziahath was putting his head to go away. He didn't know the demon was tormenting him and he didn't think to pray.

"Accept me," Uziahath repeated and continued to whisper menacing things in Anthony's ear. *"You will die!"* the demon repeated.

Anthony was breathing hard and tried to pray but he was stuttering and his tongue was swelling in his mouth. He ran for the sink to wash his face and he couldn't understand why his heart was beating so fast. He thought that maybe he was having an anxiety attack and then suddenly, there was a knock at the door.

CHAPTER THIRTY-FIVE

I was alone outside for I don't know how long. I sat under a large weeping willow that seemed to wave my discomforts away. Karen was asleep on her bed and she hadn't heard me leave. So many thoughts were whirling through my head at one time. Donyel wanted me and there was a chance that I was putting more people in danger. But then I had to realize that this wasn't even about me anymore. Donyel had to be stopped. Arquel and Shariel needed my help to find him. He had done his best to avoid their spiritual radar but I'm sure he hadn't counted on me knowing his whereabouts. I needed to talk to Anthony. I was tired of waiting and if we were going to do this, then we just needed to go.

I stood up from the spot I was sitting in when I suddenly became dizzy and my mind was whirling. I caught my balance on the trunk of the tree.

"Come to me, Andrea!" I heard in my mind. *"Come to Donyel!"* Startled, I looked around. I had caught some crazy vibe of Donyel. Either I was getting stronger or he was awfully close.

I knew it would be simple to find him. I could spare everyone if I just went on my own.

"Do you really think you can win?" another voice whispered. I stopped. I discerned that this wasn't my own mind. *"You just discovered your powers. You can not fight a being that knows more about you than you know about yourself!"*

Donyel must have sent a spirit after me. I focused to find her. I closed my eyes.

"Reveal yourself" I said out loud and immediately I saw her up in tree. I opened my eyes and thought of my plan of action. I remembered that Anthony said that this was spiritual warfare and that one person could chase a thousand demons. Well, this was just one so surely she would be no match.

"In the name of Jesus, I bind your powers. Come down from that tree," I said pointing up and I saw her fall down to the ground struggling as if some invisible chain had wrapped her up. I think my powers had forced her to materialize because she constantly tried to make herself disappear like a chameleon against the tree until I grabbed her by the throat.

"Please, daughter of Donyel, have mercy on me," she said.

"I am not his. What is your name?"

"Sorra, a demon of doubt." I squeezed a little harder and she gagged slightly.

"Did Donyel send you? Are there more? What were you trying to do, kill me?"

Sorra shook her head and tried to speak, but my grip was too tight on her cold lifeless throat. I didn't know if I could actually kill her but then maybe it was just her presence making me doubt, so I tried anyway.

"Please . . . I can't speak." I loosened my grip. "Donyel sent us to weaken you. I was not to kill you."

"Us? There are more? Where are they?" I looked around.

She shook her head some more. "Your friends."

I let go of her throat and shook my head in disbelief. This is what I didn't want to happen. She disappeared when I let her go and I ran as quickly as I could to Anthony's room. I had to warn him that he was under attack. I made it to his room and I could hear that it sounded like he was talking to himself. I knocked on his door. There was no answer. I knocked again and I heard the door slowly open. Anthony was sweating like he had been running and his eyes were red.

I gave him a hug. "I'm so glad you're all right."

"Why wouldn't I be?" he said and I got an eerie feeling that we were not alone in the room. I didn't want it to be obvious though. The room was dark and his books were scattered all over.

"I just was . . . um are you okay?" Anthony nodded and I followed him into the room and I took him by the hand. "Anthony your hand is shaking."

"Is it?" He rubbed his hands together trying to warm them up.

"Please, talk to me," I requested.

"Andrea. I don't know. I've been thinking that maybe we should just go. Maybe we should transfer somewhere else where he can't find us. He killed Dewayne and Valerie is probably dead . . ."

"She isn't dead. I know it." I stopped him. I was trying to figure what spirit was in the room. It was strong and very overwhelming and whatever it was it was blocking a lot of my ability to sense what was wrong with Anthony.

"Anthony, this is so unlike you."

"What are you talking about?"

"Anthony, when I see you, I see a strong man of God."

"I'm not strong, I'm just like anybody else."

"No you're not. Remember that we can do this together. Remember that all we need is faith." I grabbed his
Bible and handed it to him. "God is going be with us every
step of the way and I'm going to be with you."

"Did your gifts tell you that?"

"I don't need gifts to tell me that. I can see that with my
own female intuition." He smiled and I felt some stronghold let go a bit. I took him by the hand again. "When I
first saw you, I saw a man of God who was bold enough to
start a Bible study on campus and stand up and preach
about the God he loved. I know that you're scared because a lot of what you know is being tested, but you can't
run. You have to face your fears." When I said the word
fear I saw a spirit in armor fade in and out in the mirror. I
attempted to not look alarmed.

"Really? You know what I saw when I saw you?"

I blushed when he asked me. "What did you see?"

"I saw a woman who was different, special, and set apart.
I really didn't know to what extent, but you've opened a
world up to me that has made me become even closer to
God." He took his hand and rubbed my hair and it felt
good. "If you hadn't fallen into my life, I would be just like
any other guy. But now I see there's so much more. I won't
leave you to fight this alone." He looked me in the eyes so
sensitively. I was smitten by his words and I could feel his
heart opening up to me like a flower blooming in the sun
and then I saw him with his sword raised as if he was going
to strike Anthony in the back.

"Demon!" I yelled and I pushed Anthony out of the way.
I raised my hands and a shield orbed me as the sword
came down. Anthony was on the floor trying to figure out
what was going on.

"Show yourself spirit of fear!" I yelled and the demon
materialized in the room. He was a big one, as tall as the
ceiling.

"What's going on?" Anthony yelled.

"Donyel sent these demons after us" I pushed the demon back with all my might and he hit the wall. The impact made several pictures fall. "This one was sent to fill your with fear."

Anthony grabbed my hand and pointed at the spirit. "I bind your powers demon in the name of Jesus and send you back to the pits of hell where you belong!"

The demon struggled like Sorra and fell to the floor as dark shadows consumed him into nothing, "Nooo!" he yelled.

Both Anthony and I were breathing hard and I laid my head on his shoulder.

"How did you know?" Anthony asked me.

"A spirit attacked me. At first I had a hard time figuring out that there was one here with you, but as you began talking I sensed the fear and then it just let go of you."

"I guess it was something inside of me that conquered the feeling." He looked off and I felt that he meant something more but he didn't want to say.

"Oh no." I had forgotten about Karen. "We need to get back to my room fast."

"Karen. Is she sleep?" Anthony asked. "She's sure to be more vulnerable in her sleep." Anthony grabbed his stuff and prepared to walk out and I followed him into the hall.

His mind was still elsewhere, so I took the nerve to ask him, "Anthony what do you think made the fear leave you? I mean, I didn't do anything at all and I couldn't sense anything from you, but all of a sudden I felt his hold fall off you."

"You did have something to do with it," he said walking down the hall.

"What? Tell me," I asked him and he looked at me and smiled. He looked at me so deeply that my heart jumped a little at the way he stared.

He turned and kept walking. "We need to help Karen. I will talk to you about it later."

Now he was frustrating me and I wished I had more control of my gifts to just read his soul. "Anthony, you're being stubborn."

He turned around and looked at me and smiled. "Read 1 John 4:18 and maybe that will clear it up."

"You're always telling me a scripture to read. Can I just get a straight answer from you without—"

He put his finger on my lips, "Shh . . . We have to help Karen. We'll discuss this later." He smirked. Sometimes Anthony Turner makes me so mad.

CHAPTER THIRTY-SIX

The demon, Sorra, materialized back in the house before Donyel gasping for air and bowing. "Lord Donyel. She knows!"

Donyel turned around slowly and walked over to Sorra, allowing his long cape-like over coat to drape around her as he knelt to her level to look into her eyes. "What are you talking about?"

"Andrea, she is far too strong. I . . ." Sorra stumbled on her words as Donyel's eyes filled with anger and his long nail on his index finger pressed against her cheek. "I tried to stop her but she knew I was there. She held and bound me and I couldn't even move."

"Did you go to help the others?"

"No, I thought . . ."

"You didn't think." He grabbed her neck as quickly as Andrea had grabbed her and he squeezed even tighter. "Now I am sure she has gone to warn her friends and now my plan is useless" Her demon skin began tearing and bleeding its dark black blood as her bones began snapping and cracking.

She gagged for air and pulled at his shirt for mercy as her eyes bulged from their sockets. "P-please, L-lord Dony . . ."

"My plan is now destroyed and so are you. The Lord giveth you a body . . ." He ripped his claw-like fingers into her neck and ripped her head off as if she was a doll, ". . . and the Lord taketh away." He stood up and kicked the shaking body to the middle of the floor and set it ablaze with the way of his hand. Sorra's screams could be heard as her demonic spirit was thrown back into the demon realm. Donyel wiped the dark demon blood off and walked over the burnt ashes with no more concern than if it were the ashes of some burnt newspaper. He walked downstairs to find Valerie barely conscious and Tamela and Philip dozing off to sleep as well. He jumped over the remaining flight of stairs in anger and landed in front of Philip like a panther. Philip practically flipped back in his chair when he saw Donyel ready to pounce on him. He popped Tamela in the shoulder to wake her up and she fell on the floor when she saw Donyel's blazing eyes.

"Father!" Philip bowed and held Tamela down to make sure she reverenced his presence. "Forgive us. We were tired, but we won't let it happen again."

Donyel curbed his anger and stood upright, turning to Valerie. "Andrea will be here shortly. I can sense her. She has already, at this moment, rescued her friends." He closed his eyes and licked his lips. His hair was like small tentacles wrapping around his shoulders and face as he concentrated on his subject.

"Is that Donyel?" Tamela whispered, ". . . oh my God. What is he doing?" Philip covered her mouth to shut her up and nodded to answer her questions. She could see the fear in his eyes. He opened his eyes and placed his gaze on Valerie who was tired and attempting to keep her sanity.

"Dear child," Donyel whispered in her ear, "why do you resist so much?"

"Andrea will stop you," Valerie weakly murmured.

"Andrea is mine as well."

"No, she isn't. She's different than you. I can see that and you can't control her."

"Really, and what makes you so sure?" Donyel asked with a raised eye brow.

Valerie, fatigued to the point where she could barely hold her head up, looked at Donyel square in the eyes with absolutely no fear. "She loves the Lord, the one true God, and he will save her from you."

Donyel stepped back and composed himself. His anger burned deep when she told him this, but he managed to hold his menacing smile on his face. "Don't fall asleep again," he said to Philip, "you will not be warned again." And Donyel disappeared in an orb of light.

Tamela picked herself up from the floor and went to Valerie's side. "Don't worry, Valerie, soon we will free you from Andrea's spell. It's just a matter of time."

"Tamela, please let me go," Valerie whimpered.

"Valerie, this is for your own good." She tightened the roped around Valerie's wrist. Her hands had already turned colors from the bruises. Valerie cried in agony. "Valerie, now don't make a scene. You don't understand the full picture."

"No, you don't understand. Tamela, I've seen visions. I've seen who Donyel is. He is not anything good; you have to believe me."

Tamela stopped and looked Valerie in the eyes, then looked off. "It seems you are serious, but you have to trust me. Andrea is evil and you have these demon tricking . . ."

"No, Philip is evil! He's the one you should watch out for! He's a Nephilim, Can't you see—"

Philip snatched Tamela away from in front of Valerie and slapped Valerie across the face, "Shut up, devil!"

"Philip, please! Don't hurt her," Tamela cried. Philip pulled Tamela away to the side.

"What is this Nephilim that you two keep talking about?" Tamela asked.

Philip looked Tamela in her eyes. "Tamela I need you to trust me now."

"Philip, I trust you," she said back to him. Her hands were shaking and Tamela was unsure of what to think. She was at a very confusing point. She looked into Philip's beautiful eyes wanting so much to believe him, but she kept hearing what Valerie was saying to her in her head. Valerie's head was bowed over all bruised and now she had witnessed the infamous Donyel and it only proved what Philip was saying was true. She thought to herself that Valerie had changed so much and it could be nothing but the works of some demon. She wanted to help her and she felt that she could do it. She could do it with Philip. She struggled to convince herself that he was telling her the truth and the way he looked at her, so lovingly, helped. She had slept with him so many times and she was so glad that finally he could see the truth and he needed her. She didn't want to lose that. She didn't want to lose this man because he needed her and it didn't matter that she had this doubt in her mind; she would overcome it.

Valerie whimpered slightly, looking in Tamela's direction, but Tamela turned her head and hugged Philip around the neck. Her decision was made. No matter what, she would follow Philip and what he said because deep in her heart she knew he loved her. Once Andrea was out of the way they could be a normal couple.

"I trust you, Philip. I love you," she whispered and rested her head on his chest.

"Yeah," Philip placed the gun back in her hand. "keep watch over by the window."

Tamela walked over to the window and sighed. "How the heck are they gonna find us way out here?"

"Oh they'll find us, trust me," Philip said, pulling out a blade from his pocket and sharpening it. Tamela peeked out the curtains; it was a clear night. Suddenly, the wind began to pick up and a wild orb of light began forming outside in the front yard like the one Donyel disappeared in.

"What the . . ." Tamela said.

Philip noticed Tamela's distraction and went to the window to see what the issue was. Three figures materialized from the glowing orb of light. "Oh no, they're here!"

CHAPTER THIRTY-SEVEN

Anthony and I made it back to my room to check on Karen. I sensed some of the same things I felt in Anthony's room. It was a feeling of heaviness all through the room and the lights were off.

"I don't feel right in my spirit. Something is wrong in here," Anthony said, and I nodded in agreement.

"Karen, baby, you in here?" I asked and I heard her sniffle in the corner.

"Go away!" she yelled. I looked at Anthony and he looked at me. He clicked the light on and saw that Karen was hunched over in the corner hugging a picture frame. *I sensed all this depression weighing the whole room down but I couldn't pinpoint it's origin.*

I observed Karen carefully and walked over to her. "Karen, baby, I know you're down."

"Really?" she yelled back, "You understand me? You don't understand me, Andrea. Have you ever really loved someone so much and then lost them? Have you ever had that person love you so much and for no reason, they're just snatched from you? Can you explain to me, Andrea, why I

can still hear Dewayne, I can still feel him, I can still smell
him and how scared I am that I'm going to forget? No! I
don't think you can!"

A tear came to my eye when I thought about how
deeply Karen's love was for Dewayne and my empathic
powers only intensified the weight of the emotion double
time.

Anthony eased up to Karen and knelt beside her. "I
know you're upset but beating up Andrea isn't going to
help." He placed his hand on hers gently. "I loved Dewayne as well. Karen, you're right, he was stolen from us.
It's not fair. It's not even human. We can't go to the police, we can't go to FBI. Whatever happened was spiritual
and we have to go to God. Together, with the Lord, we can
at least stop whatever did this to Dewayne from happening
to someone else." His voice was so rational and I admired
how he was so open with his feelings.

"I'm scared, Anthony," Karen cried, hugging the picture even tighter. "I don't think I can do this. I just miss
him . . ." She tried hard to hold the tears in, but they continued to fall, "I miss him so much. It's like someone has
just ripped my heart out."

Anthony hugged her. "I know, Karen. I pray that God
be your strength in the name of Jesus." He rubbed her
back and motioned for me to come over. I slowly stepped
over not sure what to do.

"Karen, we've all been under attack," Anthony said,
"and I am discerning a spirit of depression attacking you.
But it's got a stronghold on you and you need to denounce
it right now." He took my hand and touched Karen's shoulder. I slowly placed my hand on Karen's shoulder. I saw
him in a vision . . . the last demon. He wore a hood and he
wedged deep in her soul. He was focusing hard, emitting
this dark light that seemed to be weakening the light of
Karen's soul.

I removed my hand. "Avraxius . . ."

"What?" Anthony asked.

"You're right, A spirit of depression, his name is Avraxius."

"How do you know?"

"I don't know how. I just do," I told him. I placed my hand back on Karen's shoulder. She kept weeping unable to really make words now.

Anthony led the prayer. "We bind up Avraxius, your spirit of depression. We bind you up and your powers in the name of Jesus." Karen cried a little bit harder and I hugged her. I didn't know what to do. All these powers and I didn't know how to make her feel better.

"Help her Jesus. Please," I whispered, because I didn't know how to help her. I couldn't help myself and I had to put faith that He could work it out. I had to have faith that He could help us defeat the demons and Donyel.

"Come on, Karen, denounce that spirit." Anthony encouraged.

"I denounce you evil spirit in the name of Jesus." Karen said through her tears.

"They are acting like you don't have a right to mourn! What are you praying about? They don't understand what you are going through. You are all alone." I could hear Avraxius talking in her head. She wept some more.

"Don't listen to that spirit, Karen. We love you," I told her and she looked up. "Karen, I love you. Dewayne was so special and I promise you, girl, we are going to get that devil that killed him. Don't give up on us. We are all sad but we need to get through this together and we are not going to let depression take you over!" There was so much passion in my voice that I couldn't hold back my tears. I could feel this warmth in the midst of us and I could feel the spirit's grip loosening. I hugged her. "I love you, girl. . . . Jesus loves you. The joy of the Lord is your strength."

I could feel her strength returning and it seemed to clear the room of the heaviness.

"Avraxius you are bound in the name of Jesus." Anthony prayed. "we cast you out now!"

"No!" I heard it yell as it too was banished into the demon realm.

Karen wiped the tears from her face. "Thanks, guys, for praying for me. I feel a lot better."

Anthony sighed a breath of relief and looked over at me. I smiled and patted his hand. "You ready to do this?"

"As ready as I ever will be." Karen stood up and laid the picture of Dewayne down on the desk. I stood up and gave her another hug.

"Let's get that devil." Karen said with more strength in her voice.

"We will, Karen, we will," I told her rubbing her back. Anthony stood up and joined the hug and then pulled away.

"So, how do we find him? I guess that's where you come in, Andrea," he said looking at me again. I knew that I could find him if I concentrated, but I had never took hitchhikers along for the ride with me.

"Yeah, I can find him. I'll have to use my powers and I've never taken anybody with me before. I don't even know if I can."

"Well, maybe you can just detect him and we'll drive to where he is," Karen suggested.

I closed my eyes and tried to get a feel for Donyel. "No, he's way too far from here. If we drove it might take us awhile."

"So how are we going to get there?" Karen asked.

"I've teleported a couple of times on my own. I think I can take all of us to Donyel without a problem."

"You *think?*" Karen interjected, not feeling so cool about my plan. "I don't want to accidentally end up somewhere in Timbuktu because you couldn't hold all of us. I'm not fat, but I'm not as small as I used to be.

"Maybe we should just trust Andrea," Anthony said, touching Karen's shoulder. "Besides, if we drove, it may take way too long and Lord knows what they might do to Valerie if they get impatient."

"But guys, what if this is a trap for all of us? What if Valerie is a part of this?" She gestured with her hands to get her point across. "Have we forgotten that Valerie is a witch like Tamela?"

"At first, I didn't trust Valerie either, but as I've gotten to know who she is, I realize that she doesn't understand the danger in what she does. That doesn't make her evil, it just means she's trying to find her way." Anthony said to Karen then he glanced at me. "I don't think she has anything to do with this."

"I agree with Anthony. Look, we are wasting time. Are we going or aren't we?" I said, taking charge. Anthony looked over at Karen with some sort of silent communication with his eyes and she nodded, placing her hand in the middle. I placed mine on Karen's and Anthony placed his hand on mine.

"Let's do this!" Anthony said.

"Hold on everybody," I said as we all huddled up, linking up our arms like a chain. I closed my eyes and concentrated and pictured Donyel. "Take us to . . ." A warm wind surrounded us and I heard Karen squeal a bit.

"It's okay, we got you," Anthony reassured her. The wind in the room picked up some more, blowing papers around and pulling even the sheets off the bed.

"Take us to Donyel!" The wind roared around us and all I saw was light surrounding us. It was so bright that I had to close my eyes and then I no longer felt my feet on the ground. I felt Karen grip me even tighter when we were no longer on the ground. I couldn't see anything, but I could feel wind passing over my face at an incredible speed. I think that Anthony was praying to himself. He may have been yelling but it sounded like a small whisper through the roar of the wind.

Finally, everything was calm. The light subsided and the wind ceased. When I opened my eyes we were all standing outside in a large field.

"Where are we?" Karen asked.

Anthony looked around and over at all the trees trying to get a clue. "I have no idea," he said. In front of us was a large condemned mansion. It appeared to have been set on fire.

"Oh my God," I said.

"What?" Anthony asked concerned.

"We're back in Heaven."

"Heaven?" Karen said, looking around. "Not at all what I imagined."

"No, we're in Heaven, Texas. "This is the old plantation that Donyel took over years ago. This old plantation is on the outskirts of Heaven. Not too many people come to this side." I walked through the tall weeds up to the house. Karen squealed again.

"What is it?" Anthony asked.

"I saw something in the window. Something was looking out at us," she answered.

"Where?" I asked Karen and she pointed to the front door. "Looks like they're waiting for us." I said, looking at Anthony.

"What are we thinking?" Karen said and stood between us and the mansion. "They are waiting for us! We don't even have a gun."

"The weapons of our warfare are not carnal, but . . ." Anthony started.

"Anthony!" she said pointing at him sternly. "this is not

Bible study! This is an angel. A real life killing angel . . . in that house! How are we going to kill it?"

"We can't kill an angel, it's immortal," I said dryly. "Maybe she's right. Maybe you guys should stay behind and I go in alone."

Anthony grabbed my arm tightly. "I'm not letting you go in there by yourself. I'm not going to lose you." His words hit my heart and I really didn't know what to say. His eyes were so serious and I felt that he would do anything to make sure I was safe. But in the same respect, I didn't want to see him hurt on my account.

"Anthony, listen to me," I pulled my arm away. "It's me he wants."

"Yes, but I see it like this. He may not be able to die, but he was mortal enough to have children and he may be mortal enough to get hurt. He has to have some vulnerability when he's manifested in human form."

"Nice hypothesis. But if you're wrong, then what?"

"I don't know." Anthony shrugged his shoulders. "I don't know anymore than you do, but I know that we can get him if we stick together."

"And I know that he won't kill you. He's not going to do anything that might draw attention to himself to the angels of the Lord. But who knows what Philip may do? Anthony, I love you and I don't want you to get hurt because of me. I will go in and find Donyel and you guys go in and get Valerie and high tail out of here back to town. I won't be alone. I have God's angels on my side."

"What did you say?" Anthony asked.

"I said that I have God's angels on my side."

"No, you said that," he searched my eyes, ". . . you love me?"

I looked around and Karen raised her eyebrow at me. "Well, I mean, I don't . . ."

"I love you too," he said. It made me do a double take.

"You can't love me, Anthony. It's not good for you."

He touched my lips to quiet them. "There's nothing you can say that's going to stop how I feel about you and how I see you. I can't explain why, Andrea. As crazy as things have been, I wish I could've realized this sooner. But I don't know what's going to happen in there. I've lost one friend already, and I made you a promise to help you through this." I swallowed and I felt my heart in my stomach. Anthony was very stubborn indeed and I wished that I could've turned back time and met him at the beginning. If anything happened to Anthony, I wouldn't be able to forgive myself.

"Guys?" Karen snapped her fingers and looked at Anthony. "Hormones later. I like Andrea's plan, Anthony. She has way more power than we can shake a stick at. He's not going to hurt her either." Karen tried to be a voice of reason, but Anthony wasn't hearing it and was beginning to frustrate me.

He never stopped searching my eyes. "I'm not going to let you go by yourself."

"Try and stop me." I closed my eyes and teleported into the house.

"Andrea!" he yelled. "I can't believe she did that." He ran through the field up to the rickety porch.

Karen trailed behind him. "Anthony, wait for me!"

CHAPTER THIRTY-EIGHT

"Father," Philip said, breathing hard in the doorway. "They're here! Tamela is down stairs waiting but I saw Andrea disappear. They must know that we're plotting against them."

Donyel sat in a larger old leather throne-like chair. His legs were crossed like a gentleman and he touched his long fingers together like he was in prayer. He looked completely sinister in that burgundy chair contrasting his white skin. "And you're telling me because . . ."

Philip appeared confused. "Because, well I've come to warn you."

"I don't need your help, Philip. You're the one who needs the help." Donyel sighed, stood, and turned away from Philip back at the window.

Philip dropped his head. "Why do you do that to me?"

"Why do I do what?"

"Constantly, reject me. I've done nothing but obey you endlessly even if it meant my own soul, and still it's never enough."

"Shut your whining, Philip. You dare defy me?"

"No, I don't. That's not my intension at all." He walked bravely to Donyel and laid his head against his back tugging gently on his shoulders. "But I love you. You are my father. I am your son. I don't care that you're an angel or what you've done in the past. I just want to please you and make you happy, but every time I try, you walk away. Is there nothing good I can do for you? All my life I have wanted you there in my life. I prayed to God that He bring you to me." Donyel's anger rose at the mentioned of God. "and as I grew older I cursed God for taking you away from me. Then you came back to me. You found me. Father, I try so hard because I just want to be like . . ."

". . . like me?" Donyel said and turned around taking Philip by the face. His entire hand engulfed Philip's face. There was fear all in Philip's eyes. "Philip, you are not like me. You are not me. You . . . are a mistake. You are not in my likeness. You are weak. What can you do for me? So many times I have wished to kill you and start over."

Donyel's words were cold, lifeless and uncompassionate. He couldn't see himself in his son but in actuality, Philip was more like Donyel than he could realize. Philip had Donyel's pain and weakness and because of that, Donyel despised him.

"Don't say that, please." Philip eyes watered.

"Can you create the legacy that I deserve?"

"I can if you help me!" Philip said, bowing to his father's feet and holding his hand like Donyel was the pope. Donyel's ego was magnified by the gesture and he softened his words to his son. "You will redeem yourself when you give me your son, a son from Andrea. Andrea has the power. Create me a legacy and a nation that will be greater than the children of God. You will be my Abraham and just as he was willing to give his son to his God, are you willing to give yours to me?"

A tear dropped from Philip's eye. "I am."

Donyel lifted Philip to his feet and wiped his face and examined the tear as if it were some foreign substance. "Still so human. But even I, your god, am merciful. I will give you power to deceive your adversary." He touched Philip's forehead anointing him with a taste of his power. "But be aware, humans are not meant to have such gifts, and this power can destroy what little bit of your soul you have."

"My soul is yours."

"So be it." And he continued to bless his son. He gripped his head and Philip began to convulse and shake. His once beautiful eyes darkened in color and even his hair lost it's luster and curl. Philip fell to the floor from his grip, shaking, unable to control his nerves. Donyel watched the spectacle and finally raised his palm over Philip's body and he stopped.

"Now go, make me proud, son. Your adversary awaits you," Donyel said, smirking slightly at the work he had done. Philip stood silently and walked out the room with no expression on his face.

Downstairs in the front room, Anthony and Karen peeked in the front door. Karen had grabbed an old splintery broom to use as a weapon. "Ow, splinter."

"I don't know what you expect to do with that broom. Sweep someone to death?" Anthony whispered. Karen wasn't in the mood for jokes and merely rolled her eyes while looking down at her hurt finger.

The floor creaked as they walked around and Karen felt wary about going any further. "Who ever was looking through the window is probably still in here, Anthony," she whispered to him.

"Yeah, that is if you actually saw someone. What if it was the wind?"

"It wasn't the wind. I know I saw someone peeking out the window."

"Well, we need to find Andrea and Valerie, so I don't have time to be scared," Anthony said, looking around at the house. It was dark, so he turned on the flashlight that he had brought with him. The ceilings were high and there were open holes where it appeared walls used to exist. There were random pieces of furniture here and there— not functional enough to be used for anything other than fire wood.

Far on the other end of the room there was a large fire place and over it a singed painting too distorted to describe. Anthony flashed his light over it.

"This place is humungous. It may take us all night to find them," Karen said.

"Yeah," Anthony flashed his light at the stairway. "My guess is that we should explore the upstairs." The stairwell coiled and curled up against the wall to the next level. From the bottom, Anthony looked and could see at least three levels and maybe an attic. He sighed and ran up the first flight.

Karen lagged behind. "Wait up!" But before she could get out the words, good Anthony's foot rammed straight through a weak step and he got his foot caught.

"Ah!" he yelled. Karen was coming up to help him but he waved her to stop. "Hold on, these steps aren't sturdy. We don't need any more weight."

"Weight? What do you mean?"

"I don't mean anything, Karen." Anthony looked at her sarcastically and pulled his foot a little bit harder, but the old wood couldn't hold and the entire three steps supporting him fell in, taking Anthony down with them.

"Anthony!" Karen yelled and she ran up the steps holding the banister. She looked down in the hole and it went deep. It was dark and she couldn't hear anything. She saw the flashlight at the bottom and realized that Anthony had fallen at least fifteen feet down.

"Oh God!" She looked around for something to go down into the hole. It appeared that he had fallen into some type of cellar. She thought to herself that he could be dead down there from that steep fall. It was so dark that she couldn't tell. She ran back down the steps. The wall following underneath the stairwell had a door. She tried opening it but it wouldn't budge.

"Anthony, don't worry, I'm going to find a way in!" she yelled at the door. She wasn't thinking to lower her voice. She didn't care that someone might be watching her— and, in fact, there was. Deep in the shadows someone was following her every move. Karen slammed at the door with the broom but it simply broke in half. She threw it down and searched for something else.

She ran into a corner room that resembled an office. There was a large dusty desk and old musty books all around the room. It was dark and only the moonlight coming in through the broken windows lit the room. She opened the closets, looking for a bat, an axe, a gun—anything she could use to get that door open. Rats scattered from the corners and Karen jumped and screamed.

"Come on, Karen," she said to herself, "get yourself together." She took a breath and continued to search in the darkness. She wished to herself that she had that flashlight. She stopped moving when she heard the floor outside the door creak. It wasn't like a mouse. It was like someone was walking.

"Andrea?" she whispered, "Is that you?" She walked back behind the desk slowly and felt around for a weapon when she didn't get a response. She thought of the person she saw in the window. "Hello? Is anybody there?" This time she didn't wait, she just started rummaging through the drawers. Her heart was beating so hard she could feel it in her throat. She grabbed an old rusty letter opener out of the top drawer.

"Hold it right there," a voice ordered.

"Tamela?" Karen said, pointing the letter opener. "Where is Valerie?"

Tamela inched into the room allowing the gun she was holding to shine in the moonlight. "Maybe you should be worried about yourself."

CHAPTER THIRTY-NINE

Darkness. Anthony couldn't see anything when he opened his eyes. He thought that maybe his eyes were still closed. A rat ran across his leg and he jumped up. A distinct pain was in his back and on the side of his leg. Shattered wood was around him everywhere and the remains of crushed boxes that must have broken his fall laid open spilling their contents. He looked around and all he could see was his flashlight, which had rolled over to the side of what seemed to be a basement. He stood up and walked over to the flashlight.

"Karen!" he yelled up through the hole he fell through, squinting his eyes to see better. He had not only fallen through the stairway on the main floor, but also the one leading down into the basement meaning he was going to need some help getting out.

"Andrea! Where are you?" He thought that teleporting would be pretty handy. It smelled awful down in that basement; like something had died. He coughed, and to his surprise, he noticed several bottles of wine.

"Wow, I'm sure these are worth some money now," he

said prying one out of its cubby hole. He dusted it off and looked at the date. He dropped it though when he heard something in the darkness stirring. He limped around, following the wall of wine trying to shine his flashlight as far as he could. The darkness seemed endless.

"Andrea," he whispered. He flashed his light to a corner and saw something run away from the light back into the shadow. "Who's there?" He grabbed a slab of wood from the ground and limped slowly to the shadowing area. He kept hearing something running around the room. It wasn't an animal—at least he hoped it wasn't. He tried flashing his light on it but it was too fast. Something touched his shoulder, "Andrea!" he said, jumping back and flashing his light on her face. "You scared the crap out of me!"

"I'm sorry," Andrea said. "I thought you were Donyel or somebody. Where is everybody else?"

"I don't know. I fell through this hole and must have been knocked out for awhile. I guess Karen is up on the main floor." He shined his light back at the gapping hole above them. "How did you know I was down here?"

"I heard you, silly. Oh, you're limping. Are you hurt?" She knelt down and rubbed his thigh, looking back up at him.

"Uh yeah, um, maybe we should find Karen. Can you get me out of here?" Anthony said, feeling slightly uncomfortable that her hand was rubbing areas of his thigh that weren't hurt.

"I will. I just want to make sure." She ripped his pants leg open, exposing his skin. "Anthony, you are hurt. You're going to need a doctor it seems."

"I'll be okay. Did you find Valerie?"

"Shhh. We'll find them later. Now let me worry about you." She kissed his thigh seductively. "Does that feel better?"

Anthony inched back because he felt she was going too far. "Andrea, what's wrong with you?" She backed him against the wall and there wasn't much more he could do than stare at her because of her strength.

"There's nothing wrong with me." She ripped open his shirt and kissed his chest, "You do like me don't you?" she smiled and rubbed his face, pulling the wood out of his hand and trying to get hold of the flashlight in his other hand.

Anthony pulled away and limped away from her. "I thought we established that outside, but uhh, this isn't the time or the place for this. Andrea, are you okay? Did Donyel possess you or something?" He flashed the light in her face.

"Get that light out of my face!" She turned away. Anthony fixed the light so it wasn't directly on her. "I know you want me. Why do you keep denying it, Anthony?"

"We need to focus here."

She walked up to him and rubbed his face. "I am focused, Anthony. I'm focused on exactly what I want. But do you know what you want?" She kissed him hard, ferociously knocking him to the ground. It felt good for the moment but Anthony gathered his wits and pushed her off.

"What is the matter with you? We can't do this!" Anthony said, lifting himself to his knees.

Andrea propped herself up on her elbows and knees with her hair covering her face. She resembled a lion getting ready to pounce. "What's the matter with me?" She laughed, tilting her head to the side. "What's the matter with you? It seems you're the confused one. Are you gay or something?"

"What? No!" Anthony said offended.

"Yeah, little Christian boy can't handle a real woman." She stood up, fixed her hair and adjusted her shirt. "Especially a girl like Andrea. Maybe . . . you would rather have . . ." right before Anthony's eyes Andrea shape-shifted into Philip, ". . . a guy instead."

Anthony screamed and fell backwards, scooting as fast as he could and shining his flashlight in Philip's face.

"I told you once, get that darn light out my face!" Philip roared and jumped at Anthony. It seemed his eyes were sensitive to the light and Anthony could see how dark his eyes had become. Philip jumped on top of Anthony, attempting to choke him, but Anthony took the flashlight and popped him on the side of his head. Philip fell to the side and Anthony crawled up to the wall and pulled himself to his feet.

"Aw, come on, Anthony. Do you think you're more man than me?"

"You're sick."

"Andrea is mine, all mine. I can sense that you like her, but I won't let you have her not now—not ever," Philip whispered getting back to his feet.

"You're not going to have Andrea. You have to get through me first." Anthony searched for that slab of wood he had before. Just as he found it, Philip grabbed him around the neck and started choking him.

"I am the son of an angel," he whispered in his ear. "You are nothing but mud. You are weak." Anthony grabbed at Philip's strong grip around his neck. "Andrea and I are one in the same and you will not stand in the way!" He slammed Anthony's head against the bottles of wine and the wine spilled against his face.

"Thirsty, Anthony? This is my blood . . . do this in remembrance of me!" Philip mocked. He threw Anthony's weak body over to the ground. "This is my body," he kicked Anthony in the stomach, "which is broken for you." Anthony hunched over and attempted to get up. Blood poured down his forehead. "Where's your God, Anthony? You going to pray yourself out of this one?" Philip taunted and walked in front of Anthony who was trying to crawl away the best he could.

"Kiss the foot of your new lord!" Philip said, placing his foot against Anthony's chin, "Who knows, I may spare you."

"You are not God and neither is Donyel. He is an angel and Jesus is Lord and no matter what you do you can never defeat the spirit he's given me," Anthony weakly said. Philip pushed his face to the ground with his foot and Anthony struggled against Philip but by this time he was too hurt to do much.

"Time for you to die, Anthony Turner."

CHAPTER FORTY

I found myself inside the house somewhere at the top of a stairway when I teleported away from Anthony and Karen. I felt bad about leaving them like that, but I figured that I could find Donyel quicker, and if we had it out, he would be too concerned with me to worry about them. I heard someone arguing down the hall so I quietly tiptoed to the door. It was open and I could tell now that it was Philip yelling at Donyel. It sounded pretty heated and I wondered what was going to happen. I sat silently and waited to see what would transpire. Then everything was silent. My curiosity was getting the best of me and I couldn't resist any longer. Across the hall was a broken warped mirror so I grabbed a piece and sat back against the wall. I used the piece of mirror to see the room without peeking my head in.

I saw Donyel laying his hand on Philip's head like he was praying for him, "Now go, make me proud, son. Your adversary awaits you," Donyel said.

I pulled my arm back and tip-toed a little bit further down the hall hiding behind the thick drapery on the window. I peeked out only a little to see Philip walk by. His eyes were dark as an eclipse and his face was lifeless. I held my breath because he stopped for a moment. I hoped he hadn't sensed me in my hiding place. He looked back and then around and continued down the stairs. I thought that Anthony and Karen would probably run into him eventually, but if I handled Donyel, then maybe I could take away Philip's new power.

I walked back to the room. "A blessing from a devil. There's got to be a string attached," I said in the doorway at Donyel.

Donyel was sitting in his chair smiling at me with his long finger on the temple of his forehead. "There always is. I see you have come back to me."

"To free my friend, Valerie."

"In exchange for you of course."

"Unlike Philip, I don't make deals with the devil. You always lose," I said back. Donyel laughed heartily impressed at my wit and stood up clapping.

"That's right! I've always liked you for this reason right here. So much spirit." He grinned like a proud father would.

"This house. This is the mansion you stole so many years ago. This is the plantation. It all started here in Heaven.

"My own personal war in Heaven. You're so smart too," he said, staring directly at me. All these secrets of his past—of my past were slowly revealing.

"It's no accident that I was adopted by a family and brought here to this town is it? You wanted me to be close so you could watch me; didn't you?" I yelled at him, realizing how scary my life really was.

He nodded and grabbed me gracefully, ballroom dancing across the room. "I will never leave you or forsake you." I pulled away. "Andrea, don't deny your legacy."

"You are not God. You are a rebellious angel and God is going to judge you for what you've done."

"And what about you? Do you think you'll escape judgment, my daughter? Slowly your spirit will hatch from that flesh into a demon. Then what are you going to do? Your children will be like me as well and their children. Quit resisting."

"I am not like you." I raised my hand at him. "My children will not be like you. I don't know what is going to happen to me, but what I do know is that as long as I am alive, I will resist everything you do until you are—"

"What? Bound? It's been done before and I will get out again. I know you better than you know yourself. I've been planning how I could reveal myself to you. I've been waiting and preserving you for my will."

"I'm only under God's will."

"Oh you're under mine too." Donyel grinned and tilted his head. "What does the Bible say? I would want to do good but evil is ever present?" He stood there proudly. "I'm always there working you toward my pleasure."

"So you admit to being evil."

"Oh, Andrea, evil is such a harsh word. Is anything evil? There are different levels of good just as there are different levels of truth. We all do what we want for one reason or another. Why we do it isn't necessarily evil. Is it evil that I want my daughter to be with me?" I was disgusted at his analogy. I walked up to him face to face to let him see the contempt in my eyes. "A half-truth is still a lie and anything lesser than the goodness of God is not good enough. Anytime we as humans submit our will to someone, we lose our soul, human or angel. If we give our will to God, He has promised us life. What have you promised me? You can't give life. All you can do is kill. Why should I fear you? Satan comes as an angel of light. But that light isn't the true light. His light—your light, your goodness compared to God's goodness is darkness."

"Nice. Seems that little preacher boy has been getting

to you." He applauded and smirked. It angered me that he failed to take me seriously. "But, you're not human." It was like a punch to my gut.

"Andrea, what human can teleport? What human has super strength like you? What human can hear people's thoughts and know everything about them without them telling you? All these are gifts of the angels. You have that blood flowing through you."

"But I have a soul."

"But your spirit . . . belongs to me." I turned away from him to keep him from seeing my tears. I didn't want to admit his truth. I wasn't sure if it could be the truth.

"Faith is the substance of things hoped for, the evidence of things not seen," I said to myself.

"Nice. Faith. What's your point? I'm telling you the Bible is a contract made for the natural not the supernatural. Your spirit is under my blood and you can't separate your spirit from your soul."

I took a deep breath trying to shut his words out of my head, but I knew that a lot of his words were undeniable. I had to remember what the other angels told me though. I had to believe that what they said had precedence over Donyel's. Besides, he was in the wrong.

"I'm not here to argue with you." I wiped my face and turned around. "I'm here to stop you."

"Stop me from what? I have what I want right in front of me."

"You speak of me like you really know what love is, but you don't. Is love when you send demons to stop me and my friends or did you think I didn't know that was your doing? Gee, Donyel, you have a weird concept of love. Seems to me that Philip pulls on you pretty hard and all you can do is make him more demon than he is human. Is that what you want to do to me? Take away the rest of my humanity, like you did to Philip?"

"What has humanity done for you? Rejected you, that's about it. I don't see your human mother looking for you. But here, your angelic father, is before you with open arms."

I curled my nose like his words stunk. "You are no father. You have no idea what a real father is. My dad is the one who raised me. He is the one that was there when I hurt myself. He was the one teaching me right from wrong. He was the one teaching me about God and how to be more humane toward others. He loved me even if he knew I wasn't really his. His love for me made me his daughter and that love is greater than the blood bond you will ever have over me. And since you brought up my mother, I forgive my biological mother because maybe she is human too. Maybe she can't deal what you did to her and I can understand that but I'm not going to hate her for that. Because now I understand how much of a monster you are. But I won't allow you to destroy me or any child I have. It all ends here."

His smile disappeared as he felt the power of my words and he knew that my mind was made up. A slight anger filled his eyes. Then I heard a crash. His eyes shifted to the noise. "It seems that your friends need you more," he commented.

"Anthony!" I heard Karen yell downstairs. I sat in the midst of a decision. Handle Donyel or go find Karen and Anthony. Her screams downstairs seemed serious and I could hear rustling down there that sounded like someone banging against the wall.

"Gee, I wonder what could be happening down there? Perhaps my son is finishing off the last of your friends like he did Dewayne. No matter what, blood is thicker than water." Donyel faded away.

"This isn't over, Donyel," I said into the air. I stepped out of the room and through the dark hall. When I got to the steps the entire middle section of the steps had caved in. "Better not risk walking on those," I said to myself. I leaped over the banister and landed on the floor with the agility of a cat. I didn't even make a dent in the floor. I listened carefully for Karen. I saw a shadow across the room heading into another room. It didn't look like Karen so I quietly walked around to the room.

Whatever it was, it didn't notice my stealth movement through the shadows. I got to the office and peeked around the corner and saw Tamela holding Karen at gunpoint.

"Maybe you should be worried about yourself," she said in a dark tone.

"Come on Tamela, this isn't you. You're not a killer," Karen pleaded.

Tamela held the gun firmly and leaned in closer to Karen. Karen backed up accordingly. "Well, if you cooperate, then I wont have to add murder to my record. Now, where is Andrea?"

"I don't know. Look, I don't have time for this. Anthony is hurt and I need to help him. If you put that gun down maybe we can help him!" Karen said. I was shocked to hear what she said and wondered what happened to him. I hoped Philip hadn't gotten to him. I had to think of a way to get that gun away from Tamela.

"Maybe you don't understand," Tamela said. "You are going to do what I tell you. All that negative karma Anthony was creating has finally gotten back to him, blessed be."

"You're talking crazy, Tamela, What have you done to Valerie?"

"We have Valerie safely contained until we can purge her from the spell of your demon."

Karen looked perplexed for a second, "What demon?" I could tell Tamela was confused with a mass of lies.

"Andrea is the demon," Tamela said and I felt slightly hurt to hear those words. All my insecurities rose back in me.

"If anyone is a demon, it's you. You're allowing yourself to be used by the devil. Andrea is more of an angel than anything else."

Tamela screamed back and shook her gun at Karen. "You are a liar! Donyel is my guardian angel and he has come to deliver us from the evil that you and Anthony allowed to reside among us!"

I couldn't take anymore of it. Karen was so brave to stand up for me and I began to admire her even more. I swallowed my insecurity and stepped out of my hiding place, "Just messy! That's why I don't talk to girls on campus cause they always talk behind your back."

Tamela turned around and pointed the gun at me. "Andrea!" That's when Karen jumped over the desk, and with the blunt end of the letter opener, popped Tamela over the head knocking her to floor. The gun slid across the floor and I grabbed it and aimed it like I was one of Charlie's Angels.

Tamela, looking defeated, laid on the floor with a bit of blood dripping from her forehead. "Look I don't know where Valerie is okay!"

Karen, acting like a Japanese Sumo wrestler, sat on Tamela's back, snatching her head firmly by the hair threatening to pull it out at the roots if she attempted to make a false move.

"How is it that you still have your powers? I bound you!" Tamela screamed at me.

"You tried to put a hex on me?" Now I was really getting pissed. The gun was sort of empowering too.

"Oh but you forgot sweetheart," Karen said, pulling her hair, "remember in the lobby? I bound your powers in the name of Jesus. So whatever is bound on earth is bound in heaven." She pulled her hair again for the mere heck of it. Those words created a flashback of what the angels told me before.

"Karen, what's wrong with Anthony? Where is he?" I asked.

"He fell through the stairway," she replied.

My mouth dropped. "That big gigantic hole? Oh my God!"

"He's probably dead by now," Tamela commented.

I knelt down and grabbed her by the hair as well, pulling against Karen's grip. "You better hope for your sake that he's not. I may not be evil like Donyel, but I do have a bad side." I looked her sternly in the eyes. "*Sleep,*" I said telepathically and Tamela passed out immediately.

"Oh my God, is she dead?" Karen asked.

"No, just temporarily knocked out. She'll wake up shortly. Come on. We don't have any time to waste," I said, grabbing Karen by the hand. We ran into the front room and Karen led me to the door on the side of the stairs.

"I think that this door leads to the basement." Karen tested the knob one more time. I grabbed the knob and twisted it with all my strength until it gave way. Karen looked at me in awe for a second. "Go head, girl, with yo' bad self."

I smiled at Karen's comment and started walking downstairs. I could hear the echo of people talking and both Karen and I descended down the stairs slowly. I pulled her back when I noticed that some of these steps had been damaged as well—not as many as the stairs on the main floor, but enough that someone could hurt themselves and fall off the side.

"Look," Karen whispered and pointed at Philip standing over Anthony with a blade in his hand. Anthony looked seriously hurt and there was no more time to waste. I jumped down the flight of steps and charged behind Philip like a bull. He hit a wall of wine face first. Karen carefully ran down the shaky steps and grabbed Anthony.

"Took you girls long enough," Anthony grunted.

"Yeah, well, we didn't want to disturb your male bonding moment," Karen commented back.

"Don't remind me. I think I've been traumatized enough," Anthony said, looking slightly disgusted. "Get my flash light." He pointed across the room where he had dropped it. "Philip's eyes are super sensitive." Karen tried dragging Anthony to safety but he only became more upset.

"Look, don't worry about me!" he snapped. "Andrea needs your help!" Philip's strength had increased almost ten times from Donyel's blessing. He picked himself off the ground and roundhouse kicked me in the chest.

"Sorry to have to do that to you, little sister," he said, cracking his neck. "I don't want to hurt you, but I will if you give me no choice."

"I don't want anything to do with this morbid family." I jumped up and backhanded him. He budged only slightly. I hit him again and he smiled. It was starting to scare me. The gun was secured tightly in my belt loop under my shirt and I didn't want to shoot him, but I would it if meant stopping him.

Karen ran to my side and shined the flashlight in his eyes. Philip screamed and pulled back.

"What's wrong with him?" I asked.

"His eyes can see good in the dark it seems. He found me in the dark without a problem, but the same thing makes his eyes sensitive to light," Anthony said, limping over. In his hands he had a large plank of wood. "I didn't appreciate getting kicked in the stomach, Philip." Anthony slammed the wood across his back knocking him to the ground.

I grabbed Philip by the collar, "Where's Valerie, Philip?"

He smiled, "Donyel has her. You know the deal. You can't have her until you give up."

"Well, the way I see it, I have you now. So looks like without you he can't do much." The flashlight was flickering on and off. Philip looked tired but his strength was coming back quickly. He growled and pushed me back.

Karen caught me before I hit the ground. "What are we going to do? We can't just keep fighting him. He's just as strong as you and Anthony's flashlight is about out of juice," she said, slapping the flashlight.

"No he's not. He's not really strong at all," I said, thinking for a moment. "Whatever powers he has, he was given from Donyel. I need you guys to pray on my behalf."

"What?" Karen said. Anthony limped over and seemed to be impressed by my idea.

"You heard me. I need you to pray. Your prayer will be like a flashlight for me."

Anthony grabbed Karen's hand. "Let's do it. I'm game." Anthony started whispering a prayer that Karen followed and then she started praying to God for my strength. I clenched my fists.

"God in heaven," I said to myself, "I need your strength in the name of Jesus. Not by might, but by your spirit." Philip's eyes grew darker. He was Donyel's puppet and I could tell somewhere in the house Donyel was controlling his actions. Anthony touched my shoulder and I felt this warmth fill my body.

"Father God," Anthony said, "I stand in agreement with her and together we bind up the powers of Donyel in the name of Jesus."

Philip screamed and ran toward me and without a second thought, I jumped forward and laid into his face with my fist. He stopped in his tracks and backslapped me. I fell back on Anthony and Karen. I didn't have time to check on them, I just jumped back up, grabbing the plank of wood Anthony had before.

"I'm tired of games." I slammed the wood across his head. He fell against the wall and turned back around.

"Is that all you got?" he mocked me.

"I got more! Don't worry, pretty boy." I slammed him with the wood again scratching his face up. He felt the blood with his hand. I could still hear Anthony and Karen praying and I knew deep inside I couldn't give up.

"My face! You cut my face!" Philip shouted, and grabbed me by the throat. Anthony jumped in on his back, and tried the best he could, but Philip flipped him back to the ground. I coughed and gasped for air. I grabbed at his wrist trying to pull his fingers from around my throat.

"Andrea!" Karen screamed. Anthony was laid out on the ground knocked out.

"Philip!" Donyel said, appearing in the room suddenly. "You idiot! You are killing her." He had Valerie clung by the neck with one hand and with the other hand he waved his fingers and catapulted Philip against the wall. He threw Valerie to the floor and walked above me.

"You're not going to win," I gasped for air.

"And who exactly is going to stop me?" Donyel said, looking around. "Your new boyfriend?" He looked at Anthony knocked out on the ground. "Looks like he is out for the count."

Philip picked himself off the ground. "Father I'm sorry but she wouldn't cooperate." Donyel slapped Philip back down. "So you would kill her after I told you not to? What would you have accomplished then?"

"I don't know. I'm sorry," Philip said, holding his face.

"You are a waste of my blessing," Donyel said, retracting his power from Philip's body. Philip convulsed slightly and was left cold and empty on the ground. He looked normal but drained. He even seemed skinnier; as if Donyel took back a loan with interest from his soul.

Philip cried at the feeling of emptiness Donyel left him with. "Why father?"

"Don't call me that."

"Why don't you love me?" Philip yelled back. "I just want you to be happy!"

"You will never make me happy, Philip." Donyel turned around to look at me. I tried running but he, without even blinking, caught me by the hair. I grabbed my gun and pulled the trigger twice in his stomach and he didn't even flinch. My strength was diminutive compared to his. He grabbed my gun and threw it behind him. I screamed and tried fighting. Karen had retrieved Valerie and shook Anthony awake to help. Anthony jumped alert seeing Donyel holding me by the hair. I was nervous that Donyel would teleport right out of there and pull me somewhere I was unfamiliar with.

"Valerie, we need your help praying." Anthony grabbed both their hands and began calling on the angels of the Lord for help. I don't know what made him do that, but in my mind it seemed like the smartest thing to do since we were battling an angel.

Valerie seemed to find a whole new belief in God after all she had gone through. "Jesus, I believe you can help us. Please help us," she said.

Donyel hesitated only a little bit and laughed. "Where is God now, Andrea?" His words scared me. We really needed something to happen because nobody could do anymore. I grew tired and I couldn't fight anymore and he knew that.

"You've just used me," Philip said faintly. I looked over and Philip walked past in a daze.

"Philip, I don't have time for your whining. The time has begun for—" Donyel started before Philip cut him off.

"All I have ever wanted was you! I have wasted my time wanting your love. And for what? All you've given me in return is hate."

"Philip!" Donyel snapped at him. The entire situation didn't look good and I looked at Anthony. He read my mind and moved Valerie and Karen further back into the shadows.

"You've never loved me! Why was that so hard?"

"Philip I don't have—"

"Time? You don't have time for your son? But you have time for her! I hate you! All you love is what she can do for you!" I looked back and forth at the two and I saw that Donyel was getting upset. My eyes opened wide at what I was beholding. Not because they were arguing but because now Philip had pulled from behind him the gun that Donyel had snatched away from me.

"You want me dead but I want her dead!" Philip said and I suddenly heard an explosion. I fell from Donyel's hands to the ground. A burning sensation was in my stomach and a warm sensation leaked from my side. I touched my stomach and my hand was bloody.

"Andrea, no!" Anthony said, running to my side.

"You fool!" Donyel said in his anger and struck at Philip so hard with his hand that Philip's head turned out of it's socket, breaking his neck. He stood there for a second with his head loosely flopping backwards and his chin resting awkwardly on the back of his shoulder; then he fell to the ground.

I was too scared to think about the gun shot wound I had. Anthony held me in his arms, which made me feel a little safer and I rested my head in his lap. "You're the fool Donyel," I held my wound. "The council doesn't take kindly to murders. You've broken another angelic law." The ground shook and the bottles of wine began bursting and pouring on the ground. Donyel's eyes filled with panic for the first time.

Shariel and Arquel materialized into the room, illuminating it like it was day. "You have committed your last offense and you shall be bound on earth as it is in heaven," Shariel said. Chains appeared out from their mouths and wrapped around Donyel's legs and arms.

"Noooo!" Donyel screamed. "You won't get away from me that easily, Andrea!" Arquel walked over and saw me hurt. I was getting cold and I looked up to see that Anthony was crying.

Arquel looked at Anthony. "Fear not, Anthony, Andrea's time is not now." With the tip of his finger he healed the gunshot wound and made me strong. His touch was tingly like warm water flowing through my veins. "Now Andrea, take them out of here."

I nodded in agreement not resisting to obey. I grabbed Karen and she grabbed Valerie and with my other hand I held it out to Anthony. I didn't grab his, I just offered mine. He smiled at me and limped over to me and grabbed my hand. Arquel and Shariel turned toward Donyel and began stating his sentence.

"For your offense the council has requested that you be bound in the earth locked away until your release is summoned," Arquel read from a fiery scroll.

"I will be summoned," Donyel screamed as he was weighed down on the ground by the chains.

"Not if you're not found," Shariel said. "And this time, we will be sure of it."

"Make no mention of this place," Arquel said to us and I speak for everyone when I say that his voice struck fear in all our hearts.

"Let's get out of here," Anthony said. The angels were raising their hands and the whole house was shaking. I took one final look at Donyel whose eyes were burning into my own. In my mind I saw this horrible monster and it scared me because somehow I knew that somewhere in me was him. I begin to say the Lord's prayer, it was all I could think of. Anthony looked at me confused.

". . . thy kingdom come, thy will be done on earth as it is in heaven . . ." I said grabbing everyone by the hands and closing my eyes. ". . . for thine is the kingdom and the power and glory forever, amen." I teleported all of us to the front yard. We stood among the tall weeds and watched as the old plantation mansion we had seen in our dreams burn for the second time in history.

There was a roar and a rumble and we all held on to each other for balance. I didn't have the strength to teleport anymore. Anthony reassured everyone that things would be all right and I heard him muttering to the Lord. He gripped my hand tight and I buried my face into his chest. The foundation of the house gave way and a cyclone of flames tore through the roof. The entire mansion began to implode within itself. The entire ground opened and swallowed it up like a hungry beast. Anthony held my hand and I looked over and saw Valerie crying hard.

"Thank you, guys," Valerie said. "Thank you for rescuing me. He said so many things to make me think you weren't going to."

Karen gave her a hug. "Shhh, it's okay." She looked so shook up. I looked at Anthony whose eyes were still on the inferno. I rested my head on his shoulder. I watched as the ground closed up and the fire sealed the ground with a perfect circle. I thought about Dewayne, beautiful Dewayne, who's spirit could finally rest. I thought about poor Philip whose love for Donyel was the catalyst for his own damnation and finally I thought about Donyel, my blood father, who somewhere beneath all those ashes and dirt was bound. And here we were, four young people brought together by this common tragedy. Who could we tell this story to? Who would believe us?

"It's over. We don't have to worry anymore," I whispered.

Anthony didn't even blink. He wrapped his arm around me and rubbed my shoulder. "I hope so."

CHAPTER FORTY-ONE

"Hello, mama," I said on the phone. I held the phone in my hand and looked out the window while sitting on the window sill.

"Hey baby, how's school doing?" I sighed a bit. I thought about how mean I treated her and how I took everything out on her. But now since all I had been through, I knew I couldn't blame her.

"School has been . . . Mama," I stopped mid-sentence. "Mama, I'm sorry I snapped at you last time we talked."

"Baby, I'm sorry. I mean I didn't want you to find out on your own like that. Sometimes, I feel like I should've listened to your daddy when he thought to tell you so long ago."

I smiled and twisted the cord of the telephone between my fingers. "No, you did what you had to do. You wanted me to grow up without worrying about anything. And you did that. I'm sorry at how I acted. You are my mama, the only mama that I have. I can't feel a bond with some other woman like the one I have with you. I know now that my adoption was God's plan and that He wanted me to be

raised by ya'll for a reason. I don't care that I was adopted.
I know that you and daddy were the best parents I could
ever want." She was quiet for a second. I wasn't sure if she
was smiling or crying.

"Mama, are you there?"

"Yeah, baby. I know that if yo' daddy was here he'd be
really proud of you." The thought of that made me feel
really good. "When are you coming home, baby?"

"I don't know mama, So much is going on. I think I really
need to focus on school for a change."

"Boys? Don't let them be a distraction now."

I laughed a bit, "Mama, you have no idea." There was a
knock at the door. "Hey Mama, let me call you back."

"Okay, child."

I hung up the phone with Mama and went to the door.
Anthony was there. "Hey. How're things going?" he said
leaning his weight on his crutch. I told him that I had
been having headaches since the incident and not to
worry. I helped him through the door and noticed that he
couldn't stop looking at me.

"How are you doing? How's your leg?" I said, trying to
not think about my problems. I hadn't talked to him in
about a week since the whole Donyel incident. I needed
time to collect my thoughts and to process if all that really
happened.

"Just a sprain. I'm trying to get things together so I can
go back to Baltimore." He limped his way over to a chair
and sat down.

"Baltimore?"

"Yeah, the school is allowing me the semester off because of Dewayne's death."

I felt slightly disappointed that he was leaving. "Are you
coming back? I mean like next semester?"

"Maybe." There was that weird silence. He looked in my
eyes and I looked in his and I wanted him to tell me what

he was thinking. But maybe I was asking for too much. all this tragedy had brought us together and I couldn't expect him to stick around. But I wanted to know what was in his heart. If I wanted, I could take the thoughts from his head but I didn't want to do that. I didn't want to steal it. I wanted him to give them to me.

"Where's Karen?" he asked.

"Oh, um, she went home for the weekend. I think she needs the most rest out of all of us," I said, trying to lighten up the situation.

"Yeah, so where do we go from here?" He looked at me. I was nervous that he was so blunt with his heart and it caught me off guard.

I looked into his eyes blushing slightly. "Wha-what do you mean?"

He cleared his throat. "I mean, have you heard from any of the angels that helped us? What are we supposed to do after all that?" I felt embarrassed because I thought he was talking about us.

"As for the angels, I haven't heard from them since. I think we should just remember not to tell anybody where Donyel is buried. He must stay sealed underground for however long it takes. I'm thinking that I may go back to Heaven, Texas to, you know just watch."

"Yeah, watch," he repeated. I looked down to avoid eye contact. I didn't want him to read my thoughts through my eyes.

"I'm going to miss you," I whispered.

"What?"

"I wanna wish you . . ." I corrected myself, "well when you get back to um, Baltimore." I fumbled over my words. He looked at me suspiciously and stood up to leave.

"Well, I won't take up anymore of your time," Anthony said, lifting himself to his feet. I was panicking and I wished that God would do something to stop him. I had made so many mistakes this semester and I didn't want to make another one. I didn't want to put my all in some guy that didn't like me. Maybe I expected too much from Anthony. He was such a good guy and maybe I just wasn't good enough for him. He deserved something better than me. Ever since I had entered everyone's life I had brought nothing but trouble.

Anthony got to the door and pivoted around and stared at me. "I was so scared."

"Scared about what?" I asked him.

"I was scared that for a minute . . . I was going to lose you."

"You mean when I got shot?" I looked up and he nodded. He limped back up to me.

"Yeah, I was scared because here I am trying to be a hero. I was trying to do everything I knew how to protect you, but I couldn't. I became aware of my own weakness. Everything seemed so unreal and I thought that maybe I could save you and then you got shot. I saw you there bleeding. I thought about Dewayne and I thought that I was losing you too. Something in me snapped. I felt like it was my fault."

"No, no." I touched his lips with my fingers and gave a bittersweet smile. "It's my fault. If I had never shared my thoughts with you guys, Donyel would have never gotten to ya'll. I should have left my butt in Heaven."

"We were already involved. He was going to get to us regardless. Through everything that has happened, you were always there for me. You helped me see the reality of my relationship with God. You helped me when I was being oppressed by a demon and you even helped me when Philip tried to kill me. What have I given you?"

I smiled and looked away. "Anthony, just be you. You are the greatest guy that I know." My eyes began to tear up. "It took me some time to see that. I think that in some way God allowed all of us to go through all of this for a reason. You've been a support system for me that kept me grounded. *You* keep me grounded. I was scared too when I got shot, but when I felt your arms around me, I wasn't scared anymore."

Anthony smiled and readjusted himself on his crutch. "You are a different girl. With all that happened, I would have never imagined that I would meet someone like you."

"I bet," I laughed. "How often do you meet the daughter of an angel?"

"Not too often. Whatever happens in my life I can never forget you." It sounded like a goodbye.

I kissed him on the cheek and opened the door to my room for him. I didn't want to prolong this anymore. It was beginning to hurt and I didn't want to cry. "Goodbye, Anthony."

Anthony limped on his crutch. "I'm still scared."

"About what? Donyel is gone and Philip is dead."

"No, not them." He stopped short of passing me and turned to look at me. He was breathing heavy like something was really on his mind. "I'm scared . . . that I'm still going to lose you." He looked into my eyes.

"Then why are you going to Baltimore?"

"You don't want me to go?" He quickly responded like he was at my beckon call.

"I want you to do what you want to do."

He grabbed my hand. "I want to do what makes you most happy." Well, at this point I wasn't sure what was going to make me happy.

"Anthony, I'm just really confused. My life isn't a simple one. Don't you think I get scared too? All of this just happened to me. I don't have too many people I can turn to. And just when I started . . ."

"You started liking me?" he asked and I stopped. I

turned away. "I'm sorry Andrea, I'm not being fair to you." He was right about that. Here he was trying to get my feelings and he hadn't told me any of his. I walked off knowing he couldn't keep up on that crutch.

"Andrea, I'm sorry. I'm going back to Baltimore because . . ." He limped over to me. "I was afraid of losing you. I didn't want to be here and get too close to you and then something crazy happen again. I don't think I can bear seeing you die. So, I was willing to leave to . . ."

"Keep from hurting?" I finished his sentence this time.

"Yeah. I've had a problem with facing my emotions, but it seems you help me to face them."

"Well, I guess we're good for each other."

Anthony smiled. "Maybe we are. Maybe I shouldn't leave. Maybe I should hang around for awhile."

I smiled back at him. "I would really like that. Thank you."

"For what?"

"For being my hero."

"But I just told you that I was upset that . . ." I walked up to him and touched his lips with my fingers again.

"Anthony," I said looking up into his eyes, "I know you're not perfect and that you're not supernaturally strong. But you are a man of God. No, you can't stop a bullet, but if you can't realize that your prayers—yours, Karen's and Valerie's, changed the outcome of what happened, then you're the fool. And if I fail to realize what important influence you have been in my life then I'm a fool."

"Have you always been so blunt?" he said smiling at me.

"I've seen demons, angels, and faced an estranged mother in the past few weeks and nothing is scaring me more than sitting here talking to you." I said.

"Maybe." He stroked my hand with his finger. "You are so remarkable, Andrea. One day you're going to be my wife."

"What?" I was choked up. "How do you know?"

"I always knew. I knew when you walked into that Bible study. I knew when you cast that spirit out of my room. I've never had one woman do so much for me. You even were willing to sacrifice your life so that we wouldn't get hurt. I love you Andrea Wallace." He stroked my hair with his hand and I did my best to not cry. "I'm tired of being scared. I'm tired of running away from my feelings. You've flipped my life so I can't go back."

I laughed and hugged him. "I don't know what to do from here but maybe we can figure it out." I looked up at him, ". . . together."

"I think I like that idea." Anthony gently lifted my chin and kissed my lips with his. It was so nice and gentle. His lips were so soft and I didn't know until then how much I wanted to taste his kiss. I felt a surge drop from my head to my toes. And for a minute I lost my mind—in a good way.

I pulled away and looked at him. "Are you sure you know what you're getting into?" I said to Anthony. "I mean, I don't know what life has in store for me or what's going to happen to me."

He shrugged his shoulders. "Don't worry. I won't let anything bad happen to you ever again."

I hugged him and listened to his heartbeat. I wanted to believe him so much, but there was still something bothering me that I just couldn't figure out. But I didn't want to ruin the moment. I just hugged him and listened to his heart. For that one moment I forgot about Donyel and everything that happened in Heaven. For one moment, I was happy.

I sighed and closed my eyes. "Thank you, God."

CHAPTER FORTY-TWO

Nine months later, in the emergency room, there's a baby coming; a very special baby to her mother.

"Push! I can see the head," the doctor said.

The mother kept pushing with all her might not even concentrating on the pain. She thought of all the things she had been through the past few months and all that she had lost. She thought about the one man she loved that she lost and how much he meant to her and she knew she couldn't give up now. She gripped down on the bars of the medical bed and closed her eyes, then pushed down. This was going to be a special child. She would make her daddy proud—her beautiful daddy. She would not let her daddy's death be in vain. Her mother would tell her of who her daddy was and how she came to be. She would know the truth, her mother would see to it.

"Keep pushing!" the doctor said.

All she wants to see is this beautiful little girl in her arms. She wants to bring new hope to her life and the world with her baby's gifts cause she knows of her hidden legacy.

"It's a girl!" The doctor held up the baby.

She cried—not the baby but the mother. The nurse wiped the baby off and handed her over to her mother. She held her daughter in her arms and prayed a blessing over her.

"What do you want to name her?" the nurse asked. But she didn't hear—she was too engulfed at how beautiful her child was.

"Ms. Jeffries?"

Tamela looked up and wiped the tears from her face, "Yes?"

"What do you want to name your baby?" The nurse repeated to her.

"Tonya. Tonya Jeffries," she said looking back at the baby. "We're going to get them for what they did to your daddy aren't we, Tonya?" Tamela rocked her baby gently.

"She's beautiful," the nurse admired.

"Yes," Tamela agreed. "she looks like her father."

The nurse pried, "Oh, is he here? I'll go get him if you like."

Tamela shook her head. "No, Philip died some months ago. But I know somewhere he's watching over both of us."

CHAPTER FORTY-THREE

And that's your story, Andrew; how I met your father and how we were met with circumstances beyond our control, but somehow found a bond of love in Christ and in each other. We married some months after the incident and I became pregnant with your brother, Antonio and you. Karen also gave birth to Courtney and dropped out of college to enroll in the police academy. She does patrol in the ghettos of West Dallas. I guess there wasn't much left that could scare her after the episode in Heaven, Texas. As for Valerie Larue, I never saw her again. She disappeared. Anthony says she left him a letter that he let me look at that I will include:

Dear Anthony and Andrea,

I am sorry for all the trouble I have caused both of you. When I saw Karen on campus going through her pregnancy alone, I couldn't help but feel bad 'cause I knew I had something to do with bringing Donyel into this realm as much as anybody else did. I can't tell you how sorry I am. Anthony, I know I haven't seen eye to eye with you that much but I wanted to really apologize to you. In the end, there is no spell or incantation that could have delivered us. Blessed be . . . to God and his son Jesus for sending his angels to help us. I will never forget that. In some ways, I do want to forget, though it's all etched in my mind and heart like a tattoo. Maybe God will find mercy on me and grant me salvation not only from my sins but from the demons that continue to follow me. I have left Texas and headed for New Mexico. I don't know where I'm going there but maybe all of our paths will cross in the future. I pray good health for Andrea and your expected child. Give him a legacy that Donyel could never give him.

   Sincerely with Love,
   Valerie

The same demons sent telepathically by Donyel who were deeply buried in his tomb that tortured Valerie out of Dallas, tortured me during and after the pregnancy. It became more intensified after your birth and I figured that it was too dangerous for us. I wanted us to live a normal life but the demonic attacks increased. So me and your dad did what we had to do; we split so that they couldn't sense your power. I returned to Heaven to make sure that Donyel stay buried and Anthony took Antonio and stayed in the suburbs of Dallas.

Donyel is still buried alive along with his dead son in an angelic-made tomb somewhere in Heaven, Texas. Sometimes deep in the night I can hear him whispering for me to come to him. He knows who you are and he wants you as well. Resist him. I see him in my nightmares and I'm scared that I'm not going to be the mother you knew. I'm losing my mind little bit by little bit, but don't remember me for what I'm becoming, remember who I was and what I've taught you. Donyel is bound in the earth, but the battle is not over. You will need your brother's help for this—I have already foreseen it . . . another battle is yet to come.